Muesli at Midnight

Aidan Mathews was born in 1956 in
Dublin. His published work includes two
books of poetry, *Windfalls* and *Minding
Ruth*, three plays, and a collection of short
stories, *Adventures in a Bathyscope* (1988),
which was shortlisted for the GPA Book
Award. He works as a radio producer with
RTE and lives in County Wicklow,
Ireland.

Aidan Mathews

MUESLI
AT MIDNIGHT

Minerva

A Minerva Paperback
MUESLI AT MIDNIGHT

First published in Great Britain 1990
by Martin Secker & Warburg Ltd
This Minerva edition published 1991
by Mandarin Paperbacks
Michelin House, 81 Fulham Road, London SW3 6RB

Minerva is an imprint of the Octopus Publishing Group,
a division of Reed International Books Limited

Copyright © Aidan Mathews 1990

A CIP catalogue record for this title
is available from the British Library
ISBN 0 7493 9135 9

Printed and bound in Great Britain
by Cox & Wyman Ltd, Reading, Berks

To Laura, my winter solstice

No one had bothered to tell the chaplain, so he just assumed it was part of an Aids awareness activity week. Why else would a couple of second-year students pedal round the provinces in the middle of June with a skeleton strapped to the saddle of a tandem? Cystic fibrosis or cerebral palsy hadn't much cachet these days; but Aids this, Aids that, Aids the fucking other – the merest mention brought a benefit do in the Concert Hall with a thumbs-up telegram from the Oval Office. It would make you want to vomit.

'This way, Father Jack,' said a nice bit of skirt on his left hand side, and she led him up to the top of the steps outside the Medical school. The Green looked lovely, but that was beside the point. He cleared his throat – not that he needed to, but microphones have that effect on people – and looked down over the hundred and forty, hundred and fifty Crusade Against Cancer stalwarts in their T-shirts and their wheelchairs, their flip-flops and their bright aluminum glasses. Some wore Crusade Against Cancer logos on the visors of their sun-hats; others were letting slip the strings on the many multicoloured Crusade Against Cancer helium balloons so that they drifted up and away and over to the Park where the punks picked fluff from their bellybuttons and hoped that somebody was looking at them.

Finally, in the slap-bang centre of the crowd were the

two college kids who were going to ride around Ireland for a host of HIV positives. Well, fuck them too; though, mind you, now that he looked a little closer, the girl had boobs so big they'd have made a perfect place for an ambush in one of those spaghetti westerns he used to watch at the seminary. Maybe this ride around Ireland was more a matter of ride than round. Maybe this guy with the earring wasn't a poof. Maybe he was going to throw his leg over more than a Raleigh ten-speed. What the fuck was his name anyway? And hers.

'Whenever you're ready, Father Jack,' said the Crusade Against Cancer PRO, and more balloons went up. The blue ones were nice.

He cleared his throat again.

'Ladies and gentlemen – or, if you prefer, gentlemen and ladies, because far be it from me to seem sexist – we're gathered here today to say a simple three cheers, bravo, the best of luck, that sort of thing, to two young medical students who are off to raise funds – and perhaps to raise hell – in support of Aids research.'

'Cancer,' said the Crusade PRO in an undertone. 'Cancer.' But the chaplain didn't hear her. Walkmans do that to you.

'Now I'm not about to mention any names,' he said. 'These two young people wouldn't want me to shunt them into the spotlight. Their individual identities are neither here nor there. Instead, they represent their class, their college, their community.'

Father Jack thought that was a pretty good sentence. Pretty damn good. And he hadn't worked it out beforehand. It had just come to him. No wonder he'd always got – or, rather, gotten; he had, after all, lived in America – straight As.

'Their class, their college, their community. Indeed,

8

they represent more than that. They represent Hope; they represent Possibility. As far as I'm aware, neither of them is suffering from Aids; but that doesn't stop them from caring for those who do. Aids–'

'Cancer,' said the PRO, without moving her lips. 'As in lung; as in liver.'

'Aids is a terrible scourge, and it must be stamped out. Ruthlessly, remorselessly, relentlessly.'

Fuck you, Jack, he thought. How many men can speak in public at twenty minutes' notice?

'But that doesn't mean we can walk away from the pathetic ruin of a man who's dying from Aids. If we can't look into his eyes, we must look into our hearts. After all, Jesus cured lots of lepers. Besides, homosexuality in itself is hunky dory. But buggery is the unacceptable face of gay love. So I say to you: chastity, chastity, chastity. One in a hundred condoms bursts during thrusting, but chastity will never leave you holding the baby.'

The PRO had her eyes closed, like she was praying. He looked at her. Was he really that good? Maybe he should be preaching the retreats at Castelgandolfo. And why not?

'The kids are going to cycle in strange company,' he announced. 'They're taking a *memento mori* with them, in the shape of a skeleton. But neither I nor the college authorities are making any bones about it. So tell us, you guys; tell us your name, rank and serial number before you disappear into darkest Donegal or wherever.'

'I'm Felicity,' said the girl, and she held a bright mint between her upper and her lower front teeth as she smiled at all the patients and physicians and pathologists around her. Where was the asshole who had failed her in Histology? Sooner or later she would have his balls for breakfast; but for now she grinned in a slow,

9

three-hundred-and-sixty-degree circle. After all, a lot of these people would be six feet under by the time she did the repeats. Let them look all they wanted. They could even examine her cleavage and get away with it, because she had a small Pope Paul VI medallion there, with a pinch of dust from the catacombs inside it.

'Felicity,' she said again, and mounted up like a man, throwing a leg over the racer. What odds, even if she was wearing next to nothing? She felt so confident after that leg-wax.

'And I'm Theo,' said the young man. 'I'm Theo. The skeleton was her idea.' His tight terylene shirt was already itching. He should have worn cotton. Loose cotton. And what about putting strips of tape on his nipples, or was that only joggers? Of course the bottom line had nothing to do with expertise, equipment, the can-do of the pros. The bottom line was the line of Felicity's bottom, the desire to be with her, beside her, inside her. He didn't care a hoot in hell about carcinoma of the rectum; he cared about the shadowline of a ghost bikini, by God he did. Yet he was sensitive, he was still sensitive. He may not have been subtle, searching, that sort of thing, but he was sensitive; and lugging a man's bones – and it was a man, he knew that much anatomy – from pillar to post around the hedgerows and the haciendas was, excuse the Serbo-Croat, a bit much.

Yet she had put her foot down, and you had to admit it was a beautiful foot. Still, she might have waited. After all, half the people present had their visas cancelled. There was one fellow with a slimline oxygen cylinder propped in a child's buggy. Point of fact, it was strapped in. When you thought about–

'Hasn't the skeleton got a name?' He looked up, looked

around. He couldn't see who'd spoken. In front of him, Felicity was adjusting her Walkman. Then she poised her bottom perfectly over the saddle and began to pedal out onto the road.

'No, he hasn't got a name,' Theo said. 'Death is all adjectives and no noun.'

They were in a village Theo had forgotten the name of; but it was no big deal. If there wasn't a train to carry, there was no need for a page-boy.

Whatever way he fiddled with the cold tap and the hot tap, the water came out scalding. Either that or it was cold as ice-cubes. You couldn't expect any better from a provincial hotel. Whatever this town was called was not Dublin anyhow. So it was better to accept the amenity of pastoral culture for what it was; all kindness and no creature comforts. Theo imagined he could live perfectly well without kindness, but two-prong plugs and cable channels were another matter. At the end of the day, life was a little more than mere existence. On the other hand, of course, the absence or abuse of complex technological aids serves to remind one of the essential fragility of all human endeavour. Homeless and helpless, the inheritors of a bleak lithosphere, we do not struggle to survive: we survive to struggle.

'Felicity. I was just thinking . . .'

'Thinking and drinking, thinking and drinking,' she called from the bedroom. 'The twin addictions of the average Irish male. Have you nothing better to do?'

And she turned up her Walkman, the better to bar him. She was angry now.

'I hate this room,' she said. 'It's like the inside of a

colostomy bag. It stinks. And I hate the woman at reception too. I took one look at her and I could tell straight away. On her bedside table, I bet you anything, she has an Agatha Christie novel and a tube of Preparation H.'

'You think?'

Theo had laid the skeleton lengthwise in the bath, and was quietly soaping his ribcage.

'You betcha. Plus I bet you anything she listens to the Gay Byrne show.'

Theo eased the skeleton's skull against the spigots of the hot and cold taps. Then he took his hands away. The skeleton seemed to be perfectly comfortable. His bones gleamed dully, the way they should. It was the mercy of God he hadn't broken some of them first thing that morning when they fell at the fork outside that godforsaken place with the three churches and the reconciliation centre. True, he had a slight little chip on his clavicle, but who was to say that wasn't congenital; and who, besides, was to know?

'What I said about the Gay Byrne show was a bit unfair. A bit below the belt. But I meant the rest.'

'Fair enough.'

The water in the bath was starting to cool. The locals must be hardy folk. Of course, now that he thought of it, the skeleton wouldn't mind. Still, the heat had helped to scrape off the dust of the roads. He was looking healthy now.

'I brought books, Theo. A book for you and a book for me. Go on. Guess.'

What the devil had he been in his own day? Curator of the Oriental collection in the Chester Beatty Library? The keeper of the Kish lighthouse? A homosexual master-butcher who recorded each and every transaction on video lest any child, sent on a summons for cocktail sausages or a slice of black pudding, should whisper impropriety?

'*Start Feeling Yourself: The Womanly Art of Masturbation*. That's for me. And for you *The Gulag Archipelago* Volume 3.'

Theo stretched back from where he was kneeling beside the bath. He could see her standing, swaying at the open wardrobe mirror. She was wearing nothing but the Pontiff.

'What do you like most about me?' she said to him. 'The mostest mostest.'

The mint taste of her mouth was one, but above all else the clash of contrasts. The hair on her head was blonde, platinum or peroxide, he never knew which; but the hairs below were black, black pussy hairs. Theo thought about them. Thinking about them was actually nicer than sitting down and looking at them. That was what it meant to be Irish. If you liked, you could call it sophistication, you could call it –

'Well?'

Theo looked at her.

'What I most love about you,' he said, 'is the charity of your openness to the otherness of others in all the plenitude of their mystery.'

That was when the phone rang.

'Don't,' she said. 'Just don't.'

But he did. Anything was better than the gobbledygook he had picked up from cyclostyled leaflets in his charismatic dentist's waiting-room. Besides, if he got into that sort of stuff about relationships he could kiss goodbye to any ass tonight.

'Uh huh?' he said.

'Theo?'

'The same.'

'Theo. It's me. Bennie. Bennie the porter. Bennie the porter from the Medical school. Are you listening?'

Felicity went down on one knee in front of Theo. Then she went down on two. She was looking straight ahead of her.

'The skeleton I gave you. This morning. For the sponsored cycle. Well, it's the wrong one. I mean, it couldn't be more wrong. And I'm fucked back and front if I don't get it back. Are you with me? Theo, I'm in the job for twenty years. If I go another five, they'll make me permanent. Are we on the same wavelength?'

Felicity drew down the zipper of Theo's fly; then she parted the flaps.

'Are we on the same planet?' The voice on the phone was not composed.

'Felicity?'

She didn't answer. She pressed her face against his crotch, burying her nose in his open trousers, inhaling strongly.

'Are we in the same fucking universe?'

'I love your man smells,' said Felicity. 'Do you love my woman smells? I want you to smell me all over, from top to bottom . . . I mean, from head to toe.'

Bennie was back again.

'The skeleton you're sightseeing with is the skeleton of Doctor –'

Theo stared at the handset blankly; but the line had gone dead.

It was the third day of their cycle, the last of Felicity's.

There must have been four to five hundred glasses in the living-room of the house where they were staying, and they were all identical. Most of them were stacked around the floor and fireplace, and more of them were ranged along the mantelpiece, the bookshelves, the twin mahogany sideboards. Wherever you looked, your image wobbled weirdly. Theo knew one thing: he'd never poormouth tupperware again.

'You get them when you pay for petrol,' the old man said. 'I preferred it when they gave out stamps.'

'You must drive a lot.'

The old man was silent for a time, prodding the plastic coalfire with the poker, staring morosely into the sentences he might or might not use in reply. Then he made his move.

'The odd bit,' he said.

Upstairs in the attic a watertank made stomach noises. Outside in the garden a few sheep coughed. Some were huddled right up at the front door, out of the way of the wind. Felicity had been examining them through the letterbox. She looked comely in the candlelight, even if it was electric. Theo studied her tush as she bent over, the intricate imprint of the webbed saddle of her bike still visible on the inner area of her thighs. He had trekked round town to find that saddle cover, but the effort had been worth while.

The old man's eyes followed Theo's. They ravished her together. It made them feel close.

'I came out of the Benedictines in 1942,' the old man said. 'Then I joined the Army. Ended up in Unter den Linden at the end of the war, playing the clarinet in a regimental jazz band. But that's another story, and it's not worth writing. What I want to tell you is that one afternoon we're waiting, me and a couple of mates of mine, outside this cinema, in a queue like, to see I think it was "Cry Havoc" or maybe it was "Hitler's Hangman",

and along come these three women. Young women . . .
well, youngish. And they want cigarettes. Nylons too,
some chocolate if we had it, but mostly cigarettes. Even
bits of cigarettes, even butts of cigarettes. And they were
prepared to do anything for them. Somersaults, soixante
neuf, you name it.'

'This is a long story,' Theo said. 'And it doesn't seem
to be going anywhere. Couldn't you quicken the pace or
delete unnecessary detail?'

'Maybe it's too intestinal,' Felicity said. 'Maybe you
should resect a few feet of it.'

'Fuck you both,' said the old man. 'This is my story.
You sit and shut up.'

So Felicity came and sat on Theo's lap.

'I hadn't one packet of cigarettes in my pocket,' the old
man said. 'I had three. Three packets. And all each of them
wanted was a single smoke.'

'It's so romantic,' said Felicity.

'There they were,' said the old man, stabbing the plastic
coalfire like he meant to. 'There they were. A trinity of
tits and zithers, waiting my will and my word.'

'You should be a writer,' Felicity said. 'You should
sit down some day and write out all the anger, all the
anguish. Because writing is writhing. You must flow with
the blow.'

The old man slowly sucked on the peppermint Felicity
had handed him. Then, with one decisive mastication of
his molars, he broke the sweet in pieces.

'Two of the three were dark; the other was fair. She
wore no lipstick. I could see the edge of a dirty bra under
her blouse . . . I could see a bulge under one of the cups
– not her breast itself, but on her breast, over her nipple.
A tea-strainer, a plastic cap from a flask, a something;
something to keep the fabric away from the nipple.'

'Cracked,' said Felicity.

'No,' said the old man. 'No, she wasn't. I worked it out a few years back. She was nursing a baby. That's what it was. And her nipple was sore.'

He looked at the two of them.

'I gave her the three packets. She gave one each to the other two. Then they went away. And I stood there, thinking.'

'Thinking and drinking,' said Felicity. 'Don't tell me about thinking and drinking.'

'The queue was moving into the cinema. I'd lost my place in it. My mates had gone in. And then a chaplain – I knew he was a chaplain because he was smiling – walked over to me. Put his arms around me. Hugged me. Held me tight.'

'Men who can manifest their anima are rare creatures,' said Felicity. 'I met this hulk from Upper Volta once. He was –'

'He smelled of pancakes,' said the old man. 'And boot polish. He said to me: "I saw. I saw what happened. But more important is that God saw. God saw what happened. I can hear him clapping. Can you hear him clapping? He's clapping till his hands are sore." After that he went on into the picture.'

Felicity made the sign of the Cross.

'I think that's the most incredibly beautiful story I've ever listened to,' she said. 'It gives me goosebumps. And whenever I get goosebumps and the hairs on my arms stand up, I know that either the room temperature has fallen to below sixty-five degrees or else the Lord is among us. That's why I blessed myself.'

'But the point is,' said the old man, 'the point is I've been regretting it for forty-four years now. I wake up each and every morning, and I say out loud: "Fool that you were! Fool that you are!" Then I put my teeth in, and I say: "You schmuck, you scumbag." You see, it's hard to say those words, to really spit them out, without your dentures. I could have had them all, all three. Simultaneously, successively, alternately, alternatively. Any way. What a piece of action.'

And he hit the imitation coalfire such a swift swipe with the tip of the poker that it perforated the plastic. Then he got up, adjusted his Walkman and pressed the play button.

'The story of my life,' he said. 'All leaf and no blossom.'

'Ruins are often more beautiful than scaffolding,' said Felicity. 'People go to Greece to see the Acropolis, not the Portakabins round the new airport. True, a narrative of failure is a hard thing; but how much harder would be the failure of all narrative?'

The old man looked at her.

'I did a year in Arts before I switched to Medicine,' she said proudly. 'And the guy I lived with was a Jesuit who liked to be paradoxical during foreplay. Anyhow, I wanted to be able to relate to my patients not only in physical but in metaphysical terms. It's a sort of totalistic approach.'

'Can you cure me?' said the old man.

'What do you suffer from?' Felicity said.

'I suffer from staring at the ceiling when I should be asleep,' he said. 'The silence is terrible: it's like the shutdown tone on the television set, but you can't turn it off because it starts inside you.'

'Have you tried counting sheep?' she asked him.

'I have, Doctor,' he said. 'Twenty times a night I get out of bed and I open the window and I count all fourteen of them. A year ago I was so lonely I would have brought one of the lambs into the bed with me, but I thought it would look a bit strange maybe, if anybody called.'

'I should be making notes,' Felicity said. 'This is all so interesting.'

But Theo was turned off. And who was this Jesuit anyhow? He'd never heard of him before. A Dominican, yes, and the guy from the Society of Asian Missions who looked like Liza Minnelli with a moustache, but not a Jesuit. Had she any lane discipline?

'Then I got the Walkman,' said the old man. 'The Walkman was a godsend. I tell you this for nothing, there were nights when nothing stood between myself and suicide but a Perry Como cassette. I'd have popped the pills like a packet of Haliborange. I came that near. But now I have myself taped. For a bout of the blues, Bing Crosby; apprehension, Charlie Kunz; and for impure thoughts, in particular the German ones, there isn't missal or medicine to match the Chorus of the Hebrew Slaves.'

Felicity and Theo watched the old man slowly walk away. They felt they owed it to him. In fact, Felicity would have clapped, the way Italians do when a plane lands or takes off. But she had something to do.

'I have something to do,' she said; and she went off to do it.

The bedroom was at the other end of the house. A print of Constable's 'Haywain' hung over a chest-of-drawers, and a 1979 Pirelli calendar was sellotaped above the wash-hand basin. Theo sat on the edge of the duvet, thinking. Why had Felicity put the skeleton into the double bed, between the two pillows? To be fair to her, he'd brought him into bed himself a couple of days before, but that was because the night had been cool to the point of coldness, and the poor unfortunate fellow looked quite wretched hung round a wooden clothes-hanger from the top of the shower-unit. Besides, Theo had left him at the very edge of the bed, with only a bit of the blanket over him. That was good manners, consideration, respect for the dead even. Felicity's propping him at centre-stage when Theo might have had plans for a little somatic gratification was quite another matter: she was definitely telling him something. Actually, he hadn't been feeling especially horny after the hard, uphill slog all afternoon; but the possibility that she might be disinclined immediately aroused him. Someday he would write a great tome about the psychopathology of the penis, someday he would illuminate –

'You're not thinking, are you?'

Felicity was standing in the doorway, naked except for her Walkman. She could never be nude, only naked. That was her destiny.

'Why did you put the skeleton to bed? I mean, into the bed?'

She smiled at him sweetly.

'Because tonight and tomorrow night and the night after that as well, my precious, my panther, you must be chaste; chaste and desperate, desperate but chaste; and the skeleton must lie between us like a sword of purity, all steel and no scabbard.'

He saw what she was driving at; and, suddenly, her boobs had never seemed barer.

'I can always tell,' she said. 'I can tell day fourteen, and I can tell when my period's coming. I got up today, I said to myself: it'll be tea-time, bedtime, round about then. And I was right.'

Then the phone rang. Theo reached for it. What in God's name was a phone doing in the spare room of an isolated farmhouse in the middle of nowhere? The whole thing was frankly unreal. All he needed now was a chorus of sheep.

'Bennie. From the Medical school. Who do you think?'

'Is this some sort of macabre joke?'

'No, it's about the skeleton.'

'Look,' Felicity said; and she slipped her finger deeply into her pussy. When she took it out again and held it up, it was slick and reddish.

'Does that disgust you?' she said. 'Are you disgusted by that?'

'Of course I'm not disgusted,' Theo said.

'You will be when you hear whose skeleton you have,' said Bennie.

'I'm not talking to you,' said Theo, 'and I don't want to talk to you.'

'You needn't fly off the handle,' Felicity said. 'I'll be all right again in three days.'

'It's the skeleton of Doctor John –'

'Fuck you,' Theo said, and put the phone down. Felicity was attempting to cry, but the tears wouldn't come. Perhaps it was harder to cry when you were menstrual. Besides, you needed the right music, something sad, something slow, something soft, 'Jonathan Livingston Seagull' maybe; not the heavy metal she was listening to. Even so, she wiped her eyes, and made her lower lip tremble.

'I wanted you to kiss me,' she said. 'I wanted you to kiss me down there. It would have been so thoughtful.'

Outside the window, the sheep had begun to baa, almost in unison.

The notices round the second next town had said *The Chieftains*, so Theo and Felicity made tracks toward the ballroom after they'd checked in, washed up, and broken the wishbone over half a chicken in a basket. The skeleton they left in a posture of defeat at the writing table in the bedroom: his left hand clutched a fountain-pen, his right a bottle of Babycham; and the solemn sockets of his eyes stared long and large at their own reflective image in the mirror. They had good reason. Felicity had been at work with her eyebrow pencil and her eye-shadow.

'I don't care what you think,' she had said to Theo. 'This man was very feminine. Or at least there was something fragile and feminine within him, like a ring in a Hallowe'en cake or a contact lens that you might have swallowed by accident. I get that ambience off him. Do you really imagine for a moment that he'd rather be back in the anatomy room with some hungover demonstrator poking a ruler into his pelvis? Will you not let the guy have some dignity?'

'I keep wondering,' Theo said. 'I keep wondering about him. Who he was, what he was. Who lifted him at night when he was little? Who taught him how to write the letter E on a green blackboard? When did he stop eating rusks and start eating rice? I can't stop . . . imagining. And it's not healthy. Imagining is the first step. Then you start the auditory hallucinations.'

Felicity was putting away her make-up bag.

'I don't mind you wondering,' she had said. 'Wondering is very feminine; conversely, femininity is a wonder. But I don't want you thinking about him. I don't think about him; what I do about him is wonder. Like was he breast-fed or bottle-fed? And who was the first woman he ever kissed? And where?' She paused. 'Her throat? Her navel?'

'Maybe he was gay,' Theo said. 'Maybe he was a motor mechanic from the midlands who dreamed about

2 2

the bondage parlours of San Francisco; maybe he sat up late at night to watch those fellows in the Levi ads with the Fifties sig tunes.'

'No,' said Felicity. 'He wasn't gay.'

'How do you know?'

'A woman can tell these things,' she told him. 'Even from a skeleton.'

And they had left it at that.

Now they were walking to the ballroom, and it was still bright. Outside a succession of small pubs Scandinavian tourists sat at the sort of tables you see on forest trails, picking tiny midges out of glasses of lager. A collie lapped at slopped beer on the footpath. Everyone stared at Felicity as she and Theo passed by. The brown of her nipples seeped through her flimsy frock.

'Honestly,' she said. 'Have they never seen a tit before? You'd think we'd arrived at some La Leche convention.'

But she went back to ask them for directions to the ballroom. She must have mislaid the little map the waiter had drawn for them on the beer-mat.

When they did get there, the Chieftains weren't playing. Instead, there was a benefit do, a Dolly Parton Look-A-Like Gala to raise funds for the erection of a solarium in the county mental hospital. The prize, according to the man on the ticket desk in the foyer, was a fortnight's holiday in Myconos; and the competition was fierce, if not formidable. His hands strayed blindly across the counter, searching for stubs and for small change.

'Your glasses are here,' Theo said to him, and offered them. But the man waved them away.

'I took them off when I saw the entrants coming,' he said. 'I've a shadow on my lung and a lousy family history. I can't afford to be waylaid at my stage in life. If I'm going, I'm going; but I want to go well. So I'm off the drink,

I'm reading Dante, and no two-bit dollybird's going to step between me and my Maker. You owe me another thirty-two pence.'

Inside it was dim, almost dark, except for the follow-spots on the catwalk where the look-a-likes paraded. Two to three hundred people were jostling on the dance-floor, the men in open shirts with the sleeves rolled up, the women in swimsuits, jumpsuits, pinafores, party dresses, a hectic, hit-and-miss, harum scarum assortment of costumes, combinations and country clothes hire.

'Theo,' said Felicity, her eyes shining. 'Babies will be conceived this evening. I feel it in my fallopians.'

Motown music blared from the monitors, and the Dolly Parton look-a-likes bucked and bounced to the beat. Some had kicked off mother-of-pearl high-heel shoes; others let down the knotted straps of their gowns, shrugging their vaccination scars at their partners. It was strange to think of them at six and seven months being inoculated against rubella, or, better still, to imagine them as pig-tailed senior infants shuffling Indian-file across a school-yard marked out for basketball, to where a Tanzanian intern from the local Health Board was waiting in a caravan, his hypodermic in hand. Ten years on and here they were, strawberry blonde in borrowed wigs, awash with sweat and discount atomisers, their armpits raw from recent shaves (though the one exception with axillary hair was quite a turn-on), jigging their boobs as if their lives depended on it; and so, in a sense, they did.

'I couldn't jig my boobs like that,' said Felicity. 'When I'm on top of you and you swing them, I get dizzy.'

'You never told me that,' Theo said.

'Women have learned to lie about a lot of things,' Felicity said. 'It makes things easier in the short term.'

Beside her a girl with a very flat chest was trying to

inflate two copper-coloured condoms; it may indeed have been her first attempt at a blow-job.

'Would you?' she asked Theo sweetly.

He blew them up, handed them back to her, and watched as she arranged them underneath her bra until her ivory blouse bulged like a primitive ski-slope.

'It's for the brownie points,' she apologised. 'There's a Greek holiday going with this.'

Up on the platform there was consternation. You wouldn't have thought it to watch the parish priest as he shakily decanted glasses of water from a stained carafe, or the senior psychiatrist endlessly polish the photochromic lens of his spectacles with the tail of his Membership tie. The first might have been Parkinson's, the second additional proof that analysts are often themselves obsessional creatures, that they are drawn to the orchard of instability because they love the taste of apple, because –

The parish priest was on the point of tears.

'I'm the External Relations Officer for the Connacht Branch of the Gay Rights League,' he said. 'What am I going to tell my member? He'll think I'm a double agent. And just when I'd finally persuaded him that his condition is a charism of the Holy Spirit.'

The psychiatrist wasn't listening. Sod queers. He'd just seen the student nurse he'd balled the night before in the sacristy; and the only reason she'd let him into her Pretty Polly tights in the first place was because he'd managed to convince her he was a militant feminist. What was she going to think when she saw him vetting Dolly Parton look-a-likes? And what was she doing here? The week before, she'd made him read two chapters from Andrea Dworkin before she'd let him leave a love-bite in her left buttock. Now she was looking like a wet nurse in drag.

'They're all cunts,' he said. 'Every last one of them.'

'Pardon?' said the priest.

'Nothing. I was just recalling a certain hole in my schedule. In fact, I was recalling quite a few holes in my schedule.'

'I wish there were more of them,' the priest said. 'You work too hard as it is: you could do with some relief.'

And if he'd wanted to say anything else, he would have had to have shouted, for by now the music had mounted another twenty, twenty-five decibels, and the Dolly Parton look-a-likes were vamping on the ramp beside the rostrum, twitching their behinds and ballooning their tits while whimpering the words of a Dolly Parton lyric to a Dolly Parton All-Time Favourite backing track.

'You know what this should be?' Felicity said to Theo. 'This should be the Feast of Day Fourteen. The priest should bless us all with the waters of the womb.'

But the priest had other matters on his mind. Was it Miss Parton, Ms Parton or Mrs Parton? Either way, she must have had incredible knockers.

'Ladies and Gentlemen,' he said, as the din died down, the strobe lights slowed and a solitary look-a-like who had staged a dramatic fainting fit was handed out over the heads of the crowd, her tresses trailing Ophelia-fashion. 'I'm delighted to be here tonight to adjudicate the Dolly Parton Look-A-Like Competition. Now I must confess that I hadn't hitherto the remotest notion of what the particular lady in question looked like. Henceforth I shall have a very ample notion indeed. As a priest, of course, I shall endeavour to keep that notion very close to my chest. For the one thing which each and every girl here tonight has in common is, or is it are, magnificent eyes. They don't glint, or gleam, or flash fire. Those are the prerogatives of paragraph transitions in the blockbusters of airport bookstores. Yet even if they don't light up, they do look up. Red with weeping and green with envy, your eyes turn and return, searching through a crust of sleep, a coat of eye-shadow. No wonder the past tense of the Greek *to see* is the present tense of the Greek *to know*. It isn't the weather that melts the snowman; it's the two coals in his eyes, make his eyes water. So don't go covering your privates when a stranger strides toward you on a beach; cover the conscientious objectors. Don't reach for a bikini-bottom, reach for a blindfold.'

The psychiatrist stared at the parish priest. Maybe it was true after all. Maybe it was true his Bishop had fucked him out of Dublin down to this provincial ashpit because he'd asked the Ursuline Leaving Certificate class to open their hearts to life and their legs to love, though the man had always denied it. Could he be a hypomanic? He might even invite him to next week's poker drive.

'Myconos,' said the priest, 'is a beautiful island. I've been there; I've been there three times. I can vouch for it. Sun, sea, sand, the whole shebang. The only thing you have to watch out for are the donkey droppings, and it's not many places you can say that about. A half hour by boat and you're onto Delos, a sort of poor man's Pompeii with lizards galore. And if your catholicity doesn't extend to our four-footed cousins, you might mosey back to Myconos and search out Paradise – I mean, Paradise Beach – where, not to put a tooth in it, a lot of the gay community wind up and wind down. In point of fact, part of the reason that I chose Myconos as the sunspot super prize in this competition was because I wanted to commit a missionary act. By sending a couple of quite straight individuals to an outpost of complete and utter poofs, I hoped to establish the simple truth – though to talk of the simple truth is a contradiction in terms – that heterosexuals have no monopoly on loving kindness.'

The psychiatrist looked again at the parish priest. Maybe not hypomanic; maybe bi-polar.

'We talk about gays,' said the priest. 'I don't like the word. I prefer queers. If you look up gay in the dictionary, it says mirthful, it says cheeky, it says offhand. Gays are none of these things. But you look up queer and you find strange; you find mysterious; you find puzzling. Now you're talking. Now you're talking homosexuality. Not an aberrant urge, but an errant demiurge.'

The psychiatrist had stopped looking. The guy was obviously schizoid.

'The great river of life has its mainstream and its margins,' the priest said, 'and those margins are anything but shallow. Gays know about the margins. Priests and prisoners know about them. The poor of the Third World could spell the word in a hundred different silences. All those for whom orphanage is a personal reality, whether by fact or by faith, the omission of others or the commission of one's self, live, move, and have their being in a world which is both impersonal and unreal. More than most, more than anyone else, the persons for whom our presence tonight is a pledge of attentiveness, a pledge of vigil, the poor patients up the road in that shithouse of a mental hospital, they understand what margins are. And I tell you this, I tell you this in your brash and trashy get-up: they are the Praetorians of the Lord, the darlings of the Almighty, the honour guard of the crucified Christ. They are not Mary Mulcahy or Ellen MacDonald, Patsy Brennan or Festus Cain. They are the first born, the first fruits of the heavenly harvest; for it is by their darkness, and only by their darkness, that we can make light of ourselves. The solarium will be ready, please God, by the time of the Galway races; those who have no place in the sun will be grateful to you for it.'

After he had sat down, everybody knew he had finished, and they started clapping. The priest was proud of himself, though he had the humility to admit it. No, it wasn't a bad speech at all, and he was glad he'd brought the dictaphone along to record it. He could listen back in his bedroom later on.

'The winner,' said the psychiatrist. 'You didn't announce the winner.'

So he got up again, and he couldn't for the life of him remember any body or any boobs in particular. At the end of the day, one milk churn was pretty much like another; it was really a question of the ratio of the pretty to the much. But then he remembered Cathy. Wasn't it Cathy had had the baby with the port-wine stain, within a week of her brother in Boston getting busted for drugs? A wee spell in a soft climate, a frolic in the fleshpots, would do her all the good in the world. But what the dickens was her surname? Nowadays you never used it, mind you, in or out of classrooms, confessionals, encounter groups. It was Martha this and Basil that, from the very first meeting. Anything would do these days to enhance a sense of intimacy in a world which lacked both.

'Cathy,' he said. 'Cathy's a clear winner.'

But there was instant bedlam, with half-a-dozen of the waxwork women shrieking and clutching their breasts as if a maniac had started shooting from a campanile. Evidently they were all Cathys. Hadn't their parents ever heard of Juliet or Randy? There should be some sort of display stand at the ante-natal classes.

'Cathy with the baby with the birthmark,' he shouted. 'Cathy with the brother who got done for dealing dope. The Snowman.'

But it turned out she was the one who'd been evacuated earlier. Some of the guys had administered first-aid in the foyer and the last they'd seen of her was when she broke free and made for home, kicking off her platforms as she went, and stepping slowly over the glass and gravel of the pathway, her wig in her hand, looking for all the world like a swimmer with a snorkel, climbing over shingle out of water that had proved too cold and too callous.

Anyhow, most everybody thought it was a good enough decision; and the glummer of the girls consoled themselves with the reflection, if not indeed the remark, that the poor, pathetic creature would be running raffles from here till Heaven knew when, to part-finance her trips to specialists and surgeons all over the world; in addition to which, it might be as much as twenty years before her brother rolled a piece of Rizla paper in the family front-room again. It would make you count your blessings to see some people, and they up Shit Creek without a paddle. So they sang the National Anthem with a vengeance, and a fellow at the back was able to give them the beat to follow because he could simulate the sound of a bodhran on his up-to-the-minute Yamaha synthesiser. Then everyone put their Walkmans on, and headed out for home.

'But for us home is a hotel bedroom,' said Felicity. 'Lodgings, a lay-by, a wayside shelter. Not that I mind, of course. It makes me feel so close to the refugee, to the displaced person. Because now I can look the displaced person in the eye.'

And she bounced up and down, up and down on the bed so the bed-springs boinged. They were back at their base, you see.

'Why are you bouncing up and down on the bed so the bed-springs boing?' said Theo. He had stripped to his novelty boxer shorts because both of the storage heaters were on; Felicity too was wearing only the Pope who closed the Vatican Council.

'I wanted to give the guy next door something to think about,' she said. 'He came up the stairs behind me, and he kept dropping his paperback. It was so sweet.'

She rubbed her finger between two of her toes, and then smelled it. Theo was down on his hunkers in front of the television set, pressing each of the sixteen stations in turn; but there was nothing on. Ceefax, test cards, tone. The most you could hope for ordinarily at this hour of the night would be some Channel Four feature on female circumcision among the Matabele, or maybe a Danish documentary with subtitles about a couple of silent movies from the Golden Age of Uzbek cinema. When were the media moguls going to cop on, and run 'Emmanuelle', or at least a round-table discussion about it, with the best bits shown beforehand?

'What are you fiddling with that for?' said Felicity.

'I thought there was a thing about the ozone layer,' Theo said.

'Forget the ozone layer,' Felicity said. 'You've always got your head in the clouds. Come to bed. But turn the light out first.'

'Why should I turn the light out?' Theo said.

'Because I thought we'd do it the old-fashioned way.'

'Old-fashioned?'

'It's an old-fashioned bed. It's an old-fashioned room. It's an old-fashioned town. So let's be old-fashioned. We put the light out, you get on top of me, we forget the prelims, a quick in-and-out, and that's it. Maybe we stop once or twice just to listen.'

'Listen to what?' said Theo.

'I dunno. To the baby. Maybe the baby's crying. Maybe she needs to be lifted. Or maybe I left the back-boiler on.'

'A back-boiler? The two of us are going to be doctors, and you talk to me about a back-boiler?'

'Just turn out the light,' Felicity said.

Theo was flabbergasted.

'You're afraid. You're afraid to let me see your body. It's this cycling round the country. The people you're meeting, the places you're seeing, the atmosphere you're inhaling. You're in a time warp. You're back in sensible shoes, mantillas, elasticated stockings for varicose veins. Admit it.'

'The light,' Felicity said.

'All right,' he said. 'All right. But let me tell you this much. Turning out the light represents more than flicking a switch. It represents a return to darkness. It represents an ideological weakening. It's like a Communist having second thoughts about price control or private property. Do you understand that? I understand it. What I don't understand is what's got into you.'

'The only thing that's ever got into me is you,' Felicity said. 'You've been getting into me for months. You're like a personal pot-holer, rummaging round inside me for rock samples. It's worse than the dentist. But our parents and our grandparents were different. Because they didn't turn out the light to hide their bodies. Christ Almighty, they knew each other better than we do. Hadn't they chamber-pots under the bloody bed? No, they turned out the lights to hide their faces. That was why. And they were right.'

'Maybe it helped them to get the job done,' Theo said. 'They were free to fantasise, weren't they? There was no one looking at them, was there? Maybe my old man was humping Betty Grable the night I was conceived, and my old lady taking the full weight of W. B. Yeats. Maybe I should ask them.'

But Felicity was engrossed in her own insight. It does happen.

'If I had a hundred Polaroids of a hundred pussies, you couldn't pick mine out of them. But the face is the final mystery because it's the first revelation. It tricks us into thinking we know it. But we don't.'

Then the phone rang. It would, of course.

'Is this a bad time?' asked Benny. He was still the porter from the Medical school.

'Go on,' Theo said.

'John Henry McHenry,' said Benny. He left a little space between each of the words.

'Benny,' said Theo. 'Either you're taking elocution lessons in an effort to disguise your social origins, which is sadly snobbish, or else you're trying to tell me something.'

'The late Archbishop of the diocese of Dublin,' Benny said. 'An ecclesiastical accomplice on your little walkabout. They're his bones you've got with you.'

Felicity lay naked on the bed, working a pillow under her bottom.

'Come to bed now,' she said. 'Come to bed. Come to. Come.'

'This is a bad trip, Benny,' Theo said. 'A bad trip.'

'What are you talking about?' said Benny. 'Sure the weather's fantastic.'

'Theo,' said Felicity. 'I give you thirty seconds, and that's all.'

But Theo was in a daze. He looked across at the skeleton looking at itself in the mirror. The fountain-pen had dropped from between his fingers. Where had it rolled to? He couldn't see it anywhere. Thanks be to Jesus he hadn't let Felicity put the tutu on the torso.

'Theo,' said Benny. 'Ahoy there.'

The Archbishop of Dublin. In direct succession to Christ, or was that only the Popes? An Archbishop anyhow. A preconciliar Prince of the Church, with a face like an elderly Albert Camus and the hands of a concert pianist. Whenever his image had appeared on the screen, his father would leave the room, talking about something called Torquemada; but his mother would switch from colour to black-and-white, because, she said, it better befitted a man of his station. A priest. A bishop. An archbishop. An intellectual.

'Holy shit,' Theo said.

'That's what I thought,' said Benny. 'That's exactly what I thought. Talk about having a skeleton in the closet.'

'Wardrobe,' Theo said. He was still in a state of shock. Christ in Heaven, the man had confirmed him. Prepared him for puberty, anointed him for the adult life. Chrism and whatever else. A day of surplices and censers, the whole church awash with the smell of beeswax and body odour; a stiff shirt collar cutting against the boil on the back of your neck, and the Bishop's entourage moving among the benches, catechising the candidates.

'There'll be no questions asked,' said Benny, 'if we get him back in one piece. He is in one piece, isn't he? I mean, you haven't lost any of him along the way?'

'How could I?' Theo said. 'His bones are numbered.' Which they were too, literally.

'The question is,' said Benny, 'the question is —'

What question had the Bishop put to him that day, his voice morose and modest? What are angels? That was it. A damnfool question if ever there was one, and Theo hadn't an iota. 'Angels,' he answered, 'are pure spirits, created by God . . .'; but there was something else, something extra, and he couldn't think of it. Up over the reredos at the back of the high altar, the silhouettes of pigeons blackened the rose window. Could his father see him stuck like this, at the back of the church? And wouldn't he be tickled pink?

'Plus they run messages all over the place for Jesus, and everybody has one.'

'What are you talking about?' said Benny.

The Bishop smiled and stroked his cheek and moved on; and Theo leaned out over the elbow-rest of the bench, and called to him: 'An angel, I mean. Not a message. An angel. Everybody has one.' But the Bishop didn't turn. Only he raised his hand and waved it ever so slightly. And that was nice when you thought about it.

'Fuck you,' said Felicity, turning over away from him to face the wall. The bottom of her ghost bikini was even whiter under the overhead light.

'I met him once,' Benny was saying. 'He'd come to the college to talk about Christian burial. It was the time that poet fellow had himself cremated, and the helicopter scattered his ashes. Tea-bags were just coming in, and he was killed dunking the one I gave him.'

'The poet?' said Theo.

'No, the Archbishop. I gave him a cup of tea while he was waiting. Then he made me tell him all about the pigeons.'

'What pigeons?'

'My pigeons. The pigeons I train. I'm a pigeon fancier. Pigeon fanciers train pigeons. So I told him how they fly to Edinburgh and Algeciras and back again, and all the while he was dunking his tea-bag, lifting it out and dropping it in again. I thought I was going on a bit much, but he seemed to be interested, so I kept on talking. Afterwards, when he had to go because the bigwigs were congregating out in the hall, I made to kiss his ring. He didn't stop me, but then he shook my hand as well. He said I'd taught him some theology. Of course, I'd be the first to admit he was a bit of a prick a lot of the time; but you have to look behind the mask, behind the membrane, as you'd say yourself; don't you? Well, don't you, Theo?'

But Theo had left the receiver down on the writing table, and gone out of the room. Felicity was already asleep, or drifting toward the darkness, a strand of her hair held lightly between her teeth, and a long-distance phone number with two crossed sevens written like a camp tattoo across the inside of her wrist. So only the skeleton was listening.

'Theo. Come in, Theo. Is anybody there?'

Outside in the corridor the heat was stifling. The radiators were on full-blast, and the windows at either end of the passageway were sealed. It was almost as if the whole place had been put on a state of alert for some nudist convention. No wonder Theo felt thirsty. Perhaps the bar was open, or at least accessible. It was way past bedtime, even for barn-owls, but he had to have a drink. So he made his way downstairs, past the pampas grass and the print of Constable's 'Haywain', and stole into the Resident's Lounge. The apostrophe, he thought, was always in the wrong place.

Then he was behind the bar, watching himself in the mirror as he jemmied a bottle of Coke. All in all, he told himself, he had rather nice nipples; and just the right amount of chest-hair, neither little nor lavish. Shame about the pimple, but there was no use pressing it. If he did, it would only come back. Let it go in its own good time.

'Are you wearing any clothes at all, or should I shut my eyes?'

Theo could see the manageress in the mirror, or at least as much of her as the light from the hall showed up. He'd never heard her come in; she must be wearing slippers. In her hand she held what looked like the head of a vacuum cleaner. Now why would she be –

'It's all right,' she said to him. 'I can't see from this side.'

'I have my shorts on,' he said. 'Sorry about the old dressing-gown, but no can do. I'm travelling light, you see. And I just came down for a drink because of the heat.'

'I know,' she said. 'They have it on everywhere. It has to do with the damp.'

Then they were silent for a few more seconds. Theo could hear his Coca-Cola tinkling in the glass. He wished she'd go away. What was she doing, just standing there in the darkness, looking at him? He would have told her about the bloody Coke the next morning. She would have understood. After all, she was almost a contemporary. She couldn't be much older than, say, thirty. Mind you, you could never tell until you examined the throat, which is why so many women wear scarves or blouses with Victorian collars. A woman could bathe in asses' milk seven days of the week, but the throat was always a dead giveaway.

'Would you believe what I'm wearing?' said the manageress.

'No,' said Theo. 'I mean, yes. Of course.' And for that matter, what was he wearing? He had so many pairs of shorts in his little Samsonite backpack: one for the morning, one for the afternoon, and one for the evening. Not that he was hung-up. He was just particular; and bicycling was strenuous. But the long and the short of it was that he didn't really know what he had on him, and he didn't dare look down. She might think he was making a pass. So long as it wasn't the Oscar Wilde ones, with Bosie on the backside.

'Under my housecoat,' she said, 'I'm only wearing a slip.'

'Are you not cold?' he said. It was all he could think of. In future he'd keep a few minerals in his bedroom.

She laughed. It was a nice laugh too. It made a sound like a wickerwork picnic basket being unstrapped and opened. And that was a beautiful image. Maybe he would say that to Felicity some day. So Theo laughed as well. But the manageress ducked down and began to look around between the legs of the tables.

'What are you looking for?' he said, cupping his hands over his crotch.

'My dog,' she said. 'He's a dachshund. He roams like a store detective. I can never find him. That's why I came in.'

She leaned across the bar-stools and peered over the counter. Then she studied Theo.

'Underpants I've heard of. They look like a shower-cap.'

It was true. Theo was feeling more and more miserable. As if the business about the Bishop weren't enough to ruin his evening. Now there was this.

'I got them in Regent Street,' he said. 'Over in London. At one of those short-lease stores.'

The design on the front showed a nuclear warhead in the firing position. The logo on either buttock simply said Bang. Actually, the colouring was quite nice, even if it had run a bit in the fast cycle. After all, Felicity was not perfect.

'You're the medical student,' said the manageress. 'The Road Runner for Aids research.'

'Cancer,' Theo said. 'The common-or-garden sort.'

She laughed again. Then she was silent. Either she was doing the Ignatian exercises, or she was a bit pissed.

Indeed, now that he edged a little closer, he thought he could smell something citric, a lemon maybe. If so, it spelled tonic; and tonic spelled gin.

'A medical student,' she said again. 'Two medical students. And a skeleton. I heard about the skeleton. The skeleton on the tandem. Do you know what I thought to myself when I heard about him? Or should I say "it"? I prefer "him". What do you say? Do you say "him" or "it"?'

'I used to say "it",' Theo said. 'But now I say "him". He's sort of grown on me, you see.'

The woman wasn't listening.

'I thought that some woman must have got upset when he bled from his navel after three days, or when he got lost at three years old outside the passport booth in Woolworth's. I thought how the same woman must have stood beside him in his academic robes in the Great Hall of Earlsfort Terrace while some doddery old fusspot conferred him with a degree in Commerce or Classics; and how pleased she must have been when his newfound girlfriend bullied him into shaving his sideburns. And then I thought that hoisting him up on a bicycle and parading him around Tipperary or Roscommon was, well, sort of shitty. For want of a better word.'

Theo's foot was sticking to a dried slop on the dark linoleum behind the counter. When he lifted it, the noise crackled like a ripped bandage. It was that quiet in the Residents' Lounge. It was as quiet as an empty birdcage.

'I appreciate your frankness,' he said. 'I really do.'

She looked at him.

'How much do you know, little student? Can you translate terminology? Can you turn Latin and Greek into English as spoken in the West of Ireland? Can you do that? Can you tell me what a subarachnoid astracytoma is?'

'It's a brain tumour,' Theo said. 'A brain tumour under the back of the skull.'

'I'm impressed,' she said. 'You'll go far. You might even end up as a plastic surgeon. You might end up trimming and tucking old women's boobs, bringing them collagen for their crow's-feet, tightening their vaginas for that second marriage. A subarachnoid astracytoma. It took me months to get my teeth into those words, months of practice and months of prayer. By the time I was word-perfect, like a schoolgirl learning the Proclamation for the school pageant, learning the big words first, then the bigger, then the biggest of all, it was too late. The curtain was down, the lights were off, the seats were empty, the show was over. All I had was a copy of my script with the same two words written out in large Roman letters on each and every page of it, a subarachnoid astracytoma; that, and an only daughter of two-and-a-half who wouldn't settle in the bed at night unless her inflatable Yogi Bear was holding the door ajar to let in the landing light.'

'I understand,' said Theo.

He didn't, of course; but that was what the surgical tutor had advised him to say whenever a patient dissolved into tears or rattled off reams about some private calamity. It was a way of diffusing potentially difficult moments; plus it saved time.

'I do understand,' he said again. In fact, running the two variations of the same verbal intention with a slight pause in between the first and the second expression, was rather nice, rather neat. Also, it had a certain authority.

'I was fine for a while,' said the manageress. 'For the first few weeks I was fine. I painted the attic, for Christ's sake; I creosoted the fence. At night I took the child into the bed with me. It was to hear someone breathing beside me, to lie awake and listen to another person sleeping. That was it. That was it, you see. Are you with me at all?'

'I understand,' said Theo. 'I do understand.'

'But it didn't work. I found it didn't work. I found I couldn't stand the room. I started to sleep in the spare bed. And then one day, one day I discovered his shaver. So I opened it. And it was full of hairs, tiny little hairs from the last time I'd shaved him. Because I had to shave him. His hair had fallen out, but his beard was still growing. It grew even after he was dead.'

Theo hated himself. Why couldn't he cry? What sort of a cold-blooded bastard was he anyway? How come he never felt the need to bless himself, like Felicity would? What sort of a doctor would he make at this rate? The woman was showing him her insides. Damn it, she was disembowelling herself in front of him. This was a kind of seppuku in the Residents' Lounge. And he was standing in his shorts, feeling a fool.

'I think I must be very young,' he found himself saying.

The manageress bowed her head. She was breaking two burnt matches between her fingers. Then she dropped them on the counter among the wet circles left by the bottoms of bottles and glasses. No way was the Residents' Lounge a tidy place after hours. But Theo made allowances: the woman was in bits.

'Come with me,' she said. 'My medical student.'

Theo thought about this. In fact, he thought twice. But what the heck. Besides, his prestige was at stake. After all, she was hardly going to maim him with a machete when he got inside her bedroom. Conversely, if she did make an erotic overture, well, he could take that in his stride too. He had his own inner resources. So he did go with her, out into the lobby and beyond, down a tilted passageway where a blood-coloured carpet soared and sagged over weirdly warped floorboards. To tell the truth, it was a bit funny peculiar; but then she stopped, opened a door, and he followed her inside.

It was some sort of chapel. That was his first impression. The semi-darkness, the smell of kneelers, the atmosphere of a modern oratory in the post-Christian era – the man upstairs at the writing table would have felt at home in here. But the back-lit mountings on the walls around the room weren't stations of the Cross, the falls and flagellation of the trek toward the gibbet on Golgotha, where Christ was always looking soulfully at the stormclouds overhead, as if he half expected an air–sea rescue any minute now. No, these were X-rays, hospital X-rays of a human skull, a skull in sections: full-face, profile, the left anterior, left posterior, lateral views, the lot. They went on and on; there were a dozen at least, a whole series of studies, each of them named, each of them numbered, each of them initialled. The thing was grotesque, it was ghoulish. What sort of freak would do this anyway? Babies were another matter, of course. If you were a fee-paying private patient, your obstetrician would sometimes throw in a couple of the X-rays taken during the third trimester. His own sister had her twins up in the downstairs loo. But to hold onto the stuff from pathology, to hang it up like it was a holy picture, to turn a room into a reliquary: that was weird. Because Theo had sussed the situation at a glance. These weren't any ordinary pics. The skull in the shots was her significant other, her lover, her husband, her toyboy, whatever. He was the guy who was gone. Finito. Fair enough, he couldn't spot the tumour; but then he was only in second Med. Give him time, and he'd be having diseases named after him.

The manageress had sat down on a simple wooden chair

in the middle of the room. She put the head of the vacuum cleaner on the carpet in front of her. Then she folded her hands and bent her head.

'Would you like me to slip away now, and let you . . . let you pray?' Theo said.

She suddenly realised he was there.

'Pray?' she said. 'I never prayed in my life. I always considered that talking to yourself is the first sign of madness.'

He took a step forward.

'I used to pray,' he told her. 'I don't mean prayers. Not even sexy ones, like the "Hail, Holy Queen".'

'I always loved the "Hail, Holy Queen",' said the manageress.

'Me too,' Theo said. 'But I can't remember it now.' If the truth be told, he was rather chuffed about that: it meant he was fully in control of his own life. He was transmitting his own strong signal; and he didn't want any breakthrough from another station. That was a nifty little metaphor – or was it a simile? – that he would try not to forget. The Student Union newsletter was always on the look-out for the sort of strong copy that would upset apple-carts in the common room. He might even do a regular column for them.

'I'd forget my own name before I forgot the "Hail, Holy Queen",' said the manageress. 'But maybe that's not saying much. Sure I forgot myself the other day when I was writing a cheque for petrol. I went and wrote my own name instead of my married name. And then the attendant wanted two proofs of my identity. But all I had was a letter of sympathy from a priest uncle of mine in the Holy Ghost, who wanted me to rejoice. Rejoice, he said. It was a wonderful privilege to die during Easter week, and it wasn't accorded to many. Well, it was accorded to a hundred and thirty-seven northern Burmese the same afternoon, when a ramshackle locomotive left the straight and narrow at a bad bend in some unpronounceable upland area; and I'm sure they all felt suitably honoured. I'm sure they all beat a path to the Blessed Trinity, waving coconut palms and autograph books.'

'Humour is a great tonic,' said Theo. 'A great therapy. I had a dark night of the soul myself, and it was Monty Python pulled me through. Anyhow, she was diagnosed manic depressive, so I was just as well off. Ever since then, I've only gone out with bimbos. Felicity's brains are in the seat of her pants, really; but it means that I'm admiring her mind whenever she sits on my face. But you must try to be humorous without being racist. "Coconut palms" is a bit racist.'

'He's happier in Heaven,' said the manageress. 'Happier in Heaven. That's what my uncle wrote. I wanted to ask him: happier than what? Happier than where? Happier than he was when he brought in coal on a Friday night before the start of "The Late Late Show"? Happier than he was when the baby couldn't get over the little chimp with the nappy up at the Zoo in Dublin? Or happier than he was when I'd let him smell my tights before I put them in the laundry-bin? In what way happier?'

She had finished. Or had she? The body language suggested that she was through; but you never knew with these people. When they free-associated, by God they took a tour of the universe. On the other hand, a silence would be worse. Theo could not cope with silence. It was nothing but emanations of id. So, when he saw another rain-belt cross her face, he jumped in.

'You have tremendous insight,' he said to her. 'You have total insight.'

She read his eyes, like they were Hebrew, from right to left.

'Say it,' she said. 'Say it with me.'

'Say what?' he said.

'The "Hail, Holy Queen",' said the manageress.

Was this for real? Was any of this for real? Why hadn't he stayed home and run kissograms for the summer, or been a Golden Oldie DJ for some pirate outfit? Even bee-keeping would be better than waking up to find yourself in your underpants in a room full of X-rays, with a Marian groupie chanting antediluvian mantras. This was not happening.

The manageress started off. Her voice was even lower than it had been. Theo had to strain to hear the phrases. When he did, he remembered them; remembered them before ever they were uttered, their stately, incantatory cadences, the way he remembered the next track on the turntable before the stylus touched the song. The whole of it was so reverent, so erotic, discourse and intercourse. How had he managed to dismember it until he had dis-remembered it all together? How? And why?

'. . . that we may be worthy of the promise of Christ.' She had dropped to a whisper; it was almost inaudible.

'Amen,' said Theo. It was true what he had read that time in one of Felicity's Fontana anthologies the Dominican had inscribed for her when she was reading English and Philosophy during the nine months she had wasted in Arts. You could no more forget what you'd encountered or endured in this world than a sycamore tree could relinquish one of its rings. Instead, you stood rooted in the rich protein of your own leaf-fall, your own successive sheddings, the flaws, the failures, the fiascos, a long and lonely earthwardness. And for a moment, a space of seconds, Theo recalled a stripped and shaggy eucalyptus, the one he'd seen in the bulletin where the state militia were beating the shit out of the steel-workers in Bucharest, and how it seemed to bend in the breeze, how it seemed almost to bow, as if saying yes to the tear-gas, yes to the picnic baskets.

But this wasn't getting him anywhere. This arboreal business was all balls. How the hell had he started into it anyway? That was the trouble when you got involved in smalltalk with a stranger. Before you knew where you were, you were copycatting the Sacred Heart, hauling out your luminous insides for inspection. Better to stick with the people you knew well, where the conversation never rose beyond a bit of bitchcraft over an Argyll sock that went AWOL in the washing machine. Theo tried to remember the number on his bank-line passcard; then he did it backwards. It was an old ploy, but a surefire way of decompressing.

The manageress was coming to.

'I don't see what's sexy about it,' she said to him.

'About what?' Theo said. Was this a come-on?

'The "Hail, Holy Queen",' said the manageress.

She was serious too. He could see that. She took everything to heart.

'Well,' he said, 'I suppose I meant that, well, you know, if I could sort of lubricate a lady with that kind of palaver, the rhythms, the rhetoric, not that I'm a lounge lizard, a ladykiller, quite the opposite, I'm an out-and-out feminist, in fact I wish I were a woman, if men could only menstruate, well, there wouldn't be half the bloodshed there is, would there?'

She made him feel so shallow. And he wasn't shallow, he was deep. Maybe not deep deep, as in washing the winos' feet like it was Holy Thursday every day of the year, the way the chaplain had been doing it ever since he came back from Nicaragua; but still deep. After all, he had loaned his Leonard Cohen compact discs for the slow sets at the Amnesty International fund-raising discothèque; he was friends with two Muslims in fourth year; and he had castigated a colleague in the dissecting room for having stubbed a Slim Panatella on a cadaver's perineum. Indeed, he had a good mind to tell her that. Perhaps then she wouldn't keep looking at him so compassionately, almost as if she were looking through him, as if she were looking throughout him. It was so patronising. Besides, it was his business if he chose to be shallow or even profoundly shallow, which at least had a certain inverted, post-modernist merit to it that someone like the manageress, with her mournful *mater dolorosa* carry-on, would never be able to fathom. Because if he were to find that Felicity, say, had decamped or defaulted, run away with that hirsute jockstrap from Trondheim who spent half the lectures sketching booby cartoons of her on geometry paper, he would just have to be far-eastern about it, to see it in hindsight, like a Hindu, before it even happened. After all, every experience was a learning experience, and the odd brush with bereavement was part and parcel of any comprehensive reconnaissance of the cosmos. If it wasn't, then you checked through the Golden Pages and you rang for a skip. So, if Felicity fucked off, he would somehow sort himself out. Then he would sort her out. Finally, he would sort out her belongings. He would make a His/Hers inventory, and forward the stuff by courier. Maybe he'd be a bit below par for a lunar month; maybe he'd find himself throwing sanitary towels into the supermarket trolley without thinking. But at least he'd have the satisfaction of knowing that he'd raised another woman from coma to consciousness, quite apart from the fact that his future love-life was bound to benefit: Felicity had taken him on trips Columbus never dreamed of.

'That's rubbish,' said the manageress.

'What is?' Theo said. She wasn't telepathic, was she? There were people who looked deadpan, down-to-earth, but inside their heads was a planetarium. If she could do this weird, wallpapering job with the X-rays, maybe she could put a kink in cutlery. That was the trouble with appearances: you forgot they were the foyer, and the film was showing inside.

'What you said about men and periods,' the woman said. 'They just don't have the balls for it.'

She smiled and stretched her fingers so that the joints cracked.

'I didn't have a period for five months after the funeral,' she said. 'It felt a bit like being pregnant.'

There was a phrase for this in psychiatry, the way she brought everything back to the death of a life, the life-time of a dying. If he mentioned fresh fruit salad or the Amazon rain-forest, there'd be a tie-in. He'd have been an anthropologist or their favourite restaurant served it for dessert. It was time to steal away.

'When did you stop praying?' she asked him. 'Or did it just peter out? They say that mostly it just peters out, and you don't notice. The way you don't notice your child's hair getting darker again after the summer; until it's Christmas, and you find a roll of film behind the candlesticks at the top of the bookshelf, and you get them developed. Then you think, gosh, she was so much fairer that day in the forest.'

Theo was thinking too, but not about solar bleaches.

'The day I stopped praying,' he told her, 'was in Pre-Med, the time I was doing my Biology paper. I took one look at the questions, and I knew that the jury was in. There was no way I could do it. So I just sat there, working the thong of my flip-flop with my big toe and

48

my second toe, waiting. All around me in the Examination Hall I could see these bright guys beavering away, with their tongues between their teeth. Even Felicity was at it, for God's sake. She had this flock of multicoloured felt-pens for doing the terminology in vermilion and the quotations in cobalt blue; and I bet my bottom dollar she was stuck into the essay on ovulation among the reptiles. It would take Felicity.'

'Were you tempted to pray?' said the manageress. 'It's always been my greatest temptation. You need to summon tremendous strength to resist it.'

'I didn't pray exactly,' Theo said. 'Not when the papers were handed out. But I had this little ink-bottle that was full of Lourdes water, and I used to swallow that. I used to take it all the time, each and every morning, just in case some smart-ass on the staff sprang a multiple-choice, continuous-assessment test on the whole class. But what I didn't know was that my mother was filling it from the tap.'

'Be innocent as doves, and wise as serpents,' the woman said. 'It's a tricky graft.'

'Graft is right,' said Theo. 'She was stockpiling her own supplies. None of her water was going walkabout.'

'Holy water,' said the manageress. 'I had so much holy water round the house those last few months before he died. As if all water weren't holy. But the funniest thing I got in the post was a papal parking sticker from the Mass in the Phoenix Park. I was supposed to put it under his pillow. Along with another hipflask of holy water.'

Theo had come forward a little. He wanted to put it on the record, about the ink-bottle.

'I didn't drink mine,' he said. 'Not that day, the written Biology day. I didn't touch a drop. Instead, I asked to go to the toilet. So the invigilator came with me, and she checked out the cubicle beforehand, to make sure I hadn't hidden a text-book somewhere inside. But I could have told her, I could have told her there are no text-books any more; there are only graffiti. And I added mine. I took out a pencil, and I wrote on the wall. There is no Temple, I wrote; and I kept flushing the john while I worked, because silence would have worried the invigilator. There is no Temple, there is no Talmud, there is only . . .'

'Only what?' said the woman.

'God knows,' Theo said. 'I didn't get it finished. I wanted a bit of a flourish for the finale, but I couldn't think it through. Anyhow, the invigilator was tapping with her ring-finger on the toilet door. So I girded my loins, and I left. For the first time in my life I felt free, because for the first time in my life I knew that I wasn't. To tell the truth, the whole truth, and nothing but the truth, it was a pretty disagreeable sensation; but Felicity was full sure it would grow on me with a little practice. She even gave me one of those bargain-basement books called *Vulnerability and the Void*. Whenever I was on a bus and I found myself sitting beside a priest, I'd take it out and read it; but they never said anything. At any rate, the long and the short of it is that, since the day I stood up and walked out of that examination, I haven't had a prayer. I mean, I haven't said a prayer.'

The woman smiled. To be honest, he preferred her laugh. That at least was above board, it was on the level. But her smile reminded him of Reformation martyrs on the covers of Catholic Truth Society pamphlets, the sort he'd won as wooden spoons at the school prize-days in a previous life, where the lips and the look in the eyes sent different messages that cancelled each other out, and left you staring into inscrutability, that left you feeling you were a bit common somehow.

'The last time I tried to pray, I prayed to try,' said the manageress. 'But it didn't work. My brothers-in-law had lifted the coffin, and they were carrying it down the aisle to the porch. I wanted to help them, but they wouldn't let me. It had to be men, you see. Death was their affair. This wasn't a maternity hospital, after all. So the mortician was a young man; the undertakers were middle-aged men; the gravediggers were elderly men; and the florist was a boy.'

'There'll be women priests yet,' said Theo. 'You wait and see.'

'In the porch, while they were arranging the bouquets in the hearse, I found all this rice on the floor,' she said. 'From a wedding the day before, and the sacristan hadn't swept it away. I kept standing on it. Then I picked the baby up because I didn't want her playing with it. And I couldn't stop myself thinking about the girl who'd got married, and about where she'd gone for the first night and whether she had a wardrobe that wouldn't shut properly like I did, and whether she'd worked it out on a pocket calculator so that her period wouldn't get in the way; and all this time there were strangers coming up to me and telling me how they had five of their own, but they'd still steal the baby.'

She rummaged in the pockets of her housecoat. Perhaps she was looking for a handkerchief. There was something about her that was more handkerchief than tissue. But all she came up with was a couple of dog-biscuits. She put them back again.

'The room helps,' she said. 'It helps a lot. Because there are times when I have to tell myself that he's dead. Not called home, not passed on; just dead. So I sit here and I say to myself: astracytoma. I say it over and over, like the Rosary. It stops you hoping, you see. Hope wears you out. Despair is so much easier. It doesn't make you do small, silly things. Like standing into a built-in press in a bedroom and smelling a man who's dead off the insides of his reefer jackets. That's hope for you. All drive and no dignity.'

From outside in the street Theo could hear faint footsteps. They were slow, slurred almost, of several people, a party perhaps. They could well be late-night look-a-likes, the Dolly Parton dragoons. Whoever they were, they were singing in a hit-and-miss harmony, full-volume, like lumberjacks in a locker-room; and, as they passed the curtained window, he could sense their fullness, their fleshiness, their smell of low-priced perfume, talcum powder, and the soft brickwork underneath bridges. They were holding on to each other; he could tell from the way they were walking, from the slick clicking of their heels. And he knew the song too. It was Tammy Wynette's 'Stand By Your Man'.

'At least I've learned something,' said the manageress. 'One thing. I learned it all by myself as well. I didn't get it out of a grammar or a guide-book, because it isn't there. It isn't even in the *Encyclopaedia Britannica* or the little brochures that the Mormons give you. It isn't anywhere, in fact, because it scares people shitless.'

But Theo was beginning to move back, back toward the door, a step at a time. They were right, those women outside. They were right to be singing. Life was the haggard and the hayrick, wineflasks, backsides, high-kicking chicitas, the blue ablutions of ordinary life, the din of what is. He could have gone on. He was feeling good again. He was feeling like Anthony Quinn. He was feeling like Zorba the Greek.

'What happens at the end of the day?' said the manageress.

What was she on about now? Of course he felt sorry for her, sympathy for her. But you couldn't just stand at the foot of the Cross all your life. Even the women who did, Mary this and Mary that, they had to go home and peel spuds at some stage. Not because they wanted to, but because that's life. Spring doesn't stop for the cardiac ambulance; it has to get on with its painting-by-numbers. So, if you must weep, weep away; but do it over the onions. What were they called, those eskimos up in Alaska who bivouacked their old folk at the foot of the glacier every autumn, and left them there, because they'd be a liability to the tribe during the lean months ahead? We do it too, of course, but we call it Homes for the Elderly. Anyhow, they were right, they were putting death in its place: as far away from them as possible. He admired that. He admired the noble savage aspect of it. That was what Zorba was about.

'I'll tell you what happens at the end of the day,' said the manageress. 'At the end of the day, it gets dark. And there isn't anything the largest light-switch in the world can do about it.'

But Theo had gone; and he was halfway up the stairs toward his bedroom before she started to cry. By the time he reached the corridor and was leaning against the fire-extinguisher to flick a fag-end from his instep, she was so deeply immersed in the reality of this world that she may safely be said to have left it altogether. That, at any rate, is what Theo would have said, and Theo is a reliable guide in these matters; reliable enough, anyhow, to have made it by now to the very door of his bedroom.

He slipped inside and stood in the darkness, listening. She must have got out of bed at some stage to switch off the light. Or else the bulb had gone, but that wasn't likely. So perhaps she was still awake, perhaps she was still alert, perhaps she was still feeling old-fashioned. She quite liked to feign sleep, an absolute stupor even, to surprise him, to take him by storm. He'd be soft-footing it around the bath-room, gargling hydrogen peroxide in a styrofoam cup, with a newspaper over the Tiffany lamp, and suddenly she'd throw off the blankets, and be sitting up in bed in a basque or a baby-doll outfit. If it happened again tonight, that would make it twice so far; and even if it didn't, what matter? Because all he wanted to do was to feel her, to fondle her, to sleep spoons, and wake up in the world the following morning, with the sound of a lorry unloading beer outside in the street. Later on in the day he could ask her about the Norwegian, and whether she'd trashed his sketches; but for now the other would be enough. For now the other would be more than enough.

But what was that noise? And there was a noise, from right beside him: a low, level rasping, discreet little teeth. Maybe a mouse, a mouse behind the beauty board. Theo hoped to the good God above that it wouldn't work its way into the room. Felicity had a phobia about anything out of *Wind in the Willows* or *Tarka the Otter*. Yet was it a mouse, after all? Somehow the sound wasn't chittery enough. Besides, there was a smell. A sort of horsy smell. But that was ridiculous. On the other hand, there were X-rays downstairs. Anything could happen in the real world. It was only in novels that you found probability.

So he touched the door behind him with the tips of his fingers, and it swung open softly to let in light from the corridor. There was Felicity, curled on the bed across the room, mooning at him. There was the skeleton, sprawled at the bureau, his bones as bleached as the Dead Sea surface. And there at his feet was a dog, a dachshund, contentedly chewing the right metatarsus. Not that the skeleton seemed to mind. He looked particularly wrapped up in himself this evening, almost as if he were dead to it all. His foot swung back and forth in the dachshund's mouth, swung back and forth to some celestial melody. Theo couldn't bear to see him mocked to this degree. Poking fun was another matter. You had to split your sides on this earth; otherwise you broke your heart, and cardiology couldn't cope with something as subtle as that. Certain subjects were off-limits, however: the Holocaust, child abuse, and whatever your own problem happened to be. A dog who was having a midnight feast by sinking his molars into someone's metatarsus, was a definite recruit to that shortlist. It was not on.

Felicity slept through it all. Tonight she was an American war correspondent turned Vietcong collaborator, carrying a wounded GI on her back through a paddyfield where she had planted mines galore a fortnight ago; his blood trickled down her battledress, but she pressed on regardless: for love, and only love, was her ultimate ideology. By the time Theo had ousted the dachshund, coaxing him into the corridor by feeding him Rolo after Rolo from a packet he'd bought that morning at the mobile van outside the megalithic passage-grave, she had made it to the safety of a ditch and was squeezing milk from her nipple onto the cut, cracked lips of the crewcut soldier. There was a pain in her shoulder, in her shoulder-blade. She must have been hit too.

'Felicity,' said Theo. He was jabbing her shoulder with his finger. 'Felicity. I'm sorry it's so late. I don't want to wake you. I mean, I do want to wake you. That is, if you don't mind. Please.'

But she was fast asleep. She might have taken pills. She did that when she was pissed. Pissed, as in fed-up, browned off, beleaguered. And sure enough there were two foil sachets on the table. But no sign of a glass of water, he thought. One of these days she'd choke, and he wouldn't be there. That'd be sure to fuck him up for the rest of his life; but that would have been her idea in the first place. It took women.

Theo looked through the window, up at the sky. You could always see more stars in the country. He didn't know why. Pollution, probably. Then again, in the city you weren't thinking about stars. You were thinking about getting a new cylinder for the gas heater, or setting the video to record the winter Olympics. In the country, on the other hand, there was bugger all to do after ten-thirty. So you could stargaze all the way home from the boozer into the marital bed.

'Orion,' Theo said. That was the name of one of the constellations; but which one? 'Andromeda,' he said. 'Cassiopeia. Sagittarius.' Or was that from horoscopes instead of astronomy? It was strange to think that he could unfold the structure of a leaf, the geography of a blood-cell, or the Keystone Cops behaviour of a trillion little sperm, but the galaxies in all their complex choreography, their grandeur and gravity, were so much wattage to him: sufficient light to change a tyre by.

Theo climbed into bed beside Felicity. If she'd taken sleeping pills, he needn't warm his hands before he touched her. She wasn't going to wake. He slipped his fingers between the cheeks of her bottom, where it was snug and moist, and lay his head against her neck. Tomorrow he would rub some calamine lotion on the insect-bite behind her ear. But now he would sleep. There was no sleeping like a baby anymore, not when you shaved twice daily and still looked swarthy; and the sleep of the just was out of the question too: but he could always try, and generally did, for the sleep of the just about.

★

They had reached the last resort on their route around Ireland; and the place was more popular than they had imagined, but then imagining is an inexact science. The streets were crowded. There was no other word for it. Felicity and Theo were quite taken aback. It wasn't so much that they'd been expecting the usual village idyll – a chicken brooding in the back seat of a brand-new BMW, inter-denominational badminton in some abandoned Anglican church on the outskirts, the parish clergy jogging with the League of Single Parents past the Regional Tourist kiosk where the Parnellites had fought, or the mountainy men with faces like a satellite shot of Europe, tapping their two Hermesetas tablets into cups of rich-roast decaffeinated coffee in plain pubs where collies begged for the scraps of smoked-salmon salads served to a Portuguese couple from the Department of Comparative Anthropology in the University of Lisbon. No, that sort of thing was pretty much par for the course all over the country. Their whistle-stop from Kill-this and Cull-that and across to the West had more or less habituated them to the signs and symptoms of immense cultural vitality everywhere. As Felicity had said not once but often on the way here, it was as if the national sperm-count had soared to new heights since the eradication of TB.

'TB was eradicated thirty years ago,' Theo had reminded her.

'I was talking metaphorically,' Felicity said. 'I was talking about another kind of respiratory disorder. I was talking about the inability to draw breath during the penal days.'

'The penal days were two hundred years ago,' said Theo.

'I'm not talking about *those* penal days,' Felicity retorted. 'I'm talking about a state of affairs, not about affairs of state. I'm trying to present the truth, not to parade the facts. Do you not realise that when you were born, the Irish penis had no civil rights? It could never stand up for itself. It had to hang its head in front of every priest, prelate and politician in the land. That's what I mean when I talk about the Great Hunger.'

'What do you know about the Great Hunger?' Theo said. 'You didn't do History at school. You did Biology instead.'

'That's the point,' said Felicity, and she waved the skeleton's hand at a nice Israeli couple who were swerving a video camera at her. 'I did do Biology. And I learned about stomachs. I learned about the large intestine and the small intestine. I did a whole project on the digestive process for the Young Scientists' Exhibition; I called it "The Odyssey of a Chicken Portion: from the First Big Bite to the Bowel Motion". Only the nuns wouldn't enter it, and that was because I didn't contribute to Sister Eithne's presentation, the time she was swanning off to El Salvador. And she was the one who always lectured us about not walking on the council flats side of the road on the way home because we might be ambushed by the types who lived there. So you see.'

'No,' Theo said. 'I don't think I do.'

'Biology,' said Felicity. 'I learned about hunger. About starvation. Then I went home and I saw it in my parents' eyes. I could even smell it off them: an atmosphere of rictus, ration books, rice-bowls. A diet of bread and water, bread and wine, bread and circuses. The only thing they ever bit was their tongue, the only thing they ever ate was their words, and the only thing they ever made a shit of was their whole lives. I'd come down at night from doing my homework, and they'd be asleep on the couch in front of "Hawaii Five-O"; and I'd look at them, and they'd be so

5 8

emaciated. But it wasn't just glucose they needed, some grub shovelled in. They needed more than a morsel, more than a meal. They needed a breaking of bread, and they never got that. All they got was an assurance that their stomach cramps wouldn't go unrewarded by the great Chef in the Sky.'

Felicity swivelled on the bicycle saddle, and glared at the skeleton. Actually, the way she swivelled was something else. It was really something else. Theo wished he could take her from behind. That would be so meaningful: to have her hair in two long pigtails, like in the picture of her with the carcass of the shark when she was only fifteen, and to hold one pigtail in each hand while you committed the sacrament of encounter. But the trouble was, he kept slipping out. Then she'd start giggling; and if there's one thing which gets in the way of the sacrament of encounter, it's a giggle. After all, some things are sacred. You can read the Sunday tabloids during the sermon at Mass, but sexual intercourse is a serious business. If it weren't, it wouldn't have such a long name.

'Are you listening?' Felicity said. 'I said that this skull-and-crossbones is part of the problem.'

'How so?' said Theo.

'Because the one thing we don't need in this country are killjoys. Killjoys see the whole world as a comic tragedy; but lovejoys understand that it's a tragic comedy. A lovejoy, you see, is the opposite of a killjoy.'

Felicity was bowled over. It was the sort of thing you read on programmes at fringe plays in theatres where you poured your own coffee at the interval and the heating was never on or at least never up so you had to sit in your coat all night. She said the sentences back to herself again in order to memorise them.

'I'm going to say that to Dolores the next time she has

59

us round for her not-so-nouveau nouvelle cuisine,' she said to Theo. 'Her and her neo-Marxist this and that. I'll neo-Marxist her.'

'He wasn't a killjoy,' Theo said. 'He wasn't a killjoy.' And he leaned out over the pew again as the Bishop was walking away, the walk of a man well used to a tilting deck beneath him, and he called out so that the acolyte turned to stare at him in surprise, and the Bishop waved, a wave that was tired and tender, mild and amused. And that was nice, when you thought about it.

'The killjoy,' said Felicity, 'is the first to remind you of the average industrial wage for a South American coffee-picker, when you're just about to make a fresh cup. The killjoy –'

'He wasn't a killjoy,' Theo said.

'Of course he was a killjoy,' said Felicity, and she smiled back at the portly Ugandan (or was she pregnant?) in national costume who was eating an ice-cream cone from the bottom up, outside a confectionery with a cardboard sign in the window, which read: "Dollars or Dinars, Everything Changed."

'This skeleton,' Theo said, 'is the key to something we may have lost.'

'Lost,' said Felicity. 'I was waiting for that word. Lose this, lose that, lose the other. The whole of Irish history is nothing other than the conjugation of the verb "to lose", from the simple present to the future perfect. Well, I want to gain. I want to gain everything. Everything except weight, of course.'

And she beamed at the Czechoslovakian dissident who was waiting for his dog to poo beside the laminated trash-can. He had a poop-scoop in his hand, and he waved it at her in welcome.

'He was a sort of Moses,' Theo told her. 'That's what

60

a Bishop is, a sort of Moses. I don't mean Yul Brynner or Charlton Heston. I mean that he had to mind a whole people who were wandering in the desert, trying to get the sun out of their eyes and the sand out of their ears, in a world that was all mirage and no maps. And what he brought them was the smell of seaweed.'

'That would have made a neat chowder,' Felicity said. 'Something to get your teeth into.'

And the skeleton's skull bobbed back and forth, back and forth as the bicycles bounded over the potholes. Some of them were so bloody deep they probably had koalas peering into them at the other end. No wonder the missing persons' list got longer and longer every year.

'Will you go easy?' Theo said to her. 'I don't want him to break his neck at this stage of the game. He's been through enough already.'

Why wouldn't Felicity understand? About the desert, that is. About how Moses had taught the Jews, or were they Hebrews then, the words for seagull, jibsail, shingle, the vocabulary of the deep, even though they were stuck in the arsehole of nowhere, an arid sierra of sand-dunes. About how –

'Through enough already, has he?' said Felicity. 'And what about us? Fear and failure, failure and fear, but that doesn't matter, does it, because the word for defeat in the Irish language is moral victory, isn't it? "We may have lost the game," said the rugby commentator that time the two of us were at home and your parents came back unexpectedly, and I couldn't find my diaphragm because it was in under the coal-scuttle, "but our defeat was a spiritual triumph." That about sums it up.'

'Nothing sums anything up,' said Theo. 'That's the beginning of wisdom.'

'It sums it up for me,' Felicity said. 'And our sleeping

partner here would have liked it too. He would indeed. The whole bench of bishops had us living with our waggons in a circle, even though the last Apache squaw had died of pneumonia in some God-forsaken reservation centuries before. That's why I wrote to the Pope.'

'You wrote to the Pope?' Theo said. He was astounded. He had never heard of anybody writing to the Pope, at least not since Henry VIII, and look where that got him. Then again, maybe the Pope was an inveterate correspondent. Maybe that was why there were so many Vatican stamps. Perhaps he should have written to Rome and not to Peking, when he was fourteen and he wanted a copy of Chairman Mao's little red book. Mind you, he'd got one in the post a month or two later, from the Chinese Embassy in London; he could still remember the sheet of tissue paper veiling the snapshot of the Great Helmsman on the inside front cover, but perhaps that was only to disguise the wart on his cheek since they'd hardly have specialist surgeons in a dump like the Middle Kingdom: on the other hand, admittedly, the Long March might have convinced him that he was Christ incarnate. At any rate, the Jesuit scholastics at Theo's secondary school had been absolutely zapped when he produced it. Two of them fought over it. The first one read from it that same afternoon during the Quiet Hour, a Religious Instruction period when the pupils did their homework and the teachers reminisced rapturously about the student-worker alliance in the Paris of '68; and the other, who always made his congregation do finger and facial exercises for twenty minutes before the Mass began, in a bid to make them be and not have a body, used it as the backbone of his homily on the following Sunday. In fact, he wanted to buy it, but Theo wasn't on. Instead, he traded it three weeks later with a classmate for a copy of a book called

Sluts in Heat: A Compendium of Edwardian Erotica. A lot of rubbish it was too. An utter violation of the Trades Description Act. How would –

'Theo?' said Felicity. She was peering at him, searching his eyes. But she didn't know him. Not really. He had never told her about things like that. Itsy bitsy things, to be sure; but they belonged to him or, rather, he belonged to them. It was strange to think that she could shove a finger up his bum when he was coming; yet she didn't know about the time he wrote off for the little red book. And he wanted her to know. At least, he wanted someone to know. Because if someone knew, knew everything about him, from the time he was little to the time he was less and right on up to the present when he sometimes felt that he was a predestined non-event, a nullity, then perhaps he could try to explain; but explain what? What was he talking about? It didn't make sense. He was twenty; that was the age of no bullshit. And he was bullshitting. There should be a law against it. There should be some sort of antibiotic that you can take when you feel the first twinges of these strange, metaphysical chest-pains. But for the time being, there was only common-sense.

'If your eye waters,' Theo said to Felicity, 'it's because there's something in it.'

'You amaze me,' said Felicity. 'You can be so common-sensical, even when you're hurting. Here, let me look.'

Already she was twisting a Kleenex. And Theo let her. There was no point.

'Whatever it was, is gone,' she said to him.

'Whatever it was, is gone,' he said.

'Crisis over,' she announced. They saddled up again. The skeleton was examining his hands, as if discovering for the first time that their flesh had been burgled, that the dry watercourse of his palm was now truly unfathomable.

There was definite anxiety in the facial expression, and Theo could empathise. When you got down to bare bones, the outlook was bleak. Tissue and tendon, liver and loin had long since been laid bare; and the body, a shrewd chronology of mumps, measles, allergies from Aran sweaters, wet dreams, laughter, ingrown toenails and the crow's-feet of a lifetime's study of scripture, had all gone up in the softest of smoke over the hurrying head of a plain-clothes policeman who was late for the bank, and could see the porter in the process of closing the doors a hundred yards ahead of him.

Such was life; and it came with the same small print to each and every one of us, from the travelling people to the Pope in Rome. Which reminded Theo.

'What were you saying about the Pope, anyhow?' he said.

'I was saying I wrote to him,' Felicity said. 'I didn't know his address, so I wrote to him care of the Vatican.'

'And what did you say?'

'Dear Pope, I am one of the petals from your rosebed. Well, I got deflowered last night. There was no blood, but that's because of what happened on the parallel bars during gym class three years ago. Anyhow, it was great. You should try it sometime. Also, if you have a moment, would you consider excommunicating St Augustine, St Tertullian, St Origen, St Ambrose and St Jerome for all the shitty things they wrote about vaginal penetration? I know they had their problems, but that's no excuse for sneering at something God obviously went to a lot of trouble about. After all, like every creative artist, He's very sensitive. Love, Felicity. PS. I thought your last encyclical was spot-on.'

'And did you get an answer?'

'No, but then of course we moved house a month later.

Not that I was expecting an answer from the Supreme Pontiff, but I thought I might hear from one of the Papabili who hang out of St Peter's. They're into marketing, they're into PR. This would have been a golden opportunity for them. They could have whisked me off to the Eternal City, the way that Brezhnev brought the little girl on an Aeroflot flight to Leningrad after she wrote to him about her stamp collection. But they missed the boat, or maybe they just felt inadequate. Not that it mattered. When I wrote that postcard, I knew what Martin Luther must have felt, with his theses and his box of thumb-tacks outside Notre Dame. Here I stand. That's what I felt. Here I stand. Not for the life of grace, but for the grace of life. So I stand for children, I sit for adults, and I kneel for the elderly. The only thing I take lying down is the sun-lamp.'

And she braked hard to stop herself colliding with a woman in wellingtons who had appeared from nowhere – phenomena of this kind are nowadays largely limited to the oldest monasteries in Lhasa; they are still known to occur, however, throughout the length and breadth of Ireland, a gnostic encampment which derides the rationalistic pretensions of the cause-and-effect model – and was trying might and main to free a choked drain outside the butcher's shop. Felicity called a greeting, Theo bestowed a smile of the sort that only saints, centrefolds, and the private beneficiaries of orthodontic dentistry can healthily hazard, and the skeleton shrieked with good-humoured hilarity as his jawbone slipped a little looser from its steel ligature; but the woman blessed herself. She actually blessed herself. Theo could see her clearly in the mirror on his handlebar. In one of her hands she was holding what looked like the rabbit-ears off an old television set; and with the other she was making the sign of

6 5

the Cross. Now why the dickens would she want to do that?

'It all adds up to the fact that I'm as free as a bird,' Felicity said to him.

What added up? He had clean forgotten what she was talking about. But the woman had blessed herself. And it wasn't because she thought she was seeing a repeat by public demand of the Corpus Christi Procession. Or because she had just got her period, the way Felicity did on the days when she kept inspecting her panties until she finally found they were spotted. Then she was like an Orthodox monk, doing the rounds of the icons. No, the woman with the rabbit-ears was a bit beyond babies; she'd be on the lee-side of her later forties at least. So why would –

'Free as a bird,' Felicity said again.

'Birds aren't free,' said Theo. 'They act according to instinct. When the housemartins migrate to Algiers in the autumn, they don't do it because they're crypto-Moslems. They do it that way because they've been doing it that way since the world first ruffled their feathers. It's part and parcel of a master-code that makes them housemartins. It has to do with climatology, it has to do with the earth's magnetism, it has to do with genetics. So, when Harry Housemartin roars down the runway off the rusted chassis of some up-ended Beetle Volkswagen at a scenic spot in Co. Mayo, and he's thinking of three weeks' time when he'll be feasting on flies around the caravans of the garbage-people who live along the coastline outside Cairo, he has as much freedom to refuse his flightplan as my tool has to stay soft when you start touching him and telling him about what the Dominican made you do in the bicycle shed after the Bible Study Group had met to discuss liberation theology and St Paul.'

Maybe she had blessed herself because of the cut of Felicity. Maybe it was that simple. You didn't have to come this far west, like some latter-day bwana with his beaters, to encounter cultural backwardness, the Stone Age forms behind the simonised surface. You could find them in Dublin too, though of course that was due to immigration from outlying areas. Theo had even known a man from Clare who had spent twenty years of his life in the United States, seven of them in the service of the San Franciscan Bureau of Statistics and the other thirteen in reducing the municipal crime rate in Minneapolis, Minnesota. Which was to say, concretely, that he first pitched about in cross-winds in a hoist a hundred feet above the northbound traffic on the Bay Bridge, counting cars, which was easy enough during rush-hour when the lanes were stationary, but a damn sight more difficult during off-peak periods when the pedals were flush with the floor and every second motorist seemed to be dress-rehearsing helter-skelter stunts for an audition that afternoon with Cecil B. De Mille; and that, subsequently, he served as a security guard in a Macy's store in a downtown shopping mall where he pocketed discount perfume from the European counter on a regular basis to award to an Austrian lady with an Afro hairstyle who used to cook him shepherd's pie every time she was between relationships, and where he had once shelled out thirty-seven dollars to save a bald-headed has-been in a wheelchair from criminal prosecution because one of the store detectives saw him stuffing flippers and a snorkel into the commode under his cushion. Yet after all that rich exposure and experience, after a quarter century in a civilisation that makes Graeco-Roman culture look like a neighbourhood crèche, back he comes to the gorse and gobshite of the family farm, believing still in guardian angels, original sin, the mystery of the Mass, the historical accuracy of Jesus of Nazareth sweating blood on the Cross, which is a haematological impossibility, and, most of all, believing still that God Almighty is passionately and compassionately engrossed in the narrative of each and every human life. The truth is, there were some people who were incapable of learning, incapable of evolving. They belonged with the fossil fragments, the Pleistocene defectives, of Death Valley. They came out of the Ark of the Covenant, or whatever Noah called it. They were strictly for the birds.

'Are you listening?' Felicity said. 'Can you hear it?'

'Hear what?' said Theo.

'Shut up and listen,' she told him. 'If only you could learn to listen.' She had taken off her Walkman, and was pointing with the headphones toward a thickly tangled creeper on the derelict portico of a Methodist hall. Theo could see it, he could see the stencilled sign that was sheathed in clingfilm, and which advertised aikido classes on a Thursday evening; but what was he meant to be hearing? There was an ice-cream van in the area, because the breeze brought him a child's tune played on a xylophone; and, now that he strained, he could almost distinguish the words of the song that Felicity had been humming, because the cassette was still running. It was country and western, it had something to do with a mother at her daughter's shotgun-wedding breakfast who stands up and tells all the guests how she was pregnant too when she got married, and how grateful she was to God that she hadn't skedaddled off to the family doctor to have a D and C, because now she could look at her baby in her Juliet cap and her mother-of-pearl bridal dress, yet it seemed like only yesterday that she'd bought her her first brassière. Where in the

6 8

name of Jesus did Felicity get this sort of chloroform from anyway?

'He's coming out,' Felicity said. 'He's not afraid of me. I think maybe he knows that part of me is a blackbird too.'

It was much more likely that he was semi-domesticated from rifling black bags left for the binmen, and that he hopped out of hiding now on the off-chance that the girl in the gingham blouse with the button-down collar was about to scrunch a packet of Tayto salt-and-vinegar before strewing it, Assisi-style, all over the footpath. Even so, it had to be admitted that he did indeed show himself; and he looked every bit a blackbird into the bargain. It was another Alpha plus for the astute Felicity, though it should be said in all fairness that her writ ran also to wrens, robins, seagulls, eagles, pigeons and peacocks. In fact, there was a bit of the spoiled veterinary surgeon in her. No wonder she always got horny watching David Attenborough stagger round the Galapagos with puffin-shit in his hair.

'Perhaps I was a bird before I was me,' she said to Theo. 'After all, Socrates used to stroll through the Forum with a Scottish terrier who he thought was his mother. Not that they knew about Scotland then, of course, apart from the people who were retarded enough to want to live there; instead, they would have called them something like, say, Budapest terriers. But you know what I mean.'

'I know what you mean,' said Theo. But he was still thinking about the woman who had made the sign of the Cross. Could she have been a religious maniac who had no power of control over involuntary reflexes, the way the laboratory technician up in Dublin couldn't prevent his facial grimaces when he snorted coke? There was the time an elderly visiting anaesthetist from Copenhagen had locked herself into the toilet when she saw him approaching, and had waited there with a sports starting pistol until he passed by. If the woman with the rabbit-ears suffered from a similar tic, then that was all right. It had nothing to do with the three of them. With him, with Felicity, with the skeleton.

'If I'd been a bird before I was born,' said Felicity, who was watching the blackbird pick at the moss on the steps of the Methodist hall, 'that would explain why I'm always dreaming that I'm able to fly. There's a logjam on the freeway, right? And the gendarmes are jabbering away, right? And the fathers, the fathers are handing the babies out through the windows of the cars so that the mothers can help them to piss against the tyres. Right? And the ice-cream sellers are working the cars the way they work the terraces at the Superbowl. But me, I throw the sun-roof open, and out I zoom. Like as if I'm Mary or one of the martyrs or Mr Spock, and I go straight up. Meanwhile, miles downstairs, all of these people are getting down on their knees, and they're waving French breadloaves.'

'What's wrong with a sliced pan?' Theo said. He was quite convinced Felicity couldn't be the cause of the woman blessing herself. To be sure, there was a side to her nature which a small number of louts and lickspittles had sometimes misrepresented as, well, exhibitionism, when in fact they were merely maligning her great good nature and generosity. The Provost had once prevented her from entering the College chapel on the grounds that the Vigil of Advent was chiefly concerned with spiritual arousal, and that her own congregational needs might be better met by the solstice shindig that the Children of Light were shortly commencing, with the full co-operation of the local constabulary, at an antiquarian site called Stonehenge. Then there was the chap who –

70

'Maybe I'm watching too much Wonder Woman,' Felicity said. 'Or perhaps it's pressure on the bladder. Pressure on the bladder can make you dream about flying.'

But you couldn't please the provosts of this world. The truth is, they were worse than wogs. They wanted their women in chadors. Felicity was never going to fit into their weirdo ways. And she didn't have to. Look at the town of Thurles only the other day. She'd been wearing a cerise bikini bottom that she said was modest, but she must have meant the dimensions. They were truly modest; even transparently modest. Yet nobody threw a tantrum. One old man was moved to the point where he took his cap off, like it was the funeral of some godfather from the War of Independence; and a middle-aged publican who was mixing disinfectant in a galvanised bucket, uncoiled his imitation tortoise-shell spectacles, studied the lens intently for a hairline fracture, held them to his face again like an opera glass, and launched into an aria from 'The Pearl Fishers'. That was nice, that was natural; but blessing yourself, that was bad karma. Besides, Felicity hadn't even been wearing the bikini bottom. She was in denim cut-offs because she had a hive on her butt from too many kiwis. She was a bit vain about boils and blisters.

'Listen,' she said. 'Listen to that.'

The blackbird had started to sing. It didn't give Theo any goosebumps, but then he wasn't heavily into birdsong. To be honest, he always found it a trifle atonal, a trifle intrusive, a note or two from Schoenberg played at the wrong speed. Of course you couldn't say that sort of thing nowadays, what with Friends of the Earth and other fifth columnists making you feel like Attila the Hun if you chucked so much as an empty tube of KY jelly into a leafy lay-by as you left it. Instead, you had to get all worked up about the white rhinoceros or a disappearing Peruvian dandelion. You might even have to sign a petition to the United Nations General Assembly because a sub-species of cockroach had been sterilised by the ammonia used in public transport toilets throughout America, thereby banjaxing the whole balance of the eco-system. Anything was possible in a world which had blurred the line between conscience and conscientiousness, and where men needed approbation like an addict needs a fix. All a Christian needed was a cross; but all a Christian wanted was a cause. Because a cause was simpler than a cross. A cause meant new clothes, a uniform even, which would be better still; whereas a cross meant that you wore sackcloth under your tuxedo, and told no one. Instead, you bopped with the band, you jived and you jitterbugged; but always, always, back of the trombone and the tuba and the clearest note of the clarinet, you could hear the wind whimpering as it searched on its hands and knees through the ruins of Carthage. A cause meant a turn-out, a ticker-tape, a triumph, even if it failed, perhaps only if it failed, because then you could run it in the private booth of your brain; you could dine on the meat and potatoes of iron rations, of no food at all. You were still confirmed, you were still elect, you were still chosen: you had your cause. It gave you confidence, it gave you clarity, above all else it gave you conviction. Everybody wanted conviction. Nobody wanted to be acquitted. But a cross released you; it released you into the loneliness of your own bewilderment. It left you in the one place worse than a world of questions without answers, and that was a world of answers without questions to make them meaningful.

'Now,' said Felicity, 'on that very note, let me put it to you.'

'Put what?' Theo said. He was feeling terrible. Had he got any Ponstan or Panadeine?

'You say it's all a matter of microchips. You say that birds are moved around the board like chess-pieces by some sort of pipe-smoking, Soviet-style Grand Master. You say they're automata. So who wrote the fiche for this little flautist? He's going to burst his eardrums the way he's going on. Nobody told him to break his heart over a beautiful day. He just wants to; and he's free to want. As free as a bird.'

Ever since they had left the centre of Dublin, the strangest thoughts had been crossing his air-space. For years he'd been intercepting them, escorting them out or shooting them down. But these were different. They came in low, close to the ground. They didn't show on his radar. What was he going to do about them?

'Birds are not free,' Theo said. 'Haven't I told you? The only free agent in this universe is a human being. That's why science-fiction writers make up monster aliens all the time. They give them webbed feet or a frog's face or a voice like second gear when you're doing fifty, because even the lowest of the low among all the hacks in Hollywood knows that there's nothing like us anywhere in the whole cosmos. We're free, therefore we're dear; we're dear, therefore we're destitute; we're destitute, therefore we invent Metaphysics, not as a branch of Philosophy, but as the taproot of the Social Welfare system. And in that system birds are not entitled to a hospital bed. They stay in the garden, even if they do burst their eardrums or break their hearts.'

'That bird,' said Felicity, 'knows more about freedom than you do. You're just coughing up sputum from some book you read. He has had sex with the wind and the rain, and now he's singing about it.'

Actually the bird seemed quite interested at this point. He kept looking from Theo to Felicity, and back again, like the heads at Wimbledon.

'That bird,' Theo said, 'isn't warbling any sort of welcome to the four elements. Wind and rain are neither here nor there. What he's doing is establishing his territory. He's got his own precinct, and he's policing it. The juvenile gangs in downtown L.A. are no different. They hustle, they deal and they racket in their own areas, but they don't cross anyone else's air-space. I mean, boundary. So maybe this blackbird has the Methodist hall to himself, with an acre either side. So he's singing to say something to other blackbirds. Something like Fuck Off, Outta Here, or Scram, you Shithead.'

And then the bird did something strange. It took off, which would be an aerodynamic miracle if it happened once or even twice, but we tend to fast-forward the commonplace these days; it hovered; and it settled. Felicity had never seen a blackbird perch on a skeleton's skull before, but the look on her face was such that you might have thought she'd stumbled on the sole surviving egg of a dodo during a photo-session for a men's Journal of Photography on the island of Lanzarote, and that she'd just been informed by a Harley Street obstetrician that the egg had indeed been successfully fertilised. But Theo wasn't too pleased. It was bizarre, it was Channel Fourish, it was like something out of a painting by that Catalan creep with the moustache.

'Isn't that wonderful?' Felicity whispered. 'Isn't it the most perfect expression of our Christian faith in the Resurrection of Our Lord Jesus Christ on Easter Sunday? And of course the first person that He showed himself to was a fallen woman. Wasn't that deep?'

It couldn't be, Theo thought. And then again it might.

Why hadn't it occurred to him before? The woman who had made the sign of the Cross didn't give a shit about the cheeks of Felicity's ass. She was doing it for the skeleton. Out of respect, out of reverence even. Because to her he was more than a novelty to make motorists honk their horns or foreigners climb out of their Escorts to have their picture taken with one arm round his nibs and the other around Miss Ireland. To her he was a presence, a person, one of God's children. What would she have done if she'd known he was the Archbishop of Dublin? Jesus Christ, she might have known the man.

Felicity was working her foot into the stirrup of the pedal. Theo stared at the skeleton. The bird had flown. What was the one that had brought something or other to the hermit? And wasn't there a bird in the story of the Flood? Or was it that birds came down and sat on the apostles' heads during the Last Supper? The trouble about Religious Knowledge classes in secondary schools these days was that you ended up knowing everything about Martin Luther King and how many pins he took out of a new shirt on the morning of his murder, but you knew bugger all about the Bible.

'Theo,' said Felicity. 'I don't want you to get worked up about this, but I feel I have to say it. I love you, of course, and with my body I thee worship. But if you really want to understand me, in my innermost innermost, you're just going to have to read Martin Heidegger. Martin Heidegger is the only man who's ever really understood me. Because *Sein und Zeit* is a love-letter from the masculine principle to the Eternal Feminine. But it's not about womanising; it's about womb-anising. So it's not just a love-letter; it's a love-cry, the soul's ejaculation.'

If you were having a nervous breakdown, would you know about it beforehand? Or was it true what they said

75

about the Blitz, that you could only hear the bombs that fell on other people? Theo made up his mind that, if he went on having these Skid Row sensations, this shell-shock in a foxhole fantasy, he was going to see a doctor; and not any old doctor either, but a man with at least two Memberships, who practised from a Georgian square and had a Protestant receptionist. Maybe he needed a tonic; maybe he needed therapy. That stuff about causes and crosses, and birds being free: that wasn't like him, that wasn't the Theo he knew, and he knew himself inside out. That was more like the guys in their dressing-gowns in the closed wards, chainsmoking from one meal to the next medication so that the back of their hand was the colour of wood preservative. But Theo was different, or rather he wasn't different. He was the same as anyone else, only more so. The time the home-kit test gave the wrong result, and Felicity had her pre-feminist panic attack, he went out and got bollocksed like any other bloke in the same bind. Afterwards he walked up Grafton Street at three in the morning, wearing one of those red-and-orange traffic cones the police arrange outside Government Buildings to intimidate terrorists. And the chap at the bus-stop cheered him, though perhaps that didn't quite count as a normal reaction because the buses had stopped running four hours before, and what was he doing there anyway in an SS uniform, three weeks after Hallowe'en? But the point was, that being tanked-up and the traffic cone were the one way of coping with crisis, the one way of being a man. And he was a man. A normal man. He could feel it in his bones.

Felicity was still talking to him. Did women ever shut up?

'If only you were a phenomenologist,' she was saying. 'If only you saw things phenomenologically. But you haven't even started *The Gulag Archipelago*. The other night, you bitched because you couldn't get ITN on this side of the Shannon, and you were going to miss a James Bond movie.'

'I missed it when it came,' Theo said. 'I had to take my nephew out halfway through. The little shit was having an asthma attack. Bang in the middle of when the girl gets harpooned in the jacuzzi after she's put the tarantula in his dinner jacket. He goes blue. He goes aquamarine.'

But Felicity had turned up the volume on her Walkman. Now she was listening to Pink Floyd. That meant it was staring-into-space time. Pastel colours and the scent of freesia. From the toilet-paper of prose to the facial tissues of poetry. Still, it could have been worse. It could have been Monteverdi's Vespers. Then he would have had to sing for his supper. When she was in a Monteverdi mood, she'd end up telling the night-porter that she'd left the convent a year after her novitiate, though even now she fretted for a game of the Jerusalem edition of Monopoly, and a bite of tough ham. If the poor man got embarrassed, that was that. But if he called her Sister, she'd frogmarch Theo to the bedroom and do a slow strip while he read her passage after passage from the Gideon Bible. It was all most peculiar, and it never ended in the sacrament of encounter. Instead, she'd climb into bed and sleep like a Paschal lamb until the windows whitened.

'I bags the bathroom first.'

Felicity was pointing as she spoke, pointing ahead of her like a comely Komsomol cadre on some stamp from the Stalin era. She must have meant the hotel, but he couldn't see any postcard stands or imitation battlements. There was only a woman watering a window-box on the second floor of the police station, and a party of East

Coast pensioners drinking stout around a replica of a cannon from the Spanish Armada. Felicity freewheeled past, and they raised their glasses to her; and even the fiddler who was cranking out some jigs and reels for the Yanks, bobbed his bow at her. So Theo raised his fist in a Black Power benediction as he belted by, and everybody was pleased. But the old man in the black suit at the back of the crowd, who'd been step-dancing to the music while the fiddler played, step-danced to the music while the fiddler paused. His shuffle was immune to the clowning of two students and a highly-strung skeleton. On he danced; and in his outstretched hand, a hand that had held more salmon than women, more glasses than girls, he kept time with his own false teeth, clicking them like castanets, the upper off the lower, molars and incisors. They smelled of cauliflower, of Steradent and fish-fingers, of a smoker's saliva. Theo was able to tell that at a glance; but he knew as well that they smelled of the Body and Blood of the Living God, eaten each morning at morning Mass, and he shivered a little.

It was obviously time to put on a pullover.

Neither of them was right about the ruin outside the town. Felicity had said it was a fort of some description. Not a Celtic fort, a ringfort, as in big bilingual plaques at every twenty paces, the sort of place where fashion photographers do cashmere shoots and MGM location crews lose their cool if it rains, their rag if it storms, and their marbles altogether if the sheep-droppings besmear their designer sneakers. She said it was a magazine, a military outpost. That would explain why it didn't get a mention in the guide-book. It was part of the past that was put in purdah. That was Ireland. But Theo said no, he reckoned it was a corn-mill or a corn-exchange, because the town grew up as a port before it grew old as a resort. Otherwise, if the ruin were historic, or is it historical, there'd be a car-park, wouldn't there? As it was, you could only get to it across the Community College playing fields and through the car cemetery behind them. Then the last leg spoke for itself. Undergrowth, overgrowth, briars and brambles: apart from the apricot tree, the place was like an obstacle course at Fort Bragg. If you raised the temperature by ten degrees and multiplied the mosquitoes, you could be out in the Mekong delta, sweltering under sniper-fire from the gooks in the high canopy of the jungle or wading waist-deep through the black alluvium of the paddy-fields, your cartridge belt on your shoulders, a blur of hummingbirds round a clump of orchids where Charlie might be waiting. Why hadn't he killed her the night before when he knew she'd betray them, the cocktail hostess from the Bamboo cabaret in Da Nang, the girl with the fluent French and the indigo toenails? But her eyes had rolled like apples in a one-armed bandit as he thrust inside her, and how was he to have known that her dental plate was in regular radio contact with Hanoi? It was too late for recriminations now. All he had to look forward to was a posthumous purple heart, and the enigmatic tears of a dozen different women. Yet this was no time for bitterness, no time to –

'Theo,' Felicity said. 'Theo, are you in pain? Or is it acidity? Your face looks horrible.'

Her own was cross enough, both cold and bothered. That was because he hadn't beaten a path for her, and the backs of her legs were scratched from the whiplash of the bushes. But he was busy enough, playing porter to the Lord Archbishop. Ever since the dachshund and the metatarsus, Theo had revised the whole security procedure. Now he was more than the skeleton's equerry; he was his bodyguard: and that meant round-the-clock surveillance. Felicity should be able to understand that. Besides, what could she expect if she traipsed through a combat zone like this, in a pair of espadrilles and teddy-bear shorts? On the other hand, there was something endearing about her, the child of nature who was neither, the streetwise sylph who could easily sweet-talk a sour-faced motor mechanic into a change of brakes, batteries and body-parts before settling the account with a large-denomination Portuguese banknote she'd brought home from the Algarve, but who was wholly at a loss for language when the Down's syndrome toddler in the Pluto tank-top offered her his bottle. That was Felicity. That was the case for the defence. On the prosecution side, it was just a pity that she always crashbangwalloped into his fantasies at the worst moment, especially when he was trying to construct an intercontinental plotline he'd never thought of before. Because the South-East-Asian scenario was virgin soil. He'd crop-rotated Stockholm and San Francisco, but never Saigon. Now he knew why the French and the Americans had dug in for so long. He would definitely get back to it.

'I'm fine,' he said to Felicity. 'I was just thinking.' And he hung the skeleton up on a branch of the apricot tree. It looked quite noble in its pink polythene suit-cover, with the front zipped up to where the skull rested on the hanger. The late-afternoon sunlight took to it in a big way. The bones positively shone.

'I knew,' Felicity said. 'I knew you were thinking. It's so selfish. I'm over here, and everything that I touch is either sticking to me or stinging me. And you, you're thinking. It's all very well to think if you're wearing long

8 0

trousers. It's all very well to grasp the nettle if the nettle isn't grasping you.'

'I was only thinking how vulnerable you are,' Theo said. 'I was thinking how much I cherish your vulnerability. How I want always to be a windbreak for you, and a breakwater.'

It had sounded better when he read the poem first, in the *New Yorker* magazine, in between an advertisement for a Bluecross abortion clinic in Ithaca and a Friends of the Earth subscription appeal for additional finance to end finally and for all time the slaughter of the last remaining ocelots in El Salvador. Now it seemed pretentious, even poetic, this talk of shelter from the storm. He should have realised at the time, but he hadn't. Of course, pretentiousness is never writ large in the *New Yorker*. In fact, they use very tiny print.

'Listen, Rilke,' said Felicity. 'Forget the hendecasyllables for a while. Go find me some dock-leaves.'

'Dock-leaves?' Theo said. 'I wouldn't know what a dock-leaf looks like. I can tell you three different kinds of weedkiller, because there's a gardening programme right ahead of that Open University series on nakedness and nudity in the Western cinematic tradition; but weeds, I know shit about weeds.'

'There's no such thing as a weed,' Felicity said, and she slashed around her to left and right with a stick shaped like a K, as she laid low honeysuckle and yellow thistles. 'A weed is a flower growing in the wrong place, like a sycamore tree in the middle of a soccer field. No more, no less. Now go get me one. Look wherever you see nettles.'

'I thought you wanted me to look for dock-leaves.'

Felicity threw her eyes to heaven. That was the closest she ever came to metaphysics.

'Theo, Theo,' she said. 'Do I have to carry jump-leads to get you started? If human nature is natural, then mother nature is human. It's a convertible proposition. Are you with me?'

This was that fucking Dominican again. He hadn't only screwed her, he'd screwed her up as well. Any other boyfriend would have made a first meeting memorable, turned a date into a destiny, by escorting his intended to some super *de luxe* rotisserie where chips emerge in a new incarnation as French fries, if not indeed as *pommes frites de terre*, and where the prices read like a logarithmic table; but this crafty cleric had been happy to hand her a Thomas Merton anthology with that hunger-strike expression sensitive people let slip strategically. After that, there was no stopping her. The human condition would be Side A, Band 1 for ever after. It wasn't enough any longer to be brainy: you had to have a mind of your own too.

'I'm with you,' he said. 'I know about convertibles. I even know about propositions.'

'People get hurt,' Felicity said, 'and they get healed. Sometimes the hurt and the healing occur in the same place. That's what's called an irony. Or maybe it's a paradox. Anyhow, nature is no different. Nettles and dock-leaves grow together. The nettles sting, the dock-leaves soothe. Sometimes the healing can be hurtful, sometimes the hurt can be healing. That's another convertible proposition. There are loads more. You might be a bit intimidated by them to begin with. I was. I'm not afraid to say it, or ashamed. But I learned; and now I can converse fluently in convertible propositions. You should see the way people look at me. They're just amazed.'

Theo decided it was time to look for a dock-leaf. If he ever did meet that creep from the cloister, he'd hurt him in a place beyond all healing. He'd show him transcendence, he would: he'd lift him out of it. Him and his breed. From the nuncio through to the least little novice skateboarding blithely down the perishing corridors of one or another diocesan seminary, there wasn't a man among the lot of them as sane or streetwise as the fellow whose spinal column swung slowly in the breeze behind him. At least he had backbone, and balls for that matter. He would have understood Theo. He would have understood Zorba the Greek. He would have understood that the world is always larger than anything that can be said about it. He would.

'Bend over,' he told her; and Felicity did. Her hair fell over her face as she bowed her head; it was almost like the pipe-tobacco commercial, or was it the pure wool one? Ordinarily, he would have found it very arousing, this primordial homage of hers, for the only other image which had ever moved and motivated him as much as a woman's bottom was his first glimpse of the Last Judgment frescoes in the Vatican's Sistine Chapel, when his parents had brought him there during the year of the three Popes. Not that the impact of Felicity's ass could be compared with an aesthetic ascension in St Peter's; that would diminish it frightfully. No, the Michelangelo moment was a mere religious rapture, whereas the cheeks of his beloved provoked a passion that could only adequately be described in terms of incarnational spirituality.

Even so, she wasn't looking sexy here and now. Theo had to concede it. If anything, she seemed tremulous, clumsy. He rubbed the inside of her thighs with the dock-leaf, but it made no difference. She waited for him to finish, like a small child being mopped after a mishap. It was that neutral. Maybe he shouldn't have sneered the way he did at her convertible propositions.

'I never knew about convertible propositions,' he said

to her. 'I never even suspected. That's why I sort of jeered when you started explaining them. I was just jealous. Because you're like Pope John, the way he ran around, opening windows. I wish I could do that. I wish I could open windows too. Yesterday morning, you told me how the incurable gambler plays to lose and not to win, and I hadn't thought of that. I mean, I've been passing bookies' shops, amusement arcades, whatever, for years now, but I never had that insight. With an insight like that, you could name your price on any talk-show. Or yesterday. Take yesterday. Yesterday you explained to me how everything in this world is sexual except sexual intercourse, which is a metaphor for everything in our life which is non-sexual. And you're right, you're absolutely right. You've got this brain like a Black and Decker when you want to. Today, you want to. Today, it's convertible prepositions.'

'Propositions,' Felicity said. 'Convertible propositions. Not that they matter. In fact, fuck them.'

She straightened up and walked ahead of him; and he followed her, the dock-leaf in his hand. And for a while after that, there was only the sound of two sticks beating a path, and the sound of the wind in the trees, like the low endearments of lovers whispering in French. There was the statutory mist of midges, but the midges made no noise. And the ruin, a building walled around to the height of its own rooftop, loomed larger as the two of them made their way toward it.

Felicity stopped and threw her stick down.

'I was imagining,' she said; but she didn't look back at him. 'Maybe because we're here, hacking at thorns and loganberry bushes and a hundred other horrid stingy things that may have lovely, long Latin decorations in the back of a botany book, but piss me totally when I brush against them here; or maybe because the sun is dancing around in front of my eyes like a yellow ping-pong ball, and I'm sticky where I love to feel dry, and every inch of me is tender like I got a bodywax at breakfast time.'

'You were imagining?' said Theo. And more fool her for doing a stupid thing like that. After all, what had imagining ever done for her, for him, for anyone? There should be a Government Health Warning on the sleeve of every record, the jacket of every book. Human nature would be grand if it weren't for imagining. Imagining fucks everything up. You never heard of a merchant banker hanging himself with the flex of the hoover, unless of course the bank went bust; but what about the poets and the painters? The poets and the painters were forming queues at Niagara Falls, and they weren't wearing water-wings. In fact, there were cliffs in North America which were so popular with the poets and the painters that the buskers had moved in. The same with Paris, France: anyone sporting tortoise-shell spectacles, with a *livre de poche* in their artist's overalls, was bloodtested for lithium levels before going up the Eiffel Tower. When they got to the top, they were given a Walkman with a tape of 'Gigi' to listen to while they scanned the skyline. Otherwise they might start imagining, and make a mess of the postcard stands below.

'I was imagining our first parents,' Felicity said. 'How they had to walk through the wilderness when Elohim expelled them from Eden. There they were, with nothing to their name except an applecore and the memories of their time in Paradise: the sea-wash and the surf-boards of their own Club Mediterranean. But that was all gone now. The world awaited them, a future of waterblisters. There was no more God the Father to play godfather anymore. They weren't going to hear his helicopter coming in low over the dinosaurs just because they

8 5

had vaginal thrush or a fit of the blues. No, they were on their own.'

'Perhaps they liked it that way,' said Theo. 'Perhaps they felt that three was a crowd.'

'They were on their own,' Felicity said. 'On their own like you and me, labouring across this wasteland.'

'I wish it was a wasteland,' Theo said. 'You can pick up speed in a wasteland. You can get from A to B in office time. Look at the Citroën team in Death Valley last year. But a wilderness says boo to the maps. A wilderness sprains your ankle, and you end up seeing stars because it's dark before you make it back to the campfire. Even then, you can't wash the weirdness of it off your body, because it's worked its way into the pores of your skin. You might as well try cleaning coal. And the city is never the same again. The traffic island, the corner shop, the paper birch tree where the secretaries eat their pineapple yogurts – things that you took for granted, they don't seem given any more; they seem gained. As if we had to win them. As if we had to wrest them. As if, at the end of the day, the human race is a race against time. Against the wilderness.'

'Wilderness, wasteland,' Felicity said. 'You sound like the minutes of a Greenpeace meeting. The point is, you put a wilderness and a wasteland together, and you get a world. Our world. You and me. We're in it; we're in it together. But to what end? To what beginning, for that matter? I mean, I was watching you in the car cemetery, and I did my mother's test. I never did it before, I never even thought of doing it; but I suddenly remembered how she washed my feet the morning after my debs, because I'd come home barefoot from the discothèque. God only knows why I took my shoes off in the first place. Maybe the strap was cutting into me. Maybe I thought it was bohemian to stagger past the policeman outside the Belgian Embassy, and wish him good evening in Irish, French and German.'

'Civility is never a minus mark,' said Theo. 'Civility is a definite plus. I would like to be able to say thank you in a thousand languages, from Hausa to Hindi.'

'But I said good evening, and this was after seven in the morning. Morning mass was over. The man who goes on and on and on about being wounded on Juno beach in the Normandy landings was coming out of the church with his St Bernard. So it must have been the thought of the little barrel of whisky that did it.'

'Did what?' Theo was enchanted. Why hadn't Felicity told him all about this long before now? It was just like the way he had omitted to mention the *Thoughts of Chairman Mao*. The truth was, they had so many depths to swap, fathom upon fathom, that it would take a lifetime to do the job justice. But that was what relationships were all about. You lived in two elements at once, in a perpetual circuit of self and other, like a salmon passing from salt-water to freshwater and back again. And what a beautiful image that was, too. If he came out with that at a dinner party, the contessa with three months to live and three Tiepolos in her Venice apartment would draw her décolletage down well below her tan-mark. Because, in the heel of the hunt, class beckoned to class.

'I got as far as the genito-urinary surgeon's garden,' Felicity said. 'Then I vomited all over his rhododendrons. The Babycham, the Budweiser, the Beaujolais. After which Brigadier Bore put his trilby round the gate. "Been in the trenches, have we? Join the club, my dear. There was a time I vomited for thirty minutes, and the only beverage I'd been drinking was the methylated spirits of naked terror." '

8 7

'Suffering jams all other signals,' Theo said. 'Not even the World Service can reach you if your head's in the toilet bowl.'

'I made it home,' said Felicity. 'That's the main thing. I made it home. And on the way I sprayed my mouth so much with a spearmint atomiser that I got anaesthesia. But my mother was nice, she was nurturing. She sat me up on the draining-board in the scullery, and she put my hair in a shower-cap so I wouldn't dirty it if I got sick a second time. Then she washed my feet in the basin; she even squirted Fairy Liquid in between my toes, because she had this notion that you can pick up rabies from dog-shit. If it hadn't been for my headache, I would have been heartbroken: she was so happy to be helping me, and I was ashamed about sneering at her the Tuesday before when the picture went fuzzy during the archive programme on the Queen Mother. And while I was thinking that, the budgie perched on my shoulder and started to play with my earring. I just felt so cherished. After that, I threw up again. Why is it all yellow, I wondered, when the stuff that I drank was red? And my mother said that our hearts are black and our stomachs yellow, and our brains a very grey area. Of course, after two years in medical school I know better, but I wouldn't want to disillusion her.'

'And the test?' said Theo. 'Your mother's test. What was that? You said you did it on me?'

Felicity looked a little lost. Perhaps she was lost for words. That would be terrible. To be lost for words is almost as bad as being lost in them. Almost, but not quite. It was a bit like the relationship between bronchitis and lung cancer. One left you silent, the other left you speechless. It was the difference between a choice and a condition, a deed and a destiny. That was it. Or that was what the Jesuit had told her, the time he blew up the novelty condoms to use as balloons for the children's street party during the Awareness of Deprivation week. He was in such rotten form too, that day, and all because the Arts Council had refused him a bursary for his new book. But who could blame them? *In the Beginning was the Word: Now We Do Impressions* was just too big of a title.

'Whenever I try and tell a story,' Felicity said, 'it keeps trying to smuggle other stories in with it. And I end up not knowing whether I should go to the green zone or the red zone, because I don't know what exactly it is I'm declaring.'

'Why don't you tell me about your mother's test? The test, the whole test, and nothing but the test. Forget D-Day, forget the budgie.' Theo had never thought much about Felicity's mother. After all, what could you say about someone who still read Georgette Heyer in the toilet, and who somehow persuaded her orthodontist to remove a gold bridge from her mouth as a contribution toward Live Aid? But a test was another matter entirely. A test was some sort of examination, some sort of scrutiny. If so, was he the scrutinised? And why? Could she have overheard that joke he told the father about the rabbi who goes jogging through Central Park when it's pouring rain, and he's wearing fuck all except a prophylactic? She did have a bee in her bonnet about God's chosen people, and how we should all go round in sackcloth and ashes because of the deathcamps. Then again, perhaps he shouldn't have corrected her when she announced that Auschwitz was in Czechoslovakia. Maybe that was when she began thinking up tests.

'Exactly,' said Felicity. 'My mother's test. That's what I wanted to tell you about, if you'd only listen. Because there I was, and my mother was steeping my feet, and I said to her: "I don't suppose you still think I'm ravishing, do you?" You see, when I'd left the night before, she'd handed me this rabbit stole at the hall-door, and then I was afraid she'd bless me with some holy water from the little green font beside the letter-box, but she didn't, which was wonderful because I would have been mortified in front of my escort. I mean, he was only back from a David Bowie concert in Amsterdam, and he had all this hash wrapped up in a Solidarity sweatshirt. I nearly died.'

'What's the big deal with hash?' Theo asked her. 'You told me you got into hash at the school sports when you were fifteen, the time you won the sack race and kept going. What's with the "nearly died"?'

'I wasn't talking about the hash,' Felicity said. 'I was talking about the holy water. The point is, my mother didn't sprinkle me. The point is, she said to me that I looked ravishing. That's why I said it back to her the next day. Did I still look ravishing? No, she said, I didn't, and she hoped I hadn't been. It took a while to sink in; then I got guilty. Because I'd let him play with my boobs a bit, in one of the telephone kiosks. I kept reading these intercontinental call codes to Djakarta and Anchorage while he went on twiddling with my nipples. But whatever he did wasn't working: they just wouldn't enlarge or get stiff or whatever. And he took it very personally. He was quite cut up. So I told him how they ice-cube the model's nipples for a Page 3 photo-shoot, and how the *Penthouse* or the *Playboy* people might have whole fridges on the beach in Lanzarote if they're doing a sea-wash and cheesecloth feature, because otherwise the nipples will not, repeat, will not erect.'

'I didn't know that,' Theo said; but he did. Had she been rooting through his magazines again? He wouldn't put it past her. After all, he'd already moved them twice, from behind the immersion to inside the wok, from inside the wok to the hood of the lawn-mower; but she could still find them when she put her mind to it. If she was in one sort of mood, she'd twist the pages into firelighters, even though he'd told her a thousand times that glossy paper won't burn; if, on the other hand, she was in good humour, he'd end up reading her the kinkiest letters from the Readers' columns. You never knew with Felicity. That was the long and the short of it. Sometime in the second term of her pre-Med year, she'd gone out in a black mini-skirt with a matching black bolero as a sign of solidarity with some wretched adolescent widow in the Punjab who was pressured by her parents to hold hands with her husband as his funeral bonfire blazed; but, two or three days later, she was stuck in a thousand-page tome about a Confederate cavalry officer who has his way and his will with one plantation slave after another before finally finding refuge and respite with two bisexual Southern belles who happen to be identical twins. Or was it triplets?

'All the time I'm telling this guy about erectile tissue,' Felicity said, 'there's somebody tapping on the door of the telephone kiosk. So I start reciting the "Hail Mary" in Latin.'

'You were frightened?'

'Of course I wasn't frightened. I just wanted him to think I was an East European on the line to Belgrade. Or something. And he must have. Because he went away. That was why I cried.'

'But you said you weren't afraid?' Theo was puzzled; or, rather, he was more puzzled than usual. Because to say that he was puzzled was to commit a tautology. Theo was always puzzled. That was what made it possible for him every so often, once in a month of Sundays, the rare and random Holydays in a head-down, headlong calendar, to find the world within him and the world without as well. They were the times his brother gave him the sick certs.

'I'm not talking about the kiosk,' Felicity said. 'I'm talking about the kitchen. I'm talking about my mother. When she saw that I was crying, she didn't know what to say. She put the budgie back in the cage, and she covered the cage with my father's barrister's gown. Maybe she didn't want the budgie to overhear us. I don't know. Then, when she'd finished, and the budgie was going berserk, she said, "Look, I don't know how to say this, I really don't; I want to be tactful." She said it seven or eight times, and then she sort of blurted it out. She said, "Did he screw you? And if he did, were you wearing a . . . rawl plug?" After that, we just hugged each other for a long time. It was one of those moments when you feel that you've moved in a subtle, shaping way from being a noun to becoming a pronoun. In fact, it was too beautiful. I couldn't bear it. Neither could my mother. So we tried to distract ourselves by writing out a list of all the people we wanted to send Christmas cards to, but that didn't take very long. Anyway, it's hard to think of Christmas when your shopping list has more protection factor suncream on it than medium sherry or Gromyko's *Memoirs*. So then we went into the drawing-room and we took all of my miniature dolls out of the cabinet, the Austrian boy in the lederhosen and the geisha in the kimono and the English girl in the sensible shoes, and we tried to remember the names we used to call them, but we couldn't, and that made us cry again. At least, my mother cried, so I felt I should make the effort for her sake. Actually, it was worth it, because I learned you can cry on cue if you want to.'

Felicity had only ever talked like this once before, and that had been the prelude to a week of bitchiness and the blues. What was he in for this time? And what were they doing here anyway, knee-deep in green gunge, trading tall stories while the whole horizon heaved under the sunset? Maybe the building up ahead had been a Trappist foundation, and there were monkish poltergeists, brothers in brown who hadn't passed wind, let alone the time of day, for half a century, reversing their rule of silence by taking possession of two simple students and using them to experience for the last time the château wines of language, the sex of words. Actually, the thought was a bit creepy. For a moment, Theo wished he was back at the apricot tree with the skeleton.

'That was when my mother started telling me about men,' Felicity said. 'About how as soon as they've come, they're gone again, and you're just lying there, beginning to drip and get itchy; but they're looking out the window, wondering where they left those tax forms. Inside the internal directory? On the radiator in the staff canteen? And two, maybe three minutes before, they were telling you that the only thing they wanted in this world was to be in your pussy for ever and ever, amen. That's men. That's what my mother said. She said there were three stages in the drama of the genitals: tragedy, comedy, and farce. First a man made love to you; then he had sex with you; finally, he slept with you, and you were lucky if he didn't snore. By two in the morning, he'd have three quarters of the duvet; by four, he'd have all of it, plus the hot water bottle. And this at the very time of the night when you were most likely to die. She had read it in *Reader's Digest*.'

'I read it too,' said Theo. 'I read it in the *Lancet*. And it bothered me. Because four o'clock in the morning is when I feel more alive than ever. I sit downstairs and I shake a little sugar on the fire to bring it up. After that, I take a few books off the shelves, anything within arm's reach, Kierkegaard, the *Kama Sutra*, and I read my annotations. If I feel I might write different annotations now, then that's a sign I've grown. A year ago I might have written "How True" against some paragraph in Sartre; but now I'd write "Peut-être c'est vrai".'

'But my mother wasn't spoofing,' Felicity said. 'She wasn't speechifying. She was drawing from her own experience. She wasn't bringing me a six-pack from the local cash-and-carry: this was home-brew. She told me about her debs. How she got pissed, how she got sick, how my father brought her back to his place because his folks were mayfly-fishing in the West, and how he inveigled her – that was her word, inveigled – into taking off her dress in case she threw up again and spoiled the material. Suddenly he was a haberdasher.'

'And then?' Theo was vexed. He had been in two such situations, and the idea had never occurred to him.

'He put her to bed in his sister's room, a room that was full of dried honesty and lacrosse trophies, and then he rang her parents. It was quite despicable. But women always draw the short straw. She got a court martial, he got a George medal, and when she did eventually go to bed the following night, there seemed to be no point in telling anyone that some phantom physician had put Cicatrin powder on the pimple under her bra strap.'

Theo was slowly conceiving a new sense of Felicity's father. Perhaps the spineless son-of-a-bitch had balls after all. Anything was possible. There were fish fossils high up in the Himalayas; opera glasses had been discovered in the equatorial rainforest; and Theo himself had recently seen a hedgehog cross a busy bypass at rush hour in absolute safety. Admittedly, the lollipop man was quite drunk. It was probably just as well that the hedgehog made it to the footpath before the police pulled up.

'If there's one thing in this world that's potentially more harmful than vice,' said Felicity, 'it has to be virtue. If he'd grabbed her, if he'd groped her; but no. He has to go and respect her. And the outcome is a couple of straight-backed armchairs in what they have the cheek to call a living-room, with wallpaper the colour of a backstreet abortion, and the arm-rests worn down to threads under the weight of wrists and well-wound wristwatches.'

Theo tried to say the last bit back to himself, but it was harder than Sally sold sea-shells. How did she do it? Maybe there was something to be said for the Montessori method after all. Him, there were times when he found most every word in the language a rogue sound, a tongue-twister. Communion, for example. Communion was a classic. And pusillanimity. Of course, you could always say weak if you got stuck.

'Which is why she told me her test,' Felicity said. 'Simple, succinct, straightforward. You're with a guy, there's a nice feeling, it may be his hand, it is his hand. So you go to the bathroom and you scrape the chilli off your tongue with a Yale key, and you try to remember which of his ears is the sensitive one. Then you come back, and the guy is opening a tube of lubricant with the point of the corkscrew. And suddenly the whole thing goes from room temperature to body heat. You feel desired. You feel desire. The night sky crowds the window, the stars close ranks around you. And your breasts, your breasts have never seemed so womanly, so worthy of Titian, even if you did forget to snip that solitary hair around your left aureole. What matter now? You are woman, the word made flesh. You stand there in your skintone strapless bra while he rubs his hands, warming the jelly. Is this the moment?'

'You betcha,' Theo said. He was, you know, in spite of himself. But they couldn't do it here. There were creepycrawlies galore in a place like this. Ladybirds he could handle, caterpillars even; but the thought of an earwig was too wet an ashtray for his cigarette. No, he would save his smoke for later on. It was all very well to take soft-focus snapshots of slow-motion streakers in a Thomas Hardy setting, but the truth was that the love of nature and the nature of love are quite incompatible. Only the other day he had wiped himself with a fistful of grass, and he was still raw.

'That's what you have to ask yourself,' Felicity said. 'Is this the moment? The answer lies in a second question. And the second question is the test. My mother's test. The acid test. It is: Do I want this man to be the person whom my children will call "Daddy"? Do I want that man to be at my side in the delivery room, getting sympathetic haemorrhoids because he's pushing every time I push? Do I want him to stand beside me when I fight the good fight for the introduction of a Comparative Religion course at a Parent–Teacher meeting? Do I want him to be the one who will comfort our little girl during the interval of "Fiddler on the Roof" because her beard fell off in the middle of the opening number? Well, if the answer is no, the rest follows.'

'You garb and go,' Theo said. 'You slip away before the jelly sets.'

'I didn't say that,' said Felicity. 'Did I say that? What I said was that the rest follows. I was being delicate. This is the age of penicillin, of the pill. Why shouldn't you share some pleasure with a perfect stranger? Or even an imperfect stranger, for that matter? It's not as if it means anything. In fact, that's precisely why it can mean so much to some people. Because if it did mean anything, it might start a relationship. It might trigger grief, longing, possessiveness, you name it. Before you know where you are, you don't know where you are. You don't know who you are. You've fallen in love, and there's nothing to break your fall. And you end up in bits. You end up with so many stainless steel pins in your psyche that you trip the alarm when you walk through security sensors at the airport. They think you're a terrorist, when the truth is that you're the very opposite: you're someone who's been terrorised. You're someone who did the most dangerous thing in the world, more dangerous than dental work on a crocodile or flying with Turkish airlines.'

'There's nothing wrong with Turkish airlines,' Theo said. 'That's more Amnesty International bullshit. Besides, where they used the rottweilers to sodomise the students was Uruguay, not Turkey. Turkey only uses the electric-shock stuff. I told you before.'

'I'm just trying to make a point,' Felicity said. 'A point about how hazardous it is to hold hands with another human being: kid gloves are called for. Two school-leavers sitting over diet-Cokes in a sandwich bar may look like a Government Work Program poster, but they're not cardboard cut-outs. They're half-ape, half-angel: they're persons. They're the image of God, and you know where He ended up. What passes between them is passion, a passion narrative, something so complicated that it makes the physical structure of the universe seem as straightforward as two plus two. She smiles at him or he shifts the ashtray downwind, and there aren't enough satellites in space to relay all the messages they're sending. You're into a zero-gravity situation at the very moment when you need to keep both of your moccasins on the lino. You're into black holes, supernovas, space-probes. You're into the Big Bang. And that's a tall order.'

Or another tall story. Yet it was easy to sneer. In fact, Theo was impressed. There were times when Felicity reminded him of himself in the way she talked, in the way she went on. Then again, he was a bit alarmed by the transfer. Could it be two-way? He had said two, perhaps even three, fatuous things since breakfast. Maybe they were merging or mixing, like the colours on clothes in the washing machine. Maybe they were leaking into each other in more ways than one. Putting a penis into a pussy was safe, it was streamlined. You had protection. The sex was a sort of controlled explosion: none of the adjacent buildings had their windows blown in. Afterwards, you could withdraw, you could even withhold. You could be yourself again. You were still intact. And the woman could douche, or whatever. But really getting stuck into someone, that was different. A fellow in final Med had told him about a couple at Christmas who were carted in on a stretcher, because her muscles had gone into spasm and the guy couldn't free himself. There they were, in the Accident and Emergency, with the noise of carols and whooping cough all around them, and a pretty intern reading the riot act to a nun who'd said they should be left to stew in their own juices. What made it worse, of course, were the stockings. It wasn't a question of perversion. You could do what you like in the matrimonial bed. They just looked damn silly on him. Everyone was tittering. The poor devil must have been praying for the muscle relaxant. And it did come. Santa wasn't stuck in the chimney all night. But what was the moral equivalent of an intramuscular shot? What did you do if you found that your feelings were roots and not branches? What did you do if you moved from making love to making beds, from quality wine with a woman to quality time with a child? It happened to other people every day of the week. It did. One week you had TV dinners in your basket, the next you had Calpol in a packed trolley. Before you knew it, you were sitting in a deckchair, downing non-alcoholic beer and trying to clean a zoom lens with a Care Bear paper tissue, while your little girl in her white Communion dress bounced and bounded in the Jumping Castle. It wouldn't be the end of the world, of course; in point of fact, it might even be the beginning of one. After all, a little girl would be rather nice; and if the mother were to die in childbirth, he would have this incredible mystique. Every woman in the country would be coming to him for a breast examination. But if the mother lived, if they ended up by starting out together on that long mortgage-to-mortuary marathon, where would it lead them? And where would it leave them? The chaplain in Dublin had said that the village of Nazareth is the closest we can come to the state of Nirvana. Actually, he had been so humbled by the significance of his insight that he had lobbied the Sunday papers to include it as a Quote of the Week. And perhaps he was right. On the other hand, the lord Buddha had begun his journey in search of the Truth by dumping his wife and kids; and even Jesus, who had made a bit of a song and dance about family life and who had changed the water into wine at the wedding feast of Canaan, had never exactly wolf-whistled at a passing yashmak. It wasn't that either of them had a bad word to say about high jinks or honeymoons *per se*; but home-life is another matter. If, at the end of the day, you want to relate to the meaning of Love at a high level, then just meaning to love your relations as well as you can is going to limit you terribly. There was that friend of Felicity's who had missed the

Medical Ethics slide-show on the sterilisation campaign in Kashmir, because she was looking after her unmarried sister's brat of a baby for the Bank-Holiday weekend; and then, to make matters worse, the sterilisation campaign came up on the exam. No, all in all, it was better by far to bow out. Not to stand aside, but to stand apart. A member, yes; but a pavilion member. That way, you could wear your whites the next day too.

'So my mother was right,' Felicity said. 'A tumble in the hay is neither here nor there, and it sure beats badminton. You feel enlarged, you feel enlivened. You just lie back, and the clouds look like Napoleon or the North Atlantic. Some of them look like clouds, they're so lifelike. Way way away, you might hear a train sounding its whistle, and you know it must be going into a tunnel, and you wonder why they do that.'

'Do what?' said Theo. It was a bit insensitive to go on about haystacks. They had never done it in a haystack, as far as he remembered. Was she thinking about the barn with all the nitrogen fertiliser and the skateboard? He remembered that all right, but no haystacks. So it must have been the tomcat with the Roman collar. Either that, or she was fibbing. Anyhow, there were no haystacks nowadays, and, if there were, you wouldn't be able to reach them through all the Japanese Summer School students with their canvas stools and their water-colour boxes.

'Why they blow their whistle,' said Felicity. 'Is it to warn the passengers or is it to warn whoever might be inside the tunnel? Or is it just the train's excitement? And you think back to *The Railway Children* and how the oldest sister rescued that beautiful boy from the public school who'd sprained his ankle on one of the sleepers while he was being the hare in the paperchase. It must have been so romantic for the Victorians, the skirts with scallops, the corsets, boleros, layer after layer after layer of lovely lacy lingerie to take off, and the whole time he'd be looking at you like Heathcliff with his nightshirt sticking out. But nowadays it's all so East European, isn't it? Y-Fronts and X-chromosomes, and the cinema usherettes practising their pubococcygeal exercises while they're selling ice-cream tubs to the toddlers during "Bambi".'

If they did, that was surely their own business. Besides, Theo thought it was rather feminine of them. So what was Felicity on her high horse about? She could crank out a lot of crap about bonnets and boudoirs when the mood took her, but she still wanted a general anaesthetic when she had her teeth scaled. And swanning around Front Square at the Trinity College Ball in her French Lieutenant's Woman wardrobe was a stylish sortie too, even if she did make a fool of herself with her prithee this and prithee that to the bouncers; but there was nothing nineteenth-century about the morning-after pill. Of course, there was no point telling her that. Pinning Felicity down was an endless job of work. It was like trying to spell Mississippi. In the end, you wrote down 'one of the US Southern states, made famous by Huckleberry Finn in his novel *The Adventures of Mark Twain*.'

'Anyhow,' said Felicity. 'The main thing about a tumble in the hay is that you're not worried. The pollen count may be hassling you, but the sperm count isn't. If you're indoors, the most you have on your mind is whether the wine's too close to the fire or if you thought Fahrenheit when you were setting a Celsius cooker. Afterwards, you can shower, you can wash your hands of the whole business. It runs off you like water. You're pure again; or, if not pure, pristine. Where he hurt you when he poked your bellybutton

will be fine the following morning. And so you tod-
dle off.'

But that was more or less what Theo had been thinking.
Maybe not as succinct, not as surefooted, but still close.
Very close. It was incredible. It was like the Americans and
the Soviets docking in outer space, their fingers touching
in an infinite black-out. Because it was one thing to feel the
same about anti-semitism or Beef Wellington, but it was
another to discover that somebody else had seen the flare
in your fireworks, that she had heard the morse among
the typing keys, and answered it. That was more than
connection, more than contact even. It was a caress. It
might pass, it might perish, but it had existed, if only for
the complex chronology of a split second. And it was the
same for others, for all others. They might stand apart,
stand aloof, but the shapely and misshapen outlines of
their lives were only half the story. The other half would
make it a history. A history of moments, of meetings,
of the kept rendezvous, when it was almost possible to
believe that two human beings could leave the same set
of fingerprints on the pane of glass between them.

'On the other hand,' Felicity said, 'you can find yourself
with a different sort of man. Not only a man you want,
but a man you want to need, a man with a voice like
crushed ice in a tall, black drink, a voice you could listen
to for the rest of your restless existence, or at least for
the rest of your two days off in lieu of overtime. I
mean, you could just curl up at his flip-flops and listen
to him reading aloud from the *Golden Pages*. Catholic
presbyteries, stud-farm stallion leasage, surveillance and
counter-surveillance communications: you name it, he'd
make the Mormon Tabernacle Choir sound like a regiment
of flush toilets. But it wouldn't only be his voice; it'd be
the way he looked at you too. If he once looked down at

you with those two palest of pale blue eyes of his, those wide, wounded eyes out of *Lawrence of Arabia*, you'd see the bereavements, the brothels, the battlefields; and you'd feel sacred and stripped, like an icon in a centrefold or a centrefold in an icon. And if you were playing doubles on the tennis court and he went to the net to pick up the balls, you'd see the way his shorts from Scandinavia tightened like clingfilm round his buttocks as he bent over. And you'd decide then that, after the wedding, you'd buy a big, mirrored bureau and station it at the foot of the bed so you could watch him clench and unclench as he came to pass inside you.'

Theo was damn sure he'd never let a woman make an ass of him that way. It was one thing to cut the cups out of a merry widow or maybe enter your one-and-only for the wet T-shirt competition in the Physics theatre. After all, that was for the tsetse-fly Flag Day, and you'd do anything to help the people in Malawi, or was it Mali? But having your backside under scrutiny while you were so exposed emotionally: that was degrading. On the other hand, there was something else she'd said, before the bit about the bureau. Something small, something slight, something not quite right, like the base of a birthday candle in a mouthful of sponge.

'After what wedding?'

'Of course there'd be a wedding,' said Felicity. 'If there's one thing sadder than a wedding without a marriage, it's a marriage without a wedding. Because there'd be nothing to stop you. To stop me. He'd have a job, a good job; permanent, pensionable. He'd make as much again on the side. If you wanted to convert the garage or go into time-share on a chalet in St Anton, you could do a month as a locum in Baghdad. I mean, everybody's wounded over there. If you're not, they shoot you for desertion. Or look at the ophthalmologist in London who made so much loot from the mustard-gas cases that he bought a Fabergé egg. But even if you didn't turn the Crescent of Islam into your night of the full moon, it wouldn't matter. The sun would still shine on you. Because his mother's place, along with planning permission for the mews behind it, is all going to be his after she dies, isn't it? Unless, that is, the silly old biddy goes and blows the lot on one of those private clinics where there's hot water in both taps, and everyone worries about your haemoglobin while they drain every last drop of your liquid assets into their profit margins.'

'Stop,' Theo said. 'Please stop.' And he looked at her; or, rather, he looked at between her eyebrows and just above them, where Hindu women wore a coloured mark, even the doctors, and he had always wondered if it came off in the shower. He was embarrassed now. He could meet a deadline, no sweat. He would eventually meet his own maker, and that was all right as well. Maybe not as perspiration-free, but in large part a simple, straightforward job of squaring the shoulders along with the conscience and attempting to walk upright into diagonal light. Yet meeting Felicity's eyes was a different, more difficult appointment than either of these. Because at times you had this strange sensation in your stomach, a bit like flying through turbulence, and you could either read the inflight magazine or actually decide to look out the port-hole and see for yourself the whole, widening world laid out below you.

'Are you telling me,' he said to her, 'that you want me to be the father of your children?'

She got a bit awkward then; or perhaps she only pretended to. She had watched a thousand such scenes on poor-quality colour sets since the time she'd started out as a baby-sitter, and each and every one of them, from weekend re-runs of *I Dream of Jeannie* to Easter premières of *Tess of the D'Urbervilles*, stood between her and her own originality. Mind you, she wouldn't have chosen the stage-set they were walking through. Not for a heart-to-heart like they were having. Delphi under starlight would be perfect. That or the place in Venice where Dirk Bogarde sits in a deckchair on the beach and dies listening to Mahler. Not dirty trees and slugs, anyhow. And yet it was here she'd felt the need to talk about need and feeling. It would have been easier to talk about a mitral stenosis valvotomy, or ask him the difference between a brothel and a ballet. It would have. She was almost sorry. But the sun was blinding her; and so she let it.

'Do I want you to be the father of my children? Of course, I want you to be the father of my children. Why do you think I was worried about the hairs on your wrists?'

'I don't have any hairs on my wrists,' Theo said.

'That's the point,' said Felicity. 'I was worried you might be infertile. Lots of men are all hat and no cattle. You can have a super-duper ejaculation, but there may not be any seed in it. Just as the heart of love is sex, so the heart of sex is seed. A man may think posteriors, but a woman has to think posterity. I'm not saying you are infertile, but I'm an oestrogen arms-dump at the moment, so we can't know for certain. After all, anything is possible. I knew a Protestant called Bernadette; she got married in a dental brace. It's that sort of world.'

'And what sort of world do you want for us?' Theo liked to pick up on the last words of whoever had spoken before him. It was something he had learned from the priest who taught him English in his final year at school, though it had let him down badly the time he was in court for switching price-tags on paper-backs.

'I want us,' said Felicity. 'To be man and woman, man and wife. Maybe mother and father. Then I could wave you off in the morning, like Snow White waving her hanky at the Seven Dwarfs, and you could sing "Heigh Ho, Heigh Ho, It's Off to Work I Go", and I'd dust the blanket-chests. I'd like that.'

Actually, it sounded okayish.

'But it's not going to happen, is it?' Felicity said. 'You may just find somebody else to staple the ends of your trousers for you.'

Now that was nasty. That was downright nasty. Because he wasn't small, he was just an awkward size. Besides, Felicity had only ever taken down his trousers. She had never once taken them up. Admittedly, there'd been a winter morning way back in week one of the New Year when she had aired his underpants at the end of a toasting fork in front of the gas fire; but that was contrition, that was lickspittle stuff. Late on the night before, while he was in the Library boning up on basic anatomy, she'd let the Licence Inspector in; and when Theo came back, the sleuth from the Post Office was writing out a docket. If he seemed to be taking his time, that was because his tankard of lemon tea hadn't cooled yet. Felicity's hadn't, either. She was sitting in a sort of lotus on the bean-bag, staring in horror as Raquel Welch struggled to preserve her hair-do from a hungry pterodactyl. And well she might. The TV licence wasn't in her name.

'Theo,' said Felicity. 'Stop thinking about whatever it is you're thinking about. You go into a think the way normal people go into a sulk. It's bad manners. I want you to come back here this instant.'

She was standing beside him. He closed in on her face. He could almost smell her lip-gloss. Yet he didn't kiss her. He didn't want to kiss her. What he wanted was for her to think that he didn't want to kiss her. That would make it advantage Theo. He looked at the redness inside her nose where she had pulled the hairs that morning. And why had she gone and done that, anyway? She was a medical student, for Christ's sake.

'I was thinking about you,' he said. Actually, he hadn't meant to say it quite that way, quite that gently. He was a bit annoyed. If you could only dummy-run the whole damn business on some other planet before beginning your actual life here on earth. Nine months in a woman's womb was a pretty lousy orientation course.

'I'd hate to lose you,' Felicity said. 'I mean, I'd hate myself for losing you, and I'd hate you too. I even hate you now, because you should be saying these things and not me, you shit. But I have this awful nightmare that I'll end up in a contraceptive counselling centre somewhere in East Africa, changing the pictures of the President every six months. Or maybe it'll be worse. Maybe I'll be here, here at home, a hospital doctor with a spot each Sunday on local radio. Ringworm at summer camp or the power of the pharmaceutical companies. Not that I give a fuck about either, but you need to combine the common touch and the crusading spirit to get ahead in broadcasting. Because getting ahead is where it's at, isn't it? Prestige, profit, the two cheeks of the one ass. The two things that make others desire us, resent us. And we need so badly to be desired, and we need so badly to be resented. We need the hosannas and the hate-mail too. Not that there's any great difference between the one and the other, is there? April or November, it's the same landscape. The landscape of the mind. The human mind. At times not very human; at times not very mindful. I don't know. I just don't know. I sound like a swami, but I feel like a pee. I can't understand why. I didn't even finish that beer, because they were out of lime.'

And she pulled down her pants and squatted like one of the pictures in the ante-natal albums. To be straight upfront, it didn't do a whole hell of a lot for Theo. If you thought about a woman going to the toilet in front of you, well, that could be quite sexy, but the greenygold gush, the bluebottles, the splash on the side of the espadrille, they were somehow too real to be raunchy. You felt soft instead of stiff; you thought diapers in the days of yore, not dildoes in the horny darkness. But that was why tenderness was a bore: it got in the way of good sex.

'You know,' said Felicity, 'there are times when I wish there was something I could still be shy about. I mean, you know me every which way. You can press all my buttons: black coffee, coffee with milk, coffee with milk and sugar. I'm like your personal dispensing machine. And you know me the other way too. The Biblical way. As in, "And Abraham went in unto some unpronounceable name, and he knew her, and she begat another unpronounceable name." It's the same with us. You know me inside out. Maybe you know my insides better than my outsides. Maybe you should be on "Mastermind", answering questions on my menstrual cycle. But what it means is that I've no more secrets left to save up for you. What it means is that we'll never have a wedding night.'

And she pulled herself together again. To be fair, she had done an awful lot. Already, two dragonflies were working on it.

'Whenever a couple goes to ground and makes love,' said Theo, 'it's a wedding night. Or a wedding morning.

A wedding tea-time, even. We've had hundreds of wedding nights, and we'll have hundreds more. I've buttonholes in every jacket. You know that.'

'It's not the same,' she said. 'It's not the same at all. Can you imagine what the bride and groom must be thinking about, up there at the prie-dieu, while the priest is consecrating the Host? Well, they're not thinking about Transubstantiation, anyhow. Or, if they are, they're not thinking about wine turned into blood. They're thinking about water turned into wine.'

'I'll tell you what they're thinking,' Theo said. 'The guy in the tux is wondering whether he should pay the priest in the sacristy or the hotel; and is fifty pounds too much or too little? The bride, she's worrying that the Juliet cap isn't sitting straight. And she's made up her mind about one thing. No way is she going to stand for any photographs her grandfather wants to take, because the avaricious old bastard never puts any film in his camera. In the meantime, unnoticed by anyone, the bread on the altar is turning into God.'

'You're always sneering,' Felicity said. 'Always the sneerer, never the cheerer. Always the cynic, never the singer. I don't know why. I really don't. You live with this old black-and-white set when everyone else is watching in colour; and, even if you do watch in colour, you notice stuff that takes the good out of everything. Like that love-scene in "Spartacus". I was so fond of that love-scene in "Spartacus", I even called my gerbil after him. My great ambition was to travel there some day, to see Sparta itself. Oh, I suppose you think I'm silly, and perhaps I did hold a candle for Kirk Douglas, but that was because there was so much politeness inside the homicidal part of him. Then you came along, just as he's gritting his eyes at the slave-girl under the olive-trees, and you showed me the vapour trail from the jet-plane in the left-hand corner of the screen. Because basically you're a bit of a knocker, you need to find flaws. I mean, if you'd written *Dr Zhivago*, you'd have had the camera panning to a corn-plaster on Julie Christie's instep when she's down on the bedspread, making babies. Just by way of reminding us that, well, we all fart on the dance-floor during the slow set, and those sardines we ate an hour ago are going to start repeating halfway through "Swan Lake". It's a sort of *caveat emptor* for you, isn't it? The smirk is your only safeguard against the unholy possibility that you might get carried away. Or carried inwards. Other folk can lift their heads, but Theo has to lift his eyebrows. Other folk can break their hearts; Theo breaks his sides. I don't know why I ever bothered to give you *The Gulag Archipelago*. *From Russia with Love* is more your style. And as for Martin Heidegger – before I find you reading Martin Heidegger, I'll find you reading tea-leaves.'

'I fully intend,' said Theo, 'I fully intend –'

'Fully intend,' Felicity said. 'Wait till you discover what Martin has to say about "fully intending". "Fully intending" is right.'

'What I meant was –'

'Don't let's get into meaning, Theo. Take it from me. Don't let's do that. Stick with pets' corner. Don't start climbing into the polar bear's enclosure.'

Theo had the vague feeling that Felicity was angry, that there was a deep anger within her. Of course, he could be wrong.

'I have the vague feeling,' he said to her, 'that there's this deep anger within you. Of course, I could be wrong.'

'Not anger,' she said. 'Something much more debilitating. Irritation. I feel irritated. I feel irritated because I have this scenario in my head, of being married to someone, not you, someone else, a nice man, a good man. When we go to bed to make love, he puts the chair against the door in case the kids barge in. The kids are twelve, ten and a half, nine and seven and a half, but he's that sort of man. Whenever he gets a hard-on, he gets heartburn, so he has to stop to spill Maalox over the duvet before we can make it one flesh for the night. But then I go to the bathroom to clean up, and I find he's replaced my toner, which means that he lost his lunchbreak; and then I really want to make love to him, but he's gone asleep.'

'You have this thing,' Theo said. 'You have this thing about men being unappreciative afterwards.'

'No, it's not that. It's not that at all. What I'm saying is, home-life can be homely, lively. And it would be with a man like that. But whenever the rain drives you indoors or the sun drives you outdoors, you'd be thinking back to the guy with the ear-ring who gave you joss-sticks to burn between your teeth while you were working in the dissection-room, so the smell of jasmin and formaldehyde became a part of your life, a part of his presence in it. A part of the guy with the ear-ring. But by now, of course, the ear-ring's out of earshot, and so's the pencil tie you chased me round the trout-farm with, when you found I'd left the bait at the bus-stop. No, now it's Oxford button-downs and a pair of trousers with a crease you could use to cut glass. God only knows what you'll be doing in them, but I wouldn't be at all surprised if the high point of your day was a matter of treating someone from Saatchi and Saatchi for tennis elbow. Then it's home to your deft designer hideaway where even the hot-press has a theme and the glass in the kitchen window is photochromic. Inside in the front room –'

This was autopilot. Worse, it was auto-suggestion. But

what could Theo do? You weren't supposed to shake a sleepwalker, and Felicity was closing in on that category fast. It would have been impressive if you'd paid into a theatre to watch an Equity actress; but this wasn't a Bloomsday reading from *Finnegans Wake*. This was Felicity, dunking the same tea-bag in a thousand styrofoam cups. The same bile, the same bitchcraft. Budgies were simpler. You threw a sheet over the cage, and they shut up. Pronto.

'In the front room,' Felicity was saying, 'you've got all those books on bookshelves, and they've been there so long they're institutionalised. You can't even take one out: they're packed too tightly. Once they were salmon; now they're sardines. But you don't notice, because you don't fish for books anymore. You fish for videos. You've got a nice one lined up for this evening, but first you have to shortlist half-a-dozen headings on genital warts for a case-session tomorrow. After that, you can put your feet up and watch "Lesbian Enemas".'

'I think you're being unfair to yourself,' Theo said. 'I think I'm coming out of this better than you are. The way you talk about me, I'm beginning to think I belong in a Sotheby's catalogue. Can't you see even the slightest little tear in the canvas? The smallest little flaw in the stone? Try to. Try hard.'

'What I can see,' Felicity said, 'is a class reunion down the road, on the other side of the century, when the year 2000 has come and gone and the bookstore bargain basements are awash with Jehovah's Witness *Watchtower*s and nobody's bulk-buying multi-vitamins for their sand-bagged cellars anymore. There'll be thirty, forty of us there at the dinner, and you'll leave after the main course to have a smoke on the street. Later, during the slide-show in Theatre B, when the lights are out and we're looking at shots of Sally and Seamus and a half-dozen others whose names are imprinted indelibly on their headstones because of carcinoma, a strong current, loose chippings, you'll put your hand up my skirt out of pure courtesy and snap my elastic. And I'll cry. I know I will. I won't even have done my eyes, because then they'd run. I'll cry because you'll be the same, you see. You won't have changed. The same split ends, the same split infinitives, the same split personality.'

Theo's face darkened. That was probably because he was standing in shadow. People's faces do redden, but they don't darken. Except when they're dead. They darken then. In fact, they blacken. They blacken as if the body itself were consumed with indignation that the children of God should die like the gods of our own childhood. And indignation was more or less what Theo was feeling. Not, to be sure, on behalf of the finite or the infinite, but because of what Felicity had said about infinitives. He had never split one in his life, even when he was under stress.

She could tell he was cross. Unless you were building bonfires at cub-camp, you didn't break twigs off trees. It was like the time he had dripped candlewax over the cockroach whose presence had put paid to a nice pre-coital scenario on the kitchen floor. But that was men all over.

'All right,' she said. 'I'm sorry. I shouldn't have said what I said. You don't have a split personality. I just couldn't think of a third thing to go with "split". So I improvised. It's that Writers' Workshop I took during the Joyce Centenary. Ever since then, I even use punctuation when I'm talking to people. Actually, when we met that woman in the mobile library the other day and you were wiring the Walkman for her, I made some comment in parentheses. It was completely natural. I just feel I owe it to the language to make an effort. I mean, you listen to

Shakespeare, and he's so Churchillian. It makes you feel like St Paul, when he appealed to Caesar to get him off the hook, not because he was a Catholic but because he was a Roman. "I am Irish, I appeal to the English language." That sort of thing.'

If this was a film, he would have left by now. Just left. Got up and walked out. Run the gauntlet of the guys with the tortoise-shell glasses who hadn't shaved for a week, and the guys with the car-keys in a cluster on their hips who thought that 'Virgin Spring' meant watersports with schoolgirls. He thought of the GI with the ginger side-burns who'd been to the Bergman season at the local drive-in on Okinawa three, maybe four years before. How he'd sat through two full-length features with Japanese side-titles, and then driven the car at the screen. Now he was a hemiplegic in Kansas, and Bergman wanted to make a documentary about him. He could stopover *en route*, and make one about Theo. It was just as well there wasn't a convertible behind the bushes. Then he'd be making a whodunit.

'But I'm not appealing to the English language now, am I?' said Felicity. 'I'm appealing to you. At least, I hope I am. I know that sex-appeal isn't everything, of course, I know it's only part of the total picture, a bit like the artist's signature, but it still matters a whole hell of a lot. If Cleopatra's nose had been full of blackheads, do you really think they would have gone ahead with the Battle of Actium? It would have sunk without trace. Or there mightn't have been a Reformation if Catherine of Aragon had only known that Henry was into fellatio, and the only woman in the court who gave great head was Anne Boleyn. Besides, the beheading business was really a castration complex. It sticks out a mile. So you could almost argue, even at the risk of being too Hegelian

114

about things that happened before Hegel was born, that the existence of the Jesuit order in the twentieth century is a direct consequence of the non-existence of sex-appeal, understand as an appeal for sex, in the ingle-nooks of Hampton Court in the sixteenth century. On the other hand, you could also argue that nowadays sex is too forthright. Too downright. Too matter of fact. Because we have this incredible microwave mentality toward any possible partner. Defrost and devour; thaw and tuck in. We know everything there is to know about excitement, but we've forgotten about desire. We don't know how to wait, how to await, how to be patient. We want Communion without having to sit through the Mass. But take my great-uncle Bernard, back in the days of bowler hats and barefoot children. He put the light out on his wedding-night and he said to my great aunt: "I think we've had enough bread and circuses for one day." Now that was sublimation. It was a sort of oriental prolongation of desire. But nobody sublimates like that anymore. Look at modern architecture. Why is it so ghastly? Because the architects are taking their erections home with them. That's why. It's all midnight feast and no midnight oil. Whereas if you look at a postcard of the Parthenon, you just know that Phidias wasn't fucking around, he wasn't perched on Plato's knee at the Hunt Ball. He was thinking concrete and cement. He was sublimating. And you can do it too, Theo. You can sublimate when you put your mind to it.'

'I can?' said Theo. Surely she hadn't heard him the time he went into the bathroom when she was too tired? Not with the taps on, and the extractor fan as well. Of course, she might have listened at the door. If she had, it was immoral. There was no other word for it.

'Of course you can,' she said. 'You've sublimated at

least three times since I met you. And I respect that. I respect a man who can have his sex and sublimate it. That time I was telling you about, that time in the kitchen with my mother, the time of the pep-talk about Prince Charming and how to pick him out, I made up my mind finally and forever that sex is to sublimation as Scotch is to soda. As Shakespeare said, "Ratio is all"; and it is. You want to get carried away, not carried out. So you want a man who's a mix of warlord and wimp. Someone with balls, someone who'll work the wipers so the parking ticket falls off, and do it – this is the test – while the traffic warden's watching. But someone who's sensitive too. Someone who'll take a phone call from his four year old at a board meeting, and not get heavy and hung-up because she wants him to talk to her in Winnie the Pooh ways before she settles down for her afternoon nap. In other words, you mix the right amount of Scotch with the right amount of soda, and there won't be a hiccup in your home-life. That's what I decided. Then, when I saw the budgie, the decision became a vow.'

'What about the budgie?' Theo said. He'd never seen a budgie in Felicity's home. The bird had obviously flown before he met her. Actually, it was a bit lower-middle-class for a family who had some pretension to style, or, at least, some quite stylish pretensions. The old man was forever walking out of the church during the sermon, even though he had to be back ten minutes later to help take up the collection. Afterwards, he'd stand in the porch and tell the parishioners why he'd done it. 'Maybe the Levite was late for a job interview,' he'd say. 'Who are we to judge? You have to be Christian about the Gospels.' And that was stylish. Plus he'd had two-thirds of a letter in *Time* magazine, where he said that he wanted to dissociate himself both as a barrister and a believer from capital punishment and the cult of the Holy Shroud. More to the point, each and everyone of his Penguin classics faced out the wrong way on his bookshelves so that visitors wouldn't read the titles and be embarrassed by their ignorance. That was called class. But a budgie? A budgie was like having your picture taken in front of Buckingham Palace.

'I don't want to talk about the budgie,' Felicity said. 'It's too visceral.'

He had taught her that word, the word visceral. In fact, he'd used it himself on the Monday of the week before. But that was in the context of Francis Bacon, a man whose catalogues were collector's items, for God's sake. Yet it wasn't the way she turned his albs into bibs that he resented. It was the endless sharing. First toothbrushes, then vocabulary. Where did it stop? He had always thought that the bit about man and woman being one flesh was Palestinian slang for an orgasm. But what if it meant what it said? What if it meant that you became an astronomer of all the freckles on another person's back? The furtive sniffer of her odor-eaters when she was out of town on business and there was nothing of her in the laundry-bin to hold to your face like a toddler's rag? Once they'd been in the bath together, and he'd weed in the water, and the bubbles from the bubble-bath bottle disappeared. Then they made mighty love, and the scent of honeysuckle filled the room like the Holy Spirit. After that, they had always bought the same honeysuckle spray, even though it was expensive. They were one flesh then. No doubt about it.

'I never had a budgie,' he said. He was too nice to say why. 'But I had a cat. It was a stray I took in. I used to talk to it like St Francis. It never talked back. But it liked dog-food. It was a very macho tom. One day he brought me a sparrow. I saw red. I left the Franciscans. I horsewhipped him with a knitting needle. He fled. I never saw him again. Such is life.'

That was how to talk. That was how to tell a story. Plain, primitive English and little Latin: all protein and no starch. How in the name of Jesus did the novels in any newsagent's shop run to six or seven hundred pages of small print? Of course, the girls who wrote them weren't really writers. They were just authors. Anyone could dash off some drivel and call it a novel. But a narrative took more than A-levels. Narrative is to a novel as a neurosurgeon is to a general practitioner. That was it.

'It was when we came back in from playing with the dolls in the cabinet,' Felicity said. 'I took my father's gown off the cage, and the budgie was lying on the bottom of it, with one eye closed and one eye open, like Long John Silver. It was very harrowing, because he never did that before. His feathers were ruffled. I think he'd had a heart-attack. The black barrister's gown must have scared him to death. He was a creature of habit, you see; he really didn't have the emotional plasticity to cope with a new experience.'

'Those of us who are vulnerable are rarely versatile,' said Theo. 'And vice versa. Such is life.' It was a grand little phrase, that trinity of three words. It sort of gave the impression that you'd been there, that you knew what you were talking about. The guys would drink their pints in silence, the girls would drag their bar-stools nearer. Then you could talk about the waiters at the Church of Satan sex-show in Amsterdam or the Cossack gatekeeper at the Russian monastery on Mount Athos, and thank God that you'd had to spend a full forty minutes over the June issue of *National Geographic* before the skin specialist could see you.

'Such is life,' he said again. It really was way ahead of 'Om'.

'We didn't bury him for two days,' Felicity said. 'I didn't want another premature burial on my conscience. Not after the tortoise. But then he went blue where he was yellow and yellow where he was blue; and he'd never done that before, either. So my mother bought a box of Cadbury's "Contrast", and we ate the chocolates except for the cherry ones that my father likes, and we buried him in the box. The "Contrast" box is black, you see, which was nice. Afterwards, I didn't go down to that part of the garden for a long time. And when I did go down, to pick some mint for the boiled potatoes, there were weeds growing over the grave.'

'Such is life,' said Theo.

'But it was chickweed,' Felicity said. 'His favourite. I used to feed him chickweed through the bars. And it was growing from the seeds in his stomach. I was so moved I went back without the mint, but the potatoes were lovely, anyway. And I knew then how the apostles must have felt on Mount Tabor. I'm not comparing the two, of course. The Transfiguration was like Krakatoa; the chickweed was just a blaze of colour. But the whole Mount Tabor thing is out of this world, whereas things like chickweed are in it. Like you and me, like here and now. Which is why, I suppose, I can make a song and dance about it. Because it's worth singing and dancing about. It's worth a hymn, but a hymn full of four-letter words, good and gutsy; it's worth a chorus of can-can girls in the blackest of mourning underwear. It's worth breathing in and breathing out, it's worth sighs and whistles. Because it's sound, it's sound and fury, signifying just about everything. You can see that, can't you, Theo? You can see that. I know you like to pretend that you're this big bowel motion, but you're not. Not really. If you were, do you think I'd be giving you this guided tour of all the emptiness inside of me? Some of the empty spaces inside of me are so vast you could find bison in them. There's only a wind looking for trees to nuzzle. And all of those spaces belong to you. You hold the title deeds. You hold the keys.'

That was it. Keys. Keys meant locks. Locks could be padlocks. Padlocks could be prisons. They had been walking toward a penitentiary. It had to be. The high walls, the lack of access, absence of signs. A ruin, of course, abandoned for ages. And of no account, amounting to nothing. If anyone of note had ever passed through, a renegade Anglo landlord who turned the west wing over to the peasants as a short-stay cottage hospital because the works of Leo Tolstoy had made him blush to his riding boots, or a curate fresh from France who'd sung the Marseillaise at the local magistrate, well, there'd be a postcard of the place on sale in the town. Or the principal of the school would have cranked out a pamphlet for the pupils to staple during detention. Because if, after all, you belonged to the brotherhood, if you'd refused the bandage and the blindfold, you only had to ease your bladder on a roadside for the local authority to transubstantiate the spots into the source of a holy well. And that was fine. It was a damn sight better than Hollywood hand-prints. But this site was no cultural waterhole. No way. This was a dried-up sewer.

Now if he said all of that back to Felicity, would she understand? First the holy well, then the waterhole, then the sewer bit. And how it all connected. There were times when Theo wondered whether he shouldn't have done English. Perhaps he ought to be writing stories and not prescriptions. His reactions were so organic. Perhaps there were good reasons why he'd been born only two days after the Feast of the Epiphany. But these things were mysteries really. Only time would tell.

'Not just the keys,' Felicity was saying. 'The master key, as well. Obviously I don't mean that in a sexist way. I mean, nobody's going to fuck with Felicity. But in the sense that other people have the key to my hall-door or my den or whatever. But you can roam. You can roam around my attic. You can roam around my cellar. I love my parents, but that's as far as it goes. You can go farther. Give me a house; I'll give you a home.'

Felicity was exhausted. In the whole of her life she had never offered the least homage or hospitality to such leanings out of late antiquity. These were Theo's lines. There must be something wrong with her. Maybe the pill was playing musical chairs with her neuro-transmitters. Maybe oestrogen was a double agent, a pharmaceutical Philby. That would explain why she had failed histology. She must be more wary, more watchful. Only that morning she had spoken of Princess Diana instead of Mrs D. Windsor. Plus she had dressed her own bed in a hotel with room service.

'It's a prison,' Theo said. 'That's all it is. A slammer.'

She would have cried. She wanted to. But the tear duct is a terrible ironist. It waits. Of course, she should have known that. She had been through the cancer wards and seen the dying sniffle over the boat people on breakfast television. If she had been elsewhere, she might have seen the boat people cry over cancer documentaries on rented portables with rabbit-ears. So she made do with looking sad.

'What did you expect?' Theo said. 'The source of the Nile?'

And he took her hand and drew her after him; and they

went in. Or, rather, in they went. The other way makes it sound a bit too climactic.

Felicity picked up promptly. She was that sort of person. She could adapt. Her tights turned into fan-belts, her brollies into parasols, whenever the need arose. Only a very versatile woman would ever have thought to use matinée coats as cosies or a dachshund jacket as a leg-warmer; and only a practical individual would have double-jobbed the Christmas crib as a bird-house in the summer months, with the Three Kings gazing reverently at the strewn pistachios.

'I'm determined to have an experience in here,' she said. 'I'm just so determined. And if I can't have an experience, I want at least to have a Kodak moment. Otherwise my legs got landed in all those thingies for nothing.'

Theo was walking along the inside of the wall to where the exercise yard would have been. He looked good too, in what you could see of him now that the light was almost gone. He looked like Page One of the modern novel, hurt and handsome, with the St Michael's label sticking up at the neck of his jumper. He was probably having an insight, or a hindsight. It was in his nature to be having insights and hindsights all the time. Felicity would just have to get used to it. One minute he'd be picking hair and dental floss out of a sink-hole; a minute later, he'd have that look on his face like a Japanese pilot in the soldered cockpit of a Zero, flying low over the flashing stillness of a limitless Pacific, blind-dating the beyond.

'It's unspeakable,' Felicity said. 'You could talk about it until there's a stopper in every single bath in the Soviet Union, and it would still be unspeakable. In fact, it would break your heart if your heart weren't already broken. There I was, moaning on about wanting a house with a name instead of a number, and all I can think of now are those poor, poor prisoners. I can see them so clearly, whoever they were. Those tiny little girls in Botany Bay for stealing a bunch of bananas, or a priest in the Penal days on the Scarsdale diet in a dungeon for spelling God with a capital G on his typewriter. I wish I had a cardigan to cover my arms. Like I did in St Mark's when the sacristan wouldn't let me in. This place is much holier than that dump.'

Theo was examining the wall. High and thick, as a prison wall must be; but a beautiful job. The strongest jails were always built by their own inmates. If you were into tennis, you could soon improve your game against this granite. The ball would be whizzing back at the weirdest angles. That was how what's-his-face had won at Wimbledon, the one who blessed himself on a second service.

And Felicity blessed herself too. You would think at times that Providence itself was pearling and plaining the strangest of patterns.

'This is where they hanged them,' she said. 'This is the exact spot.'

'This is the exercise yard,' Theo told her. 'This is where they walked in circles. Didn't the Roman who collared you have a copy of Foucault? A copy of Foucault annotated in blood or at least in red ink?'

'This is where they hanged them,' she said again. 'I can feel it. I can hear frequencies that make a dog-whistle sound like a fog-horn. Because I'm sensitive. The day I was born, I expressed milk from my nipples. Now you know.'

Theo measured the wall. It was eighteen, twenty feet. Three times the height of a man. Maybe more. And they weren't six-footers either, the cardsharps and cattle-rustlers of the early eighteen-hundreds. Not on a diet of milk with small droppings in it, and blood sucked from a cut in a cow like the Masai of Kenya. No wonder the reformers in Dublin clubs drank themselves silly with claret while their coachmen outside swabbed their chilblains with urine.

'What I never understood is the hearty breakfast,' Felicity said. 'The condemned man always eats a hearty breakfast. So you get this bizarre image of blackpudding and quicklime. It would really put you off your food.'

'It has to do with crisis,' Theo said. 'It has to do with crisis management. There was a Christian scientist in Auschwitz who spent the whole time worrying about his mortgage. That was his way of coping. In a crisis, you touch wood. Not the wood of the Cross, but the wood of your own dinner table. That time we came off the motorbike and we were in the ambulance, they wouldn't take the helmet off me. They thought I might have fractured my skull. Now that was a crisis. But what was I doing? I was counting my Chemistry notes, because I wanted to be sure that I hadn't lost a single page.'

'I was trying to check my underwear,' Felicity said. 'It wasn't easy, in a jumpsuit. In fact, it was impossible. But I knew I'd get an anti-tetanus shot, and I knew I'd get it from the guy who talks like Max Von Sydow and wears the eighteen-carat cufflinks with the wrong initials. What I didn't know was whether I'd worn the same panties the day before. Because sometimes, sometimes, I might just get two days out of them. But never again. I swore it there and then. Never again.'

Theo wanted to check out the jail itself. At most, they had half-an-hour's light left. After that, they'd be groping in the darkness. So he picked his way among planks and plant formations that were like the low-budget backdrops of science-fiction movies from the McCarthy era until he had reached the door. Then he had to go back and carry Felicity through the green rubbish, like a groom sweeping his bride over the threshold. Actually, she was heavy enough.

The passage led left. Half a dozen cell doors and a cork-screw staircase were as much as they could see. The doors were open, some of them thrown back. Names had been inscribed with nail-heads and steel combs on the stout, blue-black boards around the Judas holes; and a message in pink pastel nail-varnish at the second door-hinge read: 'Brits Out. Monica Sucks Better Than Hoover.'

'It's the very same shade that I use on my toenails,' Felicity said as she leaned forward to look closely at the graffito. 'It really is such a small world. Some day I'll get into the shower, and I'll be there already ahead of me; and I won't be one bit surprised.'

The atmosphere was dry, not damp. Of course it was summer, but Theo had expected dampness, the feel of wet wool in his throat. In fact, the place was fine. Why on earth hadn't they turned it into a writers' centre or a sort of dacha for the inter-church steering committees who spent their lives trying to agree on what Jesus of Nazareth meant when he went all mysterious over the bread and wine in the upper room? They could have played their typewriters like button accordions all over the building, and nobody would have been the wiser. After all, it was miles from anywhere. A couple of coats of whitewash and a few fax machines, and you'd be as right as rain. Admittedly, there was the odd prop from Pinewood studios – a cockroach here, a cobweb there – but nothing a few motivated mini-maids couldn't handle. Then, afterwards, if they wanted to make it a rustic retreat for the clergymen, they could call it Forty Days Farm; if for the writers, Forty Years would do nicely. Or Jordan

House for the boys in black, Hashemite House for the ones in grey.

'Do you know what it is about this that's so meaningful?' Felicity said. 'What's meaningful is that it's meaningless. It's a learning experience only because it reminds us how little we can learn. I mean, let's face it, there were people in those poky little cells who knew about pain. The two of us know about sensitive teeth. They knew about an internal temperature that was so low it would crack the mercury in your fillings. I mean, some of them were happy to be hanged. Some of them actually applied to the Governor to be hanged, like they were applying for annual leave. It was that bad. So there's no point putting on a puss, like Dolores did the time she went to Dachau on a day-trip. There's that snapshot where she's wearing a sort of Sunday school ensemble, right, and she has that fake, faraway look like she's a simple shepherd girl in a grotto and she can hold her hand in the candle and it won't hurt her. And the truth is, she's on a whistle-stop, and the next number is Neuschwanstein, because she has to see where "Chitty Chitty Bang Bang" was made.'

'Dolores has her better side,' said Theo; and he remembered the party at her place, and how he'd used the toilet after her, and the seat was still warm. To be honest, it was quite a nice feeling. But then he'd had an erection and couldn't pee. That was awful. Obviously he couldn't talk to Felicity about it, because she loathed the woman. Ever since they first met each other, they'd been inseparable enemies. But Theo had gone to the chaplain. It was on his mind, you see. And the chaplain had looked up a book on sexual perversions, but he couldn't find it listed. Theo was a tiny bit proud about that. Privately he even invented a name for it: theophilia.

'No, but what I'm saying is that there's this pressure

nowadays to pull a long face, to cancel the christening because of hurricane this or herpes that. Even the tabloids wastepaper the pin-ups if there's been a calamity, if the Duke of Edinburgh has mumps or three million farms have been flooded in Bangladesh. But people aren't like that. You can't expect them to cork the bottle because the crops have failed in a country about which the only thing they know is that it's somewhere between the pyramids and Cape Town. I suppose I'm different that way. I have a sort of automatic access. But not always. Not all the time. And not here. Now now. The characters who lived here, imagining them, it's like trying to reconstruct a skating championship by studying the scratches left in the ice. But that doesn't matter, because they're dead, and the living can't imagine the dead. Anyway, they shouldn't; it's morbid. No, what worries me, what worries me at times is that, well, that the living can't imagine the living. Each of us, say, is as complicated and as whatever as a thousand years of Russian history; a thousand years of Russia herself. Year in, year out, heat and cold, spring and harvest, war and truce. Now all of that is one of us. And what do we know about each other? Well, after a happy marriage of sixty years' standing, you might just know that Peter the Great kept his wife's head in a jamjar or that people queue for brown bread in Leningrad.'

It was true. You could experience another person's power, but not his power-cut. The most you could manage, by way of re-creating his terror in total darkness, was to scratch at the candlewax in the carpet. The Romans who crucified Christ on a refuse site outside Jerusalem were more concerned about the pus coming out of their penis than the seven last words of the Son of God. And even if the whole night-sky had gone out like Piccadilly Circus suddenly switched off, the pain of an impacted wisdom tooth would have made them think dentists first, damnation later.

Theo looked up above him. The ceiling might or might not be sturdy. It was worth a try.

'You can go first,' she said. 'Tanks after infantry, same as the Soviets. There might be bats up there. The shit who went and classified bats as mammals must have hated women. He must have been a Caesarean birth and never forgave his mother.'

The staircase was sound, surprisingly so. There was a squashed Smartie on the second step, a filter from a cheroot on the fourth. They were not the first to have found their way here.

'Imagine,' said Felicity, 'how Scott must have felt. Or was it Amundsen? Three cheers, it's the North Pole. And what do they find? Somebody else's flagpole, and a note left out for milk.'

Halfway up, above a single missing board, Theo paused. The silhouette of a flattened human hand, misted in lemon paint from a spray-can, clung to the splintered step. He manoeuvred his way around it. After all, it was one thing to tread on toes. Hands, however, were a different matter. And a strange, stretched hand, and a left hand too, was a bit unsettling. If it were a picture in a gallery, you could spear a couple of cheese-cubes, and make small talk. You could talk about the Zeitgeist while you swiped another sherry off a passing salver. But this was a bit over the top.

'Listen,' Felicity was saying. They had reached the cells on the second floor, and she was reading an inscription.

'Malachi MacMahon did a year here for what he did not commit. Assault, perhaps; battery, never. Ask Father Clancy.'

Theo pushed open the door of the first cell. It was tidily empty. Nothingness is always spick and span.

The distilleries of the underworld must bottle Dettol, he thought. Life is sputum, sediment, stains; but death and deadliness are hooked on antibiotics. It was no great wonder, when you thought about it, that those gigolos of a dark-age ideology preferred the shower-room to the firing squad when they brainstormed over Sobibor and Belzec. When they made their drafts and doodles, they were probably high on Cointreau spiced with toilet cleanser. For a moment, Theo imagined bodies on barbed wire, like staves on sheet-music.

'All cell and no blood,' he said, shutting another door behind him.

'Theo,' said Felicity. 'What smell does a bat have? Is it a bit like a wet Wellington boot? Is it?'

But he didn't hear her. He was peering into the last cell.

'Come here,' he said. 'Come over here. Look at this.'

'I mean, I know there aren't any vampire bats in Ireland. But the thought of them being snarled in your hair is enough to give you traumatic baldness. Thanks be to God I did a French braid today.'

And she peeped over his shoulder.

In the recess of the window a two-tone thermos flask caught the last of the light. A rough-cut, four-square section of patterned carpet – and Theo had seen the same red pattern somewhere else, quite recently – covered the centre of the floor, its edges raw and ravelled like the sail of a life-raft. Away from the window stood a small stack of magazines; in front of them, a large rubber torch with a strip of elastoplast that held the hood of the light together, leaned against the crumpled paper carton of a six-pack.

There was nothing else. The inscriptions on the walls – dates, declarations, Pompeian obscenities, a demand for the release of Nelson Mandela on the second anniversary of the closing of the Vatican Council in Rome, logos and slogans, and a whole series of semi-colons, twenty at least, that must have taken hours to engrave – were another day's business. The flask and the torch had nothing to do with ballpoint pens and a moment's boredom.

'One of the prisoners must have preferred to stay on,' Felicity said. 'Or maybe he sneaks back when he's feeling down. That's the way it is with people. They get very proprietorial about their bad times. And why wouldn't they? I mean, the things that dispossess us are always our most cherished possessions. A man will give you his wife to fuck and his house to live in, but he won't give you his pain. Try taking it from him, and you'll soon see.'

The torch worked. And it worked well, not weakly. Theo shone it on the wall. He made a fox with his fingers; made the fox bark. Who could have left it? Solid and shapely. Could have cost a tenner. The lamp on his own bike set him back what? And he stooped over the magazines, to make out the titles.

He gave a long, low whistle. Now he understood.

Felicity was holding her hands on her head like a POW. She was taking no chances. Bats were blighters.

'That's why Jesus would have made a good GP,' she said. 'The lepers and stuff that came to him, you know. First thing he said to them was "Do you want to be cured?" And, of course, lots of them didn't. Not really. Not when it came right down to it. Not if it meant that things would be different. No way.'

Theo looked up at her. Was she still going on about marriage?

'I'm glad I didn't bring the Archbishop in here,' he said. 'The poor man would have turned in his grave.'

'No, he wouldn't,' said Felicity. 'He was too good of a theologian.'

Theo waved one of the magazines at her. There was a very handsome man on the cover. It was strange, not because he was naked, but because he was holding the same issue of the magazine in front of his crotch. And if you examined that, then you found that, yes, there was another magazine cover inside it; and so on, and so forth, *ad infinitum.* Actually, it would make your head reel. You would end up thinking about attoseconds and quarks and the diameter of our galaxy and how the planet earth is stuck in the middle of nowhere, the back of beyond, like a solitary cigarette butt with a little lipstick on it in the sly and subtle dunes of the Sahara. After that, the newsagent would ring for an ambulance; and they would come quickly, with anoraks on over their white coats to disguise their presence.

'What about it?' Felicity said.

'Well,' said Theo, 'it's not *The World of Interiors* anyway.' Of course, he could not have been more wrong. That is exactly what it was.

'I don't see what you're getting so high and mighty about, Theo,' she said. 'Your magazines are more like midwifery manuals. In fact, your own father thought that one of them was a genito-urinary periodical. Admittedly, he didn't have his contacts in at the time.'

She picked one off the pile and leafed through it.

'See this,' she said. 'Isn't that extraordinary?'

Haughty, Hispanic, his thick hair vaselined back, the model lay in a turquoise bean-bag, holding a slim, strong penis. It had to be said that he was very beautiful, his throat a masterpiece. Bodies like that were a destiny, a deed before you did anything. But his chipmunk wasn't any longer or stiffer than Theo's on an average outing. Not by a long shot. And the circumcised look wasn't so classy anymore. Fact of the matter, it was common.

Besides, women liked foreskins. They liked pulling them back. It was a kind of unveiling.

'Not that,' Felicity said. 'This.' She pointed behind the man's head.

'You're right,' he said. 'Constable's "Haywain".'

'Isn't that sort of *mucho strango*?' she said.

Theo counted with his thumb along the tips of his fingers.

'Not in Thurles,' he said. 'There was no haywain in the hotel there.'

'Not in the bedroom, maybe. But did you never notice the place-mats in the dining-room?'

'You're right,' he said. 'You're right. And the carpet. I've seen the carpet before.'

They stared at it intently.

'The Boris Karloff guy. That's where.' Felicity's face lit up. 'The man who buggered the sheep. The reactive depressive. The one who gave the cigarettes to the woman with the tea-strainer over her nipple.'

She was right again. The guy who fucked sheep. That's where he'd seen it. A circle after circle of pale, pinched flowers, their petals nondescript now, colourless from coffee stains and weeping-fits and the grey gravel of one road after another. Were they wreaths or bouquets, those slight, stunted circles? And which of the men who came here under cover of darkness had taken the time and the trouble to knot those loose little threads that had ravelled already? In two, three, four places at the edges of the carpet someone had tied the fibres together. Who would have done that? Someone precise, someone particular, the sort of man who'd clean his nails with a toothpick, his smoker's finger with a pumice stone. Somebody deft and deliberate.

'The bank manager,' Felicity said. 'He smelled so nice,

I wanted to lean across the counter and smell his hair. He smelled like Rome late at night. And he was so attentive. Then, when he asked you for a further proof of your identity and you produced your Kidney Donor card, I had to howl. And he took his out and said "Snap".'

What sort of people came here? And what were they coming from? Were they married and mortgaged, single and singular, safe and unsound? Were they hospital porters or hotel accountants or history instructors or what? Did the veterinary surgeon blacken the curls on his chest with a sponge and some boot polish before running in the marathon for multiple sclerosis? Did the salesman in the furniture store read Rapunzel to his daughter, and walk here through the wounded wrecks of cars, the dense, difficult undergrowth? And to what? To whom?

'Or the waiter in the hotel,' said Felicity. 'He gave me his sweeteners because I didn't want sugar. And he had them in this beautiful box, with a tiger's eye on the lid. You know what his ambition is? His ambition is to go to Saigon and open an orphanage for all the American children that the GIs left behind. The ones they had by Vietnamese women. Because he grew up in an orphanage too. Except that I couldn't help thinking, unless I'm way off, that those kids would be hitting twenty, twenty-one round about now. Wouldn't they?'

Theo was trying to remember which of the magazines had been on top. He wanted to leave things exactly as he'd found them. More to the point, he wanted to leave. He had no business being there. Not because it wasn't his scene, but because it wasn't his space. There was too much grief, too much desire, too much camouflaged anguish. And it threw him. His needle wasn't finding North. The whole of what he'd been and believed for years was no help now. It was about as useful as a map of the London Underground in the middle of a South American rainforest. In fact, it was time to forget about maps as such. Like it or not, the world gave every appearance of being a globe: the curve of one horizon stretching out in all the joy of possibility toward the horizon of another curve. A flat earth made for better balance; but, all round, the odd land on your own bottom was a low price to pay for the privilege of not seeing everything when you opened your eyes.

'I don't believe it,' Felicity said.

She had unscrewed the flask and she was smelling it.

'Wine,' she said. 'There's a bit left. Red wine. Imagine.'

'Put it back,' he told her. 'Just put it back where it was.'

But she didn't like his tone.

'Well,' she said. 'It's not a chalice I particularly want to drink from, is it?'

How could anybody live like that? Silver on the sideboard in the study downstairs, a sixteen-inch set in the corner. A modern mahogany bookcase with the *Guinness Book of Records*, a novel or two by Graham Greene and a school's edition of *Henry IV, Part One*. Beside it, a nineteenth-century print of a shipwreck, driftwood and a drowning man. Behind the couch, children are cheating at Monopoly: they throw six and move seven to avoid jail. Their mother's rummaging in her handbag for an antacid, but all she can find are scratched lottery tickets and a stamp from the Cameroons that she's keeping for her godchild. And all this time the father, the man in shadow at the far side of the fire, is working the remote control like worry beads, flicking from North Sea Oil to 'Smiley's People'. Because he's hardly there. His deep, desiring self is up behind the watertank in the attic, in under the rafters like a Jew in hiding, hearing nothing of the Pepsi or the Persil jingles; but listening, always listening, for the night-sounds in the heart of Middle C, for a car-door shutting softly, a gate-latch lifted by a gloved hand, the lip of a letter-box rapped like a knocker.

'It's time to go now.'

He nodded. It was safer to wash your teeth in tap-water, to think of others as baths and basins. If you once wondered about a source or a delta, the drought or deluge within us, you could kiss goodbye to your primary fellowship and your maisonette at Joyce's tower. In fact, you would end up picketing the American Embassy, and how would that look on your application for a two-year internship at Stanford Medical Center? Goodwill was a good idea, a glamorous virtue; but the reality was that it could completely denature you. It was one thing to read the lesson at Mass, another to learn it by heart. As for the handful in a hundred years who actually took it to heart, well, suffice it to say that they might have been prophets but they certainly weren't PhDs. Oh, the saints might have filled a few begging bowls all right, but it was the agronomists who quadrupled the rice-harvests and gave people back their dignity. And what holy man had ever kept a coma patient alive on a rotary bed for over fourteen years? The most he could do was hold her hand and talk to her. That was the bottom line.

'You're right,' he said. 'It is time to get the hell out of here.'

Tap-water. That was it. Otherwise you ended up on a kissing-couch with a glacier or a monsoon. But he was still struck by the strangeness of it.

'A man's Gethsemane,' he said, 'is a walled garden. I always thought it was open plan, with plenty of parking. But no, it's not. Gethsemane has walls with glass on top of them.'

'O, Theo,' said Felicity. 'That's a beautiful thing to

come out with. That's the most beautiful thing you've said since ten o'clock Tuesday. The *Reader's Digest* would give you fifty pounds for that, not that I'm reducing it to money. It should be in the Gospels. It's much more economical than having Jesus wake his friends up all the time. And it has all those G's in it. I'm sure it would sound gorgeous in the original Arabic.'

She took out a flo-pen from her hip pocket and wrote it in Roman letters along the length of her inside wrist, in and out among the blue-blooded veins from where she would have cut herself if she had been suicidal and right on up to the fold of her elbow.

'Otherwise I'll forget it,' she said. 'Then I'd be thinking about it endlessly. The only things we ever think about in a really concentrated way are the things we've forgotten or can't find. I suppose that's why we're always thinking about God. We're always roaming round the place, thinking: Now where did I leave Him the last time?'

'Where has He left us?' said Theo.

Felicity capped her flo-pen.

'Please don't have another insight, Theo,' she said. 'The Gethsemane one is grand for the next few days. Besides, I'm hungry. And that doesn't mean I want to break bread. It means I want a Big Mac. I might even have some Chicken McNuggets. So let's go. Please.'

Theo was thinking, biting his lower lip. To be honest, it was more than he could chew.

'I was thinking,' he said. 'What if they were to arrive in on top of us? What if they were halfway here already? What if we were . . . surrounded?'

'Jesus,' said Felicity. 'It never dawned on me.'

They stood, stock-still, straining for the least sound. But there was only the distant roar of an ass. That, and their heartbeats beating away.

'Would you come on?' said Felicity. 'Come on. Let's move it.'

But they still had to take the stairs slowly, because it was too dark to distinguish the step that was missing.

'It was the fifth from the top,' Theo decided.

'I think it was the fourth,' said Felicity.

'I'm sure it was the fifth,' he said.

'I don't give a fuck if it was the fifty-fifth. Get on with it, will you?'

So Theo went down and fell on the sixth, and something that might have been rusted ripped against his inside leg. By the time they were out in the open darkness, the scrape had started to throb. He was afraid to look down.

'I don't think the bone is broken,' he said. 'Then again, I have a very high pain threshold. I played in "Waiting for Godot" with a sprained ankle. I was the boy that Godot sends to say he's not coming. But the priest who was directing said that the limp was in character. In fact, he asked me to exaggerate it. At the end of the run, Pozzo gave me two chocolate Santas. Then, the next term, he got expelled for putting a Barbie's wardrobe in the tabernacle.'

Felicity was looking to left and right of her.

'Listen,' she said. 'If we do meet anyone, then all we have to say is that we're bird-watchers. We're nature-lovers. That's better. We're nature-lovers, and we're making these candid-camera studies of otters. Otters and owls.'

'But we don't have a camera,' Theo said.

Felicity gave this a second's thought.

'That's because we dropped it,' she said. 'A badger attacked us, and we dropped it. Then we noticed that the badger had conjunctivitis, and now we're going to the chemist to get him eye-drops. After that, we're going to

1 3 7

leave town, and we're going to make the Three Monkeys look like UPI.'

She studied her breasts for a while, brushing them with the backs of her hands. 'It's a pity the sticker blew off,' she said. 'It would have come in handy now.'

'But that badge was about unmarried mothers,' Theo said. 'It wasn't about gays.'

'What it would have shown is that our hearts are in the right place,' Felicity said. 'A little to the left of centre, same as any corpse we've opened up.'

And they stopped again to listen. The ass was still roaring. Either he was very overwrought or he was thinking about another little ass. Whatever it was, he was braying at the moon as if he'd signed a contract with a record company.

'Felicity,' he said. Not the ass. Theo.

'What?' she said.

'What did I say to you on Tuesday at ten o'clock?'

'Guess,' she said to him.

'Where are you?'

'Guess again.'

'No,' he said. 'I mean, I can't see you.'

'Here,' she said. And he saw the line of her shoulder shimmy, like a fish twisting. What was that creeper or whatever beside her? It was Alice in Wonderland stuff. He should have brought the torch from the cell in the prison.

'I should have brought the torch,' he said to the shimmy.

'Why didn't you?' And the shimmy was gone. A branch cracked. Why do branches crack like a soundtrack in the darkness?

'I couldn't. Because it was the only light they had there. The only light to see by. It had nothing to do with a fear of infection.'

There she was again. The long, lenient slope of her neck. Allergic to all but pure gold. That was crafty.

'What did I say, Felicity?'

'You said it had nothing to do with a fear of infection.'

'Tuesday. Ten o'clock. Tell me.'

Now he'd lost her. And the ass was silent. Somebody had given him his oats. Or shot him with a silencer.

'You said, "I love you, Felicity",' said a voice in the darkness. A still, small voice.

He thought about it.

'I don't remember. I remember the other stuff. "I love your pussy", and you say "I love your chipmunk", but we always do that.'

'You were half-asleep,' said the voice in the darkness. 'Then you got out of bed and you shaved. You shaved because your growth was giving me barber's rash. After that, you pissed in the hand-basin because the toilet was down the corridor. And your poor pee went everywhere, the way it always does after we've made love. And then you got back in again, and we smelled of the navel orange and the Anthisan cream, and the large, electric sign of the snack-bar in the street kept flashing the three words "Morgan's Miracle Parlour" on the wall beside the other bed, the bed where the skeleton was sleeping. And something inside me was crying, but I wasn't sad. Something inside me was crying out, but I wasn't angry. And I thought of when I was tiny and my father gave me a beautiful cut-glass goblet to bring in from the car, and it seemed to take as long as the whole of my life to carry it through the hall and into the drawing-room. I was so proud and so terrified.'

The wind was rising. It had come in over the sea by stealth, in slow degrees over nets and breakers, porpoise and snorkels. Now it was combing the countryside again, stirring the sweet-pea in the graveyard, tugging at a babygro on a bent clothes-line. By such slow means it healed the hurt of the Atlantic.

The two of them, Theo and Felicity, walked as best they could toward the light. It was only the light of the overhead arc-lamps at the late-night tennis club. But it was still light.

For it was pitch-dark now, and they had lost their way.

Felicity was still sitting on the bidet, back at the hotel. Of course, she would be.

'I know what you're going to say,' she called; but Theo, who was in the bedroom, was not listening. He was trying to pour the wine without spilling it.

'Absolutely,' he said. That was almost the litre and it still hadn't burst. It was absolutely amazing.

'You're going to tell me that it was far from a bidet I was raised. Which is fair enough. Mind you, we had a tumble-dryer before most people. We had a tumble-dryer when the wife of the Papal Count up the road was still using a mangle – and he was in the Government at the time. Sure he used to switch on the Christmas lights. Plus my father has a film of his wedding on sixteen millimetre, and that was back when people used to polish their radios. But the trouble is, he doesn't have a projector to show it. Anyhow, he doesn't want to. He says there's no point picking at the scab.'

Would you get a second litre into one of them? Theo was almost tempted to open the white. Then they could drink the lot as rosé. But he couldn't pull a cork with one hand, and he couldn't put the condom down on the carpet. It was as big as a bladder. In fact, it was three times as big.

'Anyhow,' said Felicity, 'there's something civilised about a bidet. Whoever invented the bidet must have had a beautiful mind. I'm surprised the Greeks didn't invent it, what with Greek fire and Plato and the Olympics. Let's go to Greece next summer, Theo. It's so spiritual and cheap. No wonder the Persians invaded it. All they had to look at was chadors. They probably never saw a naked woman until they went to the National Museum in Athens.'

Theo swung the condom this way and that way. They were really strong. Who did the manufacturers think they were making them for? Unless, of course, he was a low-key, non-league lover, a late-start adolescent who knew shit about the press-ups and pump-action of real-life libido; but he doubted it. He was pretty representative. Not in the sense that he was average, of course, but in the sense that he was typical. There was a world of difference between the two. It was something he had said before, and he would say it again. It needed saying.

'I'm coming,' Felicity said. 'Don't be cross. I just have to get into this thing the right way.'

Theo had thought of a better word. It wasn't so much that he was representative; he was revelatory. Or was it revealing? It was one or the other, anyway. Because, yes, he'd had one fling, one affair and one relationship. That was about right. Admittedly, he'd had all three with the same woman, but that was neither here nor there. That was small print. Besides, he didn't claim to be a man about town. On the other hand, he wasn't quite the man in the street, the oracle in moccasins. No, what he was, in fact and not in fiction, was a man of the world. After he'd read Martin Heidegger, which he fully intended to do, he would be a man in the world. Then there'd be no stopping him. He'd rise to the top before he was thirty. But not so fast that he'd surface with a bad case of the bends. First the Medical Advice Column in *Cosmopolitan*; then the brain transplants. Finally, a hybrid vegetable proliferating everywhere, from the Andes to the Arctic, with a protein power sufficient to sustain the famished in four continents. Posthumously, there'd be the formula for converting human excrement into topsoil, but by then –

'You know what I don't understand?' Felicity was saying. 'I don't understand why men aren't turned on by, say, a cluster of sapphires, by a full-length leather dress from a private collection, by . . . I don't know. Nice things. It could be something small, even. A pair of eighteen-carat drop ear-rings with seed pearls or a sable stole. But no, he always arrives with chrysanthemums.'

'I never bought you chrysanthemums,' Theo said. The condom was getting a bit heavy to hold. And how was he going to get the wine back into the bottle?

'You will,' she said. 'Give it time. Just don't ever bring me fifty pounds' worth of freesias. Then I'll know you're humping the radiologist. If you did that, I swear I'd make your lithographs look like the Whitechapel murders.'

And out she came in her strapless, scalloped teddy and her burgundy-coloured self-support stockings, and twirled twice in front of him. Then she bent over and ran her hands slowly down the cheeks of her bottom. He was mad about that. Maybe he'd seen his mother do it when he was trailing after her with a blanket, back in the days of 'Mr Ed the Talking Horse'.

'Voilà, m'sieur,' she said. She could feel the blood rushing to her head. That was because her head was down almost to the carpet, of course. Figures of speech are always forgetting themselves.

'Sod the Pyramid of Cheops,' Theo said. 'And the hanging gardens.'

She straightened up again.

'Well,' she said, 'the old eighteen-carat ear-rings would do more for . . .'

He held it up proudly under the light.

'There,' he said. 'You can breathe easy.'

She was so taken aback that she put her thumb in her mouth. The last time he'd seen her do that, they were lowering her grandfather's coffin. In fairness, though, that was at the time of the gravediggers' strike, and the priest looked strange in his stole beside the JCB.

'I don't believe it,' she said.

And she reached out and touched the taut skin of the condom.

'How much?' she said.

'The whole bottle. A litre of red Pedrotti.'

'Why not water?'

'I was shy,' he said. 'You were on the bidet. Besides, wine weighs more.'

'But can we drink it now? I mean, with the spermicide?'

Theo was tilting it over the bottle. A thin trickle pattered into the carafe. Easy did it. There was no doubt about it. He had a surgeon's hand. And now he could afford to let it slosh more freely. There.

'At this stage of the game,' he said to her, 'I think you could safely say that the both of us have strong stomachs. We could swallow anything.'

Felicity lay back on the candlewick bedspread. The crack on the ceiling above her was like the coastline of Chile. But nobody who had ever slept there before would have thought of thinking that. Unless a Chilean, maybe. If, that is, the girl had been on top and he didn't wear glasses. Then he'd have got homesick and the girl would have known. She'd have licked the tears from his eyes and murmured to him: 'Qué pasa, mi amor? Are you thinking of your camaradas? Tell Rosalita, the woman of Pedro.' But his eyes would be elsewhere, back at the battle of Chico Chico, transfusing his blood into the beautiful, blind novice he had refused to rape.

'What are you going to fantasise about tonight?' said Theo.

And he turned the print of Constable's 'Haywain' so that it faced the wall. Somebody had played noughts and crosses on the flip side.

'I don't know,' Felicity said. 'But I don't want slurpy stuff tonight, Theo. I mean, I like the smell of myself when I start my cycle, and halfway through as well, but after that I don't. And even if you wash your teeth, your tongue still smells of me. Do you mind me saying that to you, Theo? Because I want you to say so if you do. I mean, it's not a veto. I'm not drawing the line; and I'm certainly not drawing double yellow lines. It's more that . . .'

'I understand,' said Theo; and he drained the cup that was at his lips. Some of it ran down his throat and his chest and into his navel. He felt a bit Biblical. He felt a bit like Barabbas in the whorehouse. That was Anthony Quinn, of course. It had to be. He was straight out of scripture, that man. Sandstorm and stubble, Mount Sinai in a pair of denims. It was no wonder he'd played the Pope in the Morris West movie, though there wasn't a Pope in the church calendar who could play Tony. Not that you'd ever call him Tony: you would call him Sir. On very special occasions, you might even call him Master.

'I'll tell you what I'm going to think about,' Felicity said. 'I'm going to think about something filthy. I'm going to think about being filthy rich. Now here's the scenario: I'm in a restaurant, a most exclusive restaurant, so close to the heart of Paris that I can hear pacemakers around me. The facial cleansers in the ladies' loo are pages torn from the wire-spine binding of sketchbooks by the boy Picasso. You can wipe yourself on his Blue period. Eau-de-cologne runs from the taps. But there are no automatic hand-dryers: you must dry your hands on linen with the late Tsar's monogram. Outside, you hear voices raised ever so slightly. You peep out. The Archbishop of Canterbury is being asked to leave. No prelate is permitted on the premises without his crozier and his cope. Proper order too. Now we're being seated at a dix-huitième escritoire, only a few feet from a string quartet, four disillusioned physicists who worked with Oppenheimer at Los Alamos. They've left titanium for the diatonic scale, and specialise with rare exceptions in the performance of lost works.'

'Hurry up, Felicity,' Theo said.

'And that's exactly what he says, in late Middle French, which is our private code. But I can't decide. Will I have the widgeon drumsticks or will I have the head of John the Baptist? A rare medium or a medium medium? What I really want, of course, is to meet the woman at the next table, the artist who had seven stillbirths on a single fertility pill and made of them seven polyurethane casts for her retrospective at MOMA. Now she's famous, too famous indeed to find any time at all for her own portfolio. She's only here in Paris to confer with a delegation of migrant workers for a photospread in *Oggi*. Tomorrow it's Vienna, a voice-over for a video on sexual harassment in the work-place; and Saturday, Saturday she leads five thousand militants in gas-masks up the steep slopes of the Acropolis to protest against pollution in the atmosphere. The only thing that worries her is how she's going to smoke with a gas-mask.'

He got down between her legs and tugged at the buttons of the teddy. She'd been shaving again. There was that lovely smell of Immac off the inside of her thighs, a scent that was more compelling than new pound-notes or the clean, cold hot-press odour of Art books. And better than any, best of all, were her own smells: home-cooking had nothing on them.

She helped him to open her.

'Masks she can cope with. Masks she can handle. She's so terrified she'll be recognised when she keeps her appointments with the psychiatrist that she wears a Donald Duck mask *en route* to the consultation. He never asks her, why not Pluto? Why not Mickey Mouse? He's a wise, healing man, not a smoothie with a grandfather clock for keeping his clubs in. He knows it was the only kind the shop had. Down a little further, Theo. And not so hard. No. No, gentler. That's it. That's nice. That's very nice. But not too slow.'

She examined the map of Chile again. Where was she?

'Where was I?' she said.

But Theo was too engrossed in what he was doing to talk to her. In fact, he looked a little like a man who's trying, digit by digit, to crack a tricky combination lock. His face was as solemn and as serious as a toddler's in an early-learning centre: it was a mix, the whole business, of *femme fatale* and Fisher Price.

'I could eat you,' Theo said. 'You're so nice I could eat you.'

Felicity thought he was speaking to her; and then she remembered.

'Now I remember,' she said. 'The restaurant. It's so classy it doesn't have a name. Cognoscenti call it the

"Raison d'Etre", and you know they go there by the way they shake your hand. And now the artist woman is leaving, and I want to tell her to stay in her studio because art begins with the world of an image and not with the image of a world, and steady, steady, steady, Theo. Nice and easy does it. Somehow, somehow I know that her studio's shut up, and the storage heaters have been left alone so long they're working in reverse. A greenhouse by day, Greenland at night. The paint is cracking on the pubis of a nude study on the easel; and a dear, dead daddylonglegs drops from the coolie shade of the overhead light. Your nail is nipping me a bit, Theo. Just watch the nail. Otherwise hold your positions.'

Theo wished she'd yap a little less. But that was Felicity. She could never concentrate. Her middle name should have been Tangent. That, or Ricochet.

'But just as I'm about to reach out to her, he passes me a cheque.'

'Who?' said Theo.

'Never you mind. A little to the left. It's for fifty thousand pounds. Twenty-five thousand for each deflowering. I look into his eyes. I hold the cheque over the candle. It begins to burn. It goes up in smoke, then flame. I can sense his manhood magnifying under the table. I stand up. No, I rise. My watered-silk dress runs off me like silky water. I am wearing nothing but a black condom tucked in an ivory garter. I've cut the top off the condom with a pair of silver scissors made by a master jeweller for Lorenzo the Indefatigable. Because I'm ready, at long last ready, to receive the sons stored in his testicles. He looks at me, this son of a Bedouin beauty and a Jewish philosopher, grandson of the one and only indiscretion of Marcel Proust, and his look is penetrating. Penetrating is the only word. Down lower, Theo. Now fast. Faster. The string quartet is playing some lovely plain-chant stuff. My nipples prick up like a dog's ears. My bush is burning . . . Shit. I don't believe it.'

The phone was ringing.

'That means I'll have to start all over again from the very beginning,' she said.

Theo was quite relieved. His wrist was sore at this stage.

'You could have let it ring,' Felicity said.

He picked up the phone with his good hand. Ten to one, it was you-know-who.

'Hello,' he said.

'Hello,' said a voice, but it wasn't a voice he knew.

'Who is it?' Theo said.

'Am I on to a Theo?' said the voice. A man's; middle-aged; lower-middle-class; Dublin; dull average to average IQ.

'I'm Theo. Who are you?'

'I'll tell you, Mr Theo, I'm a friend of Bennie's. Bennie from the Medical school. I know him from the pigeons. Are you with me?'

That was a stupid question. The man was two hundred miles away.

'In spirit,' Theo said. 'What is it you want?'

Felicity was cuddling a pillow. Any port in a storm. Yet she looked little girlish, somehow. That was the teddy, Theo thought; and he smelled his fingers.

'It's Bennie, really,' said the man. 'To be on the level, like, he's not himself. He's not himself at all.'

'I'm lost,' said Theo. 'What's the matter with him?'

There was a silence at the other end. Where was this fellow ringing from? The acoustic was sort of ecclesiastical. Big and boomy.

'I think you know what the matter is, Doctor,' the man said.

'Is he sick? Is that it?'

There was another silence. The guy must be reading from a script.

'It has more to do with bones, if you get my meaning,' said the man.

'Bones?'

'Bones,' the man said. 'As in "Give a dog a . . .". I don't want to say too much on the phone. Just in case, like.'

'You mean the skeleton,' said Theo. Felicity was pulling a tracksuit on over the teddy. Where was she off to?

'Sshh,' said the man. 'Don't say anything. Not over the phone. Say something else when you mean what I know you mean. When you mean what it is we're talking about, then I'll know; and you'll know what I mean when I mean it the same way.'

Theo felt suddenly tired. Fatigued, in fact. It was the sugar level in his bloodstream. Where were those sugar-lumps they'd crumbled into the fish-tank in the restaurant? And the owner got up on his high horse about it, too. They were right to have left without paying.

'You mean the book?'

'What book?' said the man.

'When I say book, I mean skeleton,' Theo said.

'Will you sshh,' the man said. 'I'm with you.'

'It's safe and sound. Will you tell Bennie that?'

'Are there any . . . pages missing?' the man said.

'There isn't even a comma missing,' said Theo.

'What about the ribs?'

'The only rib that's missing is Adam's.'

The man at the other end thought about this.

'Do you know where you lost it?' he said.

Felicity was stealing out. She closed the door quietly behind her. She wasn't up in arms, so.

'Look,' said Theo. 'Everything's fine. There's no problem. Unless Bennie has a problem. If Bennie has a problem, tell me about it.'

'Well,' said the man, 'there's something wrong with a man if he's in and out of churches all the time. Except he's a priest, of course. Then it's office-work. Bennie was never one for the churches. If you know Bennie, you know that much. A good man, a great man, the apple of your eye, but not a man for the kneelers. Sure, the day of his daughter's wedding, he couldn't believe the electric candles. Of course, I didn't tell him they've been in for twenty years. But that's Bennie.'

'I understand,' said Theo. 'I do understand.'

'I knew you would,' the man said. 'I knew I could level with you. Mind you, I'm no doctor. I was never even in hospital, except once. That was to put up new curtains in one of the wards. But I'm not an idiot, either; and even a village idiot would know that Bennie is, well, you know . . .'

'No,' said Theo. 'I don't. I don't know.'

The man at the other end gathered his strength in silence.

'Bennie,' he said, 'is on the brink of a nervous breakthrough.'

Felicity had been on the brink of an orgasm. That was much more important. Theo smelled his fingers again. Her absence was even more potent than her presence. If you were an intellectual, you had to get used to living in paradox after paradox. Ordinary people were just confused. Intellectuals were torn by contradiction. That was the price they paid for harnessing both hemispheres; but the price was small, compared to the prize: a deep and lasting unhappiness at the end of the day.

'Are you there, Doctor? Are you there? I didn't mean to upset you.'

Theo was getting cross. Who the fuck was this fellow, anyway? How had he found their number, and from who? Or was it whom? This was no hour of the night to be ringing anyone. It must be almost midnight. The time, of course, was less important than the timing. Poor Felicity had been on the edge of her seat, within a hand's turn of an advent if he'd gone on rubbing her up the right way. And what about him? One solitary corn-plaster apart, he was more or less the way he'd come into the world; and the shrivelled non-event he was shielding with his fist looked more like a saint's relic than a unicorn's horn. From rapier to safety-pin in a space of seconds, and all because some buffoon barged in with a lot of winks and whispers out of Cold War comics. It was more than a shame: it was a sacrilege. Christ in Heaven, they might have lost a child because of it. Felicity's egg might be weeping tears of blood over Polaroids of her sweetheart sperm; for him, a worse fate followed, a dreadful doom: death in a wet dream. For the first time in his life, Theo was able to understand what Coleridge must have gone through when the person from Porlock pushed past the butler.

'Look here,' he said. 'This whole business smells a bit fishy to me.'

'It's true,' said the man. 'I swear it.'

'Wait a moment,' Theo said. 'What are you swearing? Are you swearing that it's fishy or not fishy? Which?'

'What I'm saying,' the man said, 'is that Bennie is in a decline. Decline is a harsh word; it's a hard word. But it is the one word which puts the whole situation in a nutshell. If Bennie were himself, I have no hesitation in saying that he personally would be happy with that choice of word. I think he would go along with me one hundred per cent.

But he's not himself, that's the point. In point of fact, I have personally witnessed the decline and the fall of Bennie as we know him. He's not even feeding his pigeons. I'm feeding his pigeons. Are you with me?'

'Who's paying for the pigeon feed?' said Theo.

'Bennie is. What I felt was that it was important to involve him, so far as feasible, in normal life. Otherwise he might never make it back to the dovecote. That's pigeon talk, Doctor.'

'It's pidgin English,' said Theo.

'You're very kind,' the man said. 'But I've miles more to go.'

Felicity had been gone a good while. But where? She wouldn't have gone off jogging, would she? In her bare feet? Or were they bare? He couldn't remember. To be perfectly honest, he never thought much about her feet, except when they fought at night over the hot water bottle. Then they were cold, as cold as two trout in the freezer; and they never got any warmer, even in summer. That was why he could slowly slide the hot water bottle over to his side and not feel selfish. Yet he loved them, those hooves of hers. They were feet of clay, but she walked well on them.

'Hello,' the man said.

'Absolutely,' Theo said.

'So where do we go from here?' said the voice at the other end.

'Tell me,' Theo said, 'what do you suppose would lure the dove back to the dovecote?'

The man laughed.

'Doctor,' he said, 'you're a terrible man. Have you any yen for the pigeons yourself?'

'I have a yen for my bed,' said Theo.

'The same as myself,' the man said. 'I never burn the

midnight oil, but I always oil my midnight burns. My father used to say that. Wherever he was, he'd wait till he could bring the conversation round to saying that.'

'Dovecotes,' said Theo.

'Dovecotes,' the man said. 'The dove would settle if there weren't a ginger lurking underneath it.'

'Would somebody have written a book about this ginger?'

'They would, Doctor.'

'I think I know it. Is it called *The Skeleton Key*?'

'It is, Doctor. Bennie was afraid the book might be serialised in the newspapers. He was afraid it might be dramatised for television. He was afraid it might be the talk of the town. Most of all, he was afraid the author might have to face the press, if not the music, let alone the courts.'

Theo made up his mind at last. For weeks he hadn't been able to decide. Now he knew. It was strange how decisive a decision could be, how richly relieving. The sensation was almost sexual: after the piece of action, the peace of inaction. A closed mind might soften the brain, but an open one hardened the arteries. Ever since Bennie had boned up on the skeleton's actual background, Theo hadn't a notion what to do about the Archbishop. Day after day, he'd dithered, reflecting bleakly on the priest who slouched against the wardrobe, crouched in a carry-cot, trailed from a shower-rail, or, worst of all, whiplashed wildly over the bashed surfaces of bad roads.

Tonight he was adamant. He would bury it. That is to say, he would bury him.

Truly, he thought, there are two ways to well-being. Either you're a megalomaniac, in which case you believe everything you say, or you're a minion, in which case you believe everything you're told. In both cases, you stand –

or grovel – to achieve utter felicity. Contentment, rather. Theo would never again regard a squaddie in quite the same light; and the perfect life, by extension, would be ten years at boarding school prior to military service. For the heart of service might indeed be the masturbatory joys of servitude, an extinction of the self as radical as suicide. The ease and ecstasy of a conscript sanitising a latrine could even surpass the transcendental olés of the Spanish mystics. Because freedom – the not knowing what to do, the not doing what one knows – is only a ball until the stroke of midnight. After that, it's a ball and chain.

Somebody was whistling. He listened. It was a smoker's whistle, all larynx and no lung. Then he remembered.

'I'm sorry,' he said. 'I was thinking.'

'People are always apologising for thinking,' the man said.

'Listen,' said Theo. 'What I want you to do is to tell Bennie that everything is all right. We're with him. We're behind him; we're beside him. When we get back, we'll go see that movie together.'

'What movie?' said the man.

'Never mind what movie,' said Theo. 'The whole thing is being buried. It will never be brought up again. Do you understand that?'

'Roger,' said the voice at the other end.

'Then that's it,' Theo said.

'He would have rung you himself, Doctor,' the man said. 'But he was too afraid. Mind you, he did send the pigeon.'

'What pigeon?'

'Hound of Heaven,' the man said. 'His best. It got intercepted.'

'What are you talking about?' said Theo.

'In Monaghan,' the voice said. 'There were two kids

playing with one of those remote control model Spitfires. The lads decided to put on a dogfight. Let me say this, though, Hound of Heaven gave as good as he got. They had to send a second Spitfire up. At the end of the scrap, Hound of Heaven bought it. So did one of the Spitfires. The other one limped home. There's to be a court case. A big one. Bennie has Hound of Heaven in the deep-freezer. He's evidence, like. I think he's going to be Exhibit B. Oh, he's sure to win it. With the planes being Spitfires, you know. At the close of play, you scratch an Irishman, and Irish blood runs out. Anyhow, I don't want to bore you with all of this. The one thing that matters is that Bennie did try. To get through, that is. To establish contact. He tried when he could, and now he can't. What more can a man do in his day than that? Fate fingered his flightplan, you might say: he got grounded. Myself, I'd have given him a medal. In fact, Doctor, there was a carrier at the Battle of the Somme during the First World War, machine-gunned most maliciously by a crack-marksman on the other side. It was a shabby business, but I suppose your man was tempted by the thought of pigeon-pie after months of maggots in the bully-beef. Yet he spread his wings in a larger life, the self-same bird. The Brits gave him the DSO. They did that. I read it in Ripley. I cut it out and kept it. And it seems to me that Bennie deserves no less. It seems to me that Bennie deserves better. But not posthumously, of course. He deserves it humously, if at all.'

'Bennie will be fine,' said Theo. 'Bennie will be famous – that is, not in the middle- and upper-middle-class sense of the word, but in the colourful, inner-city Dublin working-class sense of it, as in "healthy", "hardy", and so on.'

'Replete with vitality,' said the man. 'When I say it, that's what I signify.'

'Quite,' said Theo. 'Bennie will soar to new heights. And now I must really ask you to excuse me.'

'No offence was taken,' said the man. 'By the way, there is a PS.'

'What do you mean?' said Theo.

'It's shorthand for a postscript,' the man said. 'Bennie told me to tell you that, if you can do this thing for him, you'll see every paper a week before from now until the day you're conferred. Of course, I've no idea what he meant. Not the earthliest notion.'

'Nor have I,' said Theo. 'Goodnight to you.'

'A moment more, Doctor. You've been very patient, no pun intended, and I don't mean to keep you from your pigeonhole; but, purely and simply out of scientific curiosity, I was wanting to ask you a question. I was in the toilet today, in itself a normal consequence of being a vertebrate mammal, as it were, and I noticed something strange, something which caused me to experience, well, not quite wonderment, not quite bewilderment, but a bit of both, to be honest. What it is, Doctor, was this. If a man's stool moves from mahogany to matchwood in four days flat, is it the multivitamins? Man to man, I ask you. Is my penny to remain in the warm and smelly lining of life's pocket, or is my penny destined for the great piggybank? I would appreciate any response you might feel able to make.'

Theo reached down and disconnected the phone. That way, the bloke at the other end of the line couldn't be sure that it wasn't a technical failure. It was part of his personal charm that he always spared feelings though he rarely spared time. When he did become a doctor, he'd carry a clever little bleep on his ward-rounds, one he could activate himself whenever some terminal bore was keeping him from prayer or a pot-luck. It might seem thick-skinned, but you had to waterproof yourself against a world that was continually inundating you. Even the chaplain had a Judas bleep, for God's sake. Theo had seen him gallop out of the Intensive Care Unit in order to talent-scout the majorettes at the St Patrick's Day parade; and, if you'd heard the genteel drivel of the cancer patient, going on and on and on about a shower of hailstones stripping apple-blossom until the whole lawn whitened like a winter snowstorm, you wouldn't have blamed him for bolting.

Which reminded him. It must be twenty minutes, half an hour since Felicity had stomped out. It would be just like her to have found an interesting drunk in the bar, a freelance actor planning to produce 'The Merchant of Venice' in a modern setting, with Shylock as a Wall Street wizard in man-hating Manhattan; that, or the one thing Theo feared, a priest with stubble and no scruples, an open collar and canvas shoes, the men with the Third World eyes who paused at each and every full stop in their sentences, the ones who believed that women should be priests and priests should be men. They were crafty shits, but she couldn't see that. Indeed, she couldn't have enough of them. By her own admission, she'd had three already.

Theo sat down on the bed. He was feeling blue. In fact, he was feeling ultramarine. It was that bad. It was that basic.

Call a spade a spade. She was pre-coital when she decamped. Even peri-coital. It wasn't a reasonable state; it wasn't a reasoning one, either. Not in a woman, anyhow. To be sure, it took them time to get started. Male foreplay is a matter of a French kiss or a German movie; women's extends way beyond men's, way beyond cocks and cocktails to cocktail parties, the geopolitics of a table for six. Once away, on the other hand, there was no stopping them. Look at the letters they write into *Penthouse*. You would have thought that only men were like that; but no. Women are worse; or better, rather. It was quite possible then that Felicity might have gone off and got herself into an awkward position, a tight squeeze. Not that he was castigating her. Conscience was helpless against chemistry; it was a matter of flick-knives against flame-throwers. Even the Law recognised that: you could slaughter streetloads and get off scot-free, if you were post-partem. But try telling a judge that you were horny when you nicked *Nineteen Eighty-Four*.

His penis, God love it, was very tiny. That's to say, it was very tiny now. There it was, nestling contentedly against his inner leg, for all the world like a nice little new-born puppy in a pouch, dreaming of bitches and bottoms in the land of Dog. Theo felt fond of it, fatherly toward it. At the end of the day, there was nothing to compare with an erection: it had the force and fascist purity of Michelangelo's David. But at the beginning, when you were trying to convert your fragility into fruit-and-fibre strength of purpose, that sloppy snippet down below was, well, a pal. It was nice to have one.

These were deep, delicate thoughts. Theo decided he'd earned a respite. He'd have a quick fantasy. But who would he fantasise about? And where would he situate his scenario? You had to work at everything in this world, even pleasure. God was right when he talked about sweating and browbeating. He laid it on the line. God was a great ABC man, a great man for *Appel* at cockcrow. Life would be a neat number if you were the spitting image of God.

What was he thinking about? This was not on. Was he praying to God or was he playing with himself? You couldn't be body and soul at the same time; and, if you were, you would be a very rum creature, the odd man out in the universe. No, the eyes and the anus face in opposite directions. We are not meant to be at one with ourselves. We are meant to fuck, to be fucked in turn, to be finally fucked up all together before being fucked out forever at closing time, without once knowing what the fuck it is all in aid of. To end our lives not as a noun or as a verb, but as a preposition. Such is life. And if it weren't, what would Shakespeare have written *Hamlet* about? He would have had to write a documentary about a white-haired next-in-line who spends five acts trying, in the nicest possible way, to persuade his archangelic uncle not to step down in his favour. All this, of course, while Gertie sits upstairs in a cupboard – having converted her apartments into an orphanage for blond and blue-eyed babies – and busies herself with setting the Bible in braille. Polonius would be wandering around in a Santa suit while Ophelia mails handwritten invitations to her forthcoming wedding to every man, woman and child on the register of living persons. It would, in short, be Ham without let. And it is the let – the letting out, the letting off – which is life.

So. Theo returned to the task in hand. He would think about . . . who? About Nastassja Kinski, that's who. And Tokyo Rose. Now that would be a wholesome threesome. Or Benazir Bhutto? She was quite nice. Or maybe Mary Magdalene. Rubens had done a thing of Mary Magdalene that was not half bad. Mary Magdalene must have been mighty, the honeypot of the Holy Land, a floorshow to follow. Then afterwards, when she'd turned her life inside out and right side up, when she'd be serving Mass in the convent chapel, did she ever think back to the poker drives and the peep shows, the legionaries stuffing greenbacks in her G-string and stamping the floor with their spears until she said yes, yes, and gave them her snake act.

If at first you don't succeed, think about it. Theo did. He couldn't understand why he started out in pussy and ended up in Palestine. It kept happening. The two ends of his life kept coming together like the two hands of a clock at midnight. Of course, if you were normal, you wouldn't be awake at that hour. You'd be out for the countdown. If that freak from the funny farm hadn't put a call through, he and Felicity would be sound asleep at this stage. But Theo blamed himself. He had answered the call. The truth was, he was his own worst enemy.

He would allow himself one gesture of rage. Gestures of rage are very healing. So he kicked the chair in front of him, kicked it hard and heavy with a sincerity which surprised him. And he did feel better. Admittedly, he would have felt better still if he'd been wearing a shoe. That was something to remember. He would file it away. For the moment, he sat still, listening. There was no sound from above or below. No one had heard. And he hadn't damaged the chair. He righted it and stooped to pick up the bits and pieces that had flown from it when it fell. Comb and compact, a postcard, the calculator. Felicity produced it in grocery stores and supermarkets, restaurants and reception areas. In the main, it wasn't greatly liked by chefs and shopkeepers, though one young hotel manager had shown her how to get the square root of whatever sum you liked. Of course, that was because she'd been bursting out all over in a little batik blouse.

He turned it on and worked out the day's debits. They were doing well; rather better, in fact, than need be. They could hit some high-spot on the homeward trek, and gorge guiltlessly on a host of gourmet goodies that neither of them actually liked. But Felicity enjoyed collecting menu cards. She'd slip them in her cookbooks before loaning them to girlfriends. That, of course, was only because Dolores had used a picture of Saint Sebastian as a bookmark in her copy of *The Joy of Gay Cooking*.

Theo started to work things out on the calculator. They had stayed in thirteen bed and breakfasts and eleven hotels. There'd been three unscheduled stops for running repairs, one for oral sex, and two because of downpours. Wednesday coming, they'd have been six weeks on the road. That was forty-two days. Forty-two by twenty-four would give you the exact number of hours. Then you multiplied by sixty to find the minutes. After that, you multiplied by sixty again. Or did you? Yes, of course you did. Then you had the seconds.

The sum on the calculator looked like light-years.

So he started again. This time he was going to calculate the whole of his life, right down to a T; or, for that matter, a Theo. First the years; then the years by three hundred and sixty five; then three hundred and sixty five by what? By twenty-four, naturally. Now that by sixty, and another sixty. That was how many seconds he had lived; and already, even as he was computing, another forty to forty-five had slipped by. Each separate second the length of a single human heartbeat; for even time was human at the end of all. There it was, in the neatest of numerals, a figure as long as a national debt or the estimated age of the universe: the exact number of times his heart had beaten since birth, since the moment of delivery. And delivery was the word. Not even the chaplain was calling it deliverance. You didn't have to read the Bible to know that deliverance led straight into the desert. You could watch 'The Ten Commandments' on Boxing Day.

He turned the calculator off. Anyhow, he hadn't worked

the thing out properly. He'd forgotten the heart starts beating way, way back, from deep inside the womb, when whatever you care to call it is no bigger than a blackhead but already pre-set to have prominent front teeth and to go grey same as his grand-dad before he's thirty. But you forget these things when you're working with numbers. He remembered the first time he'd tried to calculate a complex addition, and he couldn't hack it. That was when he'd had his original waking wet dream at age twelve. He'd wrapped his pyjama bottoms around the hot water bottle to dry them, and then he'd sat in the state of joy, a joy that was like the stuff he had had to learn out of 'Tintern Abbey', and he tried to add it up. Car-lights from the road below had crossed the room from left to right, from right to left, finding the tassles of the Evzone's cap and the feet of the French crucifix. They swept in circles like searchlights; he ignored them. He was busy with his wire-cutters. How many times could this great thing be brought about? If it happened even once a day for the rest of his life, then that would be thousands. More, thousands upon thousands. There at his homework table, working it out with a pencil on the cover of *Look and Learn*, he had sung to himself. He had sung 'Little Donkey', he was so happy.

The door opened and Felicity walked in. That in itself is scarcely surprising. People generally enter rooms in that way. From time to time there are rumours of crawls, cartwheels or collapses on floral-patterned carpets; but walking would appear to have won the day hands down. It is merely a convention of narrative procedure to underline the ordinary. We might otherwise overrule it.

'Where were you?' he said. 'I was worried. I was sitting here, worrying.'

She was holding a glass dessert dish with a metal spoon

sticking out of it. Her mouth was too full to speak. She pointed at it with her finger as she sat down on the bed, drawing her legs into the lotus. Because she was dressed, Theo felt naked suddenly. He pulled on his shorts, the pair with the slight steam-burn and the Byron tagline about being mad, bad and dangerous to know. When he got back to Dublin, he was going to revert to white cotton Y-fronts. Dash was less important than dignity, when you came right down to it.

'I met the woman who signed us in,' Felicity said. 'The one with the goitre and the beauty spot that's always shifting. She's quite nice, in fact, although she's got these lips like a minus sign. Anyhow, she was up a ladder, putting little dabs of Lancôme cleansing milk on that big plastic stag over the reception desk. Somebody went and wrote an obscenity on its cheek. She wouldn't tell me what, but she had a good idea who'd done it. She said he always writes his G's that way, and she was going to screw him into the ground. After that, she asked me if I could give her a ten-day cert for shingles. Now you see what happens when you do a daft thing like registering me as a doctor, Theo. You needn't deny it. I saw the book. Dr Felicity and Mr Theo. I suppose you're a surgeon now.'

And she stuffed herself again with whatever she was eating. Shitty grey gunge, with a fleck on her fringe like a speck of wet sand.

'What is it?' he said.

She scrunched, swallowed, smiled.

'Muesli,' she said. 'Muesli at midnight. My second helping.'

She looked, well, she looked lovely. Yes, lovely, in fact, in the moonlight. It sounded a bit bland, a bit bourgeois, a bit Bing Crosby; but it was true. Then again, there were times when he thought she would have looked lovely in the light of the upper saloon of a bus or the light of an open fridge. Forty-watt feelings were more Theo's style, but there were times; there were. Times when he almost forgot the real formula for the speed of light, remembering only the spurious forms of its slower disclosures. It was a bit like being in the attic, and rummaging, and finding the Christmas lights, and finding they worked, they still worked, and watching them, the greens and yellows picking out the rucksacks and the bridal dresses.

'I met a man,' Felicity said. 'An American. From, I don't remember, Minnesota maybe or Minneapolis. Are they near each other? I can never get the Midwest right in my head. But he was Irish, actually, in the sense that this is where his parents would have come from; and that's why he's here, of course. Brass-rubbing, you know. Mooching. Headstones, hospices. He got the bird shit off his grand-dad's grave with a bit of detergent, and he took some of the stones for his window-boxes. Then he visited a great-aunt of his in a home, but she's a hundred and eighty, and she kept telling him not to put his hands in his pockets before being interviewed for a job because then they'd be sweaty when he shook hands with the boss, and that was how her husband had missed out on the post-office. After that, he went off and got drunk. The American, I mean.'

She had finished the bowl, and now she licked the edges. Then she cleaned the spoon in her mouth.

'He was still drunk when I met him,' she said. 'Apparently, he had this great-uncle, a brother of your woman in the home. He was the dear and darling of the whole family, because he fought in the War of Independence. He blew up that bridge we stopped at, where the priest used the blade from his shaver to cut the corners off his sandwiches. But two months later, because he was a master mason, the local county council commissioned him to rebuild it. Then he started blowing things up left, right, and centre, and putting in the estimates before the dust had settled. Well, anyhow, twenty years ago, they erected this monument, you see, with the names of all the brave boyos on it. A plaque set in granite, and the man in the bar below was thrilled. Kith and kin in letters of bronze, like. This he had to see, but he couldn't. Money, of course. No money. He waits twenty years; he puts a little by when he can. Now he's here. A life's dream, a dream's life. Whatever. Morning of the first day, off with him to the monument.'

'It's been dynamited,' Theo said.

'That's modernism, Theo,' she said. 'Think post-modernist. The monument's there. Of course it's there. It's the only thing in the town to put on a postcard. The party politicals are held there. The Corpus Christi procession stops at it. Country and Western promoters poster the plinth week-in, week-out. It's Freedom Wall for anything from Fossett's Circus to the Sandinistas. So he's proud; pretty damn proud: there's the uncle's name, third from the top in a list of ten. And he makes a bee-line for the boozer, to celebrate. Actually, I suspect he celebrates rather a lot. His face is as red.'

She looked down at the dish in her lap, as empty now as a begging-bowl.

'I feel like Oliver Twist,' she said. 'I could go on having breakfast right through the night.'

'I'll get you more,' he said. 'I'll go down the way I am, in my shorts. I mean, so long as you cover your ass, you're safe in this world.'

Damn it, she did look beautiful. She looked like a commercial. An ad for just about anything, port or perfume. It was her way of seeming to stare at skulls and candles at the same time; that whole faraway, funnysad facial set. He'd seen a child who looked like that, walking back from the altar-rail on her First Communion day, working the Host away from her milk-teeth; and people on trains were the same sometimes, when it got dark and the carriage-lights came on, and they didn't mind anymore about the coffee-circles on the covers of their magazines because they were staring out the window at their own reflections as the telegraph poles tore past them, one after another after another crucifixion. And then they'd check their tickets for the hundredth time; but they would still be there.

'I'm fine,' she said. 'I'm full.'

She pulled down the zipper of the tracksuit, pulled it down to her navel. The teddy was itching her.

'Anyhow,' she said, 'there he was, chatting away to a few of the locals, and one of them got the knife in. Of course, he waited a while first. Our friend downstairs was buying. But when it came his turn, he told him that the uncle was shot by his own side for rape, and they only put the name on the plaque to spare the family's feelings. I was so sorry for him.'

'I know,' said Theo. 'I know.' The way she was sitting, scratching the ribs on her left-hand side, with the moonlight on her boobs like runny ice-cream, she could have sold American defence policy to the Soviets. They were welcome to Fatima, with all its apparitions; he wanted Room Thirteen, and her appearance in it.

'He was a nice man too,' Felicity said, 'and I liked him. He was on the Phil Donahue show once, in the audience. That must have been before I started watching it, because I would have recognised him. He dresses very well, apart from his shoes, which passeth understanding. But he said he wore them on his wedding-day, and he still wears them whenever he travels. In fact, he was telling me about his wife, who sounds too true to be nice, but I got distracted by a honeymoon couple in the corner. Holding hands, they were. I suppose, because they felt they had to. But they were nice as well. He looked like the sort of guy who'd have filled out the mortgage forms with a fountain pen, and she looked like the sort of girl who'd put a beach-towel under her bottom to save the sheets.'

'Spare me,' Theo said, only because he assumed that it was more or less what she wanted him to say.

'No, no,' she said, 'I was glad for them. I was glad for the American. I was glad for everybody. It was strange. I was glad for the sea and the shore and the breaking between them; and I don't know why. I don't even know that I should know why. What does the sail know of the wind? It hasn't taken an alpha plus in aerodynamics. It just fills. So, when I left to come upstairs, I said goodbye to everyone: the American, the others, the woman at reception and the honeymooners. I even looked at her ring. They'd been engaged for three years. Can you imagine their wedding night? I'm surprised they didn't end up in Australia. Though why they chose a disused bicycle-shed like this place is beyond me.'

'There's rising damp behind the beauty board,' Theo said.

Felicity looked over at him.

'That's such a beautiful thing to say, Theo,' she said. 'You have this marvellous, metaphorical thing in you. When you get going, you can reach four, four-point-five images in a minute. You're flashing, flashing, flashing away, like a photocopier. I wish I had that mind's-eye knack of knocking things together. Because you could make such a killing in graphics or TV commercials. Christ, you could make commercials they'd screen at

Cannes. You've got this little darkroom inside you somewhere; you're always developing things. I mean, I've seen the so-called writers at work, and I tell you this: the tobacco industry would go up in smoke without them. And they're sitting under the anglepoise, and they haven't any poise to speak of because they haven't any angle to speak about, and they can't even finish the sentence they've written. Maybe they've written "The tree was like", but they can't think what. What the fuck is a tree like, anyway? So they sit there while the clock smiles and frowns, smiles and frowns. O, they could tipp-ex those four little words, but no. There's pride involved. The trees outside, the ghastly, godawful trees, they're going to mean something else before they're allowed to mean themselves; because what matters most isn't, of course, the spruce or the sycamore. What matters most is the writer looking out at them. Mind you, he's only looking out for himself; but, by Jesus, he's going to stand there staring till he gets what he wants, which is an image nobody's thought of before. It's creativity by intimidation. When the tree surrenders, fine. He writes it down like the guy who's finally persuaded the pretty girl to give him her phone number. Maybe it's something like "Beware the man who is always happy: evergreens are shallow rooters." '

'That's mine,' said Theo. 'I said it to you about a fortnight ago. I remember exactly where it happened. He was a man in his fifties with three small children. I thought he was their grandfather, but he told me, no, he was a late vocationalist. And the middle child was up in his arms, and she was twanging one of his braces like a bow-string. The other two were filling a Samsonite suitcase with the softest sand they could find on the beach, because the father was making a sand-pit for them in their garden. After he fixed the tyre and they left, I said that bit about the evergreens.'

'Evergreens, everglades,' Felicity said. 'It don't matter. The point is, you write that sort of stuff and everyone thinks you're God. Or, even better, everyone thinks you're His one and only. Not alone do you get to read it at the English Literature Society at this campus or that campus, but you get to ball the social secretary when the bar closes. Twelve months later, a blurb on the hardback tells you that this work represents a great advance, but so did Hitler's invasion of Russia, and look where General January left him. Anyhow, the real advance, the one the writer cares about, has nothing to do with the account of a personal history; it has more to do with the history of a personal account. But you won't get any of them to admit it. They won't ever come down off their high horse and muck out the stables. No way. They're all Pegasus and no pitchforks.'

She shrugged the tracksuit this way and that until it slipped from her shoulders. Her breasts were beautiful, like nothing on earth, the despair of metaphor. How wonderful it would be to become a woman. Not for ever, of course; but for a few hours. That would be nice. To trade your pink and pock-marked breast-work for two suntanned tits; to swap your grubby dangle down below for a quiet little crumple in between your legs; and to switch from regulation shirts to skirts and blouses of so many pigments, camel to cobalt, the Impressionist painters might have been maddened. Not, needless to say, to go the whole hog and have it off with a man. The thought of someone else inside you was enough. But to be a woman for one day, like on a TV show where you get to be a gondo-lier or a commando for an afternoon, would be so interesting. You would see the whole world from a completely different perspective, one that hardly anybody knows anything about. Really, you would feel like Marco Polo.

'But you're different, Theo,' Felicity said. 'You don't have to search; you don't have to strain. You don't have to sit at the typewriter with this terrible, Treblinka look on your face. Other people take things on; you just take them in. Then you say something that zaps the hoi polloi. What you said about Gethsemane: wow. That's anthology material; that's after-dinner speeches stuff. And now the bit about the rising damp and the beauty board. If I was right-handed, then I'd write that down on my other wrist. I would.'

'It wasn't an image,' Theo said. 'It was a fact. There is rising damp behind the beauty board in this room.'

She was a bit taken aback. She came out of the lotus and sat up on her knees, taking off the tracksuit. It was almost a reflex with her: if in doubt, undress. She stuck to it through thick and thin, because it had always let her down.

'Images are facts,' she said. 'Facts that make us feel like fictions. Anyway, rising damp comes with the territory: this is two-star splendour. There's Christmas wrapping-paper on the window of the ladies' loo downstairs, to stop the tomcats staring in. Reindeer on the roof-tops while you're peeling skin like cellophane. But if it weren't two-star, you'd have twenty bridesmaids getting sick on the stairs and supermarket serenades up and down the corridors. So be glad.'

She pulled the teddy off over her head and threw it aside. He might not even have been there. What a sight to have seen from the window across the street, a strange woman in moonlight. The one thing dearness denied you was distance; the one thing love withheld was strangeness. In time, he thought, her dressing-gown would slip to show her breasts as she stooped at the fireplace, stacking coals; and he'd move his chair in case he missed a shoot-out in 'The Comancheros'. By then, her boobs would be a bosom, if not a chest. But here and now the moonlight leaked all over her; a bit, to be honest, like lots of bird-shit on a public statue. How did they clean the Little Mermaid, with all those gulls circling?

'I'm sorry the phone rang,' he said. 'You were almost there.'

'I don't mind,' she said.

'I shouldn't have answered it.'

'You didn't answer it,' she said. 'You just took it up, and said Hello. Answer is too big a word for phones and quizzes. Save it up for the "Who do you say I am?" situations.'

He was lost; and he tried to look it. The lost look had bailed him out more often even than his kind and caring one.

'Anyway,' she said, 'I wasn't paying attention. I was jumping from one fantasy to another, like a tourist who's trying to see all the churches in Florence in two hours. First this, then that. It was 'Time Tunnel' stuff. From Marie Antoinette to Helen of Troy in one go. You get settled into one scenario, then you're whisked off to another. But it doesn't matter. Sex isn't the most important thing in this world. If it were, it wouldn't mean six, would it? So there must be five other things on the list that mean more.'

Theo knew what they were, too. He had been living long enough in the world, and the world had been living long enough in him.

'Water,' he said. 'Food and fuel. Shelter, weapons.'

'No,' she said. 'That's for antelopes. Antelopes and jackals. We need laughter and grief, we need stories. We need more stories. That's four. And we need people we can hate. Having people to turn to, yes, we need that. But we need people to turn against as well. Otherwise, there'd be no one to deflect the blow, would there? And the blade would end up in your own guts.'

She looked across at him and smiled. Her eyes explored him, up and down, down and around, as if he were numbered dots that you could join with a type three lead pencil to make a picture. But of what? They were mostly dwarves and giants. And he thought of the Delphi Charioteer, how it stared away into the fertile crescent of the middle distances while the schoolboy coachloads pressed upon it, their Pentax cameras rising and falling like rocks at a stoning. Of course, you could only look that far-seeing if you had no eyes.

'You look good,' Felicity said. 'You look really good. I've done a terrific job on you. You remind me of the day I saw you in the Library, when I hardly knew you well enough to say Salve. You were cross because your can of Coke was empty, and you crushed it, bit by bit, in your left hand. I thought that was very male of you; it had a kind of frisson. That was the day I went ahead of you in the canteen, and I got upset at the check-out because I hadn't any money.'

'I paid for yours,' said Theo. 'Then I had to borrow from the chaplain, to pay for mine.'

'You could have borrowed from me,' Felicity said. 'I had a tenner.'

There was a silence. They tamed it, drained it, fenced it with a little laughter.

'You look good as well,' Theo said. 'You look great in the moonlight. I think it likes you.'

'It isn't moonlight,' she said. 'It's streetlight.' And she reached out to him. 'Come here,' she said. 'Little shit, little silly-billy.'

He put his hand up under the lamp-shade to switch off the light. He didn't want his bum or his boomerang to be spotted from the street. But where was the damn switch? He groped with his fingers, avoiding the bulb. The light was so strong it showed the bones of his hand against the glare, the bones he had strung together by memory-work, by dint of a dozen mnemonics for his first anatomy test.

'Jesus,' he said.

'What is it?' she said. 'What is it?'

His eyes swept the room. He bounded to the press and threw it open. It was as bare and barren as the Holy of Holies in the Temple at Jerusalem; and barer than that you cannot get.

'The money,' she said. 'Where's the money?'

'Fuck the money,' Theo said. 'Where's the skeleton?'

They looked at each other. It is the one good thing to be said for a crisis. People do look at each other. Their eyelids forget to drop; their eyebrows forget to lift. And their glances flit and flicker, like the scraps of white flags flapping in the middle of no-man's-land. They are halfway there. They are homeless. Their hands shake. Their gazes glaze, and are over.

'I'm lost,' he said. 'I can't see the trees for the wood.'

'That's wrong,' said Felicity. 'You can't see the wood for the trees. It's the other way round.'

But that was it, in a nutshell. Leaves, twigs, trees and woods. Overgrowth and undercover. A suit-cover. A zip peeling through polythene; a zip he had greased, God forgive him, with a blob of KY jelly.

'We left him hanging,' Theo said. 'We left him hanging on the wood of the tree.'

The morning after was not the sort of day the Tourist Office tells you about the evening before. The sky had gone grey as early as breakfast with a five-o'clock shadow, and the woods below were thoroughly browned off. The colour had gone out of them, and it was no wonder. This was supposed to be June, not July.

Theo put his head down. He kept digging. The ground gave beneath him. It was mostly a sort of sand, anyway. He had been wise to choose here. In fact, he wondered why murderers didn't bury their wives and girlfriends in places like playgrounds, instead of in bony back-gardens where you had to contend with gravel and gunge and builder's rubble. Each easy scoop of the earth brought up the softest of soil, or whatever the right word was. As far as Theo was concerned, if you could stand on it, it was *terra firma*; if you couldn't, you could at least stand over it. Every put-down could be redeemed by being put down to experience. That way, you didn't have to put up with it.

The skeleton would have understood these things. Theo could only squint through the keyhole. Your man had held the master key to all the locks. Indeed, in his own way, he might be said to have had a skeleton key to all the combinations in the cosmos. He could open many doors, any doors even: he could unlock the sacred mysteries of the Mass, the paperchase of scripture, the eschatological magnificence of the great God's Marshall Aid for all mankind; he could even throw open the most final and fundamental things of all – unminded hearts, disheartened minds, the unfathomable shallowness in which we sink and swim, our hurt and human nature. Because he had the key, he could do these things. Do them, and still stay sane.

'I can still feel you inside me,' Felicity said. 'It's a lovely feeling. I feel taken. Not in a nasty way, of course. In a nice way.'

Theo had never had a key. He had swallowed one when he was five, a small key to a briefcase which was empty, empty except for a plastic Remembrance Day poppy that his father, at the last minute, was too timid to wear lest his wipers got wrenched off in the city-centre. For twenty-four hours both of his parents had waited for his first motion. He had had to pass it in a collander, and then his mother had searched the shit forensically with a corkscrew. That was as close as Theo had ever got to the Keys of the Kingdom. Opening windows was a poor second to the skeleton's subtle jemmy, and even that accomplished nothing. You ended up freezing to death or chasing horse-flies with cricket-pads.

He was down a foot and a half, maybe more. The same again would do him.

'Are you thinking about last night?' Felicity said. 'I can always tell what you're thinking about. Theo, why did you never tell me before that you like it when I close my eyes while you come? Was it because you were shy? Was it? I wish you wouldn't be shy. It's a bit underhand. Anyhow, you know perfectly well I'll do anything for you, except grow the hair under my armpits. I couldn't go to a dress-dance with sooty stuff sprouting everywhere. You know that.'

She was sitting on the one swing that wasn't tied. Her sneakers trailed on the tarmacadam as she swayed slightly. Those long, those elongated legs were slick with sun-oil.

She was a child of hope, and a child of great good-nature too. As a mark of respect, she was wearing black sun-shorts and a grey T-shirt. Who but Felicity would have thought of such a gesture? Bless her, she had even changed watches. Now she had on the man's one, the one with the big, black watch-strap, the one that made other people wonder if she was hiding scars.

'If I had a proper shovel instead of this child's spade,' he said, 'I'd be done by now. But you couldn't just walk into a shop in the country, and pay cash for a spade.'

'Do you think?' she said. 'Do you think they'd start imagining things? Like you were off to bury a corpse?'

'That wouldn't bother them,' said Theo. 'But they might think you were going to dig somebody up. That's the way their mind works in the country. They live in a world of their own.'

It was almost ready, the grave for the skeleton. A good spot in a good site. He would not be lonely. The laughter of children was a better thing than the lamentations of men; and he would hear that laughter, thrown up in the air like a pearl necklace on a breaking string, peals of elation from the little ones, the little ones who would come unto him. By day, there would be youngsters, their fingers full of hangnails and ink-stains, lighting up behind the litter-bins where they could sit and study the nearly naked women in the holiday brochures; a high wind snatching at the edges, an eager, envious wind that has forgotten that the flesh, too, smells of salt. Then, later in the day, the bumps and buggies of young mothers, songbirds in the branches, a scuffle in the sand-pit, nappies thrown away among the elderberry, and a boy greasing the slide with a bar of cooking-fat while his small sister hesitates at the top rung of the ladder. In the last light of the evening, a priest might come, sit himself on the see-saw, think about a

Dimplex that won't work, an intercom for his bed-bound mother's room, or stare into the blur of his own broken state like a man reading the large and the lesser letters on the wall of the optician's clinic. And finally, under cover of darkness, the inspection of starlight, lovers would meet here and mate here, here among the creaking ship-sounds of the swings and see-saw, here in a place of possibility, a place grounded in children. Over there, where the dropped knitting-needle had not been noticed, a woman might be showing her boyfriend how to knot his new silk tie so that the edges meet exactly; or in behind the crazy concrete tunnel that has torn so many mother's tights, a girl in jeans and a jersey touches a man's penis until he comes into a piece of kitchen-roll, his hand in his mouth to stop him crying out.

He was finished. He threw the spade away. He was so pleased with himself he had forgotten he would have to cover it in again.

He looked around him. Yes, this would do, he thought. It was dead right. Even at night, he'd have noises to interest him. It would be like a radio with the volume down low. The copper tinfoil of a bar of chocolate would whack against a grass-blade, and he'd know it. He'd smile and think about the Buttons he used to give his altar-boys. And the woollen balaclava that might once have been the colour of marmalade, shagged and sodden in a corner, it would be dearer to him than any biretta. He'd wonder whether Gordon got a new one from his mother, and worry a bit about it until the boy came belting into the playground, his head a blaze of left-over balls from other patterns.

'I'm finished,' he said to Felicity. 'I mean, I'm ready.'

It was a pity about the day. The faintness of it, the feel it had of being about to rain. And the sea. The sea had the look of office-coffee on the desk for three days, a skin forming on it; but it ought to have been sparkling like sapphires. At least, that was how it struck most of the people who took the trouble to write about it. On the other hand, maybe they were cute when it came to making travel arrangements. They came at the right time, and they came prepared. If a travel writer wanted to spoof about the enchantments of Egypt, that was fine; but he took care to get his inoculations first. And he didn't write it in the commercial centre of Cairo. He wrote it in the barbaric splendour of Knightsbridge.

'There are three things I'll never understand,' Felicity said. She was off the swing and dusting the seat of her shorts with her hand. 'I'll never understand why the Pacific is three and a half inches higher than the Atlantic; I'll never understand men; and I'll never understand why the county council puts tarmacadam under the children's swings in a public playground. I mean, they can't all be bachelors, can they?'

She twisted in an effort to examine her own behind.

'Is my bottom clean?' she said.

'It is,' he told her. Fact of the matter, she was sitting on a fortune. She could have worn bin-liners for a Cosmo cover. It was no wonder so many men disliked him.

And he eased the skeleton down into the hole. He'd been a big man, the Bishop. He must have stood six feet tall in his spurs. God help him if he'd ever had to spend a night in the six by six by six of a standard punishment cell, like the poor priests in the countries Alan Whicker vets for vacations. There was even a Jesuit, back in the seventeenth century, who'd been seventy years in the one cell, reading his office from memory each morning; but, of course, a Jesuit would go one better than anybody else. He must have chuckled – no, not chuckled; smiled, a Jesuit would smile – when the other prisoners, the Franciscans, began to recant. Even in spiritual matters, there was such a thing as breeding; and the Jesuits had blue blood in their veins. That, and black ink. Actually, when you sat down and thought about it, it was pretty peculiar the skeleton hadn't entered that body. He was officer material. He had that gentle, George Saunders way of looking at you, so you felt awful and happy at the same time, like the day he had first met Felicity's parents and the family dog started sniffing his crotch while he was telling them about slow exposures in primitive photography. Eventually, of course, Felicity had brought the dog out; but, by then, the damage was terminal. There was no point telling anyone that he'd spilled sherry on his fly, especially when the mother asked him if he'd like to wash up before dinner.

'What a strange tree,' Felicity said. She was standing under one that last year's leaves had never fallen from. Shavings of rust, they drooped and dangled, dangled and drooped; and would not budge.

'This tree,' she said, 'it won't forget its past. Or maybe it can't. That's the problem. Its life died last year, and it's still in mourning for her, like a broken-hearted husband. What it needs is a complete change of identity, and a new existence in another country. As a rocking horse.'

And she twirled a leaf by its long, lean stem, so it spun slowly, like a dead parachutist from a clock-tower.

'That's it,' Theo said.

His bones were aching. They shouldn't have been, what with the cycling and the kind of Kama Sutra stuff they did in the small hours; but they were sore, damn it. The backs of his knees, the worst of all, and a lot of his upper left-hand side where he'd blundered blindly into a tree-stump the night before as he searched for the skeleton. The force of it had almost pierced his side; he was lucky not to be a hospital case this minute. Herself, of course, had never stirred, foot or fetlock. That was her way. She was the one person who would never leave the swimming-pool when it started raining. Not Felicity. Not her; or was it she? At any rate, she had left the whole business of beating the woods to him; and nobody else had been of any help, either. The one man he had met, of whom he had asked only a single, civil and courteous question, that man had taken to his heels; or, rather, he had walked away briskly and then broken into a run, as if the mere mention of bones in a bag were a menace to life and limb. The truth was, you could walk the world over in your bare, blue feet, but you'd never understand it. Undertake and undergo, yes. A thousand times, yes. But never understand.

'That's it,' he said.

The skeleton lay in a curve, curled in upon itself. It was the form the foetus takes, crouch and cuddle in one. That was fitting. The Egyptians buried their dead in that position, in the days before Osiris and Isis came to Calvary in much the manner the Magi sat in the shit and the straw of a cow-shed outside Bethlehem. The Bishop might even be pleased to be buried for a birth; he might have been something of an Egyptologist in his sparer time: he might have had Schliemann up there on his shelf alongside Spinoza. Indeed, Theo was sure of it.

'I think we should say a prayer,' he said. 'Will you say a prayer?'

'I don't know any prayers,' Felicity said. 'I used to, but not now. Not any more.'

She was a bit uncertain about this. Prayers were sort of coming back into vogue. She had been to two dinner parties in the last six months where the host had said Grace, and there wasn't a priest present, or an ex-priest, for that matter. Everybody had liked it, too. It gave the whole meal a certain amount of style; substantial style. Of course, the Beethoven piano trio in the background helped the prayer to mean more, sort of.

'I know the Our Father,' she said.

'Everybody knows the Our Father,' said Theo. 'Clever Hans probably knew the Our Father. But that's not really a prayer. The Our Father is more like talking to somebody. I mean a formal kind of prayer.'

'I think I remember the Grace Before Meals,' Felicity said. 'And if I say it, I might remember the Grace After Meals as well. You know the way it comes back to you, like when you see the ocean from up in a plane, and suddenly you remember the feel of the flour under your nails when you cooked a fish for the first time.'

'Say it,' said Theo. 'Go on. Say it.'

Felicity joined her hands together.

'You don't have to join your hands,' Theo said.

'Who's saying the prayer?' she said. 'Am I saying the prayer, or are you saying the prayer?'

'You're saying the prayer,' he said. 'Sometime. Sometime soon. Maybe even now.'

She composed herself. She was trying to look prayerful. It was rather a waste of time. God listens to our mutterings the way we listen to Mozart: with His eyes closed. From the first note of the overture, He is all ears.

'Bless us, O Lord, and these Thy gifts, which, of Thy Bounty, we are about to receive, through Christ, Our Lord, Amen.'

'Amen,' said Theo. He said it the other way, with a soft A instead of a hard one. He was careful how he pronounced words like 'homosexual', too. He had not done Greek for nothing. Medical classmates might say 'anorexic', but he would always acknowledge the genitive construction: the poor girl that had died was, of course, an anorectic patient. The hospital pharmacist had noticed, and noted, Theo's pronunciation. 'Here's a man,' he had said, 'who knows his alphas from his omegas; but does he know the difference between his omegas and his omicrons?' And, needless to say, Theo had been able to set him straight on that, as well. It was a shame, really, that Theo hadn't been in a position to sign the girl's death certificate. She would have been spared the indignity of dying of a misspelling.

The wind had risen. Felicity shivered.

'God is passing over our lives in silence,' she said.

Theo stood at the edge of the hole and looked into it.

'Are you going to pray, too?' Felicity said.

'In a way,' he said.

'That would be lovely,' she said. 'Something sincere and short. Or succinct. Sincerity is always very succinct. Like in films. You know the way the hero is always closed up, and the one who's the shit, he's always fat and fluent. Clint Eastwood's scripts are always a spit and a cough, but the men he kills, their teeth are always chattering like typewriters. Jabber, jabber. Spare me.'

And she shivered again. Because the wind was cold now, cold to the point of indifference, and the trees were throwing their hands in the air as the day went west. Down on the beach beyond, a plastic bag tried desperately to throw itself into the sea, but the sea would have none of it; and, back in the bored hotel they'd stayed in for the past two nights, kids would have cut the baize on a billiard table while their parents studied the skyline, their eyes a mix of crow's-feet and crow's-nest. Truly, the God of Abraham could have done better by the Bishop. This was a poor show, the end of the run and no first night. He wouldn't have blamed the skeleton for taking it to heart. Even if he lacked the muscle in question, he was still human. Not that he would have expected weather-conditions out of Canaletto. No; but something benign, a benediction. Larks a hundred feet high, being lyrical, which is what they're paid for; and a path of pure sunlight on the surface of the sea, a motorcade of chrome bumpers. Not this wind and stuff, this Austro-Hungarian anguish.

'I believe in God,' Theo said. 'And I like to imagine that God believes in me.'

'Hear, hear,' said Felicity.

'I believe in Jesus of Nazareth,' Theo said. 'I don't honestly know whether he proceeds from the Father or not. And I don't honestly care. In this world, most sons proceed against their father, but that's another day's doubt. What I do believe is that, if you start talking or thinking about God, you end up talking or thinking about Jesus; and vice versa. I don't know what to say about the Holy Ghost, really. He's a bit like the fifth Beatle in a way. But I will try to think about Him in future. I mean, in the future. For the moment, I'll put him on the long finger, same as a wedding ring.'

Felicity spread her fingers like a fan. Was that true?

'Apart from all of that, I suppose I believe that most everybody is broken and bewildered and that, accordingly, we should never raise our voices, except in song. Not that being broken and bewildered is altogether to be regretted. Sad, yes; bad, maybe. I mean, most of the mischief in this world is brought about by people who are very together. Albert Speer was a better provider than Albert Einstein. Genghis Khan was a family man, a better father than Gauguin. Even Hitler, when he couldn't make it into architecture, he had the maturity to say, Fine, fuck it, I'll go into demolition instead. These were well-adjusted people. They were in touch with their emotions. They knew what they wanted, and they went out and shot it.'

'Theo,' said Felicity. 'You're wrong about the long finger.'

'I believe,' he said, 'in the Mass. I believe in breaking bread instead of breaking heads, and it seems to me that the Eucharist is about that. I believe that the past can be redeemed if we forgive it, and the future brought forward if we praise it. Because forgiveness is the sacrament of what lies behind, and encouragement is the sacrament of what lies ahead; and the two together make the present what it is: a gift.'

The wind was tickling the ribs of the skeleton until its jaw shook with laughter.

'I believe too that doctors should be paid more,' Theo said. 'But I've said that a hundred times. There's lots of other things I used to believe, but you learn to travel light at a certain point. Like guardian angels. I used to believe in guardian angels. I used to sleep on the side of my bed to leave room for my guardian angel. Then I wet the bed one night. When my mother came in, I told her my guardian angel had done it. But she walloped me, anyway. Then I knew. I knew there were no guardian angels. My whole apostasy dates from that period in my potty training. Freud was right. In the beginning was the genito-urinary. Piss and shit. Amen.'

Amen was a great stand-by. There were times when you couldn't find a full-stop. A way out. The bus wouldn't brake at any of the stops, and you were miles past the part of town you knew. It would be like you were trying to type a novel on a keyboard that had only colons and commas. But then there was Amen. Period. Wherever you went, whatever you did, you could bring anything to completion, or was it completeness, by saying that one little word. It was Christianity's contribution to syntax.

Theo bent down into the hole, and put his bicycle-lamp beside the skeleton. He turned it on, and a weak, washed light picked out the bones of the fingers. It would be stronger in darkness; enough, at any rate, for him to see by.

Felicity had scooped some muesli from the pockets of her shorts. She stooped forward, letting the tiny nuts and husks trickle into the hole. Then Theo started filling it in.

'I'm your guardian angel now,' she said to him. 'Not that you leave much room for me. Sometimes you push me to the edge. You do.'

She was looking at the tree with the dead leaves. Hadn't it twigged that spring was past, and summer here? Hadn't it seen a single sunrise paint the world in its true colours? She felt like shaking it.

'Do you know what I'll let you do tonight?' she said to Theo. 'Tonight I'll let you eat a mandarin off my bottom. You haven't done that for ages. Not since Christmas.'

What he would do, he thought, was level it off with the smooth side of the spade, and then scuff the surface with his sneakers or, better still, a leafy branch if he could break one off. Because the stuff he'd dug up was a damn sight darker than he'd ever imagined. It almost stood out. With any luck, there'd be a high-density downpour within ten, twelve hours, though even a shower would help until you could mobilise a *bona fide*, North Atlantic sea-storm. If, on the other hand, some schoolboy with a library loan of *Treasure Island* happened to hit a cricket-ball off the bar of the swing before a Beaufort nine had buried the evidence, then he and Felicity were in deep shit. They could always plead insanity, of course, or blame each other, or blame somebody else, though finger-pointing was never fail-safe. After all, Adam and Eve still got the shove from I Am Who Am.

'Are you listening, Theo?' said Felicity. 'Or are you back on the banks of the Ganges again? Could you leave the corpses and the crocodiles and the great god Krishna, and wander my way for a while? I mean, you needn't answer. Blink once for Yes, and twice for No.'

He looked for her. And there she was, under the dead tree. Or was it the tree with the dead leaves? There was a difference. Failure was not death; it might not even be an illness.

'We couldn't,' he said.

'Couldn't what?'

'Mandarins,' he said. 'Off your bottom.'

'Why not?' she said.

'They're not in season,' he said.

He started stamping the ground, digging his heels in. But it meant the level sank; so he had to shovel more on top.

'Then I'll just sit on your face,' she told him, 'and you can smell me. I know you love smelling me, Theo. You do it when you think I'm asleep, but I'm not. Or, sometimes, you pretend to be asleep, with your hand on my pussy, and then you slink off into the bathroom, and I can hear you sniffing your fingers. Sniff, sniff. Anyone would think you were snorting cocaine.'

There was one thing clear. The longer he did this Hopi rain-dance, the more the ground was going to subside. It would, in fact, be better to abort. Otherwise, this sinking feeling was going to get worse; and sinking feelings were always to be avoided. The only two things in this world which you could safely sink were pints and foundations, and even they carried risks. So he would heap shingle and shale on the dark soil, and trust to the weather to do its damnedest.

'When I die, I would like my ashes to be strewn in a sand-pit,' said Felicity. 'I would like the children to play in me, to put a starfish on a sandcastle made out of my tonsils. I would like them to trot off home with a bit of my grey matter on their Benetton blouses, and sooty traces on their plaits from an ambush of my kisses. I would like that. I would. Me.'

What about that, then? Theo stood back and inspected his handiwork. Not even Agatha Christie, or even Christie himself, would have noticed more than a bit of a mess. And a mess is about as inconspicuous an entity in this universe as cement and concrete in New York city. How would Theo Kojak have reacted if the Commissioner called him, and said: 'Theo, we're looking for a block of cement'? He might have cracked the lollipop, but he wouldn't have cracked the case. No way. This Theo knew that. Besides, who in their right mind would ever connect a holy man with a place where children play? Theo would, of course, but then he was an intellectual. If, in twenty or twenty-five years, the Bishop were to be elevated, they'd probably put him in a glass case in the National Museum, and show him off as Count Ramon Diego Muchachas, survivor of the Armada fleet. And he'd enjoy that, because he was an intellectual, too. Irony and incongruity were flesh of his flesh and bone of his bone. He would stare up at the visitors staring down, and only occasional children, the oddest among them, would see for a second a tremor of yearning quicken the line of the cheekbone. Then they'd tug at the thin, transparent raincoats of the long-legged grown-ups, and, out of the corner of the case, the skeleton would watch them slip-slapping away over the wettish marble floor to where, under the bat-wings of the Great

Elk's antlers, they'd open up their guide-books and tick the things they'd seen with a transparent disposable pen.

But the child would still be watching; and that would be enough.

Theo looked up at Felicity. She was bending one of the branches on the tree without leaves. When she released it, it sprang back. It was still supple.

'Maybe it doesn't need a tree-surgeon,' she said. 'Maybe it needs a tree-psychiatrist. If it didn't grow last year, it might be ashamed. Ashamed of the size of its last tree-ring, ashamed of its smallness. Perhaps it's the same for trees as for people. Perhaps they're under this incredible pressure to grow all the time. Grow, baby, grow, grow, grow. You think? And perhaps they have these woody workshops, you know, where they all have to get into groups and talk from their timber hearts about the trauma of losing their leaves and how they find it hard to feel rooted. Then they all elect the oak-tree as Chairman and Chief Facilitator for a further twelve months, and the oak-tree says it's a great honour, and they all hate him even more. And this little fellow, who's every bit as crooked and complex as you or me, he staggers home with a bit too much sap in him. He's dreaming of the maple tree he met, and how he'd like to branch out in her direction; but all that he's got from the seminar is a rice-paper pamphlet on tree-phobias and how to cope with the sound of chainsaws.'

There were times, he thought. There were times when Felicity was dogged and fragile, fragile and dogged at the same time. And it made him want to touch her, but not in that way. In the way that you would run your hands all over a child if he'd been missing for two days; or in the way your hands would wander here and there, blindly, like dogs losing a scent, over the throat and the wires, the tubes and the earlobes of a loved one who was dead and still, and still warm. Because she seemed so naked to him now that he wanted almost to throw a blanket round her. Only her eyes were not naked. They were as difficult as the sky in jigsaws.

'If it is dead,' she said, 'it can live again. And not just a rocking horse, either. A rocking chair, as well. If there's room enough for both in one life, there's room enough for both in one tree.'

He wished that he could speak to her in French or German. In French or German, you could say Thou and you could say Thee. He wanted to Thou her, and to Thee her. But you couldn't do it in English. Of course, that was typical. The English were great at inventing threshing machines and steam engines and Logical Positivism, but they knew nothing about Thou and Thee. They had taken Thou and Thee out of the language, same as they smashed the rose-windows in the chapter-houses and the cathedrals. They had separated mystery and formality, that's what they'd done, so that mystery became occult and formality became arid. The other world guttered out into a stage-set for the blood sacrifice of Britt Ekland by a coven of Satanists; and the other person, in the makeshift miracle of his nature, had decayed into the social obligation to call him Mister. If you pointed out that man has feet of concrete, or is it clay, they would probably commission an orthopaedic shoe. That was their way; and it paid dividends – which, from an English perspective, is a rich recommendation. But was the creation of tarmacadam and Thomas Cook enough? Did it compensate for the loss of Thou and Thee?

'It did not,' said Theo.

Felicity peered at him.

'Are you all right?' she said.

'Right as rain,' he said. 'Never better. How about thou? I mean, yourself?'

'I'm fine,' she said. 'Why wouldn't I be? My pulse rate is normal; my impulse rate is normal. My brain is making waves, my bowels are making motions, and my heart is beating out the best percussion on the planet. If I were in hospital, they'd discharge me. Why do you ask?'

'Because there's something missing,' Theo said. 'There's you and me, and what we've done here in the playground; but there should be something else. Not just to finish it, but to give it a kind of finish, too. Like in a cinema, you know, when everyone senses that, yes, this is the last scene, this is nearly it, this is nearly over; and, even before the credits start appearing, there's a mad rush for coats. And you're trying to read what James Bond will be back in, but the big fellow in front of you is bickering with his wife over who had the ticket to the underground car-park.'

'You mean this doesn't feel like a film?' Felicity said. 'You don't hear any clapping or clapper-boards.'

'It's like a liturgy,' Theo said. 'A liturgy that lacks something. It's like the Mass without the Consecration, somehow. It needs something else, something done, something said; but I can't think what. Something to round it, and to round it off.'

'Would you like me to dance?' said Felicity. 'I could dance round his grave. I could even dance on it. Or you could push me on the swing, if you like. Or I could see-saw. We would have to see-saw together, of course. It takes two to see-saw.'

'I've seen it done before,' he said. 'I've seen it done twice. Once in a film about a man who dies of leukaemia and leaves two little daughters, and once in a film about a woman who dies of leukaemia and leaves two little sons. If they hadn't lived in different cities, the wife of the man and the husband of the woman could have married and brought the children up together. But those things only happen in real life.'

'You're right,' Felicity said. 'And it's only when you grow up and realise it, that you become a child again. Up until then, you were only a youngster.'

'So the swings are out,' Theo said. 'And the see-saws, too. We could have fed the ducks, but there aren't any. A walk along the beach might have been poignant, but you know yourself that it always ends the same way: if you watch for horse-droppings, you step on dog-shit; if you watch for dog-shit, you step on horse-droppings. Ergo, we go.'

'We could commit the sacrament of consolation,' said Felicity. 'But you'd have to let me change into warmer clothes.'

He thought about this for a moment; but, no, his bottom would be frozen. Besides, a man's chipmunk had a horribly hibernatory instinct in cold weather: he preferred to stay inside, curled on his store of nuts.

'I think we should observe a period of mourning,' he said. 'The skeleton is hardly stiff in his grave.'

And the two of them walked away from the playground. Walked away in silence.

'But not away from the reality which it represents,' Felicity said.

' "Leave" is a better word in ways,' said Theo. 'Not, be it said, that "walk" is wasted. But its coastal waters are quite treacherous. I might leave my wife, but I'd never walk out on her; I might relinquish my children, but I'd never walk away from them. Or from here.'

'There,' said Felicity. 'It's a fair way back already. Look.'

She was right, you know. It was already behind them

and below them, the solitary children's slide reflecting the spread, inhuman features of the North Atlantic, like a concave surface in a Hall of Mirrors. The see-saw stayed its ground as well, one shiny spar against a world of water. The kids would come to reinforce it; come with their whoops, blown noses, protestations: their din better than bugle-blasts at bringing down Jericho.

'Theo,' said Felicity, 'I've just remembered the Grace After Meals. It just came to me, out of the grey, like that. Shall I say it?'

'Save it,' he said. 'Save it for our next dinner party. We'll have coq-au-vin, an ex-priest, the choreographer who always hugs you instead of shaking your hand, the gay guy who worked as a bouncer in Berlin and who won't go for a blood-test, and that fellow from fourth year who always puts pages from *Le Monde* over his windscreen on the worst winter nights.'

'That would be so perfect,' said Felicity. 'And I'd just have to invite Dolores. It would totally devastate her.'

Back beyond in the playground, the wind was moving the swing. The seat slid forward and back, forward and back until, as if with its own momentum, it bucked into the air. You would almost have strained to see somebody on it, a child standing up, the weight of a body thrust against the weight of no body at all.

The driver of the hearse had taken another wrong turn on the home stretch. In fact, home was stretching to eternity. At this rate, it would be midnight before they made it back to Dublin. Rain or no rain, they might have done better to keep cycling. Felicity had said it was an omen when the car slowed in ahead of them on the road outside the mental hospital in Ballinasloe. The absence of a coffin was neither here nor there, except insofar, obviously, as it left space for the tandem in among the anemones in their frosted bowls. No, the hearse itself was what perturbed her.

'Perturbed,' she thought. She must use that word more often. 'Troubled', that was off the peg; 'perturbed', on the other hand, was straight from a select boutique. It was Third Programme.

'I'm sorry,' said the driver. 'It'll have to be another circle.'

Who ever heard of a hearse without a reverse gear? The thing was absurd. Maybe Theo didn't mind so much about the hearse bit. He probably thought it would make a good story. That was the way most Irishmen thought about things. They could lose their fingers and toes from frostbite at the North Pole, but you'd find them down in Occupational Therapy six months later, popping batteries out of their mouths into a dictaphone. Or if they lost their wife in labour, they'd sit and cry; but, by Christ, they'd sit and weep if they couldn't come up with ten synonyms for grief. Even the Apocalypse might be good for a few anecdotes and a free round. Felicity could just see Theo steering the conversation round to a cortège. But a cortège without a reverse gear?

'No problem,' Theo said. 'We've time enough.'

If you could only go forward, you ended up going backward. That was the whole bother. The least little mistake, and you started another slow, three-hundred-and-sixty-degree wheel over the same ground. This was the third time he'd overshot: there were forty miles on the clock with five covered. The truth was, they'd be faster on a frisbee. Jesus Christ, they'd get farther running on a treader in a gym. How the man ever found a cemetery was beyond her; and, by the time he did, the widow's weeds were probably well hoed.

But she tried hard to be spontaneous. She owed it to herself to show her teeth in a smile. It was a great responsibility, she thought, to be called Felicity. It was a bit like being a Kennedy. And you were always on show. There were no Balmorals where you could flick a nasal secretion onto the carpet without letting the side down. You were always available; you were always on call. If you were Felicity, you had to be felicitous. If you were Dolores, then you were a pain in the ass: you were, in fact, a haemorrhoid. If you were Theo, whatever it meant, you stayed Theo; you left the Dore end strictly for your birth certificate, because once you put the two together, well, you were lost to normal life and the nuclear family, weren't you?

'Here we are, then,' said the driver. 'Back on the straight and narrow.'

The driver's name was Noel. He had told them that his birthday was next week. Felicity reckoned he was Jewish, and the father had wanted to give him an alibi, or was it an alias? If you put him in the sun for a day, he would go black. Felicity would quite like to have been Jewish. Then she could have fought in the Haganah, and been tortured by a beautiful Egyptian; or she would have fallen in love with a Nazi she was sent to assassinate. After they had fucked each other into stillness and serenity, high over Macchu Picchu in Peru, or was it Argentina, he would have discovered too late that her nipples were smeared with cobra venom. Yet, nine months later, in her Paris apartment, she would have wept as she gave birth to his child, calling him Machete.

'When do they start shooting?'

It was Theo, talking to the driver of the hearse. What

were they on about now? Felicity decided she would file that fantasy under M, and get back to it later. It was a goodie.

'First thing tomorrow morning,' said the hearse-driver. 'But I like to mosey round the place beforehand. Get the feel of it, sort of thing. Of course, it all depends on the weather, doesn't it? Farming, fishing, filming, you have to ring up the elements beforehand. I remember now the time I was in "The Viking's Revenge". Oh, it must have been whenever. I was one of the Vikings, with this big bloody wig that smelled of surgical spirits or something. Two days we waited for the right weather, two days playing scrabble in a horned helmet. I ask you. Then, in the battle scene, didn't my sword bend back like a bloody boomerang when I walloped one of the Romans. Down he went, down at my feet, like a soccer player. Oh, the director was hopping. "Cut, cut, cut", he says, and he was frothing. Literally frothing. But that was the antacids.'

Theo was enchanted. He even took a cigar from the driver of the hearse, and that was something Theo had not done since he got so drunk that he put the wrong end in his mouth.

'Hamlet,' said the driver. 'The thinking man's cigar; and the favourite smoke of the late lamented Pope Paul the Sixth.'

'Have you been an extra for long?' said Theo.

'Me?' said the hearse-driver. 'Sure I was in "The Blue Max", and that was back before Walkmans. Christ in Heaven, that was back before washing-machines. I met Ursula Andress. I did. She was going to give me her autograph, but all I had was an appointments' diary, so she just smiled and moved on. Actually, I couldn't see her awfully well, because my head was wrapped in bandages. I was supposed to be suffering from the effects of mustard-gas. But you could see me properly, large as life, in "Ryan's Daughter", in "Barry Lyndon", you name it. I was in "Excalibur". I was in two commercials for Guinness, and I don't even drink the stuff; and I was in a Department of Health film about brucellosis in cattle. I was dying to play the hearse-driver in John Huston's film of "The Dead", but then I read the story, which is pretty boring, anyway, and there wasn't a hearse-driver next or near it.'

'Is this like a family tradition?' Felicity said. 'I mean, is it in the family, sort of like diabetes?'

The driver of the hearse thought about this, tapping his Hamlet off the ashtray on the dashboard.

'Well,' he said, 'it is and it isn't. There was a man who was almost an uncle of mine. He would have been my uncle if he'd married my aunt, but he didn't. Instead of that, off he went to America. He used to send us oceans of postcards, and the aunt would use them as fire-lighters. Anyhow, he was a galley slave in "Ben Hur". He was two rows behind Charlton Heston, with this glazed look on his face. That was because he wasn't wearing his spectacles. When he came home again, years later, I remember they showed the film in the Marian hall; and the projectionist stopped it at each of the six shots he was in. Everybody clapped, even the aunt. She got up out of her seat and helped the baby in the pram to clap, too. Then the uncle made a speech about biremes and triremes, and he hadn't lost a trace of his accent in the years he'd been away. The whole hall gave him a standing ovation. I think it was less to do with being in "Ben Hur", really, and more to do with being Ben.'

'And he was your role-model?' said Felicity. And she waved to the child who was waving at her from the back of the car in front of them. The child shook his mother's shoulder to tell her what had happened, but the mother wasn't interested. The only wave which moved her was a wave of tiredness, sweeping her slowly out to sea.

'He was, in a way,' said the hearse-driver. 'He was a model for all the roles I ever played. Not that I'm the sort of fellow who'd shake the dust off his shoes and steer for the bright lights. It wouldn't be a case of shaking the dust off, anyhow, would it? More like scraping the dirt off with a steak-knife. But, no, I'm a quiet sort of customer, really, a biddable enough bloke. I'd go down the gears at a green light, you know. Then, of course, I'm used to driving slowly, I suppose. There was a time, back during the winter, when I stopped at a red light, round about four in the morning. No traffic, of course, but I waited. We were there, maybe, three or four minutes; and my wife, she was weeping. As in, you know, weeping. She said I wasn't timid at all. She said I was terrified. A terrified person.'

'Perhaps she meant it as a compliment,' Felicity said. 'Perhaps she was weeping for you, and not at you.'

'Perhaps,' he said. 'Then again, she's different. Very strong. Strong teeth, strong hair, strong stomach. She'd have a couple of those complaint cards filled out in a restaurant before we'd finished our main course. It could be embarrassing, you know, especially when she'd ask one of the waitresses how to spell "dishevelled". I'd go to the toilet then, and spend ages there, washing my hands again every time somebody walked in. Because I get so anxious, like. I went into a book-store once with a book in my pocket, and I didn't know how to leave. I was there all afternoon, thinking to myself: did I write my name on that book? Eventually, the shop closed. I took the book out, looked at it. No name. So I had to go and pay for it, hadn't I?'

'Was it a dirty book?' said Felicity. 'That would have been awful.'

'No,' said the hearse-driver. 'It was a book about Lourdes.'

'Lourdes?' said Felicity. What an artful Jew.

'Lourdes,' he said. 'It was for somebody else I went. For a little girl who used to put Muppets in the crib at Christmas. Kermit and the Kings; Miss Piggy standing guard over Jesus, with one of those little bottles that never empties. But when I got on the plane to go to Lourdes, I got anxious. Was this the plane to Lourdes? So, after about half-an-hour, I couldn't stand it any longer. I leaned over to the man sitting on the other side of the free seat, and I said to him: "Excuse me, sir, but is this the plane to Lourdes?" "Of course, it is", he told me; but he got anxious too. He leaned back and asked the person behind him. Within five minutes, there was pandemonium. The stewardesses could do nothing. The captain had to make an announcement. Then the captain got anxious. He radioed Paris. Of course, I didn't know that at the time. I was up and down the aisles, trying to reassure people.'

'I don't mean to stop you in full flight,' said Felicity, 'but you turn left at the next junction.'

He slammed on the brakes, swerved sharply left, and made it. The wheel spun fluently through his fingers. Felicity was not about to mention that the handle-bar of the bicycle had made a lasting impression on one of the misted bowls that were so like cake-covers in the window of a tea-shop. For one thing, the dent was on the coffin-side, and so it wouldn't be seen by the immediate family; for another, it wasn't as if the hearse was pristine in the first place: there was a blue rubber bone down at her feet, and half a bale of briquettes wedged in the glove compartment. Now who would be lighting fires in the middle of summer? Unless, of course, it had something to do with the Passover.

'Now the wife is another breed,' the hearse-driver was saying. 'Or she was, at any rate, until, well, until things got on top of her. They're very Catholic, troubles and such like. They always assume the missionary position. In fact, I said it to her the other day, to make her laugh, like. But she didn't. Laugh, I mean. She didn't, really. Of course, there's only so much anyone can take. Even a dartboard falls apart at a certain point. In her day, though, in her day she was mighty.'

'Right,' said Felicity. 'I mean, turn right.'

The hearse-driver lit his Hamlet again. Why did they keep going out on him? That was the second time he'd done it. Would he not just smoke the damn thing like a normal person? Or maybe he was used to snuffing it when the service ended and he had to go in for the coffin. It was just as well that the priest used incense. Otherwise, there'd be ructions, especially if it turned out to be a case of lung cancer.

'Take my daughter,' said the hearse-driver. 'The older one. She was mad about ballet. Certifiable. Tutus and things. Then the Bolshoi came to Dublin. Tickets were ten-a-penny, the Russians had marched into Czechoslovakia and nobody wanted to be seen booking a balcony seat. Jesus, there were priests on the picket-line outside the theatre. I kid you not. Howandever, it didn't stop the ballet brigade. Maybe it thinned the ranks a bit, but that's about all.'

'Your wife and daughter went?' said Theo.

'The daughter was off to it, anyway,' said the hearse-driver. 'Because one of the girls in her class was having a birthday party, and the birthday party was the Bolshoi, followed by a bunfight. But what happened next was that

199

my daughter and the birthday girl had a row. And when I say a row, I mean intercontinental ballistic missiles. It was over the History teacher, and which of them was to sit beside her on the trip to Yeats's castle at Thoor Ballylee. Then the teacher got glandular fever and couldn't go; but the two girls were still sworn enemies.'

'I had a crush on my Biology teacher,' Felicity said. 'I used to carry his briefcase down the school avenue as far as his bus-stop. During class, I was always asking him questions about seminal intromission, but he never seemed to cop what I was talking about. You see, subtlety will get you nowhere in this world. If I'd been a few years older and wiser, I could have asked him to wait for me. As things turned out, he had to get radiation for something or other, and all of his hair fell out. I found the whole thing very aging.'

She seemed to have finished. Certainly she had paused for the statutory few seconds. He might safely intervene now.

'Go on,' he said to the driver of the hearse. 'It's clear now.'

The man took him at his word. He shot forward and nearly killed them all. Three cars sped by, blaring their lights.

'You told me to go,' said the driver of the hearse. 'You told me and I trusted you. I let my guard down.'

He was groping between his feet for his Hamlet. Of course, it had gone out again.

'I'm sorry,' Theo said. 'I was being figurative.'

'Well,' said the hearse-driver, 'that's all right. But the next time you want to be figurative, make sure you're standing on the ground, not sitting in a car. Just come down to earth if you want to go around with your head in the clouds.'

'Hear, hear,' said Felicity. 'Thinking and drinking.'

Actually, it was all Felicity's fault. Theo had been afraid that she was going to talk about the Vice-Principal. There was no statute of limitations on that kind of absurdity. Besides, if she'd mentioned his name, it would probably turn out that he was related to the driver of the hearse. Everybody in this country was related to everybody else, just as everything in the world was related to every other thing. No wonder the scientists at Los Alamos had been knotted up inside when they detonated the first atomic device. There was, after all, an appreciable mathematical possibility that the consequent chain reaction would more or less incinerate the universe. In much the same manner, the beat of a bird's wing in a backyard in any place beginning with a B could, and did, have a direct effect on cloud-formations over the Andes. He had heard that on the BBC, and the BBC always tolled the truth. Why, even a white lie lost you an increment if you were working for the Beeb. There was a chap from 'Blue Peter' who had jumped the turnstile in the Underground, and had the cheek to boast about it. But where was he now? At the bottom of the Thames, that's where, weighed down by two electric typewriters.

'I'm sorry,' Theo said. 'I was afraid that Felicity was going to break the seal of silence on a teacher who was found playing blind-man's-buff with the fourth years in the school gym. Blind-man's-buff with, as it were, an emphasis on the third syllable.'

'Right,' said Felicity. 'No, second right.'

Theo was wondering about the first atomic device and the beat of the bird's wing. Had he or had he not said those things to Felicity in the recent past? It was so important always to be original. Even one's sins, if sufficiently original, intrigued the Almighty. What He could not endure was the sin of imitation. Theo had tried hard all his life not to imitate anything. When other people wore broad ties, he had always worn thin ones. At Bohemian parties, he had inevitably worn suits; at a stylish do, he had just as inevitably arrived in denims. In his heart of hearts, he was quite looking forward to the day when nobody went to Mass anymore. Then he would become a daily communicant. In the meantime, he must beware and be aware. To copy others was bad enough; to plagiarise from oneself would be worse. Envy was venial; pride was mortal.

But it didn't ring true, any of it. Not really. In fact, it didn't ring at all. It rattled. It was a mix of death-rattle and baby's rattle, of something in a bad way deep inside him, something dying to be done with; yet something living too, new and noisy, still unspeaking, speechless even, all throat and no tongue. The whole of Theo was wondering.

Am I a bullshitter?

Could it be that? Could it be that simple? Were they the missing eleven letters at the heart of the crossword? Was that the word that was the key to the clues across and down? The one that gave you 'cardiac', 'Celt' and 'modern'? That won you invitations to an opening night at the theatre, where the loathing among look-a-likes left the end of *Hamlet* standing? Or that sent you a box of Beaujolais for your next black eucharist with a circle of short-lease allies?

Am I a bullshitter?

'Right, right, right,' said Felicity.

'I hear you,' said the driver of the hearse.

'Forgive me,' she said. 'But I hate getting lost. I don't know why. It may be that I was lost as a child in a supermarket. That would have been a powerful and primordial lostness for a little girl, to be stranded among dead cucumbers and the corpses of cod, with many male voices murmuring at me from the public-address system, adding an element akin to auditory hallucination to what was already an experience of drastic de-realisation. Little wonder I pooed in my pants.'

'Quite,' said the hearse-driver. He always said 'quite' when he didn't understand. Or 'indeed'. But 'quite' was better. It was a bit English. Whenever he did a Church of Ireland removal, it was quite this and quite that, with never a trace of a tear; whereas the other lot would blather and blubber and tuck cigarettes in the small of their hands, like policemen do, during the prayers at the graveside.

'You were saying,' Theo said.

'Quite,' said the hearse-driver. 'I mean, quite what was I saying?'

'About the Bolshoi,' Theo said. 'And your daughter.'

'Before you cut me off in mid-sentence?' said the hearse-driver.

'It wasn't me,' said Theo. 'It was Felicity. She's a compulsive rambler. She does it to everyone. She does it to me, for God's sake. I don't know why she does it. Why do you do it, Felicity?'

She was penitent.

'When somebody runs a tap, I suddenly need to wee,' she said. 'Story calls to story, narrative to narrative, until the Word is broken like bread, the daily bread of the language we live within and die without. Be it soda or sliced, scones or . . . what other kind of bread begins with an S, Theo?'

'Quite,' said the driver of the hearse. 'But I don't hold with two people telling stories at the same time. It's unnatural. It's like, well, it's like group sex, isn't it?'

'Listen, Felicity,' said Theo. 'I appeal to your better

203

nature. Here we are, the three of us, thrown together by chance, huddled in a hearse, driving to Dublin. We've never met before; we may never meet again. Who knows? It's at least unlikely. Noel lives and works in the country, making a living from the dead. We live and work in the city, making a living from the dying. There are obvious social and educational disparities which I won't labour. Anyhow, they're immaterial. To be sure, we have certain things in common. All of us watch "Dynasty". None of us can speak a word of Irish. Yet the divergences too are legion. I look out my window at the glare and grime of an inflamed capital. Noel hears the twitterings of birds. I can't think offhand of any of their names, but you know the ones I mean. The ones that aren't classified as vermin.'

'Actually,' said the driver of the hearse, 'I look out on a bowling alley.'

'And I'll thank you to remember,' said Felicity, 'that my house – my family home, that is – overlooks a cricket club which is five-point-two acres big, with thirty-two adult trees, three of them copper beeches and all of them preserved. By court order.'

'What I'm trying to say,' said Theo, 'is that here we have this opportunity to listen to each other, to share something.'

'You can start by sharing the petrol,' said the hearse-driver.

'Do you realise,' Theo said, 'that between us, or is it among us, we have, gosh, about ninety years of lived human experience.'

'It's among,' said the hearse-driver. 'Anything over two is just among.'

'Speaking for myself and from myself,' said Theo, 'I would be very grateful to learn exactly what happened to your daughter at the Bolshoi.'

'Me too,' said Felicity. 'I love stories, especially when they're parables. The parables go on and on inside you for years. They stay there like shrapnel.'

The hearse-driver made up his mind.

'All right,' he said. 'What happened was that the girl who had the fight –'

'With your daughter,' said Felicity.

'Invited the whole class to the ballet, but not her. Not my daughter. So my wife went and bought tickets for the row in front of the party. The party party. But she didn't just buy two tickets, one for herself –'

'And one for your daughter,' said Felicity.

'She bought the whole row. Twenty-eight seats. Just so the parties in the other party, in the row behind them, would notice. That's it. That's the story.'

Felicity let a few seconds elapse.

'Christ,' she said. 'That's one story.'

'It would make you think,' said Theo. 'It would make you go away and think.'

'It makes Medea look like Mother Teresa,' said Felicity.

'It was better the last time I told it,' said the hearse-driver. He was a bit miserable.

'It's still sinking in,' said Felicity. 'I can feel it going down like a lump of an ice-pop.'

'It's an alpha plus,' said Theo. On the other hand, would he understand that? The last thing he wanted to be was patronising. But how could he get out of it dexterously?

'What Theo means,' said Felicity, 'is that it's an A plus. Ten out of ten.'

'I used to think so,' said the driver of the hearse. 'But I see now it's only a delta. At most, maybe, a delta commendation.'

'I never heard of a delta commendation,' said Felicity; but she said it nicely. She was sorry for him. She was even sad for him. The man was way down. If you dropped a pebble into him, you would not hear it hit the bottom.

So she decided to change the topic of the conversation. It was like when you visited a friend in the mental hospital. You might want to talk about the healing power of the Holy Spirit, but it was wiser really to stick to the weather and how depressing it was.

'Your daughter must have loved the Bolshoi,' she said.

'One thing I have never seen is the Bolshoi,' said Theo.

'How many of them have defected now?' said Felicity.

'The ballet died the death,' said the hearse-driver.

'My God,' said Felicity. 'I never knew that. What happened? Was it something like Legionnaires'? You really don't know the hour nor the day, do you? Private medicine or no private medicine.'

'She went to London,' said the driver of the hearse. 'For tests and things. For an audition. But when they went and X-rayed her hands and feet, you see, they were able to tell her that, well, it was more a case of camogie than Covent Garden. She was all Eliza Doolittle and no Professor Higgins, sort of thing. And after that, she went into a decline. Gave her leotards away at the door to someone who was collecting clothes for the chronic unemployed. Went sort of hard and headstrong. Found a boyfriend, a fellow who wore goggles on a Honda 50, and called everybody "mate" because he'd been out to see his uncle in Australia. But then there was this mother and daughter of a row, because the wife started snooping, didn't she? Rummaging round in the daughter's bedroom, one weekend. That was the same weekend the Pope came to Ireland. The same weekend the shit hit the fan. Because what did she find inside the balalaika, only letters.'

'French letters?' said Felicity.

'Exactement,' said the hearse-driver. 'The fellow was off in the South of France, picking grapes. Probably picking pockets, too. But he missed her, he said. He missed her smile and he missed her singing; but most of all he missed her Prudence. The touch of it, the smell of it, the shyness and the secrecy of it. Of course, the daughter was down in the kitchen, weeping she was, swearing curses and swearing oaths that, no, what he meant was her hair; and the wife said nothing, but she went on hitting her fist off the wall under the spice-rack, wallop, wallop, until she'd crushed each and every one of her knuckle-bones. The doctor did an X-ray, same as they'd done in London on the daughter, and he told her that when she was sixty, she'd suffer terrible pain. From the calcification in her bones. Because photographs may lie, but an X-ray doesn't. You look at your bones, and you see your whole future fleshed out: "Swan Lake" down the rubbish chute, arthritis in the service hatch. Wishbones sucked and broken.'

'I think Prudence is such a lovely name for your little wound,' Felicity said. 'I think it's so romantic. It's better than all those Beatrix Pottery names that people think up.'

'But they made it up?' said Theo. It was strange, when you thought about it, that you used a phrase like that to describe a reconciliation. When he was little, it had always meant to pretend.

'Did what?' said the man.

'Made it up?' Theo said.

'Not a word of it,' said the hearse-driver. 'Scout's honour, it is God's truth. The only time I ever made anything up was when I made up my mind. Twice.'

'But your wife and daughter, they smoked the pipe of peace?' said Theo.

'Alas,' said the driver of the hearse, 'in these matters

my wife is a non-smoker. She fumes, yes. She lights up constantly. But she doesn't smoke.'

Felicity was thinking of the names that Theo called her parcelled parts. Some of them were nice; others were strictly for the point of precipitation, to be used spasmodically, or was it sporadically? There were a few which were blue, a few which were purple, and one or two which bordered on she didn't know what. But they bordered; that was the point. So it might be a thought to set up some checkpoints. Theo had told her they were only diminutives; but 'diminutive' appeared on the same page as 'diminish' in her dictionary. 'Dim' was there too. She wasn't sure what 'utive' meant, but she would find out. If it had anything to do with the uterus, that was the last time she would let him call her Lady Macbeth, diminutive or no diminutive.

'I went to the Mass in the Park,' Theo was saying. 'Of course, I didn't go to Communion. I just went to observe. I wanted to be able to tell my great-grandchildren that I'd seen the Pope, when the office was still held by a person who was male and ordained. Actually, I kneeled down when he passed in the Popemobile. Pandemonium exerts fierce peer-pressure. I sometimes imagine I might have saluted at the Nuremberg rallies, only I would have been in Dachau at that stage.'

'Dublin would have been nice,' said the hearse-driver, 'but Galway was nearer. As well as that, it was specially for the teens and twenties. So we packed her off. When she came back, two days later, she was a Buddhist. More to the point, she was with a Buddhist. Now who the hell let Buddhists into a Mass, even if it was open-air? Can you imagine what they'd do with a Christian in Mecca?'

'Was he a nice Buddhist?' said Felicity. 'Some Buddhists are lovely, a bit like Friar Tuck. And the way the snakes come out of the hat and dance for them is amazing. I'd love to go to London and see it sometime.'

'I showed him where the loo was,' said the man. 'I showed him where the ashtray was; and then I showed him where the front-door was. I even shook his hand. The wife couldn't, because her hand was still bandaged. In the meantime, the daughter fled upstairs. Off with the third degree of concentration, and on with the third degree of pure pain. For weeks on end, there was neither peace nor ġuite. I mean, quiet.'

Theo was beginning to feel sleepy; and why not? The day was getting on; it was old enough by now to have taken early retirement. Already, many of the cars that were passing had their dims on; he had even seen one with its headlights shining. That sort of driver would leave the polythene seat-covers on in the car for a month or two after the last valeting; or perhaps she'd killed a child on a hairpin in among hedgerows, early or evening of a day that was now forever floodlit, hearing a smudged thud and a cry like a matchstick striking as she held receipts to the wheel and read off hairspray, kiwis, Jelly Tots. They were the times to watch, darkness and dawn, the times when shadows were shapes and shapes shadows. In between, from the morning milk-round to the message left in a bottle late at night, was plain and pasteurised; but, at either end, it was best to smell the jug before you poured it.

'She was in a sulk?' said Felicity.

'She was in a sulk with six bedrooms and bathrooms *en suite*,' said the driver of the hearse. 'It was a sulk that came with carpets and curtains. She'd sit there for hours, you see, in the lettuce position, meditating. And she had these tapes she'd listen to, full of gongs and boings. Oh, she'd wear her Walkman, but you could still hear them.

Goat-bells and groaning. She told me she was searching for the Way, for this Way and that Way and I don't know what Way. But would she set the fire for me? No way.'

'And you coming in frozen from your funerals,' said Felicity. 'Because cemeteries are such cold places, aren't they? You can feel the cold of a cemetery in your bones, even if somebody gives you their coat to wear over your catsuit. Mind you, it can be perishing at a cremation, too. I was at a cremation in January, and I was hoping the business of burning would help to heat the room; but it didn't. And to make matters worse, half the people present wanted to say a few words. It was mostly baloney, of course, because the creep in the casket was a total invertebrate, a yes-man of the first order anybody barked at him. In fact, this was probably the first time in his whole life that he'd stood up to any heat. But I wasn't there for him. I was there for his wife, a wonderful woman who was also Assistant Examiner in three of my mid-terms. Even so, I decided there and then that, in future, crematoria were off my list. Once frostbitten, as they say.'

'She's doing it again,' said the hearse-driver to Theo. 'I mean, she's worse than a pirate radio station. I'm the broadcast, and she's the breakthrough. Now she's talking about crematoria. Next thing you know, she'll be introducing John Wayne to the Western.'

But Theo was feeling far too comfy to say anything. Besides, he was watching the driver of the car in the next lane. Was he or was he not singing along to the same song that was playing, albeit with the volume down to the point of disappearance, on the radio in the hearse? Was the same vintage vinyl from the Beach Boys making their toes tap under shoe-leather and the canvas of sneakers? Were they strangely equal, equally strange, blood brothers in a commonwealth of the medium wave? Were they, in fact, on the same wavelength? It seemed possible, even probable, because Theo didn't need to lip-read now: the guy was slapping the wheel in perfect time to the tiny notes he could overhear himself. And that was nice when you thought about it, even if the other car did put on speed and pass them out. A fellow always drove faster when they played a song that slowed him down inside, that brought him back to tennis-hops, stag-nights, buskers at a cinema queue, the whisky and elastic of first-love in a bed-sit. Memory Lane was Formula One territory. It was a pity they didn't remember that when they handed down convictions for dangerous driving.

'Never mind him,' Felicity said to the hearse-driver. 'Theo thinks you're an intellectual if you never hear what people are saying to you. But that's just because he's always watching current-affairs programmes where they're trying to do a link-up between London and Leningrad, and the poor unfortunate at the other end keeps dropping his earpiece and asking the interviewer to repeat the question. Then you discover that he learned English from a physicist in a labour camp, and that his only textbook was a complete Shakespeare. Can you imagine letting him loose in Leeds or Liverpool? Sure the most modern English he knows is probably *perestroika*. But Theo is a guru's groupie. He'd give his vocal chords to have a mid-European accent.'

'Does he want to be a Buddhist?' said the driver of the hearse.

'No,' she said, 'he wants to be a neurologist. I want him to be plastic or genito-urinary. Neurology has more prestige, of course, because it's more healing and harrowing, and sort of Christ-like; but the pay is shit. Whereas the genito-urinary stuff brings in big bucks. It's not glitz, it's not glamour: the bottom line is, you're clearing the drains. But for every roof that a storm rips off, a thousand toilets get badly blocked. So the neurologists sail dinghies and think about St Jude, the genito-urinaries sail yachts and think about St Tropez. Neither thinks about Buddha, believe me. If you're a child of the Accident, the Orient is beyond you.'

'I brought some books home from the local library,' said the hearse-driver. 'Books about Buddha. *A Child's Guide to the Great Religions* and *The Book of Amazing Facts*. And they were, too. Did you know that Buddha was a married man? Maybe not a valid marriage, you know, from a Christian point of view, or even from a Buddhist, because he wasn't a Buddhist yet. He was still plain Buddha. But he walked out on the wife and a child as well. Never looked back.'

'In his heart of hearts,' said Felicity, 'he might have felt remorse in later years. Remorse, or even an anxiety depression.'

'No,' said the driver of the hearse. 'I mean that he never looked back, literally. Left a wife and two children. Like that. Went off whistling into the woods. And why?'

'To roger one of the white women,' Felicity said. 'Indians have a thing about blondes.'

'To seek enlightenment,' said the hearse-driver.

'Same thing,' Felicity said.

'Enlightenment, no less,' said the hearse-driver. 'Well, I thought to myself: that's a strange bloody way of looking for enlightenment. I mean, if you don't find it at home, where else are you going to find it? There's your breakfast, lunch and dinner if you want enlightenment. There's your feast and famine in one. A home, a wife and three children, and he throws it all up like vomit. To seek enlightenment. As if he didn't have a light-switch in every room already. As if you have to walk to the Dead Sea for salt, when the cellar in the press is full to flowing; as if you have to climb the Himalayas for a mouthful of snow, when there's cool water at the twist of a tap. No, no, it's a long word, enlightenment is, but I think I'd trade each letter of its length for the chance to put a small child on a potty at two in the morning, or the chance to wake up and smell my wife in the bed beside me, a sleep-and-vodka smell, you know, when light from the sun itself has taken the trouble to travel, Christ, thousands of miles to my discount shaving-mirror on the window-ledge, and make it brighten like, well, like a monstrance.'

'Jesus left his family,' said Felicity. 'He left Bethlehem for the bright lights, same as Buddha. Lots of people have. Look at Florence Nightingale. Some people have a sense of mission. Most people don't. Most people just have sense. That's the way that God intended it. There are loads of ordinary mushrooms, a few poisonous mushrooms, and a small number of magic mushrooms. People are the same. Most of us have dandruff in our hair; some of us have stardust.'

'Don't talk to me about stardust,' said the driver of the hearse. 'I've seen stardust. At least, I've seen moondust; and the moon is a star. I know you meet these clever-dicks from time to time, the ones that tell you whales aren't fish and bats aren't birds; that they're both mammals, same as ourselves. But where does that leave you? A child of five can tell you that we don't spout or hang from the rafters. But you check out any basic biology textbook the kids are using nowadays, and what do you find? You find that we're in there, you and me and Rip Van Winkle here, in among Labradors and orang-utans and ant-eaters; and nobody's going round like a bear with a sore head about it. Some Nazi numbskull four-letters the Israelites and he ends up stitching mail-sacks; but a Harvard high-brow brings the ant-eaters in to hear the

2 I 3

will of God being read, and, lo and behold, he's a Nobel laureate.'

'All the same,' said Felicity, 'we have to make discriminations. Think how a person with red–green deficiency would fare as a fashion designer. Or a Christian sitting as a Judge in an Appeal Court. They would just not be able to discriminate. Everything would go to Hell. It would be like a wine-cellar without labels. Nobody would be able to tell the difference any longer, not even by the dust; because nowadays the dust is put on afterwards. And if you couldn't tell the difference, you couldn't see the similarity either. Metaphor would be changed beyond recognition. In fact, you'd end up losing everything: first the figures, the ones that add up, and then the figures of speech, the ones that do all the multiplying. Anyhow, the fact that I'm a mammal makes me feel a sort of ineffable affinity with the whale, even if I can't spout or fill an oil-lamp in an igloo. On the other hand, of course, my affinity doesn't mean that I don't approach the whale without a strong sense of its Otherness. A quite brotherly Otherness, you understand, but an Otherness which, howsoever brotherly, rests and remains essentially Other, notwithstanding its surface appearance. I may have a whale of a time, but I also have time for the whale. And a final footnote of lunar length. The moon is a planet, not a star.'

Felicity was starting to feel quite drowsy herself. Maybe the man had the heater on, or maybe her determination always to be alert and articulate in order to represent her kind as resourcefully as possible was beginning to tell. Even Simone de Beauvoir could not be the burst water-main for a thousand-and-one street parties in the space of a single day; why, even Martin Heidegger, than whom no one, with the possible exception of his wife, could be more heroically *Herrlich*, must, at moments, have relaxed his rigour sufficiently to chat up a useful contact at a faculty shindig. You might call it Being-in-the-right-place-at-the-right-time.

'I was there,' said the driver of the hearse. 'I was there on the day. I queued with a little girl whose plaits kept coming undone, because I'd made them. And she was excited, she thought it'd be like something out of "Doctor Who", this Lunar Exhibition up in Dublin. You know the way they have these stones that are magical and light up, and you can look into them and see the Professor that's trapped, and the beam from them carbonises the monsters that are wearing the chainmail out of last week's episode of "Robin Hood". Well, that's what she thought, so she put on her pretend sunglasses. But the queue took forever, it must have taken three ice-pops and a packet of Opal Fruits; and she was asleep in my arms by the time we reached this moondust. I was half expecting Lenin's Mausoleum at that stage, a sort of Seventieth Wonder of the World, a cornerstone; and it wasn't either. It was just dust. If you saw it on the carpet, you'd make everybody show you their shoes.'

'I was at the Exhibition, too,' Felicity said; and she pursed her lips, as if she was sucking in lipstick. It was not nice to yawn, either from a social or a sexual point of view. People might think they were boring you, which could shatter their self-confidence; or they might start stiffening downstairs, because a yawning mouth was an immediate metonym for a yearning vagina. Felicity remembered yawning her way through a long evening with a nice boy whose thumb was deformed because his parents didn't believe in soothers. He had been at her to go to bed, that boy had. But they were all alike: the brains of Yogi Bear with the sprint-time of Speedy Gonzales.

'What I couldn't understand,' said the hearse-driver, 'was the waste of money. These crewcut college guys coming back like Captain Cook, but where's the tree that nobody's named? Where's the koala bear? Where's the aborigine, prodded down the gangplank to have his picture taken with a ga-ga dowager? He blinks and beams, but the whole of him is hidden: his language lies within him, in under his tongue like a cyanide pellet. And the band plays "Waltzing Matilda" because Australia has been discovered, and isn't it marvellous? But these guys step off the plane with a capsule of dust, and I queue for three hours to examine a bit of wet sand from Brittas Bay. So much for stardust. Well, if that's stardust, then the earth is a star. Maybe we should put the earth on top of the Christmas tree. Maybe that's the star we should steer by. Street-signs instead of Sirius. Any one of them would bring you to a place where a baby was being born in conditions that would call for a steward's inquiry if it were a foal instead of a foundling.'

Felicity yawned again. She just couldn't help it.

'I've never seen an ox or an ass in a maternity hospital,' she said. 'A hamster, once. They had to cover it in a labour gown in case the other mothers miscarried.'

'Maybe the mother is the ox,' said the driver of the hearse. 'The father would be the ass. But there are no more stables, anymore. No more stable places. Only cribs. People cribbing endlessly. And no more stars. Sand from the strands. Beached bits and pieces.'

His voice was low and level. She liked that. She liked the long approach to shut-eye, the cosy cabin-pressure of it. You were aware, but not awake; loaded with a lens-cap on: ready, steady, stay a while. The cat's eyes might be quite unlike the eyes of any cat you'd ever seen; still, they made you think. They made you think how much would the man who invented them have made after tax? Because zips had made more than trousers. That was a fact. Felicity would like to have invented something. Could she invent a car for the blind? You could sneer all you want, but it was probably round the corner. Nietszche said that Our Lord was dead, and there was a rush on Penguin Books. But then the British created the National Health System, or was it Service, and that was surely more Bible than Beveridge, straight from the Sermon on the Mount, in fact, and therefore the greatest Christian achievement of the age, even if the fountainhead of the Reformed Church was a syphilitic shambles. Thanks be to goodness Shakespeare had not been a playwright when Henry VIII had a box at the Globe. He would have been burnt before he had finished his Middle Period; and the pain of the faggots would have hurt him less horribly than the realisation that he would never write *The Tempest*. Perhaps he dictated the storyline to his secretary as the flames flamed flamingly around him. That would explain why it is such a short play.

'Shakespeare believed in the stars,' she said to the driver of the hearse. 'He developed a philosophy which was called The Great Chain of Being. It influenced everybody until Karl Marx came along. His philosophy tried to forge links with a new beginning. I won't try to summarise it because it's ineluctably complex, but, basically, he felt we had nothing to lose but the Great Chain. When it was lost, we were left with Being, and that's what Martin Heidegger spent his life writing about. Actually, he wrote even more than Karl Marx had. He must have written, maybe, fifty books; and each of them is thicker than *Gone With the Wind*. That may help to give you some idea. Of course, Shakespeare proliferated a lot himself. He has something wise and wonderful to say about everything, though he concentrates a good bit on sex and violence, as well as on the Great Chain and stars. The tit and bum is really for the tabloid toughies in the parterre, the vinegar regiment; but the Great Chain and stars is strictly for the samurai. The real stars, that is. I don't mean horoscopes, of course. How anybody can read a horoscope is beyond me; and, no matter how many you read, they're all the same, anyway. No, I mean Vincent Van Gogh stars, like at the Post-Impressionist Exhibition, where I was with a member and I didn't have to queue. Those stars were out of this world; they were unearthly. As long as I live, I shall hold a candle for those stars.'

'If people believe that the stars influence them,' said the man, 'then they will be influenced by the stars. That's what I think, anyhow. Belief creates faith, and faith creates fate. If a patient believes he has cancer, that patient will die. If, on the other side, a terminal cancer patient doesn't believe that he has cancer, well, he'll die too; but he'll die much more happily. His death will be shrouded, the same as for anyone, but shrouded in mystery. One minute he'll be trying to remember the capital of Panama; the next, a brain-cell blows like a lightbulb, and his daughter's thinking, can she call her brother in Canberra on the hospital phone without having to fork out a fiver? And will they let her call free if she donates his corneas? If only he'd asked her, she thinks, if only he'd spoken out sooner, she could have been there for him. She could have told him that the capital of Panama is Panama City; then he would have died in peace.'

'I never knew that,' said Felicity. 'About Panama. That's because I dropped Geography to do Greek. The nun who taught Geography began with the A's, and went on from there. She had a crush on the alphabet. She even taught us the meaning of every single Christian name, starting, of course, with A. She said it was for when we had babies, but who'd call a boy in a bouncer Aethelred? So, as a result, I know heaps about Afghanistan and Barbados, but shit about France or Germany. By the time I decided that I could be a lover of all things Greek without any of this heavy breathing bull, Sister Penny had done a second Phineas Fogg on the nations of the world. When I repatriated to the Geography class, she was up to Qatar, and trying to explain that God put the oil in the Moslem countries because He really thought the Crusaders would clinch it.'

'God is brainier than that,' said the driver of the hearse. 'Why He put the oil there is because He wanted them to westernise themselves. When they're up on their camels, they have a different perspective, don't they? Give them some money, and they don't know themselves; so, already, they're halfway to being like us, aren't they? Bowing to Mecca five times a day is great gas if you're wearing sheets and blankets; but you feel a bit of a fool in a handmade business suit and a briefcase stuffed to Kingdom Come with the day's faxes. They may have stood their ground against bows and arrows, yes; but a year or two of strong satellite telly, and they'll be every bit as Christian as you or me. All you need to do is show them Christendom; you don't have to sell it. Christendom is well able to sell itself. Now, the people who market our kind of culture, the people who pros . . . who pros . . . what is that word that begins with Pros?'

'Proselytise?' said Felicity, and she squirmed her bottom because it had gone to sleep; it had gone all pins and needles. The rest of her too was bone-tired in a nice, nice way. Her eyelids felt so heavy she would have needed sellotape to keep them open, like Aristotle who-the-hell-was-he Onassis, yes, the poor man; or was his name Plato? Plato Onassis? That didn't sound right, but Theo would know, because Anthony Quinn had played the part to a T. Felicity had never understood Theo's thing about Anthony Quinn. Perhaps it was a homosexual hangover from adolescence. Of course, there were as many hangovers from adolescence as from alcohol. Each commenced with staring into wishing wells, and each concluded with staring into toilet bowls. Such was life, though she could not say so anymore, now that Theo had a relationship with that phrase, a relationship which had entered the heavy-petting stage.

'Proselytise,' she said again. It was a horrid word for a horrible job of work. Thank goodness Jesus did his thing before you had to go to briefing sessions with image consultants or press the flesh on 'Meet the Press' before planting six stupid trees that hooligans would douse with gasoline the next night. Actually, if he were here now and called to the door, you would probably think he was just another of those Christian fundamentalists and not a Roman Catholic.

'Precisely,' said the hearse-driver, though he didn't say 'Proselytise', because it was something of a sword-swallow. 'Even the ad-breaks on a European station say something to Islam. Sure, you meet these yahoos from the university who like to jeer at Windowlene and washing powder, but they wouldn't last long without soft toilet paper; and they don't like using the hard stuff in the men's toilet, because they know that everybody can hear. Then you find the soft bits in their bottom drawer, and they tell you they've a cold. So, what am I to think? Is that hygiene or hypocrisy?'

Felicity was seeing stars. Lots of them. It was just as well they only came out at night. If they came out during the day, you would never get from A to B. You would be welling up inside you everywhere: at the pass-link, at the photocopier. And if you saw them and didn't have a sensation, you would feel so proletarian. You would realise that, inside, you were a vacuum, a vacuum cleaner at best, a mouth that gathered dust: a Hoover in hiding. That was Dolores. Within herself, Dolores was without. She didn't follow the stars, or, if she did, they lived in Beverly Hills. No, she followed the road; she followed the cat's eyes. That was Dolores.

'Hypocrisy and hygiene have a lot in common,' Felicity said. 'But that's an insight which I've just had, here and now, so it'll be a few days before I can understand it. I'm sorry to tantalise you. It's my nature, you see. I'm like the woman whose waters broke at the infertility clinic. One baby, no bump. So she had to think the whole thing through again, but backwards. Signs and symptoms, probable causes. It would have been like putting a court case together. Actually, she was putting a court case together. But the point is, I have these insights all the time, and most of them don't make sense. What you have to do is stick with them. It's good gardening, really. The most earth-shattering act of all is to go and plant something. A stick today, a shoot tomorrow. You have to be patient with everything, especially your insights. You have to take the view that, well, you never know. I'm pretty sure they would have chucked a can-opener in the bin two hundred years ago; but they would have been sorry when cans were invented. My mother is great that way: she had a brush for cleaning toasters twenty years before toasters appeared; even now, she's kept an unused pocket-diary for 1986 because she can use it again in 1998.'

'My mother was great as well,' said the hearse-driver. 'I put that on her grave, under the other bits. "She was a great mother". Just that. I thought it said everything.'

'I think I may be having another insight,' said Felicity.

'About what?' said the driver of the hearse.

'Hypocrisy and hygiene,' said Felicity.

'Fire ahead,' said the man.

'I would not be surprised,' Felicity said, 'if you found that men buy less deodorant in American states with no gun-control laws. What would surprise me would be the opposite.'

'I agree,' said the hearse-driver.

'It would be an astonishing insight,' said Felicity, 'if it turned out to be true.'

'It rings true,' said the man.

'I think I may try it out on Theo when he wakes up,' said Felicity. 'Swift used to read everything he wrote to his servant, to be certain sure that even a complete and utter imbecile could understand it. You can imagine poor Patrick, having to sit there in the Cathedral while Presto was up in the pulpit, declaiming the Collected Works; and, every quarter-hour, he'd bellow at him: "Can you construe that, Patrick?", and Patrick would be cracking a head-louse in between his thumbnails, and he'd look up and say, "Oh, I think you're chipping away, Bishop, chipping away. What else can you do with a baby-mountain? Only I don't see what you have to be modest about. If I were you, I'd just call it 'A Proposal'. Modesty will get you nowhere nowadays." So Swift would bung it off to his editor at Macmillan, and the two of them would go and get sozzled in "The Fox and Chicken". Theo's a bit like Patrick that way. If he misses the point, I know I'm on to something.'

'Maybe you'd tell him what I said,' the hearse-driver asked her.

'About Buddha?' said Felicity.

'You could start with that,' said the hearse-driver. 'But the bit about the Holy Ghost working through Western technology to Christianise the Arabs.'

How many stars were up there in the firnament, or was it firmanent? One after the other after the other. They were like the lighted ends of cigarettes in a dark theatre, and more and more of the audience seemed to be smoking. Whenever she looked through her own reflection out into the night, tiny pinpoints glinted back that had not been there before. Had it taken God a trillion tests, light years in his laboratory, adjusting atoms and mixing molecules, before finally, fantastically, he got it right, and there was life; or, rather, there was Life? Leaves leaving, badgers badgering, stones stoning down, and Adam seeing how far he could piss in Paradise, pissing farther in fact than any of the gorillas, with an archangel using a retractable measuring tape to certify the distances for the Garden of Eden *Guinness Book of Records*. He would have been proud as punch then, Adam would. He would have summoned Eve in under a tree that was still nameless, and he would have treated her like an object. Or would he? After all, this was pre-Torah. This was the Indian summer before the Fall. So perhaps he would have treated her like a subject instead. Of course, that might have been worse. But because he had said 'You' to her, in under the tree with no name, it would have been known thereafter as a yew-tree. Felicity didn't like to think what had happened in under the birch. Unless Eve had given Cain a few marks there.

'That's the way the Holy Ghost works, of course,' said the hearse-driver.

'I don't think so,' said Felicity. 'I think the Holy Ghost is a pet. Imagine coming third through all eternity. There are never many photographs of a third child in a family album. And you can always tell a third child when he's grown up. He dresses badly. That's because he's used to hand-me-downs. I bet you anything the Holy Ghost wears Jesus's old jumpers.'

What was that lovely light out there and in among the stars, between the stalls and the lower balcony? When she was little, she would have thought it was a shooting star or an unidentified flying object. Now she was old; she knew better. She knew it was an unidentified flying plane. Shooting stars were for the stage-sets of West End musicals. She would not demean herself by thinking about them. It was nicer to think of all those ordinary people, heading off to Spain with their duty-free and their Diocalm. God bless them, they deserved a break from the mundanity and the meaninglessness of their lives. She wished them well. When she had graduated as a doctor, she would walk on tip-toe through the wards late in the evening, and she would kiss her patients goodnight, one by one, on their flushed foreheads, especially the ugly ones who had never known love. They would watch her through a blur of tears as she left the male surgical after another five-hundred-hour, twenty-day week. But she would not be bunking down. No, she would be in the research reading room, preparing a complex chemical formula for turning black skin white. For those who were tortured and traumatised by their negritude, this would be salvation indeed. And the formula would work in reverse, as well: liberal whites who loathed their plucked-chicken pigment could be blackened until they were truly at one with the cultures they liked to describe as colourful. They wouldn't have to worry anymore if the mandatory mulatto failed to arrive at their cocktails and canapés; they could still demonstrate their inordinate loving kindness by being the mandatory mulatto themselves.

'Don't go left again,' she said to the hearse-driver. 'Left again will take you the wrong way. There are two more right turns; then, when we hit the first traffic jam, we're almost home. If we're stopped for ages, that means we're headed in the right direction.'

Yes, thought Felicity, when we patent that procedure, there'll be a stampede to the surgeries. All the Left Bank sorts will come back from the private East Coast colleges, those harassed, hard-working poets and priests and philosophers who've given their lives so selflessly to another day at the Amstrad, writing about the deprived and the dispossessed. Now they can become what they love: the Jew among the Gentiles, the pigeon among the cats. Oh, they won't know themselves. They'll be so happy, they won't ever feel the same again. No more conference papers with the smell of sherry on your breath: you're free as a bird to live like one. From hand to mouth, from beak to claw. Bin-liners and Bovril. Plus you can paper over the cracks with the xeroxes from the Strasbourg seminar, the one where you lectured for ninety minutes on 'Street Riots: the Mass, the Masses and the *Kermess*', and then met the delegate from Madrid, the woman who swallowed her wedding-ring before you balled her, the one with the hairy bottom who got on the phone to her toddler and babytalked to him, standing there naked beside the bed; naked except for a bra that was open but didn't fall off.

It was queer, really. Always she began off with a big thought, the full orchestra; but it ended with a sexy situation, a frisky little piccolo. She knew she was complex, creative, and cosmopolitan. Loads of men had told her that, even the ones who did not want to sleep with her. They would be the homosexuals. But she was basically an Earth mother. Her brain might be heavier on the scales in the Anatomy room, but her womb weighed more with her. In, of course, a very feminist way: blood, tears, sweat, and coil. Still, it was just as well she had never worn her two Puritan collars in seventeenth-century Massachusetts. They would not have seen behind her bosom to her Abraham. They would not have seen her thinking big thoughts about chemical colordosis.

'Do you think,' she said to the man, 'that you could change the colour of a man? I don't mean sins. I mean skin.'

'Well,' said the driver of the hearse, 'why not? If you can change a man's mind, you've as good as changed his brain, haven't you? There are people going about these days with a pig's heart inside them, and it doesn't seem to make them any less heartbroken, does it? Although I wonder how they feel when they pass a slaughter-house or when they're at the Past Pupils' Reunion Dinner Dance, and they're served pork.'

'It would be just a dinner, not a dance,' said Felicity.

'Exactement,' said the hearse-driver. 'Très exactement. And the same applies to sex-changes. You can have a sex-change nowadays. So they think of everything. These scientists we have, they're always one step ahead of the possible. They'll think of a cure for Aids next. In fact, they might even be working on a disease that doesn't exist yet. I'm a bit like that, myself. I never get headaches. Why's that? Because every day I take ten Anadin, regardless. I keep the Anadin in one pocket, and the antacids in the other. A bit like pistols in a holster. The least twinge, and I give myself both barrels between my eyes. So I understand how the scientists think. In leaps and bonds.'

'Bounds,' said Felicity.

Where was that lovely light? The airplane glow? But it shouldn't still be there, and it was. Unless that was the return flight from somewhere in Spain, full of widows called Carmen with a flock of famished goats in the stowage bins, and their dark-eyed daughters in the loos, calling 'Momento, momento' as they stashed the facial cleansers and the soap-bars inside their mantillas, or was it tortillas? And maybe the last surviving English veteran of the Spanish Civil War was in the first class, on his way to Wolverhampton after having hidden out in a dry watertank above an English pub in Torremolinos for half a century, wholly unaware that the Fascists had handed in their last Toledo sword. If the *Sun* reporter to whom he'd sold the story didn't get him too jarred, he would probably expire with elation when he stepped off the plane and touched again the dear, democratic tarmacadam of his native land. He might even die on the bit that said 'Strictly No Stopping Here'. That was where the *Sun* would have stationed its photographers, anyhow. They probably had the sniper in the conning tower.

'You might get some blacks going for it,' said the hearse-driver. 'Because of History, you know. History did some pretty dirty, drastic, dreadful, downright deplorable things to the blacks. A lot of things that begin with D were done by History. I reckon the fellows in "Hill Street Blues" should put out an APB on History, and bring him in for questioning. He doesn't have much of an alibi, but he does have this incredible system of aliases. In fact, I wouldn't be surprised if he ended up using your name, or mine even. Oh, he's a black bastard, the same History. So I can understand why your average black might want three coats of whitewash. Life may imitate art, but it also imitates chess. White opens. As well as that, white's nice. A white woman with a strong sun-tan looks a picture; if she's really deep brown all over, a white woman looks a portrait. But then, of course, you stand into the shower with somebody who's mahogany from his midriff up, and you look at his bottom. And, by God, you could shove a sprig of parsley up it, and flog it in the deli as rhino rump.'

That wasn't any sort of star, shooting or still; and it wasn't a plane or a helicopter, either. It was the reflection of the hearse-driver's Hamlet, or the tip of it at least, lodged in the spokes of the steering wheel, a little like the fag-ends stuck in the frets of a mandolin at Woodstock. It was a long while since reality had tricked Felicity. She was foxy in a twofold, transatlantic manner: pussiable, yes, but perspicacious too. Still, she didn't mind. If you kept confusing things, that meant you were thinking clearly. Anglo-Saxon might call it a muddle, but Anglo-Saxon also called a come an ejaculation, which sounded like a word you would hear on a construction site. Greek, on the other hand, would translate a muddle into a metaphor. In fact, that was the word they used for porters and baggage-handlers: they were metaphors. You would go up to one of them, and say: 'Mr Metaphor, I have mislaid my Samsonite suitcase on the carousel in Terminal B'; and he would go find it for you. But that was what metaphors were good at: finding things you had lost, bringing your longings and your belongings back together again. It was really rather French of the Greek to make a metaphor out of metaphor itself. At least something had come of Napoleon invading them.

'I remember waiting one time in a church porch,' said the hearse-driver. 'Waiting for the Mass to be over, so I could bring out the body. Not, of course, that the Mass can ever be said to be over; in the sense, I mean, that the Mass is being said every split second of the day and night, somewhere or other: in Swiss, Swahili, Sanskrit. It's a great comfort, in a kind of way, a kind way even, to know that there isn't a moment of our lives when Christ isn't being broken into bits, privately or publicly. But the point is, I was there in the porch, and one of the little kids whose daddy had died was playing with my hat. Then he started playing with a black toddler, a girl it was, two, two-and-a-half. And a couple of women who were wearing black, were watching them play. One says to the other: "Isn't she sweet? What a shame she has to grow up." The other got a bit snooty, then. "They're in the same playschool," she said. "They sit together all the time. I think it's lovely, as a matter of fact." "They might even grow up and get married," said the first, sort of innocently. "My dear Gwen," says the other. "I have always said that I am a liberal. I have never purported to be an anarchist." That was when I stepped inside to collect the body. Straight down the aisle with it and out the front, where the two of them burst into tears. It was a real stopwatch start. If you needed to know which of the two of them was first off, you'd have to play it back in slow motion, like a track event.'

What was nice was not sleep; it was sleepiness. You could slip to sleep anywhere, a depot, a divan, but it was always the same place, the same bunk, the same bedroom: it was always the nursery with its nursery light in the corner. When the darkness brushed against you and the small gleams danced before your eyes, that was your mother's long pearl necklace swaying above you; and the moment of sleep was the slow enfolding in her sable wrap, the blue-black crush of it. Which meant, Felicity realised, that Shakespeare's mummy must have been very poor, what with her ravelled sleeve and all. Yet she was well-off enough to have a soft nurse. Or maybe the soft nurse had the ravelled sleeves. That would make sense. It would also explain why Shakespeare has lovely nannies in his plays, while the mothers are not what you could call pally-wally.

The stars were still there. They must have thought they were fucking fantastic, but they weren't. They were shit. Plumstones without the plum, that's what stars were. God's origami, scrunched up and swept aside. The whole cosmos was not, in fact, a wilderness. That would ennoble it. No, it was a ginormous waste-paper bin. If you opened up one of those balls and smoothed it out, you would find it was a foolscap page with the words, 'In the Begonninh'. Open another – say, Uranus – and, again, it'd be, 'In the Beginning was the Ward, and . . .', with a Prontaprint phone number in the margin.

Felicity had never quite realised it before. Oh, she had realised it in a perfunctory fashion, of course, but she had never realised it in the way in which you cannot be said to have realised anything until you have really, really, really realised it; or until it happens to you. If you wish to familiarise yourself with the aesthetics and the anaesthetics of totalitarian culture, it is deeply meritorious to sequester yourself in the Bodleian for a sabbatical. But it saves time to apply for a ten-minute pistol-whipping. Similarly, Felicity had always entertained a strong suspicion that perhaps God might have had a hand in the preliminaries. She had often felt handmade; she had sometimes felt a hand-maiden. She had never considered that putting an universe together might have given God grey hairs. He did look a bit, you know, in the pictures. Well, weather-beaten, to say the least. Mind you, His hair did have a spring in it; He was not dirty. But, to be blunt, you would not see Him at a society wedding, unless He was a distinguished film director. He would get away with it, then.

She looked up through her half-closed eyes. Was it

possible that God knew what it was like to lose some-thing? To lose heart, to lose hope, to lose out, to lose all? Even, perish the thought, to lose face? If He did, then he was no better than us, and what the shit was she doing, praying to Him? She might as well be praying to the hearse-driver, or to himself in the playground. She might as well be praying to somebody who was heading off to the gas-chamber or the firing squad or death by crucifixion.

But He hadn't lost everything. He had made it happen here. The earth was moving for everybody. It wasn't origami; it wasn't even blank paper: it was a blank cheque. Obviously, Felicity didn't know whether it was all by design or default. Maybe it was an accident, like penicillin, not that the guys with gonorrhoea give a damn. Perhaps one of the assistant angels in the laboratory spilled some Fairy Liquid in a test-tube full of carbon monoxide, and, Bingo, you had a human brain. That was the main thing. That was the headline. The small print may have muttered this and that about a thing called planned obso-lescence, but the noun meant nothing and the modifier meant the reverse: it meant that somebody else had done the preparation. After a time, you discovered that men were dying like flies, and, what was worse, that flies were dying like men. Even a thumped mosquito managed more grace than a guy with gall-stones. And, yes, it was hard. It was hard for an artist to paint a mountain, and then die, but the mountain would still be there. Not, of course, that there was any necessary connection between painting the mountain and dying. You did not die from painting mountains, unless you did it on a cold day and caught a kidney-chill, or unless the locals thought their God lived there, in which case they would run an assegai up your arse. Still, if you lived as long as a mountain does, you would end up turning into stone. Indeed, some people have achieved the consistency of stone by the time they're thirty. How much stonier would you be at your millionth birthday party? Your heart would be as heavy as lead, that's what. But you could show the same result simply by living a normal span at a normal pace as a normal creature of flesh and bloodshed, foosthering around your own furlong in some part of the Bush called Greyview Glen. Anyhow, who wants to be a mountain? So long as they're sacred, nobody scales them, which is how the mountains like it. The mountains probably enjoyed being above everybody else, back in the Bronze Age or whenever, in the times when the timber-line was territorial, and the least little avalanche from on high meant that another missionary had to be mutilated, and the video sent by scout to an altar halfway up the southern ascent. Nowadays, it was different. It was all après-ski and funiculars to the top, and men who had a complex about the size of their tools tap-tap-tapping with chisels and ropes in regions of rock where even the vultures got vertigo. And meanwhile, downstairs, you'd have geologists with their geiger counters, thinking to themselves that, yep, this is the world's richest supply of stainless steel, so let's destabilise the government and then destabilise the mountain. And the mountain hears them thinking, and wonders out loud; but all the geiger guys can see is a glazed look on the summit, and all they hear is the ping-pong noise of enormous boulders blabbering down into the glacier, into the elk-horns and the tea-leaves.

No, three score years and fifteen was a better brief. Less, even. Seventy would do. Because you could not cope with more. If you had the right support mechanisms, if you had a private room in a nice nursing home, if you had television and time to yourself, and if you had vitamin supplements, someone to hate, Plan D Health Insurance, belief in the hereafter, no visits from any of your grandchildren, paperbacks aplenty and selective amnesia about most of your life, then maybe, then perhaps you could cope with the grief of how many days and nights: twenty-five thousand days and nightmares in this world. But you could not cope with the joy. The joy of being in this world, the joy of being this world. Sooner or later, it would kill you. Sooner or later, you would push your way from the dance-floor, breathing in through your reddened mouth, your dress sticking to your hips and bottom, the strobe-lights sweeping the room, violet, ochre, as you stoop under a chair for your shawl and shoes; and out, out into the garden. There, out there, the cool of midnight would pick at the tiny hairs on your arm, and the taste of salt, like a single lacquered hair, would grain the tip of your tongue. A moment of the small hours would suffice. You'd turn again, to return; but the place would be empty, and the hostess would be down on her hands and knees, working on a wine-stain.

'I don't know,' said the driver of the hearse. 'I don't know what to think.'

That would be that, then. No wonder the dead stuck out their tongues in *rigor mortis*. It was not a Fuck You; no, they wanted flesh and blood and bread and wine. They wanted fish-fingers and lipstick, painkillers, pretend cigarettes, a man's tongue. Unless, of course, they were men. They wanted everything that had broken their hearts, because the things that break our hearts are always our most treasured possessions. A man will wear around his neck the bullet that the surgeon dug out of his side. It will be his lucky charm forever. There was even the case of the woman who put fresh flowers on the grave of the abortion she had gone for, in her fifth month. She had had to die with it for the restless rest of her life. When Felicity found the pigment formula, she would go into counselling and help everybody. She would show how, really, the joy of life is not only to be enjoyed, but to be endured as well; and why, at the end, it doesn't matter how we are broken, so long as we are broken open. Because life is not a *non sequitur*; it is a *res ipsa loquitur*. That is its meaning.

Felicity had not expected to stumble on the meaning of life in a hearse. She had thought it would dawn on her, late at night, in a church, after fasting for an eternity, maybe even a full day. But that was no sweat. Shostakovich had written the Leningrad symphony in a roadhouse. Even Hitler had written *Mein Kampf* in a prison, although that didn't really count, because he had only dictated it. He had not stared at the typewriter, the way he stared at everybody else. He had not shouted at it, the way he shouted at everybody else. And he hadn't ever thrown it across the cell. Marks on the wall were the mark of a real writer. Plus the shouting and the staring. They gave rise to beautiful works about inner peace. But Hitler could only dictate. That was how he would be remembered, and serve him right, too. She was never going to read the book, anyhow. She just liked the look of it, up there on the shelf, alongside *The Rule of Saint Benedict*. No wonder people who saw it gave her a strange look. They knew she was hot shit, culturally.

'Mind you,' said the hearse-driver, 'I get a week out of a pair of black trousers, and I only get a day out of a pair of white ones. So there's another perspective.'

What was the man rambling on about? Maybe you became weirdish in a business like his. Because most of the time you would have nobody to talk to, would you? If you started chatting to the corpse in the coffin, well, that would be certifiable, perhaps even criminal. And who else had he to talk to? He was alone with the dead all day. Of course, he might be a necrophiliac. Or, rather, a clever necrophiliac; one who had worked out ways and means of flashing in mortuaries. Yet, if he were a necrophiliac, he would be making a song and dance about how much he hated the work, because, as a rule, we always denounce the things we most desire. Perhaps he was legit. That would be boring. Then again, the truth generally is. Lies and falsehood are much more interesting. That was why you never got tired of people.

'It all depends,' said the driver of the hearse, 'on what you believe. I don't mean it like in the way that somebody says, "I believe there's a phone-call for you." Or, "I believe the chihuahua has gone and done it again." I don't mean that.'

'You mean,' said Felicity, 'what you believe inside of yourself.'

'No,' said the man. 'I mean, what you believe outside of yourself.'

Felicity did not correct his grammar. He was a nice man, poor fellow.

'Beliefs are too important to be left to yourself, or to be kept to yourself, either,' said the hearse-driver. 'That's why I took the Buddha books away from my daughter. I told her she could have them back when she was old enough to be bewildered by them. Otherwise she'd have all sorts of ideas, and they'd run away with her, wouldn't they? Having an idea, it's a bit like coming into money, isn't it? Ruin your life, it would. Alcohol's the same. One man can drink down twenty pints, no bother. Knew a navvy in Penge, used to fry his sausages in axle-grease. He'd knock back twenty-four pints in as many hours. But another fellow would be different. He might keel over if you spiced the fruit cocktail. Ideas are the same. Origen, he cut off his male member because of something in scripture about eunuchs. What happened, you see, is that he got an idea into his head. That was all it took.'

'Do you let your daughter read the Bible?' said Felicity.

'Here and there,' said the driver of the hearse. 'But the Bible's different. Jesus didn't walk out on a wife and family. And St Joseph was there to mind the mother. Obviously, he couldn't call them every night, but I'm sure he kept in touch by letter. And I have a theory, you know, about the parts in the Gospels where Jesus just disappears, and not even his disciples know from Adam where he is. Back home, that's where. Maybe the dad took a turn. Maybe he died. There's an ancient church tradition that says Jesus was at home when his dad passed on; and I believe it. In fact, I imagine that Jesus buried his father himself. Perhaps I think that because I want to be able to identify with him. Because it's my line of country, isn't it? They were simple people, so a simple grave. A wooden cross. An inscription: Joseph of Nazareth, born BC whenever, died AD whenever. No Saint this or that; no Patron Saint of Workers. Joseph wouldn't have wanted that. He was my kind of man. Lived quietly, loved quietly, died quietly. You know what I like to think? I like to think that when Jesus was on the Cross, and he was talking to his father, he was thinking of Joseph too. After all, your real father's the man you call Daddy, not the man you call Sir.'

'What does your daughter call you?' said Felicity. 'Does she call you Godfather or does she call you God the Father?'

'She calls me all sorts of names,' said the hearse-driver. 'It's a phase she's passing through. If your adolescent daughter doesn't hate you, there's something terribly wrong. But she'll hug me for ten minutes before she leaves the wedding reception.'

'Is that when you'll slip her a Gideon bible?' said Felicity. 'When she's married and mature, and able for it?'

'She's able for it now,' said the man. 'But she's not able and willing. Anyhow, I only ever censored the strong bits.'

'Your breasts are like antelopes,' said Felicity. 'Your in-between is like Gideon. Gideon must be gorgeous. They're the parts I want read at my wedding. Them, and "Love Me Tender, Love Me True" at the Communion.'

'I don't mean the Song of Songs,' said the driver of the hearse. 'The Song of Songs is mighty. I mean the Sermon on the Mount. If you took that to heart, you couldn't go on living. Not the way we survive, anyhow. You'd have to commit a kind of suicide, and start all over. From the foundations. Which is fine, of course, except that you have to clear the site first, and the site happens to be your home, a house on a twenty-year mortgage.'

That interested Felicity. She had always imagined that people like hearse-drivers would live in local authority housing. This man obviously had moved up. Either that, or this man earned more than you might imagine. Of course, between one thing and another, a lot of people did die. Winter must be a windfall for them, too. Asian flu must be the apple of their eye.

'You have to interpret sacred scripture sacredly,' she said. 'Sacred means mysterious, obscure, semi-unintelligible except to the inner eye which, thanks be to goodness, turns a blind eye to a great deal, because the inner eye is full of Christian love. It is much more concerned to secure free specs on the National Health for the peering multitudes than it is to wipe the wool and the sleep from its own lids. So you see.'

'I do,' said the hearse-driver, squinting into the darkness.

'On the other hand,' said Felicity, 'you can sometimes interpret scripture according to the letter, though according to the spirit is safer, as a rule. For instance, I had a great aunt who was greatly troubled by the "eye of the needle" business. She was, in fact, filthy rich.'

'There is no other way,' said the hearse-driver.

'You're right,' Felicity said. 'There's no point being rich, unless you can wallow. But she blew it. Not the money so much as the means to enjoy it. That she blew. She grew to be scrupulous. The eye of the needle was always there in the background, and it panicked her. What should she do? Should she invest in Heaven or swell, Paradise or premium bonds? Was a death-bed donation a safe bet? Should she instruct the mortician to dress her as a bag-lady when she died? Finally, a nice Monsignor told her that the Eye of the Needle was a name given to a gate in Jerusalem, a gate that was so narrow all the camels and the water-buffaloes had to be unloaded before they could pass through. Three days later, she threw a party that was so out of this world it passeth understanding. But she was still uncertain. Her spirit was still unquiet.'

'That is the nature of the spirit,' said the man. 'It will toss and turn until the alarm goes off.'

'It was only a matter of time before she went to Jerusalem,' said Felicity. 'And straight the next morning to the Eye of the Needle gate. On the fifth attempt, she squeezed through on a camel, carrying three suitcases and five handbags. After that, she never looked back. She spent her last twelve years in the lap of luxury in a Swiss psychiatric clinic that was designed by Le Corbusier.'

The driver of the hearse was blessing himself. Was it something she had said, or were they passing a church?

She twisted slightly to see better, and, sure enough, there was a monstrosity on the side of the road. If God ever dropped down again, He would not stay in a place like that, all cold and candle-droppings. He would stay in the presbytery and play poker with matchsticks while the curate re-wired the spare electric blanket in the guest room. But why would the driver of the hearse have blessed himself when he wasn't on duty? It was like a doctor prescribing for scabies in the foyer of a theatre. He wasn't on call; therefore, there wasn't any call for it. Or was he a religious maniac? Worse than that, was he spiritual?

'Are you very spiritual?' she said to him.

'Jesus, no,' said the man. 'Spiritual? You can be spiritual if you're a beggar or a billionaire; but, if you're just about managing, you can only afford to be religious. I'm religious, all right; but that's my business, even if it has gone to the wall once or twice. Of course, I can live with that because, well, giving up the ghost is more or less my line of territory. I mean, I don't go overboard about anything. I might do, if I could see any lifeboats on the trestles, but I never have. Sure, I have some attitudes, a few assumptions, that sort of thing. No opinions, though. I just don't like the word. I never did. I have this image in my head of someone weeping as they skin a pair of spectacles. Then again, if I were Dutch or Danish, I might well opinionate like mad; but the word you were doing would be different, wouldn't it? Well, the long and the short of it is that I don't have any opinions. I have a conviction, but that's for drunken driving. I won't go into it. Anyhow, it's in the past; it's behind me. Just behind me. Overall, I would say that, yes, I'm religious, definitely, but not indefinitely; because my full stops keep turning into trailing dots and then repeating decimals, until they end up looking like the Northern Lights. You can imagine how much worse it would be if you were spiritual. No, I'm happy enough to be one of the maintenance engineers in Bomber Command, instead of a Spitfire ace in a fighter-pilot squadron.'

'But do you believe?' said Felicity. Her drowsiness was oozing into her like the sludge from an oil-slick sloshing slowly into the white wing-feathers of a cormorant, or was it an albatross? There were so many birds, she thought. Too many, really. It must be a frightful headache for birdologists. And there were sixty-five thousand different kinds of beetle all over the world. She had seen that on 'Sale of the Century'. Thank goodness Ireland was an island: thank goodness she lived in an age of pesticides. Anyhow, sixty-five thousand was nothing. There were over three billion different kinds of human being. Plus we had flame-throwers.

'I do and I don't,' said the driver of the hearse. 'I reckon the god you know is better than the god you don't. So I haven't gone the whole hog, the way my wife did when she took her name off the baptismal register. That was a sort of Hell-hath-no-fury affair, but the priest said that only love could hate that deeply. I don't know. Maybe, maybe not. The thing is, I suppose, that God is our biological parent, but you get fierce attached to the people who adopted you, the folk you live with. Now, I can live with Christianity most of the time; what I need, though, is to go away for the odd weekend, the out-of-town affair, and have mindless sex with my doubts. On the bed, in the bath, on the floor. Love-bites and bruises. It isn't that I don't have time for God. The problem is, you see, He doesn't have time for me. What He has for me is Eternity. All I want is five minutes. Five minutes of Mean Time.'

Wasn't there a song called 'Five Minutes of your Time

would be the Time of my Life', or did all the words have capitals? A soft, smoochy Motown murmur, where you could get in close to the guy and feel his erection? Now that she was monogamous, Felicity sometimes felt a twinge of sadness for all the other twinges of yester-year, the pithy twitches of young passion. How many greenhorns had she blooded? How many boys had she drawn out into full manhood? Not that it mattered. She was committed to Theo. She had committed him like a sin, and he was hers. She had no doubts.

'What made you?' she said to the hearse-driver. 'Doubt, I mean.'

'Little things,' he said. 'Small wonders. As small as white blood-cells. It went on from there. There was an elderly woman I liked, who died and was brought to the church without being swabbed and staunched the right way. Halfway through the Requiem Mass, when the priest was talking about how we die to sin in the waters of Baptism, the coffin started leaking. It hit me hard. It hit me hard enough to hurt. She was a nice woman. She was more than that. She was a nice lady. She was so lady-like she could have been a Protestant. Maybe she was a convert. She deserved better. Better than what happened, anyway. She taught me everything I know about the best way to use your castle in chess, and she would have got on to the Bishop, if it hadn't been for the stroke. She was really lovely. It hit me hard.'

'I miss church, mostly,' said Felicity. But that was not what she meant. 'I mean, I miss going to church. What I mean is, I don't go.' And she yawned, until you could see her tonsils if you were sitting on the bonnet, looking in. 'But I would go to church in Rome. I would go to San Clemente. San Clemente is built over a Temple of Venus. It is the wisest church in the Vatican, although it is not in the Vatican. It is near the Colossus instead. The Colossus is beside itself, beyond the shadow of a doubt. The shadow of a doubt is San Clemente.'

'I would prefer a shadow of a doubt to a shadow on the lung,' said the hearse-driver. 'But the doubts get more and more substantial. After the lady and the leaking coffin, I found out that Thomas Jefferson owned one hundred and eighty slaves. That was another body-blow. It didn't make sense, did it? How could you own slaves, and design a University?'

'How could you build it otherwise?' said Felicity. 'How do you think the Acropolis was built? Diogenes was staying in his barrel.'

'But that was pre-Christian,' said the man. 'There's an amnesty on everything that happened beforehand.'

'But this is post-Christian,' said Felicity. 'The whole world's been post-Christian since Jesus died on the Cross. So there should be an amnesty for everything that's happened behindhand, as well.'

'But Thomas Jefferson,' said the hearse-driver. 'He had a responsibility to live his life as if he were someone of the stature of, well, Thomas Jefferson. And he was, or should have been, but he didn't, did he. He ended up as plain, ordinary Thomas Jefferson instead. I just hope to God he had the grace to be a bit ashamed about it.'

'He never whipped his slaves,' said Felicity. 'Not once. Maybe his manager did, but that's different. Jefferson was inside at his escritoire, trying to think of something to go with "pursuit of". He probably would have gone for Felicity, if his wife's maid hadn't been called that. So he was stuck with Happiness; unless, that is, Happiness was his pet-name for his wife's withers.'

'That's not the point,' said the driver of the hearse. 'The point is that coffins leak and Thomas Jefferson owned slaves. They don't have that in the penny Catechism. Some Catechism; some penny. It isn't worth a brass farthing.'

'You should talk to a priest, or a rabbi,' said Felicity. She was still not quite sure about him. Most Catholics never talked theology. Theology was for retreats, not for advances. Issues were different. Of course, women should be priests, though they might have to think of another name for seminaries. And, yes, of course, it was nice to know something about iconography, which was why she had gone to see that dreadful film about Andrei Rouble, and Dolores had been there with the Slav in final year, and when Felicity had asked her what she thought of the pseudery on screen, Dolores had said that, really, what she felt was very Orthodox. Which was totally typical of the Southern belle with the Northern balls, the bitumen Barbie doll; though it had to be said she was playing it by the rules. She wasn't embarrassing any of her peers by billing and cooing about the Blessed Sacrament; if she did talk about it, she would be at least level-headed, if always lacklustre. She would be interested in a sociological break-down of the statistics. Who received in the hand, who in the mouth? And why? And was it hygienic? But this guy was going on about internal bleeding. It just wasn't done. It was like passing a sanitary towel round for inspection. Maybe he was a Christian, even a Catholic, but there was something not quite kosher there. Being a hearse-driver didn't help. He should do arrivals as well as removals, and weddings. Why not weddings? That would turn his mind away from metaphysical quickies with his inner quailings. He would climb out of sackcloth and into the sack. All you needed in this world was somebody to get on with, and get into.

'Then there was the bunker,' said the driver of the

hearse. 'Now I grant you I may have been a bit out of sorts when it happened. I was supposed to be in "Zardoz", but I got a streptococcal throat. So I brought the television up to my bedroom, and I stayed between the sheets. Afterwards, I never had the heart to see that film. I would have watched all the extras, and wondered how I'd have done it different. Maybe not better, but different. My way. Instead, I sat in bed and heard about the bunker.'

'Hitler's?' said Felicity.

'No,' said the man. 'The Pope's.'

'The Pope's?' said Felicity.

'Him,' said the hearse-driver. 'They've built a nuclear bomb shelter under St Peter's Square, and the plan isn't to airlift two of every kind into it. No, it's for the High-ups. The Cardinals and the Bishops and the Concubines; and the Pope. I was so astonished I couldn't speak. I mean, I couldn't speak anyway: I had a streptococcal throat. But I thought, you know, I just thought that, if the guys in the officers' mess are putting on their water-wings, why is it full steam ahead down in the boiler-room? And what about this business in the Bible, where the number-one Navigator says, straight down the line, He's with us all the way? Or is that just Perry Como on the public address?'

Felicity had had enough. She was asleep. It was like white rum rising in a tall glass, rising and darkening as a dark mixer mixes in. She was content. She let it happen. And she dreamed she was a dog, a dog among dead explorers and a flapping flag, somewhere so far North that one small footstep would set you South again; and the snow fell steeply and silently over her, in a flurried blur of big flakes, until she was no longer a dog but a snow-dog, a huskie hidden under snow shedding still more snow. But was it huskie or husky or huski, and the eskimos would not know because they could not spell. If they could, they would spell disaster in everything they saw, and they would move down to the Smithsonian Institute and ask for sanctuary. She would never write that word for an eskimo's dog until she had found out how to spell it. Otherwise, Dolores would think she was an ignoramussssss . . .

'What mattered most,' said the driver of the hearse, 'was when the shoes were taken from the grave. They were the first she'd worn, after the booties stage. I used to hang them from the crucifix in the bedroom, where we have the thermometer for the central heating now. You could always smell her off them, even years later. Her little feet used to be wringing. So I put them on the grave, with a perspex yoke to keep the rain off; and they were taken. When I went one day to lay some bedding plants, they were gone. All I could do was sit there, not saying anything, not saying her name over and over.

'After that, I had the plot filled in with white stones.'

He had lost his way again, but he didn't dare wake them. They were in another world. They were sleeping like lambs.

'It was because of *The Elves and the Shoemaker*,' said the man who was called Noel. 'That was her first and favourite. I must have read it to her a couple of hundred times, a Ladybird book with the last two pages stuck together from a spoon of honey stuff for a child's cough. I used to say to her mother that she'd grow up and marry a cobbler; that she'd be pushing a trolley through the supermarket, and she'd see an old man in the shoe-repair shop, and in she'd go and have her heels done, even though they were fine. Of course, the wife would get on her high horse then, because she had other ideas. That was her way. A practical person was how you would sum her up. Not that you should sum anybody up, I suppose, because we're not invoices; but she did have a practical side. I was with her one day when she bought a Mickey Mouse nightshirt and three mousetraps. The same year or maybe the year after, she left a watercolour out in the garden, and it started raining. She tried drying it under the grill, but it was still, you know, blotchety. It didn't stop her, though. She entered it, anyhow, and it came third. "Stillness of Summer, Left in Light Rain". The local paper thought it was quite Japanese in a way, and they ran a picture of it, although the picture was wrong, really. They had the side at the bottom, and the bottom at the side.

'That was the wife back then. In the old days. When they didn't seem old at all.'

Felicity shifted her shoulder slightly, and Theo's head lolled forward. It gave him a bit of a double chin, in fact, when he did that. Still, he looked well. They both did. She, with the lip-gloss on her wide-open mouth; he, with the strong, long lashes you could sell to a beautician's. And they smelled nice too, not like the former Garda he had ferried to the inter-provincial match a month or two ago, with his socks and his salt-and-vinegar crisps. But these two smelled of unpronounceable perfumes, scents so expensive you could probably get away without washing. Babes in the wood, they were, for all their yackety-yak. Of course, even Burke and Hare would have looked like cherubs when they were snoozing.

'She doesn't sleep much anymore, my wife,' he said. 'Me neither. I woke up once in the middle of the night, and she was on the phone, but she wasn't saying anything. So, after a while, I took it from her, and I listened, and it was only the speaking clock. That was because she'd cleaned out the car that afternoon, when I backed it to the hall-door and she brought out the vacuum, and she went in under the seat and she found a Smartie. I can understand that. I can understand it because I did the same thing myself. I came in late one night and I went to the toilet to have a leak. And I always used to piss on the side of the bowl, so it wouldn't wake her, because her cot was on the other side of the bathroom wall, and she might have heard, she might have woken, she might have called me, called out to me. But then I realised. Then it came home to me, the going away, the homesickness. I pissed straight down onto the reflection of my face in the bowl.

'And I was so much on my own after that, I couldn't believe it when my hands and my feet did what I hoped them to do. They brought me into the bedroom, and undressed me. My fingers opened the laces of my shoes, and my arms reached up to draw my singlet over my shoulders. They were so good to me, so understanding. They never said a word. But I was on my own inside my body, like a trapped miner with a broken back in the tunnel they never cleared, hearing the drills stop and the pumps cease and the feet of the rescue-workers fade away, until there was neither the noise of a sound or the sound of a noise at all.

'I sat up all night in the darkness, beside the shaving mirror. That was for the company. It made a difference, you see, to feel that there was somebody else in the room.'

What he needed was a sign. Kinnegad, Kilcock, anything. Miles or kilometres, it didn't matter. How could a tourist be expected to cope, or was it deliberate? Were they meant to get lost, and so spend more money? But it was one thing to go astray on your holidays. Holidays were intended to expand your horizons, and being lost opened up a whole new vista. Being lost meant that wherever you stopped, out of breath, out of water, you had a brand-new, purpose-built viewing stand to step into. But this was not a holiday. It was not even a holiday weekend, or an ordinary weekend. It was the working week, make no mistake about it. He was not pony-trekking. This was fast-lane, foot-on-the-pedal, fuck-everybody land. It was not, on reflection, the optimum habitat for a man without a gear that could bring you backwards. Noel had always reckoned that the single most useful component of a car was a brake. Now he knew better. Reversal is the key to rapid progress. Whether you're reversing positions or charges, a reliable stick-shift separates the sheep from the lambs.

'Hardly anyone understands,' he said. 'Having a child, it gives you a reason for putting on your seat-belt. You never had one before. Afterwards, when the child isn't there, it leaves a hole; it leaves a hole that no amount of earth and flowers can fill. Because you can only fill a future: you can't fill an aftermath. That's what people don't understand. They tell you to look forward and not back, but that's what we're doing every day. We're looking forward to no child tomorrow, no child the day after, and no child when the next-door neighbour asks us for a loan of the Moses basket, and she's using it six months later to store cooking apples. My brother, he's a priest, he stood beside me, the day she was buried. He said to me that I was a very positive person, that I answered the phone to him late one night, at five past midnight, and I said "Good morning". He said I was an optimist, that I'd build apartment blocks in Beirut, if I had the chance. Then he said that the dolls in a child's bedroom have a lot to teach us, because the ones she loves most wear out quickest; as if God were a little girl, and a little girl was mass-produced in Taiwan. But he was the same in his sermon. He went on about how the seed has to die so that the wheat can grow; and that's fine, except we're not cereals. We're not like anything at all, even ourselves. We're beings, that's all we know. Human is only an adjective. But I didn't say that. I said nothing. I was watching my wife's grandfather streel around the cemetery with a Polaroid, taking snapshots of pals he hadn't seen since the year dot. And I wondered was it the same one he'd used at the christening, when we had to stand and smile, and stand and smile again, for a picture he finally took that came out all dark.

'And a tiny friend of hers came up to me, who wanted me to arrange the thread of her mittens for her. Around her neck and down her sleeves. And, while I was doing it, she said to me, "She'll be gone forever, and then she'll be back," and I said, "That's right, now," but I meant the mittens.'

Felicity was winning at Wimbledon. Her partner hadn't appeared for the final of the mixed doubles, so she was shattering the opposition single-handedly. In fact, it almost surprised her. She still felt slightly weak after having donated her kidney to the premature infant of a Vietnamese boat-person at Charing Cross Hospital the night before; but she wasn't about to let it show. Her balls left scorch-marks on the surface of the court, and the crowd gave her another standing ovulation. But now her bra was pinching her; she called for another. The stewards raced into the changing-room, returned with a mauve Maidenform, and handed it to her. She opened her shirt and shrugged it off. It slid like ice-cream down her sides, and pooled at her beautiful sneakers, no, her beautiful bare feet. The men were throwing their credit-cards like flimsy frisbees at her. Only Theo walked from the court, the smear of a three-day stubble on the sallow surface of his cheeks, his flannels flapping; but could that snooty bitch beside him really be Aquaplane Le Chic?

'What happened to my wife,' he said, 'is that she went into herself. It's not safe. You're better off on safari or sailing solo round the world. At least, that way, you've got your fire-arms and your weather forecasts. But she went in, into herself. And I lost sight of her. It didn't show, at first. She was absent-minded, maybe. She'd slip out for coal, and take the fire-guard instead of the scuttle; or I'd find her polishing the backs of the books on the bookshelf with deodorant. But, I mean, we all do that. Before ever anything wrong happened, I put a louvre door on the cubbyhole under the stairs, and I sawed three inches off the end for ventilation. But it was more than absent-mindedness with her; it was more like absence. I talked to her about the garden. The garden was always a thing with her. Roses galore, with their names in Latin on metal tags. She was rose-mad. But, no, she wasn't interested, and we argued over it, and she started to cry. It came out her nose, and she was wiping her face with the sleeve of her cardigan; and I couldn't stay. I went out for a walk, I don't know where. I don't know where I went, I don't know where I was. I came back later, and the cardigan was in the kitchen, with these snail-paths up and down the sleeves, and there were no roses out the kitchen window. Each and everyone was gone. Hundreds of them. Three, four hundred. She'd cut them with the bacon scissors.'

The skeleton was still smiling down at Theo, so there wasn't one good reason to be afraid. Yet he was afraid. How deep was this lift-shaft? Already he had passed lobster and squid, and a drowned parachutist with a face like the face of Albert Camus. But the parachute couldn't be large enough, light enough. It looked like a pair of Felicity's panties; yet, as he barely brushed them in passing, passing onward and downward the length of this bottomless ladder, he couldn't smell that shy, shoreline scent of hers, the spoor of her lips and her cheeks. It was too cold, he thought. It was too cold to smell anything. And he squinted up at the skeleton, and the skeleton raised his hand and waved it ever so slightly. And that was nice when you thought about it.

'I was in Dublin on a job,' said the man who was driving in the darkness. 'After it was over, I thought I'd wander round for a bit, and I ended up in O'Connell Street. And they were showing "Lady and the Tramp" in one of the cinemas. I thought about it for a while, and then a while longer. Not that I was just standing there, like a fool. I stood into one of the bus queues, where you could be waiting for a dozen different numbers. I'd taken her to see it, you know. What, maybe a year and ten months before. Oh, she loved it. The thing she loved most was the men's toilet. The urinals. But the film, too. Adored it. Wanted to stay and see it again. Wanted to be the woman who sold ice-cream, when she grew up. Either that, or God. Holy God.

'Then a bus-conductor was talking to me, so I decided. I went in. Sat in the same seat. Asked a fellow to move. I said it was my sight, that I couldn't see properly. He didn't mind. The place wasn't full. It was half-full, two-thirds, maybe. Of families. Mothers and children, and one little fellow in a wheelchair who had to have his head supported. Everybody cheered when it started, the same as she'd done. And there I was, watching away, the Tramp doing his mosey round the restaurants, and the ushers came up to me, men flashing torchlights. They'd been keeping an eye on me, you know; they had their suspicions. Because middle-aged men don't come in off the street to see a Disney cartoon. It's weird, isn't it? Maybe it's wrong. So, of course, they wanted identification. I showed them the stub of my ticket, and that annoyed them. There was an off-duty policeman a few rows back, with his wife and most of a Montessori class. He came down, and himself and the ushers and me, we talked, but people said Sssh, so we went outside; and the only child who was watching us as we left was the bloke in the wheelchair, with a grown-up trying to move his head back towards the screen again.

'She was her own woman, my child was. She did it in her nappy at her baptism. You could tell, because of how her face went. And the day of the Lunar Exhibition, I brought her to the sea. I wanted to show her what the moon does, how the tide comes in and the tide goes out. But she didn't understand. She kept looking at the tide coming in over the sand, and then she said to me, "The sea is trying to get out of the water, because it doesn't like being wet." That's what she said. And she was right. Because I thought of when I was small, how much I dreaded the sea. It seemed to me at the time that nothing could be more awful than to drown in the ocean. But you can drown as easy in your own bath, without salt or seagulls near you. You can drown in three inches, the same as in thirty fathoms. The deepest part of the Deep is always the shallows.

'But he didn't understand me when I said it, my brother didn't. He reached over and he squeezed my knee, and he told me I was a Trojan. An absolute Trojan. I didn't know, and my wife didn't, either, so I went upstairs to the Buddhist daughter's bedroom, to look it up in one of her dictionaries. She must have four or five. She's bright, you know. Perhaps that's her problem. Bright people have very dark outlooks. But, whatever. Anyway, I found it.

And who do Trojans turn out to be? People who got sacked, enslaved and massacred. That's who. And my daughter had written in the margin that a Trojan was also a novelty condom with thingies on the end of it. When I went down, I told my wife that Trojans were one of the tribes of Israel. I had to make something up. Because she was just sitting there, staring into space, saying nothing. And looking at nothing, but looking at it hard, as if there were something there, there in the nowhere, a face she could almost remember the name of. If you'd seen her, you would have thought she'd been beaten, raped. You would have thought that the doctors had told her she was dying.'

What in the name of the loving God was directly ahead?

He braked, brutally. The wheels shrieked like the long italics of vowels. It was a truck, a truck without tail-lights, carrying cattle. No, not cattle. Sheep. Sheep shoved together, steaming and shorn. Whoever was driving should be put against a wall.

It had woken Theo; it had woken him rudely. That is in the nature of awakenings. They are often rude, and sometimes obscene. He was disoriented, or is it disorientated? He had heard a scream in the lift-shaft, and, thinking it must be himself, he had let go of the ladder.

'And everybody has one,' he said. 'An angel, I mean.'

'What the fuck are you talking about, Theo?' said Felicity. She was vexed. It had been match-point on centre-court, when a blood-curdling cry from one of the linesmen made her look down. Her waters were breaking. She stretched to serve.

'I'm sorry,' said the driver of the hearse. 'I couldn't see him. Not without lights.'

'Sheep,' said Felicity. 'Thank goodness we didn't plough

into them. I'd hate to have it on my conscience that I killed a sheep.'

She studied the driver.

'It's all right,' she said. 'Don't be frightened. Why are you crying? Lord, if you can cry this much in a matter of moments, you should go to Central Africa. You could solve the drought problem just by standing wherever they tell you and thinking of something sad. But I'm only joking, amn't I? I mean, aren't I? Because you may be in a state of shock, you poor man. Would you like to stop for a moment, and smoke a Hamlet? Would that help? My diagnosis is that you have had an intimation of mortality. You might have made a shish kebab of all three of us, back there. But you didn't, and we aren't. We're fine. So please stop crying.'

She gave him a Kleenex and he wiped his face. His throat was wet, too; even his shirt-collar. That was not crying. That was lachrymating. The man was a prodigy. He wouldn't die in a dungeon. He would drown in a dungeon. There were legends about the likes of him, about tears that hollowed out boulders of granite. Or was that a tap-drip over decades? Or was it Saint somebody who used to weep about almost everything, and what he was weeping were pearls from no earthly oyster? The truth was, Felicity had read so much that, by now, she was a bit confused. It was the price you paid for devouring books; and Felicity had devoured and digested so many books, it sometimes surprised her that she didn't pass motions the colour of printer's ink.

'I'm all right,' said the hearse-driver. 'I'll stop somewhere soon, and check the video. It's back in the boot, and it might have got a clunk or a thwack or even a bedoing. I wouldn't mind a clunk or a thwack. It's stood up to those before. But a bedoing could easily be lethal.'

'What is it for?' said Theo. He would love to have had a video camera. He would love to make a video of Felicity in her most felicitous moments. But who would develop it? That was the question.

'It's for the film up in Dublin,' said the hearse-driver. 'What I do is, I look for someone in the crowd. Not the crowd of extras, but the crowd of others who'd be watching the extras. I usually pick a priest, because a priest isn't going to skedaddle with the camera. Of course, it's a bit difficult, sometimes, since priests don't always wear their canonicals these days. If you see someone, though, who dresses sort of down-and-out, but whose teeth look American, very white, very regular, then, ten-to-one, he's a priest. Sandals and socks is another sign, but you have to be careful. Sandals and socks is not foolproof. The guy in sandals and socks could be arty, and the arty chaps are Artful Dodgers. In fact, an awful lot of them are Bill Sykes, posing as William Shakespeare. To be fail-safe, so, I check it out beforehand. Then, afterwards, I have a record of whatever I did on the day. It may not be a hill of beans, you understand, but it means that you can say to yourself, "I have run the race, I have fought the good fight. Je ne regrette rien." A lot of what they film may never be used. Between the rushes and the wrap, your finest hour may end up on the cutting floor, the killing fields of tinsel-town. But you still have it on video. That's the main thing. It's like, you know, "veni, vici, vidi". I came, I overcame, it's on cassette.'

And he beeped his horn at the truck in front to make it move aside.

'You'll frighten the sheep,' said Felicity. 'They can die of fright, sheep can. They can drop dead on the spot, of heart-failure. Try to show some consideration.'

'It was talking about the film,' said the man. 'Talking

about the shoot, it bucked me up. I needed a bit of a buck.'

'I have a soft spot for sheep,' Felicity said. 'When I was at school, I was a lamb. Each of us was. There was a plasticine path on the classroom window-ledge, which led from a flag called Here to a flag called Hereafter. These wee woollen lambs moved from one to the other, a square every school-week, if you were good. When you reached Hereafter, you started from Here again. The first time you reached Hereafter, you were a saved soul; the second time, a Blessed; and the third, a Saint. Then you were given Enid Blyton books as a prize. I collected the whole of Malory Towers, except the fourth-year one. I was a Saint twelve times, which meant I was three Lamb of Gods. Every time it was Easter-time, I used to watch them, humble poor people from the backwoods, giving a lamb to the Pope on the steps of St Peter's. They would do it every year. There must be more lambs in the Vatican than there are sheep in Australia. The chaplain says that's why the Pope can pull the wool over everybody's eyes, because there is so much of it to go around. But I think lambs on the altar are lovely. They just lie there, and blink, and wag their tails if the Gospel is about them. But I think they should do the same with a donkey. When it's Palm Sunday, there should be a little donkey in the church. A lot of what I do from day to day is donkey-work, but then I remember that a donkey was chosen to carry the Lord into Jerusalem on Palm Sunday, which was not, of course, Palm Sunday then. It was the day after the Sabbath which was the last Sabbath before the Passover that fell on Good Saturday. And do you know something? That donkey knew he was carrying Jesus straight to an abattoir. He knew that the hullabaloo was all bullshit. That's why donkeys look so sad. They bloody well know. Same as the one on Palm

Sunday. He knew; it wasn't donkey-work for him. So, when it seems like donkey-work for me, the nothing much of my own life, well, I try to remind myself that I may be carrying more than I can bear; and that makes it difficult, yes, but sort of dignified, too. Because way down inside of the tedium, you can just about hear your own voice singing the Te Deum out of tune. Not that it matters, mind you, being out of tune. This life is about music, not about music-lessons.'

She would love to present the Pope with a donkey or a lamb; or, better still, the two together. They had had their differences, obviously, she and the Pontiff, but she was prepared to set them aside. They had more in common, the two of them, than what each had been through. If you set aside all of what he had written and most of what he believed, there was an amazing co-incidence of commitment between them. She hated to think of those hoodlums in the headquarters of the KGB who whiled away their tea-breaks at the samovar by sticking syringe needles into effigies of *il Papa*. She did not really believe in vodka and voodoo, but it would explain why he looked so pained a lot of the time. Not after five, not after hours, to be sure; but, by then, the secret police had gone home to watch 'Sesame Street' with their children. It would have red Russian subtitles, of course. She knew that. Felicity was not an eejit. But even if they watched something else, even if they watched 'The Cosby Show', it would furnish a respite for the Pope, a siesta from his sufferings. He could walk through the high-ceilinged halls of the Vatican, and think about things. And God would meet him halfway, at a side-altar, and they would sit and say nothing for ages and ages, the two of them. And they would go over the holy books together, and maybe God would have to explain something weird out of Meister Eckhart that the

257

Pope couldn't crack. And then they would sit and say nothing again for more ages, until God would ask the Pope if he had any Otrivine for a blocked nose; and they would be going to get it in the Pope's bathroom, when a Cardinal would see them, and send for the Swiss police, and have God removed. Then he would tell the Pope, the Cardinal would, to go to bed at once and to stay there. And God would have gone by then.

'You like lamb, do you?' said the driver of the hearse.

'I love lamb,' said Felicity. 'I love it with a nice, light mint sauce. Only I still can't make it the right way. Intellectuals make lousy cooks, I'm afraid. They are too busy gourmandising great works. Bread and water is their daily diet, bread and wine their daily dream. They are the trenchermen of thin air.'

He smiled. It was the first time she'd seen him smile, and she didn't like it. Besides, he was wearing a black tie. He should look shattered. He should look as though his world had fallen apart.

'They were lambs, and now they're sheep,' said the hearse-driver. 'Black or white, it makes no difference. They've all been fleeced out of just about everything. But I tell you this much. One of them is baaing to another, and I don't need a translator to tell me what he's saying. "It can't be any worse than what's happening now," he's saying. "We may have to rough it a bit in the transit camp, but, God above knows, we're used to roughing it at this stage. I tell you, there'll be pleasant waters. There'll be green pastures. Trust me." Baa, woof, hiss, neigh, twee-twee, whinny, moo, no.'

'No,' said Felicity.

'Yes,' he said.'

'Yes?' Felicity said.

'Yes,' said the driver of the hearse.

258

'I'm lost,' said Theo. 'What the fuck are you talking about?'

'Sheep to the slaughter,' said Felicity.

'Jesus Christ,' said Theo. 'Are you still on about the bloody Bible?'

'They're going to be slaughtered,' said Felicity. 'I thought it was only a figure of speech. I thought it was harmless.'

'Now you know,' said the driver of the hearse who was called Noel, though he had not been born at Christmas. 'And, in case it escaped your attention, we're following close behind.'

Felicity knocked, and knocked again; but it was still not opened unto her. So she pushed the door ajar.

'Tar-ra,' she said. 'We're back. The odd bruise here and there, but no bones broken. Home again, home again, jiggedy-jig. How about that, then?'

The chaplain was sitting in his swivel chair behind the photocopier. He was wearing his skull-cap that the Jews for Jesus had given him, so he must be reading his journal. Felicity had seen a couple of the entries, four or five months ago, the time she was turned down for the Samaritan switchboard, and the chaplain had helped her to cope with a sudden storm of low self-esteem, because he had been turned down, too, in his day, by the Anglo-Catholics, the Benedictines, the Blackfriars or was it the Blackshirts, the Dominicans, and whatever Order began with an E and had their headquarters in a catacomb. He had shown her the entries he had written at the time to tide him through the rocks of rejection, and they were so beautiful she had had to boggle. Later on, though, she discovered that he had lifted two of the loveliest lines from a Lancôme ad, which was a bit cheap, and a bit paradoxical too, because Lancôme was very dear.

'How about that, then?' she said again, because the chaplain hadn't said a word, not even 'Ciao' or 'Ça va'. In fact, he hadn't even looked up.

'How's Benny?' said Theo. 'How's he doing?' But then he stopped, and stared, because he'd never before noticed the print on the wall beside the blow-up of the ad from a Lonely Hearts column that was looking for pen-pals for a softly-spoken Galilean carpenter with a criminal record. He squinted to see it more clearly, and, yes, it was Constable's 'Haywain'. And that was incredible. It was like something out of Hitchcock. In fact, it was incredibler than that. With a name like Constable, it was more like a police presence. But was it surveillance or a bodyguard?

'Fuck Benny,' said the chaplain. 'Who gives a shit about Benny? I just think there's something so self-important about people who have nervous breakdowns. Who the fuck do they think they are, anyway? Fyodor Dostoevski? The way they sit around a closed ward, rolling threads off their dressing-gowns around their fingers and thumbs, cursing the darkness but never lighting a candle. Matches, yes. Matches for cigarettes. Smoke, smoke, smoke, like they were sending up signals to the Lone Ranger. But who's out in the rain, bringing his P45 to the Tax Office? Moi, that's who. And meantime, he's staring out a shatter-proof window, stroking his three-day shadow, and thinking how sad the rain looks. Well, I could tell him how wet it feels, and I don't have to stroke any three-day shadow, either. I've got a forty-year shadow at my heels, and, if I try to stroke it, it'll bite my fingers off.'

Some deep-down sixth sense told Felicity that the

chaplain was off-form. Or was she perhaps being too subtle? Maybe he was colour-carding some ideas for his journal. After all, the more dazzling the battledress, the more distant the battlefield.

'Some deep-down sixth sense tells me you're off-form,' she said to the chaplain. 'Or am I being too recondite?'

Recondite was better than subtle, whatever it meant.

'I'm not off-form,' the chaplain said. 'I'm just off. Not as in milk, mind. I'm spilled, not spoiled. The Bishop was in. He said I was fired. With energy, enthusiasm, egomania, and ignorance. That made me think. Ignorance doesn't start with an E. But he told me Exit did. He must have come in the front way, which was pretty sneaky, and seen the Exit sign in the corridor, the one that's always flashing like an SOS at sea. So, when he said that, I was speechless, though I didn't let on. I pretended I was just bemused. Actually, I don't much like being speechless. Silence, fine. Silence is fine by me. It's the aristocracy of speech. You remember that silent sermon I preached on "What have we to say for ourselves"? People were talking about that for weeks. I even had requests for copies. But speechlessness is something else.'

'It is,' said Felicity. 'The difference between silence and speechlessness is the difference between the same woman's behind, photographed first in pristine colour for the cover of *Penthouse* and later in clinical monochrome for a *Lancet* supplement on skin-cancer. One is a tush, the other a posterior. That is the bottom-line on silence and speechlessness.'

'Absolutely,' said the chaplain. 'But that would be utterly lost on the same episcopal ass who was in here today. I was sitting in that swivel-chair, feeling out-manned, feeling out-manoeuvred, and he was bullshitting about Constable's "Haywain" and the Cult of Nature, and how we should fix our sights instead on the Nature of Cults; and I was tearing round inside my head like Davy Crockett at the Alamo, standing the corpses up and tying their arms around their rifles. That's the sort of day I've had, while Benny's been playing pontoon with a staff-nurse. They've taken the ties and shoelaces away from the wrong guy. Nobody ever told Bennie that his mind amounted to the sum of all the fortune cookies he'd ever read. Nobody ever told Bennie that his breath smelled of a stack of bogus books that kept repeating inside of him, the way a battery chicken smells of the fish it's been force-fed. I had to endure that from a man who looks so sinister that, I swear it, Mossad would abduct him if they had an agency in Ireland. I had to let him tell me that I couldn't see straight. Well, I bloody well told him back that no way had Father Jack lost eye-contact with the basic message of the Gospels: Have a nice day; God will if you do. But the Reichs-marshall barked back at me that I hadn't only lost eye-contact with the Gospels, but I'd gone and lost radio contact with the gospel truth. And I was taking all of this from a blind bigot who probably thinks that Deconstructionism is a demolition manual. I tell you this, the Book of Life can be a real page-turner at times.'

Theo was astounded. Fr Jack was an intellectual. The man had an umlaut on his typewriter. He had written a book about Jacques Derrida, called *Kaddish for Judaism*; Derrida had sent it back to him with a personal message, saying that it was an experience he would never be able to erase from his mind. Jesus Christ, he had a Christmas card from Rudolph Hess which he always included in his *curriculum vitae*. Actually, he had been a tiny bit annoyed when Hess died, because it meant he couldn't talk about him at Mass any more. At marvellous Masses the Bishop had never been to. Reggae, jive, Albanian Orthodox, and the string quartet from Budapest who had played so beautifully that even Father Jack forgot about the Consecration. If a bastard like the Bishop had found the time to attend any of those eucharists, he would not have arrived in here today with a wooden spoon. No, he would have brought a wooden stake. Theo could not understand it, try as he might, every minute of the day. Why had the Church decided that the best kind of in-law was an outlaw? It was either a complete cock-up or the work of the Holy Spirit.

'Why?' he said. 'I mean, why now? Why today? Or is he just back from his holidays?'

'It was a sermon I preached,' said the chaplain. 'A mighty one, though I say so myself. The mouse produced a mountain, this time round. A hard enough birth, as you can imagine, but nothing is impossible with God and a good back-up team. Me. My past, my present, my future. The three of us.'

'What was your sermon about?' said Theo.

'Tell us, Father Jack,' Felicity said. 'This is so moving. I feel so drained and rained on. If I met that odious little man –'

'He's six-two,' said the chaplain.

'Well,' said Felicity, 'if he's larger than life, he's less than human. I would take his Bishop with my Queen; I would take his night with my day; I would take his arm and guide him into the traffic.'

The chaplain was searching for his sermon.

'I've given away my last copy,' he said, 'and I keep my originals in the Anatomy room. It's the one spot they'd never think of looking, if they tried to subpoena stuff.'

'You mean,' said Theo, 'the Inquisition?'

'Libel lawyers,' said the chaplain.

'Was there anything libellous in the sermon that buggered the Bishop?'

'Not a bit of it,' said the chaplain. 'Only the odd hint of heresy. Nothing you wouldn't find in the New Testament. Basically, there's something in the Gospels to offend everybody. It's a good thing Jesus wasn't born during the Reformation. They'd have eaten him.'

He looked over at Theo, who was looking up at the 'Haywain', which was looking at the particulars of nothing on the opposite wall.

'You can have that,' said the chaplain. 'I'd like you to have it. I can see that you love it.'

'But I was just looking –' said Theo.

'Yes,' said the chaplain. 'But a look can lead to love, and love to blind love. Vision begins in a light glance, and ends in heavy fretting, a gaze into darkness. St John of the Cross knew that, and so does Alex Comfort. You should read them, the mystics, Masters and Johnston. In the meantime, take the picture. Instead of my sermon. Trees and water, instead of roots and drought. Take it.'

'Did you give your roots sermon?' said Felicity. 'Was that the one? About how the carrots started rooting in the boot of your car, because the boot was broken, and light got in; and that made you think how humans root in the strangest of places, bistros and monasteries, but also it made you think about Bugs Bunny and how we never see things from the perspective of the carrots he chews, and how awful it must be for them to be bumped off by big buck teeth.'

'I gave a sermon about the Wheat and the Tares,' said the chaplain. 'About how we must let them grow together; because, if we pull up the weeds, we might damage the good grain. We might even destroy the . . . what is bread called before it's bread, before you can put it in the toaster or make sandwiches?'

'Corn,' said Felicity.

'Corn,' said the chaplain. 'You might destroy the corn all together. There was a farmer in the church who got up on his two hind legs with a practical reservation. Being a farmer, I suppose, he would have had a mystical sort of attitude toward the fields; but I stopped him. I said that we weren't here to be practical; we were here to be practically.'

'Practically what?' said Theo.

'Precisely,' said the chaplain. 'Practically what? That is that I said, or practically. I said that cleaning up our act is like cleaning coal. It's not on. You can only clean coal by burning it, and that gives light and heat to others. In the home-fires, the bonfires, the watch-fires. D'accord? If, like a lump of coal, you reform your blackness by transforming it into warmth and illumination for others, then, at the end of your blaze, you achieve –'

'The presence of God,' said Theo.

'Cinders,' said the chaplain. 'And I believe that prospect would motivate anybody. Alas, we're not coal. No, we are wheat and tares. Virtues and vices. But our virtues can defile us, as much as our vices. They may make us right; but they can also make us righteous. The Good Book is important, sure; on the other hand, good books are just as important. And good books are about wrongs and righteousness. They are about life. And life is not a theological termite colony, full of whiter-than-white ants, shaking collection boxes outside termite take-aways in order to raise revenue for disabled ant-eaters. Perhaps life should be like that, but it isn't, thank God. And thank men and women too; all of them. Because there's no rhythm and blues in a termite colony. Life may be red in tooth and claw, but a lot of that red is nail-varnish and lipstick; and nail-varnish and lipstick are good theology. Let us therefore be gentle with the selves inside us and outside us. Pills first and scalpels second, surgery as a last resort; and let that last resort be entered into as if it were Raffles of Singapore. Let us, in fact and fiction, live in sin with the world, and thereby save it. The desire to lead an irreproachable life is the second symptom of moral morbidity. The first is finding out about being irreproachable. That's so fucking unhealthy. Because a vice can strengthen a virtue. A man with a blind spot may hear more sharply. A woman with a deaf ear may see more clearly. Closed minds and open hearts bathe in the same bloodstream. The left hemisphere doesn't know what the right hemisphere is doing, but they sleep on each other's shoulders. Let them. Leave them. Leave them alone.'

Felicity was enthralled. Or, rather, she was elated. No, not elated, because, of course, elation was one side of a psychiatric coin, the other being depression; and that would not do. The nearest Felicity had ever come to a depression was when she shared a fairy cake with an akela at a brownie brunch in a glacial moraine. On the other hand, enthralled was wrong, as well. There was a thrall in there, wasn't there, between the en and the ed, and she knew from *Richard II*, or was it *Richard the Lionheart*, that thralls were horrible, hairy, hunchbacked half-wits who spent their whole lives dropping out of trees and missing Charlton Heston. But, if she wasn't elated or enthralled, what was she? There was a whole galore of pretty words, but the deeper you dug, the more dirtier they got. Adam meant soil rearranged, and soil itself went back to when you wiped yourself with an oak-leaf cluster. Sacred used to be about curses, not blessings. Really, there wasn't a single Aryan male or female in the whole of the Indo-European extended family. Every last member was a mongrel. God only knew what Felicity signified, and she would leave it that way. There were some things it was better not to bring out into the light of day. Was there a florist, far or near, who sold the root along with the rose? The ugh of the clay with the *voila* of the petal? No way.

'I'm so happy,' she said to the chaplain. 'I'm so eponymous. If only you'd said it that way to the Bishop, he would have understood. He would have handed you his crozier, like the Japanese did with their samurai swords. He would. Or he would have gone down on his hands and knees, and kissed your sneakers, the way Alec Guinness did when St Francis came to see him in the film about himself, where Mr Guinness was playing the Pope. Not that you would play the Pope, of course. Because the Pope does not play, and he cannot be played with; plus, I am pretty sure they insisted that a Catholic be the Pope, or at least a lapsed Catholic, so Mr Guinness split the difference. He is a convert.'

'What did the Bishop say to that?' said Theo.

'We weren't talking about conversions,' said the chaplain. 'I was kicking for touch. He was just kicking. And he got in a fair few swipes. He said that, if he breathalysed any single sentence I'd spoken, he would find it was footless. I reminded him that a certain Simon Peter had been accused of drunk and disorderly conduct in the opening chapters of the *Acts of the Apostles*. It just came back to me. I mean, I haven't read the *Acts* for ten years. I haven't had time. You don't, if you're trying to keep abreast of all the international theological breakdowns. But the Bishop didn't like it. He did not. And I felt sorry for him, this strange, solitary man who takes his coffee like medicine, his medicine like coffee; this flatulent, plum-pudding fart of a fellow, the whole of whose life is a whites-only neighbourhood, where he stands with a shotgun loaded and ready, in case some dark idea might streak past his porch-front. I wanted to say to him, Hey, man, mellow out. Turn your reservoirs back into lakes. Lakes are lovely. There aren't any postcards of reservoirs. And turn your canals back into rivers. Canals are clever; rivers are wise. Rivers wander, they go walkabout. But they get there. They get to the sea. They make a sound like "Thalassa, Thalassa". Try to like them. Try to be like them. The plot thickens as they pass, as they process like dignitaries in open cars, the crowds crushing the barricades, the tall trees tickertaping greenness from Eden into their banks and borders, the brambles roaring in a breeze no human buttons his coat against, the wildflowers darting in and out, like children among the legs of adults, to see something, to see her dress, lift me, show me, and the grasses bending at the brink to sip a shivery sliver of glass-white wet from the weird onwardness of it, a wet that tastes of kingfishers and tin-cans and the continental shelf.'

'I can understand that,' said Theo. 'I grew up beside the Dodder. My mother used to make my legs dance if I went near it. Maybe that's why I hate ballet. She was afraid I'd drown in it. So I never got my feet wet. But I used to listen to it, at night. It wasn't doddering then. It blabbered and blubbered like a whole bloody classroom of kids when the teacher goes to the toilet. I had a mad aunt, the statutory mad aunt everybody likes to think is barmy, because barmy is a nicer word than endogenous depression; and she thought it was a tributary of the Jordan. She used to wade into it, with her suspenders dangling, to collect Lucozade bottles and egg-boxes. She said she owed it to Jesus, because of his humility in accepting baptism, when he had no earthly reason to be ashamed of anything. And the strange thing was, she had a varicose vein on her left leg that was like a river itself. Not like the Dodder or the Jordan, but like some river you might just come across someday. And then you would think, Why, yes; yes, of course.'

'Well, the Bishop isn't a river,' said the chaplain. 'And he isn't even a canal. I don't know what he is, but I shouldn't be surprised if you found that he was baptised in an ice-bucket. Old style, old school, old school tie. I swear he thinks that God wants to be worshipped. All poor old God wants is to be wanted. He doesn't give a tuppenny shit about anything else. I mean, the ritual and stuff, it's like a vote of thanks, a note of appreciation. But a lover wants more, and He's in love with us, for Christ's sake. How would anyone feel if he loved a woman to the point where the goddamn grace and goodness of it was as close to sickness as to strength, and she said to him, "Look, I respect and value you more than I can say, but", and he had to sit through the arid, arctic etcetera of her kind indifference? Well, that's God. And the whole Church, the bricks and mortar-guns, is a way of keeping God at a safe, social distance. Because if we once let Him love us, we are totally fucked. You can't invite the Pacific ocean to a tupperware party, without running out of glasses.'

'I ran out of glasses at my last party,' said Felicity. 'And nobody wanted to drink out of the same bottle. It was all cake and no ale. Really, Aids has it in for the Latin Quarter. It's more like Dodge City, these days. Irish dancing, of course, is on the up and up, and why wouldn't it be? It's the native expression of the rhythm method. Noli me tango.'

'You should have told the Bishop about the river,' Theo said to the chaplain. 'He's a fisherman. He caught the first salmon of the season in the Liffey two years ago. So he would have understood. Because fishing is only a pretext. If you stood at a river from dawn to dusk, with your two hands empty and outstretched, people passing by would think you were a Hindu. They'd write to the county council or call the police. But, if you stand at the same spot from sun-up to sun-down, with worms and hooks and whippy rods, then you're a Christian, and you're gutting a good-sized trout while you work it out in your head how best you can gut the Assistant Marketing Manager at nine sharp the next morning.'

'I did say it,' said the chaplain. 'Sort of. I said that he should let the river be, because it'll find the sea in its own time, in its own turning. Let it wind and waterfall, and burst its banks and sink in the dry season. Sooner or later, it will taste salt on its lips; sooner or later, in the white wholeness of whenever, it will surge, splurge, splash out, the champagne running from the rusted hulls of boats that know no better than to call it waves. They have made their meeting; they have met their makers. It is begun.'

Felicity had never thought of rivers in quite that way before. If you lived in Venice, perhaps, or in Vienna, it would be different. In a gondola, you would be floating on air; and 'The Blue Lagoon' would dance you into moods of devilment beyond the power of all discretion. You would be one ruined Rhine maiden. But Dublin wasn't Italy, or Austria-Hungary, either. It was only where you lived, because your father was too small-minded to transfer to Strasbourg. And the Liffey was so polluted she wouldn't even piss in it. Some of the salmon had started sail-boarding down the last laps. If a child fell in, she would have to have her stomach pumped, and that was only after the trauma surgeon had seen to the multiple fractures. Now, could you ever feel pathos or a pre-coital palpitation for something like that, fish leaping through bicycle wheels like dolphins through hula-hoops?

'And?' said Theo to the chaplain.

'He said I had allowed myself to be swept out to sea,' said the chaplain. 'And he went on to remind me that there are rivers in the Australian interior which simply disappear in the desert. He was holding that card to his pectoral cross, you see, as I went on, meandering about sources and streams. He was biding his time. He was building his dam. But I wasn't surprised. He thinks deserts. He thinks deserts are Biblical. I wish to Christ that Jesus of Nazareth had been Jesus of Newhaven, Connecticut. You know, ivy, Ivy League, League of Women Voters; neighbours, neighbourliness, Neighbourhood Watch. Because, when people start imagining God, they get into sunstroke and sand-dunes. And where do they end?'

'The Promised Land,' Theo said. 'That's where.'

'I wish it were,' said the chaplain. 'But the Bishops have it in their heads that the Promised Land is out there, somewhere; when, in fact, the Promised Land is in here, everywhere. We've landed, we've landed on our feet, and it's bloody promising. If you're not happy with it, try the New Jerusalem. It's only four hours away, on a Club Class El Al flight. Of course, your man who was in with me this afternoon wouldn't buy that. As far as he's concerned, this is the Valley of the Shadow of Death.'

'What he needs,' said Felicity, 'is a woman. Celibacy is very bad for Bishops. What does it profit a prelate to have no buttons on his shirt-cuffs, prostate problems, and to share a space with priests who always want to watch the other channel?'

'But he's right,' the chaplain said. 'This is the Valley of the Shadow of Death. It is. And what of it? Valleys are nice places. Things grow in valleys. Barley and grapes and pot. Valleys are on the level. Valleys are meant for men and women. The tops of mountains aren't. Kilimanjaro,

Tabor, they're for the birds. You climb a mountain, you make it to the peak, and then what?'

'You hold the bottle of Coca-Cola high up so the camera-team in the helicopter can get a close-up. And tiny toddlers all over the world sit up and listen, and they sing the Coca-Cola song for their babysitters. It gives you a lovely Family of Man feeling. Like pins and needles.'

'No, no,' said the chaplain. 'That's not what happens. Anyway, the Coca-Cola is too far down their rucksacks to go rooting for. No, they search for the book to sign it, and maybe write a comment, like, "I have now done something that bastard my father never did, God be good to him". But then what? They can't see through their goggles, because they're misted; they can't smoke, because they're breathing through an oxygen mask; and they can't do Zorba's dance, because they've really shot themselves in the foot this time, with green gangrene in a pair of their piggies. Do they look up? They don't. Do they look around? Yes, they do; but once you've seen a single snow-field, you experience a sort of epistemological burn-out in relation to other snow-fields. Because they are identical, they can never be the same again. So what does the mountaineer do? He looks down. He looks way down. He looks way down at his valley. And he thinks, "Fuck me. That is one hell of a valley. That is the Valley of the Shadow of Death, where I live and move and have my business. And I love it. Why has it never won the Tidy Valleys competition? It may be a mess, but, by God, it is the neatest valley this side of the Vale of Tears. And it loves me. How many years is it now since I lay on my back under Pumpie the milk-cow, and squirted the milk from her teat into my mouth, so that the nice lady from Germany could take an interesting photograph of a typical inhabitant of the Valley of the Shadow of Death? And then I ran home and washed out my mouth with Jensen Violet, because I was afraid that I might die of cow bacteria. Yes, the Valley of the Shadow of Death was a good place for a boy to grow up and run wild. Why am I not there now? What am I doing up here in this shitty place, this bollocks of a bare mountain that would blow me from its summit as lightly as a woman might blow a hair from her lip? Get me out of here, fast." '

'Proper order,' said Felicity. 'That shook him.'

'Down he comes, at a canter,' the chaplain said. 'To the backsides and honeysuckle of his own unearthly element, the Valley of the Shadow of Death. There's meat and potatoes in it, there is eating and drinking. It's a sabbath slap-bang in the middle of the working week; it is a sanctuary under shellfire. To which my answer would be the short and simple prayer: Well, fuck it. Amen.'

Felicity had seen the Valley of the Shadow of Death, in a spaghetti western, but she couldn't for the life of her remember any honeysuckle. It was more cactus and scorpions, and a beautiful woman with breasts like a bottom, who was held by two whiskery sombreros while Ramon Rod-something-or-other burnt her cheek with the end of his cigar. After the intermission, she had cut off his balls; fair play, only you did not see much, which was a pity. But perhaps there was another Valley of the Shadow of Death. There was a Dublin in Argentina, except it had lots of O's in it, and there was a Disneyland in Paris, as well as in Disneyland.

'No more driving motorways through our private and personal deserts,' said the chaplain. 'God has already invented the camel. No more transforming the forests within us into quick-yield, conifer cash crops. We are acorns, sodden grenades with the pins pulled out. There is a wilderness within us all, and the Bishop wants to turn it into a Botanical Gardens. There is an eco-system that doesn't understand itself, on the inside of our outside self. It survives the loss of our hands and feet and the lower half of our bodies; it survives strokes, senility, amnesia, Alzheimer's. It balances the whole of what we are, the steppes, the falls, the rifts, the frozen north of our nature. And the Bishop wants to turn the entirety of it into an airport for some eventual Ascension. But I say: Kill the psychologists. Torture and kill the bereavement counsellors. As for the Bishops –'

'What about the Bishop?' said Theo. He was thinking about the playground in the far-flung sea-front site. He might as easily have buried him anywhere: the whole planet was a playground for those who lived by water and lived wholly.

'Well,' said the chaplain, 'he may be doing me a favour. There aren't any left-turns in this world, you know. And he diverted me, in both senses. I was amused by the skeletal sang-froid. In fact, I had this terrible urge to say, "Bishop, did you ever go down on a French woman?" Because he was telling me, you see, that my work in the School of Medicine was all lab and no oratory. What it means, in effect, is that my river floods another plain. A new one.'

'I hope,' said Felicity, 'there aren't too many, well, people living there. People love disaster movies, but they're not really, sort of, orgasmic about being flooded.'

'Alluvium to the arid,' said the chaplain.

'And where do the arid hang out?' said Theo. 'Waiting, that is, for the light relief of rain, its very welcome wee-wee?'

'On the other side of the river,' the chaplain said. 'Out by the airport. A community of enclosed nuns. The

274

vow-of-silence sort. Sure, they couldn't talk even if they wanted to; the planes fly so low over the convent you could almost see the bulge of a boiled sweet in a child's cheek. Amsterdam and Istanbul, and they're sitting on benches, making hosts for the mystery of the Mass, saying nothing, saying everything, while the Jumbo up above is carting cretins like moi to a conference paper on penance in Johns Hopkins.'

'I know the convent,' Felicity said. 'Dolores has a second cousin there. And there's another lady, Sister Something, late middling to early old, who has binoculars that she plane-spots with. When Frank Sinatra came for a concert, the nuns were up on the wall, watching, and Dolores's cousin was hogging the binoculars until Sister Somebody had to intersect. Dolores went up to visit her, and the cousin was trying to squeeze a video under the grille, but it got stuck. "Two Mules For Sister Sara" it was, and they all thought it was a howl. So the cousin asked Dolores to get "Hang 'Em High" and "Fistful of Dollars" for her, because she wanted to get back in with Sister Somewhere or other after the ructions over the binoculars. They just think Clint Eastwood is so funny. They think he's funnier than Jack Lemmon.'

He thought about this, the chaplain did.

'I sort of thought they'd be solemn,' he said. 'But now you tell me what you have told me, I see that they're obviously quite serious people. What I'll do is, I'll bone up on a few joke books. I've some rag mags back in my bedroom. I'd like to think I could make them laugh, the odd time. Trouble is, I was never really a funny man. I just don't have a sense of the ridiculous.'

'You pay a price for being profound,' Theo said.

'I don't know,' the chaplain said. 'I always had a hunch that a sense of the ridiculous was a large part of being profound, the way a Department of Education is a division of Government. Anyhow, I must away. Work awaits me. That's the way it is, if you belong to the Order of Melchizedek. If, on the other hand, you belong to the disorder of matrimony, then you say that the wife will be worried. For a priest, though, it has to be work that gives you an out-clause. Then you go back to the presbytery, or wherever, and you think, That was a lie, wasn't it? Impure and complex. So you write to your relations in New Zealand, until two in the morning. When you finally quit the priesthood, they're baffled. You were such a wonderful Jesuit.'

'But you're not a Jesuit,' said Felicity.

'I might have been,' said the chaplain, 'if I hadn't mixed up Francis Xavier and Francis of Assisi at the fourth interview. That was when the guy from personnel got the knife in.'

He was easing Constable's 'Haywain' off the wall. It left a sort of scummy square behind it, like when you peel a plaster off a wound. It was a bit disgusting.

'Think what it was like when Stalin died, and they denounced him,' the chaplain said. 'Rectangles of dust and dirt from Checkpoint Charlie to the Bering Straits.'

How many 'Haywains' were there in the world? In homes, hotels, factories, furniture stores, passenger liners, interrogation cells, concentration camps, psychiatric hospitals, psycho-geriatric institutions and the postcard stands of the Metropolitan Museum of Modern Art? Theo was slowly beginning to consider the possibility of, yes, an intercontinental conspiracy theory. If it were true, it would make Watergate look like a molehill.

'Yours,' said the chaplain, handing it to Theo. 'Strange to think that the same picture is halfway across the cosmos now. Deep in the vaults of Voyager, with a baseball bat, a compact disc of "The Marriage of Figaro", a human skeleton, an Esperanto copy of the Bible, a sachet of contraceptive pills, and I don't know what else. Oh, and a pair of reading glasses. God must be wading out to meet it, like a man retrieving a model sailboat from a pond in a park in the centre of a city at the edge of a glittering ocean.'

Come to think of it, what was a fucking haywain, anyway? Was it a haystack or the person who made it?

'First,' said the chaplain, 'I have to talk to Ooze. You know, the new band out of fourth year. They want to write a few new songs for the benefit, but they don't know what. I mean, the market's cornered. Whales, the Third World, Fascists, child-abusers, additives in food. What's left? They want to strike the right note, you know, so the audience can feel vanguard instead of on guard. But the megastars have beaten them to the big subject matter, because the megastars have taken that subject-matter, and really subjected it. The new number two, you know, "A Blast of the Begging-Bowl Blues", about starvation and stuff in the sub-continent. Well, in less than two months, they've trebled the million they put in promotion, though it hasn't helped the bass guitarist much. He crucified his hip, doing a tricky stem-christie on an off-piste run in Aspen. I mean, that's two private nurses for at least a year, plus he has to delegate his whole investment portfolio to his broker, because, obviously, he can't vet any real estate when he hasn't got a leg to stand on. Admittedly, it leaves him time to think about numbers. It'd be nice if he could do another, bigger "Begging-Bowl" for the world tour, though it may be selfish to say that, because it puts him through so much pain to think about the Third World. Still, we're banking on him, and he's banking on us, too, for support. We're all in this together.'

'I love "Blast of the Begging Bowl Blues",' said Felicity, 'but I prefer "I Am Ashamed".'

'Right,' said the chaplain, 'right on. "I am ashamed when I think, They have nothing to drink, And I have a six-pack beside me." That's the one he dedicates to Kahlil Gibran.'

'I think we should go now,' Theo said. 'The Haywain' was heavy enough. Was that the picture or the frame?

'Fine,' said the chaplain. 'And, you know, well done. The Aids people will be grateful. Very grateful. You've helped to heal them. You've helped to show them that, no, they're not lepers. Social lepers, maybe, but that's a trifle. So they sneeze at a party, and the guy who gets snot on his shirt-front does a lightning strip. At least, they don't have to walk up Grafton Street, shouting "Unclean", and getting stoned with croissants and Walkmans. And, you know, after the hot-air balloon, they may not even have to worry about the party situation. Two guys and a girl in third year are going to fly a hot-air balloon to Iceland. Reykjavik is preparing a reception. They don't have too many problems up there, apart from a spattering of suicides during the winter, so they really want to get involved. They may be a bit ashamed they're not doing too badly. You never know. Myself, I thought Iceland was a good idea, as ideas go, and I felt this one could. I suggested a whip-round, you know, twenty quid from everyone attending the school, but they wanted the bigger sacrifice. They wanted the hot-air balloon. So, Operation Hot-Air is well underway. But I really must go.'

'To Iceland?' said Felicity.

'No, no, no,' said the chaplain. 'To my sister's. Her dog died. He choked on a Bisodol tablet. She was stricken. They were terribly close. He slept with her for years. He

278

used to answer the phone for her. I mean, he used to lift the receiver and bring it to her. O, Shit was great.'

'Shit?' said Felicity.

'That was his name,' said the chaplain. 'His real name was Pride of Place, but that was very horsy. Anyhow, he didn't answer to it. But the sister, you know, she swears a lot. And she says "Shit" this, "Shit" that, and "Shit" the other; and the dog, Pride of Place, when he was still a puppy, well, his ears would prick up and he'd answer her. He'd shoot down the stairs and sit at her feet. So, "Shit" sort of stuck. You got used to it, after a while. Except when you had to say something like, "Sit, Shit, and shut up". That took a bit of time. Of course, when I took him for a walk, I never called him Shit.'

'You called him Pride of Place,' said Felicity.

'No, I called him Faeces. That's his name in Latin. And he always answered. I bet you anything he knew he was canine, and not just dog. He was cute, but he was clever too. And she'll miss him, my sister will. That's why I'm going to see her tonight. I'm going to lead her through it. We'll think about Shit, and we'll talk about Shit. It'll be a sort of Pause for Prayer. It'll be his evening. An evening given over to the Shit we knew and loved. Because, you know, strange as it might seem, our lives became entangled over the years. So that, almost without knowing it, Shit became a part of our days and nights; and we, in turn, became a part of what Shit was. He's there still, in the house, in the woofs you wait for, but you don't hear. He's there in his lead that dangles from the hat-stand in the hall; he's there in the tennis-balls with the tooth-marks in them; he's there in his big, brown bowl in the scullery. Oh, I imagine the sister will get rid of them. She'll give them to Oxfam or some other charity. But there's one thing she won't be able to jettison. However hard she tries, the smell of Shit is going to be there, in every room in the house, for a very long time to come.'

Theo stood on the steps of the Medical school, with Constable's 'Haywain' under his arm. People who were passing by, or was it on or into, looked at the picture as they neared, narrowed, and were gone again. Was it the cover of a chocolate box or a celebrated masterpiece? That would be what they were wondering. When they got home, they would hoist themselves into the attic to take a second look by torchlight at the Madonna and cherubs with the suction circles from their children's bow and arrows. They would think about cleaning the dribble of milk from the year of the flu vaccine, and wonder was it a y or an ie at the end of Christie's. They would sleep under starlight, dreaming about garage-conversions and grandmothers, and was it worth it, anyhow, because her heart might not make it to the winter solstice, let alone to the Ireland–France match. And all this time, in the pitch-black of the box-room, an oblong igloo of sheets of asbestos, milk would be oozing from the painted nipple of a painted Virgin, dropping as slowly as the mercury in a thermometer, in under the breast and over and down the dark length of her cloak, past the outstretched fingers of a God with a navel, through the worked wood of a gilt frame, and, drop by drop like a medical drip, to the plastic Pooh Bear saucer with the pink pellets of rapid rat-killer.

The sun was setting, painting the whole town red; and the wind too was stirring, playing in the trees like tomboys, making the strangest of sub-aquatic sounds, gargling the names of Welsh villages, Llandudno in a mouthful of oloroso sherry. In Portugal, the wind would be Russian; in Egypt, Norse, or was it Nordic? Or was it Norwegian? At the end of the day, the wind was something else.

Where the fuck was Felicity? It was getting cold. The time was coming, coming sooner than he had ever thought likely, coming sooner than the sky and sea and the good ground suggested, when you would have to turn from the window you were watching from, and summon the strength to ask yourself, in good faith and with good will, where you had left your electric blanket. For such, indeed, was life.

'Did you do that?' said a middle-aged man who had not shaved for about a day and a half.

'Do what?' said Theo. It was too bad about the day and a half. If you were young or youngish and didn't shave, except at the weekends, then you were an intellectual; but if you were middle-aged, as this man was, it meant you were unemployed.

'The painting,' said the man.

'I did,' said Theo. He didn't like to lie, but it saved time. It saved having to talk about haywains, when you weren't really sure whether it meant the doing or the done. Though, now that he thought about it, wasn't a wain a man of some description? Or was that swain? A swain swived with a wench through her placket, and, behold, bairns were born. Bairns, of course, were Scottish; and so, too, was Wainscot, meaning the waning of Highlands culture after Culloden. In that case, a haywain might mean a bad harvest instead of a bumper harvester. Whatever the case, it was no wonder Theo had said, 'I do'; or, rather, 'I did'. The truth took forever. You could spend your life telling the truth, but it would tell on you, sooner or later. You would be a broken man, health-wise. Because the truth went on and on, and we do not. If it is a line, it is a longitude, running from Pole to Pole, Maypole to Maypole; and, if it is a longitude, latitude alone can take its measure. What, Theo thought, was the precise latitude and longitude of the sunny side of Stephen's Green? The lie of the street in front of him was as true as God made it. That was why the wires were humming up above him, like a string section. That was why the leaves were clapping madly, gloves applauding at a concert, ovations of doves. They knew this place, this shortfall, this landfall, was the ends of the earth and the centre of the world. That was why they came back, the leaves did, year after year to the same tree. To the same branch. To the same bud.

'I hope it blossoms,' said the man. 'Your talent, I mean. It's not bad, that picture. It's not half bad. The greens are just the way the greens should be, in a picture like that. It'd look well on a green wall, it would. Restful. The Amateurs are having an exhibition around the Green in a few weeks, you know. If I were you, I'd put it up on the railings. You might even sell it.'

And he stood for a moment, trying to decide where he'd been going when he stopped.

'Yes,' he said. 'That's not half bad. The picture. If I were you, I'd go into it. Take time off, and go into it.'

Theo watched him walk away until he was no longer lost in the crowd, but a part of it, a part of its procession, safely and shabbily inconspicuous as the letter e in a large novel. The pages were pouring past him: children of six and seven, children of seventy, too. A man stopping to search his pockets, his face dismayed. He takes out keys, a pencil sharpener, a half-eaten sweet he was given at work but didn't like, a cheroot case with chalk-prints on it, and two, three, four pound notes. He hasn't lost them. Thanks be to the good God above. He'd have had to leave his car in the underground car-park overnight.

But he can rest now. Now he can breathe again. He draws deeply on his cigarette, walks on, bumps against a plain woman in plaits and tight cotton trousers, a woman with a beautiful bottom, a lift-and-separate sort. If she sat in wet plaster for twenty minutes, they would hang the mould in the Louvre; but she moves on, checking to see that her engagement ring is still hanging from a knotted ribbon round her neck. She must work with her hands in a canteen or a cake shop. And now she was tired. She was going home to price another fifteen hotels. They were all so snotty, too, because her accent wasn't posh. You would think she was asking for a discount.

'The Haywain' was too heavy to hold. He put it down at his feet.

The woman from the country glanced at it as she passed. She must be from the country, because only a country-woman, single and thirty-fivish, would wear caramel and mustard. She would be off to the ballroom, he thought, in the hope of meeting someone nice, someone gentlemanly, someone who would use a nail-brush, and leave light between them during the slow-set. If she didn't meet him, she would end up dancing round her handbag on the dance-floor, telling Cliodna she'd kill him for not remembering it was this week, and not next week. She would tear out his eyes, so she would.

The people passing, they cast shadows, each and every first one of them. They cast such shadows, but, by God, they cast them in bronze. If you looked at them long enough, if you yearned enough and yielded enough, your eye all pupil and no master, they would teach you, they would tell you how to keep going, how to keep faith, how to keep body and soul together. They would tell you the words of the song and the steps of the dance. They would. And your mouth would fill with the bittersweet smells of

283

vowels you had never thought possible. There would be blood on your tongue, though you had not bitten it.

Theo was coming to his senses. Sight, sound, taste, touch and smell. He could never remember the sixth. Had it to do with breathing, or sex? Or was it the sense that refused to make sense, the sense that made peace but would never make pacts? The other five, they kept us on our toes; but the sixth, whatever it was, it kept us on our feet. Theo was damned if he could name it. After all, it was the pianist who came forward and took a bow when the recital was over, not the shadow in the shadows who was quietly turning the pages. He might have been anybody at all. And he probably was.

'Look what I have,' said Felicity. 'Look. Smell it.'

It was a mandarin. He looked at it, and at her. She smelled like the colour mauve. Her smile was the end of civilisation as he knew it. They would have many children, at least two. When they were ninety, she would die, feeding the peacocks in the lower orchard. By the time he had run to her, apple-blossom would lie on her head like a lace mantilla. In the pocket of her Provençal apron, he would find a shopping list and her last haiku.

> When I have finished feeding the peacocks,
> Let me die in the lower orchard
> With a lace mantilla of apple-blossom.

There would be a solemn High Mass, and his mistresses would have to stand in the porch.

'Tonight,' said Felicity, 'I will prepare you a dish fit for a king.'

He pecked her on the cheek. It was a bit too public to give her a smack or a smacker farther down. She turned the other, for a second kiss, so that people passing might think she was French. In France, of course, she would say the Our Father in Irish, until the garçon turned out to be a student from Belfast.

'It's lovely to be back,' she said. 'And everything's the same, the trees and the buildings, even the clouds. I feel like Noah must have done, when the Ark of the Covenant finally moored on Mount Cavalry, and the stoats and the stingrays started sitting on their suitcases to try to get the zip to go round.'

'Where did you get the mandarin?' Theo said. 'Mandarins are out of season.'

'Ah,' said Felicity, 'wheels within wheels. Before man invented the wheel, woman invented wheels within wheels. Ask me no questions, and I shall tell you no truths.'

So he reached down and gathered up the 'Haywain'.

'It comes down,' Felicity said, 'when we have people round for an eucharist. Especially Dolores.'

The two of them, Theo and Felicity, crossed the street as best they could, dodging a fast fruit-and-vegetable van with a slanted slogan on its side, which read, 'Fairfield's, Full Of Folk Wisdom', and then getting stopped in the middle lane when the lights changed. They were stuck between a bus and a four-door hatchback car in which the driver was a bride, and the groom seemed groggy in the front passenger seat. That was strange, when you thought about it, because, if you were the groom, well, you were also the jockey, weren't you? But Felicity had total insight.

'Domination,' she said. 'She cracks the whip, in more ways than one.'

'Maybe he can't drive,' said Theo.

And then the lights changed, and the two agency models went on to the Wedding Fashion Fair at the Mansion

House; and Theo and Felicity made it to the other side. Two men in overalls were walking past, gently and gingerly manipulating an enormous pane of glass with the one word 'Glass' painted in big, bold capitals on either side, so that, in point of fact, it was impossible to make out the word at all. And everyone who was passing slowed or stopped to look at it, a large, lengthwise transparency; and Theo could hear a number of them say to one another, 'Glass, I think. Yes, glass, that's it', but he didn't know if they were talking about the pane or the painted word.

'The way in is down here,' he said to Felicity.

He wanted to go into the park. He wanted to see the people who were sitting there, pretending to be waiting for someone. He wanted to see the young warden, the one who put the brooms up the beech tree at the children's playground when it was near to Hallowe'en; the one who paced the park each evening with a ski-stick that he got from God knows where, spiking the dropped cones and the breadcrusts, the maple leaves and the ruined cassette, skewering them the way you would drive a knitting-needle through a ball of wool. Because you could use a ball of wool. At a black time, in a dark place, you could unravel it behind you as you went. Then you would always know your way back to where it was only grey.

'It's a short-cut,' he said to Felicity.

There would be birds in the bandstand, too, larking about, flummoxing the music-stands, like kids from the ghetto, kicking up a racket in Carnegie Hall. There would be this, there would be that, there would be the other. Truly, it was a world of milk and honey.

'Well, a world of cows and beehives, anyway,' said Felicity. 'We're sort of halfway there.'

And she blessed herself as she walked along.

'Why are you making the sign of the Cross in the middle of St Stephen's Green?' said Theo. But it was all right. There was no one looking.

'I wasn't just making the sign of the Cross,' said Felicity. 'I was blessing myself. There is a difference. I was blessing myself because I wondered who else would.'

'I would,' said Theo. He said it quietly, but that didn't mean it was spoken in an undertone. He couldn't have said it in a normal voice, because there were two joggers walking past at that very split-second. They should be fucking ashamed of themselves, too, the same pair. If they were out for a stroll instead of a sprint, they should dress like strollers, and not traipse around, la-di-dah, look-at-me, like a couple of sportswear coat-hangers. If they hadn't barged in and brutalised the moment, he would have said what he wanted to say, straight out.

'What did you say?' Felicity said.

'Me?'

'Uh huh.'

'Nothing.'

'You said something,' Felicity said.

'What?'

'That's what I was asking you,' Felicity said.

Theo thought about it. He could be about to come, and say to her, 'Your pussy feels so soft and nice; nice, nice, nice pussy'; but it meant not a great deal, really. In a few seconds, you were trying to get the skin back down without touching the glans. It was harder to come clean than to talk dirty. Reversely, if there was such a word, it was easier to rise before dawn than to sleep before sunset; easier to do everything in your power to make a woman happy than to say anything out of your powerlessness to make her pause. To wait for the commercials, and then say to her, 'I love you. When I met you, I was no one. You made me one. You made me at one. Now I'm two; the two of us. And without you, it would be like the mosquitoes without the Mediterranean.' By then, hopefully, the commercials would be over, and you would be more tired than you had ever been in your life.

'Well?' said Felicity. 'I'm waiting.'

That was why men had invented God. Because they could not tell women that they loved them. All they could do was stand in a church and recite the 'Hail, Holy Queen'. Then they went home and asked what was for dinner.

'I'm blessed if I remember,' Theo said. 'As blessed as you are.'

But he did bless her. Inside, in his heart of hearts. Nobody would ever find that. He didn't know where it was himself. In a sweat-gland, a skin-pore, the parting of his hair. Or a tiny spittle-spider on a petal of the iris of his eye. Wherever it was, he blessed her there. Blessed her in the name of the father and of the son and of the daughter, if there was one, and there might have been, but, most of all, in the name of the Holy Ghost who puts the burden and the blessing of so much flesh on our bones.

And he would go on blessing her, he thought, until he did it out loud, and his life would fall silent around him. He would bless her until Kingdom come, which would not be too hard, seeing as how it had, already.

'That'll do,' said Felicity. 'That'll do to be going on with.'